The Potato Patch

L.E. PEEPLES

Dear Matt,
thank you for being a blessing. Please enjoy and God Bless
Lori

Revised Edition

ISBN-10: 0-9710571-1-7
ISBN-13: 978-0-9710571-1-1

DEDICATION

To our Mother, Elease Peeples Porter, who opened **The Potato Patch** in the 1950's. The business did not last because she gave away more food than she sold, forever her memory and love will live in our hearts.

CHAPTERS

Create a playlist and take a nostalgic journey to the 1950's

ACKNOWLEDGMENTS

Adrien
Akimme
Tiffany
Michel Ange
Joy
Kadrian
Adynne
Kalynne

1 PESKY FLY

Warm and cozy in bed, Violet feels something rubbing against her ear followed by an irritating sound. *Bizz!* Brushing the side of her face, half-asleep, she murmured, "did someone leave a window open?" No one responded. Slowly she drifted back to her dream of lying in a field surrounded by purple flowers blowing gently in the breeze, as white fluffy clouds floated through the skies, slower… and slower… and *Bizz!* Suddenly awake, frustrated, turning desperately to locate a comfortable position, not ready to start the day. She hated flies.

Adam smiled as he watched her chest rise and fall with each breath, the white cotton sheets outlining her curves like a well-rounded cello. Propped up on his elbow, he little by little outlined her ear with his finger making the sound… *Bizz!*

This time she sat up, "Where's that pesky fly?"

"Ain't no fly," he said in a sultry low southern voice gently kissing her on the neck. "More like a bee looking for honey."

"Umm," she whispered relaxing into her husband's strong arms, allowing herself to enjoy his caresses for a moment. "So that's what that was."

"Ain't that better than a 'pesky fly'?"

"Much better, I should have known it was you all the time," she smiled attempting to get out of bed.

"How about five minutes of honey… *Bizz!*" he said pulling her closer.

"Baby I got so much to do this morning before we leave."

"Then four minutes? … *Bizz!*"

She longed for the intimacy of his embrace, but time was not her friend, so she attempted a compromise. "How about…" trying to sound firm amidst his kisses, "this weekend… I make it up to you."

"You promise?"

"I promise, and by the time you get out of the bathroom, I'll have some hot cakes and sausage ready."

"Hot Cakes!" he shouted quickly kissing her one last time and jumping out of bed. "And sausages…I'll be ready before you know it!"

Violet lay there for a moment wishing he had insisted on more hugs or more kisses, but knew romance was hard to come by when they both left so early and returned so late. "Oh well," she sighed as their brief interlude floated away like the fluffy white clouds of a dream long past.

"You know that's why I married you," he shouted amorously from the bathroom.

"Hot cakes and sausage?" she smiled getting out of bed and putting on a pink housecoat. "That was the only reason?"

"Yup, that and them big thighs," he responded. "And also, your…"

"Adam!" She quickly interrupted. "Watch your mouth, the children can hear you!"

"Hear what?" responded Lil' Adam standing in the doorway between his parent's room and the bathroom rubbing his eyes.

"Never mind." Violet smiled warmly at their middle child as she tied her robe around the waist. He was only fifteen but already stood over six-feet tall, well over her small five-foot frame. She knew he would surpass his father in height and stature, but dared not mention this to either of them, else both their heads would explode with pride. "You can lay back down until breakfast is ready, if you want."

"No that's okay, I couldn't sleep much anyway."

"Excited to start school now that you're a big high school man?" She reached up to hug him before heading into the kitchen. "I will be so proud when you graduate and head off to college."

"Momma, don't push it, I don't like school *that* much to be thinking about college. Besides, some of the fellows quit school over the summer and told me they intend on getting jobs at the mill. The pay is good. Maybe I could quit school, get a job, and help you and Big Adam with the bills. We really need a car, everywhere we go we have to take the bus or catch a ride."

His father pulled the bathroom door open practically face to face with his son, "what's that got to do with liking school?" Not waiting for a response, he continued. "Boy, I won't have you talking that mess. School is the best thing for you. Nobody is going to work at no mill. Vee, maybe I better knock some sense back in his head before school starts, seems he lost what he had over the summer."

Getting into a boxing stance, he threw jabs lightly towards his son's shoulder and stomach, each time coming within inches of contact. Being highly competitive, Lil' Adam quickly reciprocated jab for jab as they zigzagged back and forth around each other in the tiny hallway.

"Son, don't mess with me. I was the high school boxing champion with a mean right hook. I knocked so many fellows out - they called me the 'mean, lean, fighting machine'."

"I bet I could take you," he said bobbing his head right and left as his shoulders moved up and down. "That 'mean, lean, *fighting* machine' is old and rusty."

"Boy, what you call me." His father quickly responded attempting to bob his head faster and faster as his feet shuffled back and forth. "I'll show you 'old and rusty'."

"I see y'all," said Violet peeking around the corner from the kitchen. She enjoyed watching their playfulness, but not this early in the morning on a school day. "Stop all that messing around before somebody gets hurt."

"Won't be me," said Lil' Adam.

"Sho' nuf' won't be me," quickly responded his father.

She smiled to herself and shook her head as they both continued trying to outdo each other. "Adam let that boy get started in the bathroom, ain't no telling how long it will take his sisters to get ready".

"Okay Vee," he smiled proudly before giving his son one actual punch in the arm.

"Oww, that hurt!"

"Told you I had a mean right hook," rubbing the top of his son's head. "That was a light jab, keep talking about quitting school and I'll give you the *real* thing."

"Yes sir," he answered solemnly, rubbing his arm as he went into the bathroom.

"Don't let them boys fool you son filling your head with nonsense. Working down at the mill is hard work and no place for a chile' of mine. The railroad is hard work too, but I need to feed my family. We expect you three to go on to college and be something special. School is where you need to be. Stop worrying about the family, we fine. Now get finished so your sisters can get in here before your momma starts hollering again."

* * *

Squeezed into the small kitchen was a metal framed yellow laminate table with matching chairs, and a modern refrigerator and stove, purchased used but in good condition. Above the sink were two sets of white cabinets with silver handles, and short handmade yellow curtains framed a picturesque view of the back yard. Everything in the room sparkled with cleanliness and a hint of pine-sol filled the air.

It did not take long before the hot cakes and sausages were on the table, smoking hot ready to eat, as the William's family arrived one by one for breakfast. Adam was first to sit down and pile a large helping of everything on his plate.

"This is good," he said pulling his wife around the hips and sitting her on his lap. "Nothing like a full belly and a soft woman to start the day," kissing her on the neck before she squirmed away.

"Stop now" she giggled, handing him a glass of fresh squeezed orange juice. "And stop eating so fast before you choke."

"Why that boy saying he don't like school?" he quickly gulped down half the juice and stuffed a forkful of triple-stacked hot cakes into his mouth despite her warning.

She sat next to him still in her housecoat fixing a small plate for herself. "He'll remember how much he likes school once he gets there."

"Nobody cares what he likes. I told him we expect all our children to go to school, then college, *and* like it, and that's that," he replied with authority.

"You know how much college cost," said Lil' Adam entering the kitchen, apprehensive about speaking up against his father, yet hoping to appeal to his practical side.

"I know you're concerned about helping out and having enough," added Violet reaching over, affectionately rubbing her hand against the side of his cheek. "The Lord will take care of everything."

"But Momma you don't understand. There is tuition, room and board, books, and the…"

"That's enough! You heard your mother, she said don't worry, and I said that's that."

One thing the William's children understood was their father's tone. When his tone sounded final, continuing to speak was at your own risk. Lil' Adam decided to hold any additional comments for now. The kitchen became quiet except for the clinking of forks as they cleared their plates.

Finished eating, Adam sat back in his chair rubbing his completely flat stomach. He was in great shape for a thirty-five-year-old. "Baby I keep eating like this, I'll lose my ripples."

"Ripples?" laughed Lil' Adam, "that's what you call that." He pulled his shirt out of his pants. "Now these are ripples!"

"My goodness, stop bragging, you *both* mighty fine," laughed Violet taking the plates and washing them in a sink of warm, soapy water. "Here Adam, take your lunch before you miss your ride. And son, tuck your shirt back in, I won't have you at school showing all those *ripples.*"

They threw jabs at each other from across the table, play boxing, twisting in their squeaking chairs, unable to reach each other, but coming close.

"Y'all break my chairs, somebody will be in trouble."

"Won't be me."

"Sho' nuf' won't be me."

"Here Adam," handing him one of four brown paper lunch bags, knowing it was hopeless to ask them to stop.

"Sweetie, what I got today?"

"No peeking," she answered winking, "let it be a surprise."

"You know how I love a surprise!" He puckered his lips and playfully kissed her on the cheek while simultaneously pinching her on the backside.

"Adam, you see your son looking at you," she responded, outwardly protesting yet inwardly enjoying every moment.

"Nothing he hasn't seen before. Besides, he needs to learn how to treat a woman, especially if he wants to keep her. My job is to show him what he needs to do."

"I already know how to treat a woman," he confidently interjected while drinking his glass of orange juice.

Both parents looked at each other for a moment and burst out laughing.

"What's funny," he asked seriously.

"Vee, first he said he's quitting school to work at the mill. Now he tells us he knows how to treat a woman. Which one are you getting first son, the job or the woman?"

They both continued laughing and the more they laughed the more frustrated their son became which caused them to laugh even harder.

"Boy, you funny, I'll have me a good laugh all the way to work."

"I still don't see what's funny?"

He turned to kiss his wife before heading towards the backdoor. "We'll talk later if I get home before you go to bed."

Violet waved good-bye as Adam continued chuckling down the driveway. He only had to walk a half-mile to the highway where he caught a ride with his friend Fred. She turned her focus to the two members of the family who were yet to make their appearance in the kitchen. "Y'all sleepy heads better get in here, food's getting cold and school will start without you."

Lil' Adam lovingly shook his head watching his mother clean the stove and dry the pots in the dish drainer. Smiling, he remembered the same scenario from last year of his sisters taking forever while she yelled for them to 'get in here'. "Why was that?" he thought to himself. To keep doing the same thing repeatedly, year after year, didn't make sense. Maybe he did not *really* know how to treat a woman, but pointing this conundrum out to his mother, would probably get her upset and him in trouble. For now, keeping quiet was the best way he knew to treat a woman.

"You hear me calling you?"

After a few seconds, "Yes ma'am," sounded in unison from the rear of the house.

Rose was the first to enter the kitchen. She had on a pink poodle skirt and a short-sleeved white blouse she made herself, with her hair neatly pulled into a ponytail. Almost eighteen, everyone said she was the 'spitting image' of her mother, beautiful, sweet, and quite the young lady. Violet's only worry was that her daughter would meet and fall for her high school sweetheart and have no interest in college. She smiled, thinking she probably felt the same way her mother did when she met Adam. Her mind drifted:

Back in High School, Adam was such a charmer, tall, dark, and very handsome, with a smile that melted the hearts of many girls. He lived a mile down the road from the family's farm and everyday he would come by to walk her to school. At first Poppa disapproved, 'here comes that William's boy again.' This did not stop Adam. Rain or shine, he was always at the front porch waiting to escort her and her sister to school. After a while, Momma would have a plate ready at the table for him to eat breakfast. This infuriated Poppa even more, 'big as that boy is, he'll eat us out of house and home.' Momma ignored him. She enjoyed feeding people. Many nights they would hear a tap on the door as someone from the neighborhood would ask if she had any food to spare. Poppa always complained, 'Mae, we barely got enough for ourselves, let alone feed the whole town.' She would respond, 'the Lord will make a way.' Violet understood how Poppa was cautious especially with the depression going on and people not able to take care of their families. Many of her friends moved north looking for work. However, Poppa was determined to stay in the south and work the land. Farming was the only way he knew to support his family. He would always say, 'I'm in charge of my own destiny, I won't have folk running me off and telling me what to do'.

Every morning Poppa would ask him the same question, 'Boy what you doing here so early?' Adam would always respond respectfully, 'I came by to walk Ms. Violet to school, Mr. Johnson, and make sure she gets there safe, sir.' Poppa would frown at him and reply, 'That best be all you making sure of.' 'Yes sir, Mr. Johnson.' Adam would wait patiently for permission to go in the house. Poppa would make him stand there for a few minutes hoping he would eventually keep walking. Finally, he'd say, 'Go on then, reckon Momma fixed you something to eat.' 'Ms. Mae is awful kind,' said Adam, always the charmer. 'Thank you, Mr. Johnson sir.' Poppa would roll his eyes, shake his head, grumble, and walk away towards the back of the house to smoke his pipe before breakfast.

But Poppa loved baseball, and when he found out the Kansas City Monarchs, a Negro League Baseball team, was interested in Adam, his feelings began to change. 'Mae, maybe that boy's not so bad,' he finally said one morning. Violet smiled. She knew then he was destined to be part of their family. From then on, her love for him continued to grow until he became the center of her life and existence.

"Good morning," said Rose, kissing her mother on the cheek. "Why was everyone laughing earlier?"

"Your father and brother acting silly," she answered, walking over to kiss her on the cheek. "You look nice. Where is your sister?"

"Still in the bathroom," she answered, disappointed she missed the fun since she barely saw her father except on weekends.

"Lillie Mae Williams, don't make me come get you!"

Now Rose *and* Lil' Adam looked at each other, shook their heads, and shrugged their shoulders.

"Don't make any sense," she said mostly to herself, while wiping the stove and washing the dishes. "Don't you want to go to school, or maybe you want a job at the mill like your brother."

Rose turned to him with a questioned look on her face.

"Don't ask," he said motioning for her to keep quiet.

"Lillie Mae, you hear me talking to you!"

"Momma just let her be late," said Lil' Adam, no longer able to keep quiet.

"Then who will make sure she gets to school?"

No response came from the back of the house.

"Lillie Mae? Lillie Mae!" She angrily threw down the dishtowel and took off her apron. "That's it! Chile', you got three seconds to get your behind in this kitchen, because if I have to come get you…" She walked behind the kitchen door to hang up her apron, not noticing Lillie Mae slide into her seat at the table, rushing to put hotcakes and sausages on her plate.

"Calm down, Momma," she said stuffing her mouth full of food. "It's only school."

Turning around she was surprised to see her daughter's smile, Adam's smile, beaming up from the kitchen table. How could she remain upset? What a charmer, just like her father, she thought. She walked over and kissed her lightly on the forehead. "Don't you start, I had enough already from your brother about school." Before walking back to the sink, she popped her youngest daughter on the back of her head.

"Oww, that hurt!"

"Not as much as it would hurt if I came in that bathroom to get you! Do you want to be late your first day?"

"Momma, how many times was I late last year," she asked boldly pushing her mother's already thin patience to the limit.

"Girl, I don't have time to try and figure out how many times you were 'late last year'," she mocked her, shaking her head from side to side.

"Take a guess," she persisted looking up at her with twinkling eyes and a captivating smile.

"I don't know, maybe ten or twenty."

"You are way off Momma, guess again."

"I will *not* 'guess again'," answered Violet, taking the empty plates from Rose and Lil' Adam who watched in amazement at their sister's bravery. "And if you don't finish eating by the time I wash these plates, you can guess how many times I tap your behind right on out that door!"

Lil' Adam laughed as he playfully pushed his sister on the shoulder leaving the kitchen to get his books. "You heard Momma, move it."

"Leave me alone," she said trying to hit him before he jumped out of her reach.

"Lillie Mae, what I tell you!"

"Yes ma'am," she responded quickly putting the last piece of sausage in her mouth as she got up to get her school satchel. "I was only late two times last year, because of Rose."

"Don't bring me in your mess," she responded heading towards the living room unable to take her sister's antics any longer. Since they obviously had time, she decided to listen to "Earth Angel" by The Penguins on her record player. She loved music. It helped her to escape into a beautiful, loving, imaginary world, different from her own.

"See what she doing, Momma? That's why we were late. Rose in the mirror fixing her hair, singing some song about angels that live on earth, as she dreams about that new boy who moved down the road."

"How does your being late have anything to do with me," said Rose, waving her hand to dismiss her sister as she continued checking her ponytail from all angles. "You're losing your mind!"

"What new boy?" asked Lil' Adam, taking his brown lunch bag off the counter, finally interested in something they were saying.

"You hope he walks with us to *school,* Rose," taunted Lillie Mae, pulling her sister's ponytail and running back into the kitchen.

"Who... Juan?" asked Lil' Adam.

"I saw her looking at him the other day when you were playing baseball in the yard."

"Girl let's go. Nothing is wrong with Juan, mind your business." He kissed his mother on the cheek no longer interested in his younger sister's distractions. "Bye Momma."

"I didn't *say* anything was wrong, just that *Rose* likes him!"

"I do not." Aggravated, she turned off the record player.

"Do too!"

"Lillie Mae, leave your sister alone. There is nothing wrong with fixing your hair and trying to look your best, even if it is for a boy. Maybe you should try it sometime?"

"Eww, not for a boy, I don't need lipstick and fancy hair do's, know why?" She paused to look in the same mirror recently vacated. "I have natural beauty." She put one hand on her hip and the other to her face, posing. Everyone stopped and shook their heads in disbelief as she switched her hips from side to side walking back into the kitchen.

"Get to school Chile', all y'all gone crazy. Take your lunch and leave Rose alone. Hurry up. You got a long walk to school and I got to finish getting ready myself before I miss the bus."

"Why do we have to walk way across town and there's a school right down the road?"

"Baby, you know that's the white school."

"And you colored, so you go to the colored school," said Lil' Adam as he pulled her hair.

"Leave me alone, I ain't talking to you," she said pushing him.

He reached around his mother and pulled her hair again.

"Mom-maa," she whined trying to catch him but this time he escaped her reach. "Why?"

"We don't have time for this Lillie Mae." She kissed her daughter wishing she had a better answer. "It's just the way things are, that's all."

"What's for lunch?" Lil' Adam asked, hoping to change the subject.

"Bet I know," said Lillie Mae distracted.

"You know everything," said Rose under her breath as she followed her brother out the door.

"Forget you." She rolled her eyes returning to her thoughts. "An apple and bologna sandwich, am I right?"

Violet smiled and tapped her lightly on the behind, "get going Chile' and be nice to your sister."

She watched her three children head down the road, Lil' Adam leading the way, followed by Rose walking carefully not to stir up any dust, and Lillie Mae skipping in the rear throwing up as much dust as possible. Smiling, she shook her head and waved at the three of them different as night and day. "Hurry up so you won't be late."

"Bye Momma," said Lillie Mae running past her brother and sister to catch up with a group of friends further down the road. "Wait up," she called.

"Lillie Mae don't you go too far ahead," her mother shouted from the porch.

"I won't," she answered finally catching up with her friends.

Violet felt an overwhelming sadness watching them walk, knowing what her daughter said was true, a school was 'right down the road'. "If they could go there they wouldn't have to get up so early," she said aloud waving good-bye to the children almost out of sight.

"Why *couldn't* all children go to school together? At least whichever one was closest." That made sense, she thought. Were other children in the neighborhood better off than her children? Why did being white provide extra privileges in addition to school, like using public restrooms, drinking from water fountains, eating in restaurants, sitting in the movie theater, or riding the bus. Even attempting to obtain justice, colored people had to sit in the back of the courtroom. Everything was separate.

Violet remembered as a child looking up into the faces of white people wondering why things were different for them, was it only their skin color. Most people ignored her gaze as her eyes followed them until they passed by, others would return her stare with a look of disgust that made her stomach turn uncomfortably into knots. "Momma why they hate us," she asked as they hurried down the street to the colored section of town.

"Hate is a mean word," she answered. "Jesus loves you and that's more important than all the hate in the world. Gently squeezing her hand, she would start to sing:

'Jesus loves me, this I know,
For the Bible tells me so.
Little ones to him belong,
They are weak, but He is strong.'
Violet began to sing with her mother.
'Yes, Jesus loves me,
Yes, Jesus loves me.
Yes, Jesus loves me, for the Bible tells me so.'
She smiled - Momma's songs always made her feel better.

Finally, the children were out of sight and Violet finished getting ready for work, which didn't take long since everything was prepared, and her makeup consisted of a small amount of lipstick. Her uniform, pressed and hanging in the closet, consisted of a plain short-sleeved navy-blue dress with a hemline slightly above her knee, black stockings, and oxford shoes that were more comfortable than fashionable. She pulled her hair up into a round bun with neatly curled bangs above her eyebrows, placed a black bonnet on her head in case it rained, and dashed out the house to catch the bus.

2 SCHOOL DAYS

Forrest Middle and Freeman High, faced each other, separated only by a playground in the middle with a few broken swings, some rickety slides, and a difficult to push merry-go-round. Rose and Lil' Adam watched their younger sister join others struggling to move the contraption fast enough for those in the middle to have an enjoyable ride as those pushing attempted to jump on without falling. Walking across the field, they noticed the high school students separated into small clusters around the front of the building waiting for the bell to ring.

"Who is that with your brother?" whispered Margie, Rose's best friend since grammar school. "He's the most! Check out those threads. He rich?"

"I don't know if he rich!" she replied, annoyed by her questions. "All I know is he walked with us to school and he moved down the road last week in the ole' Murray house with his dad…"

"I didn't ask you where he *lived*! I asked who he was, what's his name?"

"Hey y'all," said Naomi walking up to them. "Who is that dreamy looking boy with Lil' Adam?"

"That's what I been trying to find out. He came with Rose."

"He didn't come with me."

"Rose, that your new beau?"

"No," she replied disgusted at the thought. "He walked with us to school, his name is Juan."

"Wan?" said Margie with a puzzled look on her face. "What kind of name is that? Never heard of nobody name Wan', is that Wan', like a magic wand? I can be Cinderella." She twirled around hoping he would look her way.

"No! Juan with a 'J' not a 'W'," corrected Rose wondering if she needed new friends.

"Then wouldn't that be John or something?" said Naomi confused.

"Forget it," she said, frustrated.

"He must not be from around here with a name like that, looks like he mixed or something."

"Who cares, he's so fine." Margie started swaying her hips and snapping her fingers as she sang, "…send cold chills up and down my spine, oh yeah, so fine."

"I love that song, 'So Fine' by the Fiestas."

"Ain't he fine Rose?"

"Y'all crazy, stop dancing 'round here. Everybody is looking at you."

"Come on Rose, get the beat."

"No way," she interrupted, hoping to change the subject and stop the singing and dancing. "He has an accent, I heard him tell Lil' Adam that he used to go to school in Chicago."

"Chic – Ca – Go, Chic – Ca – Go," sang Margie swaying her hips from side to side.

"Shh, he'll hear you."

"Chic – Ca – Go, Chic – Ca – Go," she continued ignoring her friend as she snapped her fingers. "They say there is a lot of jazz and blues up in Chic – Ca – Go, home of the Big Bands."

"How you know? You never been further then the city limits," laughed Naomi jokingly pushing her friend.

"You don't know where I been," said Margie pushing her back harder.

"Maybe he's a gangster?"

"He too young to be a gangster," said Rose shaking her head and looking over at another group of girls who seemed to be having a more enjoyable conversation. "He is only sixteen."

"How you know?"

"Bet he know some gangsters," said Naomi. "I heard Poppa talking to my Uncle Buddy after he came back from my cousin's funeral in Chicago. He said women sell themselves on the streets for money. My Uncle Buddy seemed interested in that part because he asked, 'for how much?' Then my Aunt Lucille slapped him upside the head."

"What's that got to do with gangsters?" laughed Margie, watching Juan and smoothing her hair, hoping he would look her way. "You just silly!"

"You the one silly, I'm trying to tell you what I mean if you'll let me." She breathed out a deep sigh attempting to gather her thoughts before continuing. "My cousin lived in a neighborhood called 'Black Belt'…"

"Is it because colored people live there?"

"I guess," hunching her shoulders. "All I know is Poppa said police didn't care what happened in that 'Black Belt' on the Southside of Chicago, and how white folks hated colored folks so much, at night, they would drive around hunting people like rabbits."

"Eww, you eat rabbits," interrupted Margie flattening out the pleats in her skirt.

"Who says?"

"Don't you?"

"Just because my father hunts rabbits, don't mean I eat them."

"Then why he hunts them?"

"What happened, in the 'Black Belt', Naomi?" interrupted Rose wanting to hear the end of the story before the bell rang while still noticing the other group of girls. "I wonder why they're laughing," she thought to herself.

"Coloreds were being shot, beaten, and jumped on by gangs of white folks. It got pretty bad."

"Is that why they call them gangsters?"

"Margie, please, let her finish."

"Thank you Rose, where was I?" she said, with a questioned look on her face. "Oh, okay… back in the 'Black Belt', they were scared to go outside."

"Why didn't they call the police," asked Margie taking a small compact mirror from her purse. She began puckering her lips making kissing sounds as she reapplied her bright red lipstick. "Maybe he'll look over here now."

"Now that you put on more lipstick," said Rose, sarcastically shaking her head. "Surely the other girls were laughing *at* them", she thought.

"You not listening, I said the police didn't care."

"Same as here," she added fluffing up her hair in the back again. "How I look?"

"Forget it, nobody is listening."

"I'm listening," said Rose watching Juan toss a baseball with her brother and some other boys, feeling sorry for him. "No wonder he left Chicago, with all that going on."

"The colored folk tried to fight back with protest signs and marching through the streets. It was on the news and everything. One night, a carload of white folks drove by and killed several people including our cousin. That's when Poppa had to go up there."

"Was he scared to go?" said Rose wondering how Juan survived such an awful place.

"Who knows, but he went anyway."

"So, is Juan a gangster or not?" said Margie putting a stick of gum in her mouth. "He still is fine, even if he is a gangster."

"And you said I'm silly," said Naomi shaking her head at her friend. "Give me some."

"Please?"

"Please."

"Maybe that's why Juan's dad moved back home. I wouldn't want to live in that 'Black Belt'."

"Y'all party poopers, forget that stuff and get with the sounds," chimed Margie moving her hips again trying to change the mood of her friends. "Forget the bad, what about them good ole' blues from Chic – Ca – Go, Chic – Ca – Go!"

"Let's go Rose, before we're late!" said Naomi walking away. "I told you she's not listening to a word we say."

"I heard what you said." She hurried to catch up, before taking one quick glance at Juan who still would not look her way. "Only I don't want to think about no 'Black Belt' or white folks and colored folks or anything like that, before class. Have you ever thought that might be where good blues came from? Colored folks treated badly in the 'Black Belt', or the South, or wherever, then singing about it… *the blues.*"

Rose looked at her, "that's the first smart thing you said today."

"I ain't stupid, I know stuff. Bad enough I got Ms. Jennings again this year. She really knows how to rattle your cage first thing in the morning. Don't want to get all shook up ahead of time."

"Umm 'all shook up', that's the song by that white fellow that does all that shaking."

"He kinda' dreamy too," laughed Margie, "and he got the moves."

"You silly," said Rose as the first bell rang and they headed towards the school entrance. She looked over and saw the students of Forest Middle heading into school. Not able to make out Lillie Mae, she waved anyway.

"Lil' Adam!" someone shouted. He turned to see his friends, Tommy-Do and Richy-Rich, pulling up in a 1950 black Ford Tudor with "Get a Job" by the Silhouettes ironically playing in the background.

"Man, where you get this boss set of wheels," he asked walking around the car to get a closer look.

"Man, come hang out with us," said Richy-Rich. "It's too hot to be in school, we headed down to the water hole to have a swim."

Lil' Adam knew him since first grade. His real name was Richard, but he hated that name, said it made him feel like his old man. When he got older, he always managed to have money but never a job, so everyone started calling him Richy-Rich, like the cartoon. He was happy with that.

"Man, later we'll sneak into the show and catch a flick," said Tommy-Do who always wore his hair slicked back since he got 'the process'.

Lil' Adam smiled to himself as he thought of the night when he watched Tommy's sister put some white paste called 'conk' in his hair.

He screamed something awful, 'it's burning'.

She laughed, 'Lye is supposed to burn if you want your hair to be straight, gonna' leave it on for another fifteen minutes. You'll get used to it.'

'My whole head will burn off by then.'

'You want it straight don't you, the longer it stays on the straighter it will be.'

Tommy took a deep breath fighting back tears.

'Man, you going through all that pain for straight hair like a girl'?

When she finally washed the lye out, he apparently forgot the pain, because he spent the next ten minutes looking in the mirror. 'Gimme' a comb,' he grinned fixated on how straight his hair was. 'Chicks will flip over me.'

Lil' Adam thought for sure he would object when she said he had to wear rollers to have curls ... Nope. The next day his hair was curly and straight. 'Man, you look like a boy-girl.'

Tommy shrugged his shoulders, 'Man, chicks dig my new do! Everywhere I go, they want to touch it.' Ever since then they called him 'Tommy-Do'.

Stirred from his thoughts as "Come go with me" by the Del-Vikings playing on the radio, Lil' Adam wrestling playfully with Tommy-Do and Richy-Rich. "Man, I'm not going down to no water hole! Today's the first day of school. I'm cranked up! Barely could sleep last night. Man, we in high school, y'all better come on. I'm sure you can sign back in."

"Man - school ain't *no* fun," said Richy-Rich putting his arm around Lil' Adam's shoulder heading away from school towards the car. "That's why we quit. We'll show you how to have some *real fun.* Come on, we'll even let you drive."

Lil' Adam stepped back with a serious expression on his face. "*Drive!* Man, Big Adam would tan my hide if he knew I even *thought* about skipping school… I couldn't have any *real fun* driving… I'd be dead."

"We didn't say skip school forever, just one day." Richy-Rich attempted to put his arm over his shoulder again but Lil' Adam waved his hand at the two of them and turned back towards school.

"Man, you scared," said Tommy-Do as he walked around him in a circle flapping his arms and making chicken sounds, "balk, balk, balk, little chicken, balk, balk, balk."

"Nah man, I got plans and all."

"Man, we got *plans*, big *plans*!" said Richy-Rich. "We are blowing this town and heading up north!"

"Yeah man, up north is where the *real fun* is."

"Nah man, I'm heading to school…"

"Forget it, let's split," he interrupted sarcastically. "He got a new friend anyway."

They both stared at Juan who stood quietly nearby looking uncomfortable.

"Yeah man, looks like he found him a high-yellow friend."

"Come on Man, let's split, they big-time high school Negro's now. We're not good enough."

"Man, you know it's not like that," he called to them as they walked away.

"Later man, call me when you ready for some *real fun*."

His two friends got in the car and drove away not bothering to look back. "Sorry man," Lil' Adam turned to face Juan embarrassed. "They shouldn't have said that."

"Man, don't sweat it, I'm used to people calling me 'high yellow' or 'light-skinned', and since my mother was white, I guess they could have called me worse."

"I thought she might have been Spanish because she named you 'Juan'."

"No, she just liked that name, I guess. She had a hard time living in the colored section of town in Chicago. People called her all kind of names. I hated it, but I learned to ignore that type of stuff a long time ago and keep on moving."

The second bell rang loudly. "And that's what we better do," said Lil' Adam running up the steps. "Man, you don't want to be late on your first day."

They both looked at each other realizing they used the word 'man' far too much. "No man, I don't."

Laughing the two boys ran down the hall to catch up with the other students before the last bell rang.

"Can you help me find my class?" said Juan taking a piece of paper out of his pocket. "I got to find Ms. Jennings class."

"She's the senior class teacher. They say she mean as tar. Rose in that class, you can go with her."

"Wait," said Juan pulling his shirt before his friend turned away. "I don't think your sister likes me. She did not look my way one time all the way here. Then when her friends came around, they *stared* at me all morning, talking, and laughing, and making weird gestures."

"Rose isn't like that. She kinda' shy, that's all, and her friends… they stare at *all* guys. It'll be okay, you'll see."

The high school was a long flat redbrick building built in the early 1950's for colored students. The front entrance divided the freshmen and sophomores to the right and the junior and seniors to the left. Each classroom had six windows, open wide on hot days or shades drawn on sunny days. The used desks came from the white high school, but they were better than the old wobbly wooden tables from before. Connected in the rear was a large two-story gymnasium for physical education and basketball games, converting into an auditorium for special events. The boys walked quickly, cutting through students busy putting things into their lockers, heading to their classrooms, waiting for the final bell.

"Hey Rose, wait up."

She turned puzzled wondering why he called her. The rule was, once they got to school they went their separate ways until the end of the day when they met at the playground to pick up Lillie Mae.

"Here he comes, here he comes!" said Margie gleefully elbowing Rose.

"Can Juan walk with you? He's in your class," Lil' Adam asked in a very hurried voice.

"Oh, okay," said Rose reluctantly wincing from the pain of Margie elbowing her in the side.

"See yah' after school," he added, quickly turning to leave before anyone could protest. "Hey Sam, wait up," was all they heard as he ran to the opposite end of the hall.

"Ahh, he's excited," said Rose awkwardly not knowing what to say. "This is Margie and Naomi."

"Hello," he said nervously attempting a smile that looked more like a grimace.

"You welcome to walk with us."

"Th-thank you," was all that managed to come out.

They all headed towards class, Rose and Juan in the front trying desperately not to bump into each other while moving through the crowded hallway, Margie and Naomi giggling and whispering behind them.

"Why do you call him 'Lil' Adam?" he asked trying not to look her directly in the eyes, not knowing what else to say. "Because he so tall?"

Rose looked at him strangely, "Then wouldn't we call him Big Adam?"

"Oh yeah, right."

For a few moments, they walked in silence, Juan feeling awkward in his attempts to start a conversation and Rose feeling uncomfortable regarding her response. At *least* he tried she thought. She attempted to make it up to him with a softer tone. "At home we call my father 'Big Adam' and we call him 'Lil' Adam."

"I think my father knows your father."

"Oh," said Rose stepping away from Margie who had begun to elbow her again. "This is our class."

The third and final bell rang loudly. Approximately twenty students sat in Ms. Jennings twelfth grade classroom. More registered, but some chose to leave school to get jobs as domestic help, to work in the mill, or to relocate north. Others refused to come to class because of horrible rumors circulating from the previous senior class that she was 'mean as tar'. To the current class, she looked pleasant, tall with glasses, hair pulled back into a bun, wearing a white shirt, blue jacket and matching skirt with black shoes, nothing scary so far, they thought.

"My name is Ms. Jennings," she said writing her name on the board in large cursive letters. Once she finished she turned to face them smiling slightly as other students began to arrive. "Sit anywhere you like. We will figure out seating arrangements as time goes along. Some of you knew me from last year and are excited to have me as your teacher again."

Chatter began.

"Who could possibly be excited?"

"Maybe she's not so bad after all."

"Who said she was 'mean as tar'?"

"She seems nice to me."

Feeling more comfortable, the students began looking around trying to determine who was there from last year and who was new. Finally, all eyes turned to Juan who slowly sank in his chair, not daring to speak or make eye contact with anyone.

"Quiet down everybody, quiet down," she said, softly tapping a long ruler on the blackboard that got everyone's attention. "This is a very important year in high school, your senior year. Some of you might be the first in your family to graduate. Some of you will be going on to seek employment or raise families. Some of you might have the opportunity to go to college. And some of you might not make it *out* of my class."

"What does she mean?" Everyone looked around at each other with puzzled looks.

Ms. Jennings paused for a minute allowing them time to talk amongst themselves despite her telling them to 'quiet down'. Then she SLAMMED the stick down on her desk. All the students JUMPED in unison. "The CHOICE is YOURS," she shouted with a grin that confused and frightened them. "CHOOSE the road to graduation, employment, and happy families, or DROP OUT and be ignorant and lazy!"

"I will help you either way," she said pleasantly, her tone once again gentle and easygoing as she walked through the aisles looking each student in the face, "Any questions?"

No one made a sound. They all sat stunned, puzzled, wondering how to react to an apparent split personality.

"Good!" she turned with a snap of her heels. "Let's get started on your final journey of high school. Remember what you make of it… is up to you."

No one dared move or speak, they did not know whether to laugh or cry. 'Mean as Tar', appeared to be an understatement. They sat terrified waiting for the stick to SLAM at any moment.

3 FRIED CHICKEN

Violet began working for the Gist household as a maid before Rose and Lil' Adam started school. Working there was not bad at all, she thought as she walked to the bus stop. Many of her friends told awful stories of harsh treatment, name calling, even physical abuse at the hands of their employers, but she felt accepted as part of the family. Initially Adam protested, 'not having my wife working for white folks.' He had a good job at the railroad, but times were tough for everyone, especially colored people, and when Violet found out she was pregnant with another child, the additional income was welcome despite his protests. The bus pulled up and Violet climbed the three steps, paid, and quietly went to sit in the back.

After thirty minutes, she arrived in a part of town with streets lined with large majestic oak trees, lawns glistening from the morning dew, and immaculately kept flower gardens surrounding perfectly manicured shrubbery. The regal homes stood proud encased by white pillars of grandeur, welcoming visitors with neatly aligned rocking chairs, as porch swings swayed gently to the cool morning breeze.

Violet opened the tall wrought iron gate and headed towards the back of the house. Mr. Gist usually left for work before she came leaving the door open, otherwise there was a secret key hidden under a frog-shaped stone in the garden. Quietly entering, her heart sank when she saw the cluttered, disorganized kitchen.

"Hello, anyone home?" Immediately she heard Carl Jr. running down the stairs.

"Ms. Vee! Ms. Vee!" he answered practically knocking her off balance as he squeezed her tightly around the hips, his curly blonde hair unkempt.

"My, my, you're mighty glad to see me. I've only been gone two days," she said warmly examining him as she put on a white apron and tied it neatly behind her back. "Carl Jr. why aren't you ready for school? The bus will be here soon, and you're not dressed. Did you wash up yet?"

"No ma'am," he smiled up at her with bright blue eyes that warmed her soul. "Soon as I heard you open the door, I jumped out of bed, ran down stairs, and here I am."

"Yes, here you are." His innocence wiped away all Violet's thoughts of scolding him. He was only eight and not to blame for circumstances within the Gist family. "Okay then, let's run back upstairs and get cleaned up and ready for school. Is your momma and Lizabeth up yet?"

She knew the answer to that question before asking. After working there for over ten years, she rarely saw Mrs. Gist before breakfast, especially since the accident.

"Nobody up but me," he hugged her again glad to have someone to talk too. "Poppa left off for work and said you'd be here directly."

Violet took his hand and walked up the stairs while he happily chattered on and on, apparently a squirrel was collecting nuts outside the front window and hiding them all around the yard. "I watched him all morning Ms. Vee. Can you watch him with me?"

"Maybe, after school," she smiled and nodded as he continued the story while she picked out clothes for him to wear. She loved him like her own son.

He could barely contain himself as she filled the tub with water and poured in bubble bath as foamy soap lather quickly filled the tub. He took off his pajamas, ready to dive in.

"Yippee, I love bubbles."

"You only got a few minutes," she said trying to sound firm. She stood watching him as he splashed under the water, bubbles everywhere.

"Can I have some hot cakes and sausage for breakfast? Please, Please, Pleeease?"

"I think I can fix up a few hot cakes, if you promise to wash up really good, especially behind your ears."

"Yes ma'am, I promise," he answered taking his washcloth and scrubbing behind his ears.

"With soap," she handed him a bar from the sink.

"Thanks," he smiled, normally no one noticed, and he could complete his entire bath without soap. "Don't forget fried chicken for dinner?"

"Carl Jr., you haven't had breakfast and you fretting about dinner."

"Fried chicken is my favorite, Ms. Vee," he said scrubbing behind his ears, this time with soap. "No one cooks fried chicken like you. Momma tried yesterday, but nobody ate it because it was black on the outside and pink on the inside. Ms. Vee there was so much smoke in the kitchen… I thought the fire trucks would come."

With a fully lathered washcloth, he scrubbed his legs while continuing his weekend update. "But Poppa wasn't mad, 'at least she tried', he said. Momma looked sad, but she got happy fast when Poppa said we were going to dinner, and guess what Ms. Vee, we had fried chicken."

"That doesn't surprise me."

"It wasn't as good as yours, Ms. Vee. Maybe you could work there so everybody can taste your fried chicken, yours is the best."

"Thank you, Carl Jr., but I am *not* trying to cook fried chicken for the whole town, got my hands full with you. Now go on and get finished in that tub without spilling every drop of water on the floor you hear?"

"Yes ma'am," he merrily scrubbed away thinking of hot cakes and sausage with fried chicken for dinner. Once he was full of lather, he dove under water splashing water and bubbles everywhere.

Violet walked into the baby's room. "Ma Vee," the little one said reaching up both arms from the crib, her big brown eyes sparkled with happiness. She rushed to pick up the youngest member of the Gist family, who at two could not pronounce 'Ms. Vee' like her brother, but Violet loved 'Ma Vee' even better.

"Good morning Lizabeth," she said kissing her on the cheek. "You are such a good girl sitting here so quiet, I thought you were sleep."

She hardly ever cried despite spending plenty of time in her crib. Everything changed when Violet came to work, they were inseparable, wherever one was the other was nearby. She loved her like her own daughters.

"Let me change you honey, so we can get some breakfast." Her crib sheets were soaking wet. "We'll clean those later. Once your big brother is off to school, I'll give you a nice bubble bath, so you can play with your ducky in the water."

"Ducky," she said pointing to the yellow toy on the dresser.

Before going downstairs, she peaked in the bathroom and said firmly, "Carl Jr., that's enough playing."

"Yes ma'am," he answered startled.

"Your clothes are on the bed, dry yourself off and get dressed, then head downstairs for breakfast."

He pulled on the chain to lift the stopper letting the remaining water out of the tub. "Be ready in no time."

Violet stopped dead in her tracks as she looked around the kitchen. Pots were all over the stove, flour all over the table, plates filled the sink, and the fried chicken Carl Jr. spoke of, sat abandoned on the counter burnt to a crisp.

"Oh my, looks like a hurricane hit this place!" she said taking a deep breath. "Sit in your chair while I move this mess out the way until later. I will rustle up some hot cakes and sausage for you and your brother." Dusting off flour from a doll thrown in the corner, "here, sweetie, play with this; we got lots of work to do around here."

She quickly fixed the hot cakes and sausage for the grateful Gist children, and soon waved good-bye to Carl Jr. as he got on the school bus. "Let's get the kitchen cleaned up so we can say morning to your mother."

"Mor-ning," she smiled reaching for Violet to take her.

* * *

Mrs. Gist used to keep everything nice and clean the way Violet left it on Friday, but after the accident, things changed. As she cleaned, she thought of the events leading to that tragic day.

Three years ago, the Gist home was full of joy and laughter. Their two sons, Frank age seven and Carl Jr. then five, were typical well-mannered boys only occasionally getting into mischief. She remembered one summer night watching from the kitchen window as the whole family played football in the backyard, laughing and running around chasing each other, having a great time. Mrs. Gist had Frank on her team and Mr. Gist had Carl Jr. on his team. Carl Jr. barely understood the game, so he would always end up running the wrong way with the ball, helping Frank and his mother win. No matter how many times they explained the direction to run with the football, he always ran the opposite way yelling, 'Touchdown!' They all tackled him rolling around in the grass laughing merrily, not a care in the world. Not at that time anyway, she thought.

The circus came to town later that week on a warm summer day in August. Excitement filled the air as Violet stood on the sidewalk with Frank and Carl Jr. next to her while a caravan of horse-pulled wagons rolled down the street. The boys watched in amazement. Frank danced happily as "Maple Leaf Rag" by Scott Joplin played in the front of the procession. Carl Jr. held tightly to Violet's leg, afraid to move, he was too young to appreciate the hustle and bustle of the circus. Crowds of people hurried along the street trying their best to keep up with the rickety-rackety wagons as the festive music filled the air.

"Ms. Vee, that sign says, 'the greatest show on earth', reckon Poppa will let us go," asked Frank, his eyes stretched with amazement.

"You have to ask him sweetheart."

"I don't want to see it Ms. Vee," said Carl Jr. as tears filled his eyes.

"You act like a baby," his older brother scolded. "Don't you want to see the 'greatest show on earth'?"

"No," he said shaking his head grabbing Violet's leg tighter.

"Baby," he taunted sticking out his tongue.

"Am not," tears rolling down his cheeks.

They all continued watching as elephants, horses, clowns, jugglers, and beautiful girls in sparkling costumes merrily paraded down the street, as children from the neighborhood ran alongside. Finally, the last wagon rolled by with colored musicians sitting in a wagon playing "Ragtime Piano" by Scott Joplin as more people danced behind the caravan. The three of them stood there until the sounds slowly faded in the distance and the parade turned the corner.

Once Mr. Gist came home Frank began his quest. "Poppa, Poppa, the circus is in town! The circus is in town! They said it's the 'greatest show on earth'. Can we go, Poppa, can we go?"

Violet heard Frank's voice trailing into the distance as he told his father how the circus came right in front of the house. She closed the gate and headed towards the bus stop. She did not know she would never hear that voice again.

4 SAVED BY THE BELL

Rose yelled out the front door as her brother headed down the road tossing a baseball with some friends from school, including Juan. "You better not forget to meet Momma at the bus stop or Big Adam will tan your hide!"

"Don't tell me what to do!"

"You better be at that bus stop."

"I said don't tell me what to do!"

"Okay, get in trouble, won't be my fault."

She slammed the door, briefly catching a glimpse of Juan waving before running to catch up with the other boys. Wearing dungarees, a white shirt, and black loafers, dressed too nice to be playing outside, she thought.

Taking hamburger out the refrigerator, she decided to call her friend Margie. The cord was long and stretched so she could continue fixing dinner while talking. She picked up the yellow rotary dial phone, excited to discuss who the girls watched googly-eyed in school, careful since it was a party line and you could never tell who was listening.

"Juan really looked good, today…"

"Girl he looks good right now."

"How you know?"

"I'm looking out the window at him."

"Boss Cat, you so lucky you see him all the time."

"He waved at me a few minutes ago."

"I am so jealous."

"He is sooo fine."

Margie began to sing, "so fine, so fine." You could hear her snapping her fingers through the phone. "…send cold chills up and down my spine, oh, oh, yeah, so fine."

"Don't start that song again."

"You know you love it."

"He stared at me the whole class." As she talked, she began chopping the green peppers and onions for the meatloaf.

"Wonder if he likes me?"

"Does *who* like you?" Lillie Mae said coming around the corner headed for the refrigerator.

"Girl I got to go, somebody in my business."

"Is that Margie," asked Lillie Mae trying to grab the phone before she hung up.

"Never mind, you want to help make the meatloaf?"

"No way, cooking is for girls! Can I have an apple, I'm hungry?"

"If you helped I could finish faster."

"I said cooking is for girls." Taking an apple from the fruit bowl on the table, she left the kitchen.

"You are a girl!"

"Not a girly-girl like you."

"I'm not a 'girly-girl', I just like to cook."

"And sew, and fix your hair, and stare in the mirror, and wear skirts all the time, girly-girl things."

"You'll do the same thing one day."

"No I won't," she answered slamming the screen door.

Rose thought back to when her grandmother took care of them while her mother was at the Gist home. She would hum and sing while working around the house. Lil' Adam stayed occupied with his toy soldiers and cars. She had her baby dolls, but when her grandmother cooked, she remembered being right at her side. Grandma Mae would explain how to prepare each dish, step-by-step. 'You'll be the best cook when you grow up,' she would say, then gave her the biggest hug that seemed to envelop her entire body in warmth and security. "Nobody hugs like Grandma," she said to herself.

"Rose!" shouted Lillie Mae from the porch swing startling her. "Some strange car pulling in the driveway, you better come and see who it is."

"Girl, I'm cooking and you out there doing nothing! *You* see who it is." Her mind focused on completing dinner, putting the meatloaf in the oven and a pot of water on the stove to boil potatoes. "Momma will be home soon, and supper is not ready. *No* thanks to you."

Lillie Mae did not listen to her complaints, her mind focused on the car and its occupants. She could tell there were two women in the front seat and somebody tall in the back seat. "Why they just sitting there," she asked herself.

After a few minutes, the tall person got out the car. It was Lil' Adam tossing a baseball in the air as he headed for the porch.

"Where you been? What are you doing in that car?" she nagged with her hands on her hips. "I'm telling. You know Big Adam's rule – no riding in cars with strangers. I'm telling soon as he comes home!"

"Girl, shut your mouth," he snapped at his sister. "That's not a stranger in the car, that's Momma with Mrs. Gilmore. You know who she is don't you, maybe you need glasses."

Lillie Mae froze, unable to move or respond. She could see them both clearly now. They looked to be having a very serious conversation. "Why was her mother sitting in a car, in front of the house, with her teacher?" She wondered nervously.

"And by the way," Lil' Adam said as he reached the top step of the porch, "you in *trouble*!"

She jumped from the swing when the screen door slammed behind him. Panicking, she ran in the house demanding answers. "What you mean, *trouble*? Why would Mrs. Gilmore give you and Momma a ride? Does she live around here? Why you say I'm in trouble?"

Lil' Adam ignored her, looked in the refrigerator, grabbed the jar of milk and drank from the container.

"Eww, I'm telling. He's drinking milk from the jar again!"

"Give me that milk." Rose snatched the container. "You know better!"

"You both need to mind your own business," he answered wiping his mouth on the back of his hand leaving the kitchen.

"What Mrs. Gilmore tell momma?" following behind him. "Is she mad? What did she say? Answer me!"

Lil' Adam walked straight to his room and slammed the door in her face. She did not follow him since she knew the rule was his room is off limits to her and her sister. If she opened the door, she knew she would be in more trouble than she figured she already was. She needed assistance to get answers from him.

She stomped back into the kitchen. "Rose, he won't tell me why they were in the car with Mrs. Gilmore, make him tell me!"

"Girl you not making any sense, isn't she your teacher? Go sit down somewhere, you see I'm busy, and you know I can't make Lil' Adam do anything." She added milk, butter, and salt to the mashed potatoes, stirring and tasting to see if the ingredients were coming together correctly.

"Yes, Mrs. Gilmore is her teacher," said her mother entering the kitchen and handing her coat to her son who had ran back into the kitchen when he heard his mother's voice. "Hang that up Lil' Adam and put my purse on the dresser."

"Yes ma'am," he replied moving quickly, enjoying the sight of his youngest sister squirming with anxiety.

"Here Momma, taste these potatoes."

"Mm-hmm, that's perfect baby. Hand me a glass of water please," she said a weary look on her face.

Rose hurried to get the water, "what's the matter Momma?"

"I'm fine baby," she said sipping the water and taking her shoes off under the kitchen table. "But I am disappointed in your sister."

"Momma, I'm sorry!" cried Lillie Mae as she kneeled in front of her mother laying her head on her lap.

"What happened?" Rose said irritated by her sister's behavior.

"Well, according to Mrs. Gilmore, during recess, the janitor caught your sister and a new girl named Juanita Nesbitt, behind the school house, smoking.

"Whaaat!" said Lil' Adam overdramatizing his response to aggravate his sister since he heard the story earlier in the car.

"Momma, I'm sorry!" she cried without tears.

"Lillie Mae stop!" said Rose growing more frustrated with her.

"Buford, the janitor, your father's cousin, didn't take her to the Principal, thank the Lord, but to Mrs. Gilmore, that's what she was telling me in the car."

"Girl what were you thinking?" glared Rose looking up from chopping spinach.

"She doesn't think," answered Lil' Adam with a smirk enjoying every moment of her misery.

"Leave me alone," she sulked looking up from her mother's lap, still without tears.

"Now here I am worried that your brother will run off with them no 'count boys, instead you go off with some girl…smoking."

"Who is Juanita Nesbitt? Is she related to Juan, the new boy that walks to school with us?" asked Rose adding fresh cream and butter to the spinach while it cooked. "I didn't know he had a sister."

"He told me he had a younger sister," added Lil' Adam sitting across from his mother. "I think she'll be walking with us next week, their pops is looking for a …"

"If she smokes," interrupted Violet. "I don't want her walking with Lillie Mae. No telling what her older brother does if she's already smoking. Maybe you shouldn't walk with them at all."

"Momma, he's not that kind of boy," said Rose not wanting her mother's impression of Juan tainted before meeting him. "He seems pretty nice to me?"

"Yeah, because you *like* him," said Lillie Mae looking up from her mother's lap.

"If I was you, young lady, I wouldn't say anything about anybody," her mother said looking down at her. "You in enough trouble, if your daddy finds out, Chile', I don't know what will happen."

"Momma I'm sorry, it won't happen again," cried Lillie Mae hugging her mother around the waist still kneeling at her feet, suddenly tears beginning to fall. "Please, please don't tell Big Adam!"

"Tell Big Adam what?" Their father stood at the door filling the entrance, jacket thrown over his shoulder, muscles bulging beneath his white cotton t-shirt. He avoided the drama, greeted his wife with a kiss, and complemented his eldest daughter. "Rose, the food smells so good, I smelt it way down the road. I knew it was my baby cooking. Hey son."

"Hey Pops."

"So, what's going on?" His voice strong and deep rumbling with authority.

Before anyone could say anything, Lillie Mae ran over and hugged him around the waist. "I'm sorry daddy."

He knew right away that she must be in trouble. Since his children could talk, they called him 'Big Adam', his name from baseball. That did not bother him. He knew he was their father. Nevertheless, whenever they were in trouble, they called him 'daddy'.

"Wait a minute, Lillie Mae," said Adam removing her arms from around him. "Sit down. Let me hear what your mother has to say, before we find out how sorry you are."

"But Daddy I…" she continued trying to make a final plea.

"Hush girl," he said firmly, "let me hear your mother."

No one moved. Who would speak first? Silence engulfed the kitchen like a courtroom before a verdict, even the pots on the stove simmered softly...waiting.

"DING!" They all jumped as the loud oven timer broke the silence.

"Cornbread's done," said Rose matter-of-factly. Everyone looked around and began to laugh. The tension in the room immediately gone, they relaxed.

"That bell almost made me run and get my gun," laughed Adam.

"You don't have a gun," said Lillie Mae relieved to see her father laughing.

"You don't know what I have," he responded giving her a look that she was not out of the woods yet.

"Yes sir," she said with downcast eyes standing in silence.

"That bell," he continued shaking his head, grinning as he reflected. "Sounded like a round from the boxing rematch of Joe Louis and Max…, Max something or other, back in '38."

"DING! The bell rang," he got into his familiar boxing stance, throwing punches in the air, bobbing and weaving around the kitchen. "Joe Louis pounded on Max's head so much the only thing saved him was…"

"The bell?" answered Lillie Mae with a worried smile.

"Just like you," he added to taunt her.

His theatrics and jovial banter made her feel safe enough to attempt another hug. This time he did not object.

"Vee, what's got my baby so worried?"

Lillie Mae relaxed as he patted her on the back, confident that when he referred to her as 'baby', she might be out of the woods. But that would depend entirely on her mother, since the rule was that Violet did the spanking if the problem was with her or Rose, and he did the spanking if the problem was with Lil' Adam but spanking only commenced when both parents agreed. Her destiny still lay in the hands of her mother.

"Your 'baby', said Violet sarcastically, "was caught smoking with some girl behind the schoolhouse…"

"What?" he said surprised, removing Lillie Mae's arms from around his waist.

"…by your cousin Buford."

"Did he take her to the Principal?"

"No. He knew you would tan her hide in front of the whole class if you came from work. He took them…"

"Them?"

"…yes, her and some other girl, straight to their teacher, Mrs. Gilmore, who told me what happened when she gave me and Lil' Adam a ride from the bus stop. I didn't know she lived right down the road."

"Lillie Mae, what were you thinking," he asked sternly, lifting her chin up towards his face. "You know the rule…No smoking and No chewing tobacco. That stuff ain't good for you. I told you fellows on the team had rotten brown teeth from all that smoking and chewing tobacco? You want your teeth to look like that?"

"No sir," she answered putting her head down, but he lifted her chin up again.

"Them fellows at work smoke too. They clothes smell, they breath smell, and they teeth brown. That's what you want Lillie Mae?"

"No sir."

Adam paused a second, then continued. "You best be glad Buford, part ways my cousin on my daddy's side, was there or you'd be in a heap of trouble, especially if your Principal called my job and I had to come to school. This better not happen again!"

"Yes sir."

"I tell you, Buford saved you like that bell saved Max…, Max something or other from Joe Louis knocking him into next week. Now go on and get me a glass of lemonade or something, all this here talking made me thirsty."

"Yes sir," said Lillie Mae with a big smile knowing for sure she had made it out the woods. She did not understand the 'bell', but somehow it saved her, Max, and the cornbread, and she would leave it at that.

"Buford only got that job after ole' Mr. Jesse couldn't halfway see no more," he continued hanging his jacket behind the kitchen door. "I remember when he'd tell us stories at recess, he had to be close to ninety years old, been working at Forrest Middle since it was built."

"Back then it was plain Forrest School for all grades," added Violet rubbing her feet. "You need help, Rose?"

"No ma'am dinner almost ready," she answered taking the meatloaf out the oven.

"I'm so hungry," said Adam reaching over putting his wife's feet on his lap to continue rubbing them. "I could eat a whole cow."

"It's not the whole cow, only meatloaf," laughed Rose, pleased her father enjoyed her cooking.

"What stories did Mr. Jesse tell Daddy," Lillie Mae asked affectionately.

"Stories when he was a slave picking cotton until his fingers bled and his back ached from bending over as the sun beamed down, whipped, spit on, and hated by people that reaped the benefit from his labor. The worse part, he said, was the name calling. I remember asking him why he was smiling and not angry. I never will forget what he said..."

"What did he say?"

He paused real long before he answered his daughter, reliving the moment. "He said, 'no matter what they call me, I know my name'."

"What names did they call him?"

"Names we don't use in this house young lady," interrupted Violet sternly looking at her daughter with a look that conveyed she was *not* completely out of the woods.

"A name that hurts so bad it stings on the inside deep in your gut," answered Adam rubbing his stomach as if in extreme pain, his face twisted in agony. "What he told me still helps me down at the railroad when the boss calls me names."

"It tears me up inside to even think of how much you go through," said Violet visibly shaken. "Let's not talk about this."

"I know it's painful, but my children need to know what helps me through…," he paused solemnly continuing to rub her feet. "Just thinking about Mr. Jesse and his big ole' smile with hardly any teeth, the pain I'm feeling eases inside. I say to myself, 'no matter what anyone calls me, I know my name'. If he could go through all he did as a slave and still have a smile on his face, then I can hold my head up and respond 'yes, sir' no matter what."

Violet reached over to hug him tightly. She knew he faced many hardships and difficulties. Things were not easy for colored people, especially colored men who often had to work twice as long for less money. "I'm sorry honey," she said turning sympathetically looking at each of her children. "Your father has told me stories of how men lose their jobs for getting angry and talking back. He goes through a lot to take care of us. Things haven't changed much from back in slavery times."

"Are you a slave?" said Lillie Mae as tears rolled down her cheeks.

"Come here baby," he said softly motioning for her to sit on his knee. "I don't want to make everyone sad. I'm not a slave, but I do work real hard."

"*And* get paid," added Lil' Adam hoping to lighten up the conversation, "which is the main difference from slavery."

"Anyway, slavery is illegal," added Rose as she started putting the plates and silverware on the table. "Ever since the Fourteenth Amendment, anybody born in the United States becomes a citizen."

"… And didn't Abraham Lincoln free the slaves," said Lillie Mae proudly. "We learned that in school."

"Yes he did, but white folks in the south loved slavery," added Adam. "I know that much."

"That don't make it right," added Violet.

"Far as I can tell they'd bring it back if they could."

"For the free labor," said Lil' Adam.

"No matter, the whole thing was wrong, it divided the country, and during the Civil War thousands of soldiers died from the North and the South," said Rose as she sat the final bowls of food on the table.

"Soldiers dying over a country divided" said Violet shaking her head sadly. "It wasn't right."

"Well let's eat."

"Adam, don't be so uncaring."

"I care, but my daughter prepared this great meal, and I can't wait to eat it."

"Me either," added Lillie Mae reaching over to grab the bowl of mashed potatoes.

"Wait!" said Violet softly slapping her hand, "until we say the blessing."

The aroma of meatloaf, creamed spinach, mashed potatoes, and cornbread filled the air as everyone joined hands around the table and bowed their heads. It was always a tradition to give a prayer of thanksgiving before eating.

Adam began, "Dear Lord, thank you for this family and this food my daughter has prepared. Thank you for keeping us strong through tough times. And thank you for saving Lillie Mae from getting a beating from her momma, Amen."

"Amen!" everyone responded in unison with an extra hearty 'Amen' from Lillie Mae.

"Don't think you getting off the hook that easy young lady," said Violet who could still alter her fate. "Let me hear someone else say you smoking again and I will tan your hide myself sho' as you born, no questions asked."

"Yes ma'am," said Lillie Mae careful not to aggravate her mother.

Eating was a time of enjoyment with family that outside turmoil could not alter. For now, no one thought of names, slavery, smoking, or other disappointments. The kitchen was silent of conversation as they reached for different bowls filling their plates with second and third helpings, appreciating the food and each other's company.

"Rose, you put your foot in it girl," said Adam breaking the silence taking another helping of mashed potatoes.

Lillie Mae looked confused, hunching her shoulders.

"That means the food is good," agreed Lil' Adam through a mouth stuffed with meatloaf.

"Your grandmother taught you to cook like this?"

"And momma," added Rose.

"Don't know if I recall your momma cooking like this," he said with a smile as he reached over and pinched Violet gently on the thigh.

"You up and married me while I was a child. I never had much time to learn to cook like Rose."

"Excuses, excuses," he laughed reaching over to kiss her on the cheek. "Baby you know I love your cooking and them…"

"Adam, what I tell you," she giggled like a schoolgirl enjoying her husband's boyish ways. "Besides, the Gist family loves my cooking, thank you very much."

"Yeah, that's because Ms. Daisy can't cook at all and the whole family nearly starves waiting until you get back on Monday."

"I know," said Violet joining everyone's laughter. "But Ms. Daisy was learning to cook pretty good before the accident."

"How is she doing?" he asked more seriously.

"She's the same," she answered with a sigh sitting on his lap while the children cleared the table and washed the dishes without request. Since they were younger, they all knew their kitchen duties, Rose washed, Lillie Mae dried, and Lil' Adam put away.

Laying her head on his shoulder as he rubbed her back, Violet reminisced about the Gist family. *Ms. Daisy, once so vibrant and full of energy, now stayed in her room most days staring out the window. Violet wished she could turn back the hands of time on that fateful day in August. She remembered it like it was yesterday, waving good-bye to Frank still excited about the circus, focused on coming home to her family and enjoying their time together. After settling in for the night, there was loud banging on the front door. Adam alarmed and ready to defend his family, leaped from the bed to the front door in two steps.*

"Who is it!" he shouted with a voice of power that radiated throughout the house.

"It's Carl," the voice responded with a slight quiver.

"Who," Adam reached for the bat next the front door?

"Mr. Gist, its Mr. Gist. Please, please I need to speak with Violet."

Adam snatched open the door. "Mr. Gist you know Violet don't work on the weekend."

Mr. Gist held on to the doorframe gasping for air as if he ran all the way to their house without stopping. His face beet red and his hair and clothes drenched with rain. "Adam, I'm sorry for disturbing your family. Please forgive me, but there's been an accident."

"Come in, please, come in," he responded this time with sympathy and concern.

Violet ran into the room barely able to recognize the man standing in front of her. His face distorted in anguish. Immediately she knew something was wrong. "Mr. Gist, what happened?"

As soon as he heard her voice, he began to sob uncontrollably. She looked up compassionately at her husband who nodded his approval for her to console him. "Please, sit here on the sofa."

Mr. Gist continued to cry unable to speak. The children came into the room dressed in their pajamas wondering what was going on.

"Rose, get Mr. Gist a glass of lemonade," she said rocking him gently with his head on her shoulder as if he were a little child.

After taking a few sips of lemonade and drying his eyes with the handkerchief Adam gave him, he finally gained enough composure to speak. "You know how excited Frank and Carl Jr. was with the circus coming to town. Mostly Frank, he really wanted to go, telling me repeatedly how the circus passed right in front of the house as the band played along the way. He could barely sleep last night. First thing this morning, he started again… the circus this and the circus that. In the end, Daisy and I decided to take the boys downtown for tickets. Vee! We should have never left the house! It's all my fault!"

Violet continued to rock him back and forth, tears welling up in her eyes for the grief he displayed, afraid to know why he cried. "God will work it out. Don't worry."

"Thank you Vee." He slowly took several more sips of lemonade and continued explaining the events of the day. "Daisy wanted to drive, so me and the boys headed out the front while she brought the car around. While we were waiting, I knelt to tie Carl's shoes. Frank could barely stand still. Not waiting for her to bring the car around, he ran around to the side of the house. Everything happened so fast, Vee! All I heard was tires screeching and Daisy screaming. By the time we reached the back, Frank was lying on the ground next to the car, not moving."

Mr. Gist began sobbing again.

"Oh Lord!" cried Violet, gripping him by the shoulders and shaking him. "Carl what are you saying!"

"Vee, we rushed Frank to the hospital, but they couldn't save him. He was gone. My son is DEAD! Vee, he's dead!"

"Oh Lord, NO!" cried Violet as they both held each other.

Adam stood behind the sofa with one hand on Mr. Gist's shoulder and the other on his wife's shoulder. Rose, Lil' Adam, and Lillie Mae stood watching quietly, everyone crying.

"Where is Daisy now?" Violet asked trying to be the strong one.

"She was so hysterical she had to be sedated. They're going to keep her overnight in the hospital."

"And where is Carl Jr.?"

"Oh my God!" frantic Mr. Gist jumped up heading for the door. "I left him in the car. He was sleep. I didn't want to wake him, oh my God, I left my son!"

"Wait! Just stay here," said Violet in a very calm voice turning towards her husband. "Adam can you get Carl Jr. out of the…"

Immediately he headed out the front door before she could complete her sentence, quickly returning with five-year-old Carl Jr. sleeping in his arms.

"The Lord will help us get through this." She motioned for everyone to gather around Mr. Gist and Carl Jr. as she began to pray. "Dear Lord, we don't understand your ways, but we know they are right all the time. Please Lord,

strengthen this family during their time of sorrow and keep your loving arms around them. In Jesus name we pray."

"Amen!" they all said softly.

"Mr. Gist, go back to the hospital with Ms. Daisy, we'll take care of Carl Jr., there's no need to worry, he'll be fine right here."

"Thank you," he answered with tears in his eyes.

"We glad to help," said Adam patting him on the shoulder, "go on and take care of your wife."

"Yes, yes," he appeared to hesitate not wanting to leave his son.

"He'll be fine," reassured Violet. "We got plenty of room."

Adam carried Carl Jr. into his son's room and laid him on the extra bed. Violet came over and pulled the covers up over his shoulders as Mr. Gist watched from the door.

"He's sleeping so peacefully," he said looking at his son, tears quietly rolling down his face. "Been through so much today, yet he never cried."

"He is a mighty strong boy." She leaned down to kiss him on the forehead as he slept quietly.

Violet and Adam stood on the porch as Mr. Gist walked towards his car, solemn and grief-stricken, appearing to age twenty years right before their eyes. They watched the car drive away, thankful for their family and praying for his family.

Later during the night Carl Jr. woke up with a scream, "Momma, momma!"

Violet ran quickly into the room scooping him up into her arms as he began to cry.

"There, there baby," she said rocking him back and forth as tears ran down both their faces. "Don't cry. I'm here with you."

"Ms. Vee?" said Carl Jr. squeezing her tightly, confused and looking around the room wondering where he was. "Where is Frank, Ms. Vee?"

"Frank went to be with Jesus," she said without hesitation slowly caressing the back of his head lying on her shoulder.

"Why he had to go with Jesus?"

"I don't know baby, I guess the good Lord and all the angels wanted him up in heaven with them."

"Is Jesus taking me up to heaven too?"

"Not today," she answered kissing him on the forehead.

"Will I see Frank again?"

"He will be around."

"Like an angel Ms. Vee?"

"Yes baby, like an angel, looking down from heaven smiling that big beautiful

smile of his, you remember that smile?"

"Yes, but I still miss him Ms. Vee."

"Yes baby, I know." She continued to rock him back and forth in her arms. "I miss him too."

Violet began to hum 'little ones to him belong, they are weak, but he is strong'. Carl Jr. slowly drifted back to sleep. A tear rolled down her cheek as she prayed, "Lord please help this family, they need you now."

"What's the matter," asked Adam lifting her chin up noticing her tears. "Why are you crying?"

"Momma, I'm sorry I smoked that cigarette," said Lillie Mae hugging her mother. "I won't do nothing crazy like that again, please don't cry."

"Oh baby, I know you sorry, these are tears of joy. Thinking of the Gist family made me realize how blessed our family is to have each other."

"We are blessed," he said kissing her on the cheek. "What made you think of them?"

"The way we all sitting her laughing reminded me of Frank, he was a happy child. He had the biggest smile I ever did see. Look at me making everybody all sad."

"Sometimes you need a good cry, even when you're happy…tears of joy."

"Tears of joy, reminds me of a new record by the Orioles called "Crying in the Chapel"," smiled Rose timidly. "You think I can buy it when we go to town Saturday?"

"How does it go?" her father asked.

Without hesitation, she began to sing, "You saw me crying in the Chapel. These tears I cry are tears of joy."

The children watched as their father stood, put his hand out to their mother requesting a dance, she gracefully accepted. One hand holding hers, the other around her waist, he twirled her around the small kitchen changing the atmosphere from sadness to joy. The other two children sat watching, while Rose sang, "I pray the Lord I grow stronger, as I live from day to day."

"I like that song," said Violet, feeling better.

"Plus, I want to get "Money Honey" by the Drifters, it has a snappy beat," she continued excited when she saw her mother's smile. "They got this new cat that sings with them named Clyde McPhatter. He is sooo dreamy."

"Oh no, I can't take anymore," said Lil' Adam shaking his head standing up from the table.

"Son this is all part of how to treat a woman," dipping his wife down low to the floor.

Lil' Adam smiled and shook his head, knowing he would never hear the last of 'how to treat a woman'. Being the center of ridicule did not bother him, especially if that restored the family's jovialness and made his mother happy. He waved to them turning to leave, "I'm going out back."

"Okay now that's enough," laughed Violet attempting to pull away. "I don't want to stay up too late. I have to roll Lillie Mae's hair."

"Just like a woman son," he said giving her one last dip. "Soon as you get started good… they done for the night."

"Who said I was done?" laughed Violet winking at her husband. This time she dipped him down low to the floor. "Now that's how you treat a man."

"Yeah baby, now you got me started," he said enjoying her teasing him.

"Adam, go on so I can finish what I need to do," she giggled as he kissed her on the neck. "Hard enough to get Lillie Mae up in the morning…"

"We'll finish this later," he said with a wink. "Let's toss a few balls son before it gets too dark."

"Boss man!" said Lil' Adam excited to spend time with his father.

Violet and Adam looked at each other, confused.

"It means 'great'," said Lillie Mae matter-of-factly from the table.

"Oh," they said in unison unwilling to admit their inability to keep up with the latest teenage terminology.

"Come on Lillie Mae."

"Yes ma'am," she said groggily, her stomach still full.

Every night her mother would comb, brush, and grease her hair with castor oil before going to bed. On the weekends, Violet took a brown paper bag from the grocery store and tore it into ten-inch strips, roll a large strand of hair around each strip, then twist the end securely. The next day Lillie Mae would have lots of long flowing curls she despised, but her mother loved.

5 THREE STRIKES

Three bats of varying weight, four balls reddish in color from the southern soil, two gloves, and his favorite, a tattered catcher's mitt from the Kansas City Monarchs, lay neatly behind the porch behind the swing. At first the mitt, a past birthday gift, was too large and heavy, but now it fit perfectly.

"Big Adam, the fellows want me to join their baseball team down at Willow Tree Field."

"I know where that is, I played down there when I was your age."

"They practice a couple times a week and have a game every Saturday."

"You saw them play?"

"Yes sir, they pretty good."

"Show me what you got."

"Yes sir!" shouted Lil' Adam enthusiastically tossing his father a baseball glove.

The length of the driveway was approximately the same distance as a pitcher's mound is to home plate. They threw the ball back and forth with precision, speed and accuracy, hindered only by the slowly setting sun.

"You pretty good," Adam said proudly. "When you were a little chap, before you could walk, all you wanted to do was play with a ball, any kind of ball. I remember telling your mother you would be a great baseball player."

"Like you?"

"Well," he laughed, "I don't know if I'd say all that."

Lil' Adam took a step back, rubbed the ball into his glove, focused. He lifted his front leg, high, and threw his father a fast curve ball that almost knocked him off balance.

Adam felt a slight burn through his glove when he caught the ball, amazed at his son's power. "Pretty close, I'd say," he beamed taking the glove off to massage his hand. "Pretty close."

They both laughed and continued throwing, each one attempting to outperform the other as dusk approached and the sky filled with amber and orange streaks from the descending sun.

"Great catch!"

"Boss throw!"

"What position you want to play on the team?"

"I was thinking, maybe I should try out for catcher. Isn't that the position you played with the Monarchs?"

"That was a mighty long time ago," said Adam rubbing his shoulder heading up the steps to sit on the porch swing. "Let's take a break son." No way would he admit that he was tired from a few throws, it must be the long hours at work, he thought. "Bet the girls at school think you the stuff?"

"Some of them do," he responded wondering what his father was getting at as he put the gloves and ball behind the swing. He knew his father was tired. No way would he push him to throw longer. He was glad for the time spent together.

"You got a special girl?"

"No sir," he answered slightly embarrassed by his question. "Not really thinking too much about girls right now."

"Your mind only on baseball," said Adam sarcastically with a smirk and a raised eyebrow. "Don't try to fool me son, wasn't long ago when I was your age."

"Well," he said hesitantly. "Chicks seem to like me, can't say there is a *special one*, they all look good to me. Don't rightly know which one I like the most."

Adam laughed heartedly. "Boy earlier you said you knew how to 'treat a woman' and now you say you don't even have one yet."

"But when I do, I'll know how to treat her."

"How will you know that son?"

"I'll keep watching you."

"Then you'll be fine," he smiled.

They both sat silently rocking as the moon glowed brightly, the sun only a memory.

"Momma told me you played with the Monarchs in the Negro League," he started thinking now was a good time to bring up a topic he longed to ask for many years.

"What else did she tell you?"

"She said you were the best baseball player ever."

He smiled and nodded, "pretty much."

"And every time you were at bat you'd hit the ball clean out the ballpark!"

"Almost every time."

"And if you got a hit to first base, you would always try to steal second."

"Sure did try," he laughed.

"And as catcher, you were so fast, no one stood a chance making it to home base."

"Boy, sounds like your momma might have stretched the truth a bit."

"Not one bit," said Violet standing in the doorway carrying two glasses of lemonade, "thought you boys would like a nice cool drink."

"Thank you," they both said.

"Your son gave me quite the workout. You might have to rub my shoulder tonight."

"Pops still got it."

"I know he does," she smiled.

"Come join us," said Adam.

"No, finish your baseball stories. I'm turning in as soon as I finish Lillie Mae's hair. I need to rest my feet." Before closing the screen door, she turned smiling warmly at her husband, "And you *were* the best ballplayer ever, even better than Jackie Robinson."

He smiled up at her, "And you still my biggest fan."

"Always will be," she said as the screen door closed gently behind her.

"You knew Jackie Robinson?"

"Yup, played with him in the Monarchs."

"*The*, Jackie Robinson?"

"Yup, '*The*' Jackie Robinson."

"Boss man!"

"He joined the team around 1945," he continued, enjoying his son's reaction as much as he enjoyed telling the story.

"He played for the Kansas City Monarchs?"

"Sure did," continued Adam rocking back and forth on the porch swing. "He played shortstop and boy I tell you nothing was getting past Jackie. He was fast as lightening. He made catching easy, because if someone was trying to run home, BAMM! He threw that ball to home plate so fast, nearly knocked me off my feet, 'bout like that pitch you threw tonight."

Adam jumped to his feet, startling his son. He stood erect for a moment both hands clasped together in front of him, staring slightly over his left shoulder. Slowly he raised his left knee up towards his chest perpendicular to the ground, as his right arm wound backwards, then threw an imaginary ball, SWOOSH! "You're Out!"

"Boss man!"

"But Jackie had his eyes on bigger things," his excitement diminishing as he sat back on the porch swing. "He wanted to play in the Major Leagues."

"Why you sound sad, wasn't that a good thing?"

"That was good, but back then they had what you call a 'color line', where Major League owners didn't want colored boys on their team."

"But you were so good! How could they not want you?"

"Sometimes people don't want you even if you're good, because of the color of your skin," he said, turning to look at his son with hope in his eyes. "But never give up, that's what helped Jackie."

"How," he asked trying to understand the complexity of the situation.

"He never gave up his dream to be in the Major Leagues. He kept playing hard as he could, game after game. Then one day, a general manager named Branch Rickey came to watch Jackie play and he didn't care about the color of this skin. We always saw the two of them talking. By and by, they became friends. Next thing we know, Jackie said he was going to play up in Canada with a team called the Montreal Royals."

"In Canada? That's another country."

"Yup," he continued his excitement rising. "First time he played, he had four hits at bat, one was a homerun with two men on base, plus he stole two bases. They loved him up there in Canada, called him 'the colored comet'."

"Boss Man!"

"But Jackie wanted to play in America."

"Did he?"

"What I tell you, never give up," he said, eyes filled with pride. "In 1947 Jackie got his chance, Branch Rickey got him signed with the Brooklyn Dodgers."

"Boss Man!"

"Our team got the ole' bus and went up to Ebbets Field in Brooklyn, New York, to watch Jackie play. The whole family went, including you, to see the first Negro, we knew, play in the Major Leagues."

"I can't remember," said Lil' Adam squinting his eyes trying to recollect the slightest memory. "And I was there!"

"In his first game with the Dodgers…" Adam stood, this time clinching both hands over his right shoulder as if he were holding a bat. Left elbow up, hips pivoting forward, he swung with force, BAMM! "Jackie knocked that ball clear out the park! Folks yelled and screamed with excitement."

"Colored and white?"

"Yup, colored and white," he continued gleefully. "That first year, he stole twenty-nine bases and was named Rookie of the year!"

"Rookie of the year?" he nodded in amazement.

"Yup, and the next year he stole thirty-seven bases and had sixteen homeruns."

"Boss Man!"

"But all that came at a price," his father's tone changed as he sat back on the porch swing. "His team members wouldn't even talk to him. In the dugout, he sat by himself. No one wanted to sit next to him. The saddest part was the other teams and people in the stands called him names, spitting and throwing things at him when he was on the field."

Adam paused as they both sat quietly rocking, the swing squeaking rhythmically from their weight, as the crickets chirped, and the owls echoed 'who, who' in the darkness. "But Jackie never quit," he continued slowly nodding. "He held his head up and lived out the dream he always wanted."

"To play in the Major Leagues," finished Lil' Adam.

"Yes. Last time we saw him was in 1949 when the Monarchs got together to celebrate Jackie being the National League's Most Valuable Player. Boy, I never saw a man so happy. We were proud of Jackie that day, real proud!"

"Boss Man!"

"Time to come on in," Violet called to her husband and son on the porch. Without waiting for a response, she finished placing the last roller in her daughter's hair. "Lillie Mae, pick up them scraps of paper and don't forget the hair grease."

"Yes ma'am."

"Where is your head rag, so I can tie up your hair?"

"In my room," she stood for a moment half-asleep, not recalling what she was supposed to do next.

"Get the head rag Chile'. I'm not trying to stay up all night fooling with you."

"I'm turning in Vee," said Adam kissing his youngest daughter on the cheek still standing in the middle of the floor. Winking at his wife, he added, "don't be long."

"I'll be in directly," she smiled thinking of his playfulness.

Lil' Adam sat on the couch, still puzzled from talking to his father, "Mom why didn't Big Adam go to the Major Leagues like Jackie Robinson did? Everybody says how good he was."

"Your father was a great baseball player, as good as Jackie Robinson, even better I thought."

"Is that how he got the name 'Big Adam'?"

"I don't know exactly who started calling him that first, maybe other baseball players, but he didn't mind and the name kinda' stuck. Did he ever tell you why he stopped playing baseball?"

"No ma'am."

"At first, he played on a local team and the whole town, colored and white loved to see him play. Soon word spread and people from other towns came to watch 'Big Adam' play. Before long, the Kansas City Monarchs asked your father to join the team. Everybody in town went crazy when they found out. Guess who was his biggest fan?"

"Poppa John," they nodded, responding in unison.

"Yes, he wanted to drive up to all Adam's games, but I was still in school."

"Big Adam didn't finish school? Maybe I can…"

"Don't start with that young man," interrupted Violet. "Yes, your father finished high school and so will you."

"Yes ma'am."

"*After* I graduated high school, your father asked me to marry him, and I got to travel all over the country with him and the Kansas City Monarchs."

"So why did he stop playing baseball?"

"I remember it like yesterday, "she sighed sadly, shaking her head with her eyes closed. "The Monarchs traveled to Pittsburgh playing against the Homestead Grays at Forbes Field. They were winning the game but some of the white people in the crowd seemed angry, more than normal, shouting hateful things during the game."

"Why they come see colored baseball players if they didn't like them?" wondered Lil' Adam, "that makes no sense."

"Sho' don't," said Lillie Mae lifting her head from her mother's lap, practically asleep.

"I didn't understand it either baby. Once the game was over, everybody wanted to get on the road as quick as possible, but we were hungry and wanted something to eat. Finally, we stopped at a place, but the restaurant had a sign in the window, 'Coloreds served in rear'."

"I would drive away if it was me," said Lil' Adam with a frown.

"Me too," said Rose, sitting in her housecoat with her feet stretched out on the loveseat.

"Even if we stopped somewhere else, it would be the same. So, we went around back..." She paused, not wanting to relive the pain, but knew it was important for them to know what ended their father's baseball career.

Seeing how upset she was, Lil' Adam put his arms around her shoulder, "what happened Momma?"

"It's a long story..., promise you won't give me any trouble in the morning for keeping you up so late?"

"We promise."

"Okay," she continued. "When we came back with our food order, your father and I sat at this picnic table on the side of the restaurant. After a while, a group of white men leaving the restaurant saw the bus with 'Kansas City Monarchs' on the side. Walking past us, one of them said to your father, 'Boy don't you play on that nigger team'?

Your father stopped eating and looked up at them. Then another one said, 'yeah, he plays with them, I remember him, he's pretty good'. Another one said, 'Yeah, good playing other niggas' but ain't no match for Lloyd Waner of the Pirates. 'Now he's a real catcher,' someone else said.

It took courage not to respond to their insults, but we knew it was time to leave and started wrapping up our food. As we headed for the bus one of them said, 'Boy that's a mighty fine heffa' you got there'. 'This woman is my wife,' was the first thing your father said. My heart sank. I knew from the sound of his voice, they had crossed the line. I tried to hurry him on the bus, hoping he would ignore them, but the men came over closer and said, 'hey missy come on home with me, I got what you need'. All the other men started to laugh. Before I knew it, your father turned and punched him dead smack in the face, POW! After that, everything happened so fast! He yelled at me to get on the bus as the other men ran towards him and started punching him, or trying to punch him, but your father was strong and able to get the best of them, until one of them hit him upside the head with a bottle. Then the others shouted, 'Hold him'. Someone grabbed a baseball bat and yelled, '*Catch this* nigga'."

"Jealous," said Lil' Adam angrily.

"I heard a loud crack, BAMM! Even today, that god-awful sound haunts my dreams. I started screaming! By then the team members came around the corner, but the men ran. Your father never cried out, but I knew he was in an awful lot of pain. You could see his knee mangled and twisted through his pants leg."

"Did you call the police?" said Lillie Mae sitting up, wide-awake.

"Yes. We waited two hours for a couple deputy sheriffs to come and say they were going to fill out a report. You could tell they didn't really care what had happened. When they left, I heard one of them laugh and say, 'good for that uppity nigger."

"By that time," sadly she continued, "your father's knees had swollen to the size of watermelons. I wanted to drive all the way home, but we had to find a hospital somewhere in that horrible town."

"How bad was it?" said Lillie Mae worried for her father.

"They told us what we knew," sighed her mother. "Your father's knee was pretty smashed up, and he wouldn't play baseball anymore, maybe never walk again."

The children listened in silence, heartbroken, their faces mixed with sadness and anger as their mother finished the story. "But you know, the Bible says, 'all things work together for good to them that love the Lord."

"You always say that," said Lil' Adam with tears in his eyes. "How could this be for good? Big Adam lost his chance at the Major League because of mean hateful people. There is nothing good about that."

As the tears began to roll down his face, Violet put her arms around him and squeezed tightly. "You right son, hate is never good. Your father was a great baseball player and it wasn't fair, but sometimes we don't understand God's plans."

They all sat quietly, saddened how the story ended.

"I do know this," continued Violet in an uplifted tone. "We found out that the Kansas City Monarchs had insurance on the team."

"What's that?" said Lillie Mae.

"Insurance is something you get to protect property," said Rose.

"Not that slave thing again, I hope."

"No," she smiled, for once not angered by her sister's inquisitiveness. "This insurance would be for the players on the team in case they got hurt, to pay medical bills and stuff."

"You right Rose," said Violet, impressed by her daughter. "They acted like they didn't want to pay the doctor bills, since your father hit the man first. But your grandfather, Poppa John, who lives in Kansas City, went to the NAACP."

"What's that?" said Lillie Mae.

"It stands for the National ...Association ...for the Advancement... of Colored People," she said carefully pronouncing each word. "Poppa John told them what happened and how the Monarchs did not want to pay the doctor bills."

Violet kept holding her son as tears began to roll down her face. "And you know what; the NAACP put together a lawsuit against the Kansas City Monarchs. It took a few years, but the Monarch's lawyers did not want to go to court, so they agreed to pay all the doctor bills, *and* give him extra money. And you know what your father did?"

The children looked at their mother with hopeful eyes and lifted hearts. "He bought this here house for our family and helped purchase the Potato Patch, the store your Grandma Mae always wanted."

The children looked at each other impressed by their father's love and generosity.

"After some time, he was able to walk," her voice grew stronger. "And one of the lawyers from the NAACP helped him get a job down at the railroad to take care of his family. Do you think God turned hate to good?"

For a moment, everyone sat quietly pondering her question, sad for their father, but proud of him at the same time. Ultimately realizing how things turned around.

Lillie Mae looked thoughtfully at her mother, "do you think it brings sad memories when we call him 'Big Adam', because of all that baseball stuff?"

"It would if it was me," added Lil' Adam, "maybe we should call him something else."

"Like what," said Rose wondering where her brother was going with this idea.

"Like Pops?"

"I like that," said Violet proudly.

"Me too," said Lillie Mae feeling much better inside.

"Yeah until you get in trouble and cry 'Dad-dy, Dad-dy'," teased her brother.

"Will not."

"Stop, it's too late to start bickering. I think your father will like 'Pops' or 'Daddy', either one." She kissed each of them, "now let's get to bed, or I won't want to get up myself."

The three William's children headed to bed prouder than before of their father knowing all he went through, so his family would have a better life.

Before Violet got into bed, she knelt to pray softly, "Lord this was a busy day. Thank you for my family, I am so proud of them Father. Please keep your loving arms of protection around us, in Jesus name I pray." She slowly crawled into bed and snuggled up close to her husband.

"What took you so long baby?" he whispered putting his arms around her.

"Shared some family history with our children," she answered relaxing in the warmth of his body.

"Um-hum, that's good," he responded already dozing back to sleep.

"Good night sweetheart," she whispered. Hearing no response from him, she smiled and slowly drifted to sleep.

6 GRANDMA'S HOUSE

Once a month, the children visited Violet's parents, Grandma Mae and Poppa John, for the weekend. When they were small, they enjoyed going, but lately they preferred staying home with friends. Despite their wishes, Violet insisted the tradition continue, since she knew her parents longed to spend time with them and appreciated their help in the store with ordering supplies, cleaning, cooking, and waiting on customers.

"You not ready, Lillie Mae!" shouted Rose already frustrated with the slow-moving pace of her sister.

"Don't worry about me, worry about *your…self*," she said rolling her eyes contemplating whether to take one doll or all of them.

"Poppa John is picking up momma at the bus stop. They'll be here any minute, and you not trying to get ready."

The two sisters shared a small room together barely large enough for the twin beds and dresser. Anyone entering the room could tell where it divided. One bed, neatly arranged with a homemade quilt and a teddy bear resting comfortably on the pillow. The other had a similar quilt but it lay crumpled and lopsided on the bed with dolls scattered everywhere. Squeezed next to the beds was a dresser. One side had a comb, a brush, ribbons, lipstick and lotion, arranged in a straight row against the mirror. The other side had scraps of paper from used rollers, jacks, a small ball, ribbons, and open lotion bottles.

Annoyed, Rose hurried around the room putting clothes into a small carrying bag. "You need to put those dolls down! You too old to be playing with dolls anyway?"

"No, I'm not too old," mocked Lillie Mae defiantly. "That's why Lil' Adam always tells you to mind your business'."

"Okay, if you not ready, it won't be my fault." Rose headed to the living room to listen to her new song "Only You" by The Platters as she secretly dreamed of Juan, which was the least she could do since he had not spoken to her since the first day of school. Maybe Margie and Naomi scared him away.

Lillie Mae looked up, thinking glad she left, now she could focus on what was more important than packing, deciding which doll to take for the weekend. Sitting on the floor, surrounded by all her dolls, some hand-made and some store-bought, she had a hard choice to make. "Too old for dolls, no way," she said aloud. "I'd rather be with my dolls than you."

Her favorite, designed by Sara Lee Creech in 1951, had dark skin and curly hair. Once her parents found out there were dolls especially for colored children, they purchased three. Her next favorite were the ones made by Grandma Mae from old clothes, with pieces of yarn for hair, braided into pigtails, and button eyes on beautiful brown faces. Most were hand-me-downs from Rose, but she did not care.

"Lillie Mae, you better come on here!"

Startled from her thoughts, she yelled back, "Leave me alone, I'm trying to get my dolls ready!"

"Dolls ready, you better get *yourself* ready."

"I said, I'm getting my dolls ready," rolling her eyes. "Just because you think you so grown, sash-shaying around here with your music all loud singing 'only you can make this world seem right' and dreaming of Clyde McPhatter, wishing he was your boyfriend…"

"I do not!"

"Oh yeah," continued Lillie Mae peaking around the living room door. "Oh yeah, I forgot you got a new boyfriend now. That pretty boy with his hair all slicked back. What's his name… Juan?... Only you can make my dreams come true…" She laughed and ran back into the bedroom.

"Get back in here!" Rose started to run after her, but shook her head and yelled, "He is *not* my boyfriend!"

"Who?" said Violet walking in the house carrying a bag of groceries.

"Nobody," Rose answered surprised to see her mother, "Lillie Mae fooling around, as usual. I'll take that."

"I *know* she ready to go!"

"I told her to get ready before you got here, but she never listens to me," she smiled glad to direct the focus away from the 'boyfriend' comment and to get her sister in trouble as well. "You know how she is."

"Lillie Mae!" yelled Violet sternly, heading towards her daughter's room. "I know you not just sitting there playing with them doll babies."

"No ma'am," said Lillie Mae looking up, amazed her mother knew exactly what she was doing.

"No ma'am what," she responded quickly, trying to stay firm despite her daughter's charming gaze. The same gaze Adam used to melt her heart.

"No ma'am. My bag is not ready."

Violet stood looking at her sitting on the floor surrounded by dolls, her anger returned. "Well young lady, you got three seconds to clean up this mess before I help you. And, I promise you won't like my help."

"Yes ma'am," she quickened her pace knowing her mother's help normally involved discomfort to her behind parts.

"What's all this fuss?" said Poppa John with Lil' Adam right behind him.

"Trying to get these chaps of mine in line."

"Let them be, seem to me they in line," he said walking into the bedroom to hug Lillie Mae. "Hey sweetheart, how you been?"

"Fine Poppa John," she responded happily hugging her grandfather.

"Now hurry up and get ready so your mother won't be yelling like the house on fire," he whispered in a soothing voice.

He was always calm, no matter what. At times, it was ironic, since Grandma Mae moved at a fast pace, always fussing. Yet he would slow things down with his famous, 'now Mae', and tranquility immediately entered the equation.

"Yes sir," she laughed squeezing him tighter. "I'm almost ready."

"Hi Poppa John," said Rose coming into the bedroom.

"There's my other sweetheart," he said giving her a hug. "You both get more and more beautiful every day. Get a move on, your grandmother 'bout to worry me to death if we don't get there soon."

"Lil' Adam you ready?" Violet turned to her son.

"Yes ma'am," he answered sitting down on the couch. "I got my bag together last night."

"That's my boy," said Poppa John sitting next to him. "Be prepared, that's what I always say. It will cut down on a lot of problems son, especially with the women folk in your life." He smiled with a wink.

"Yes sir," he nodded in agreement.

"Poppa you want a glass of lemonade while you wait for the girls?"

"Sounds good, a little refreshment before we hit the road is fine."

"Is Momma intending on spoiling them all weekend?"

"Ask me no questions and I'll tell you no lies."

"What that mean, Poppa John?" said Lil' Adam with a smile, always amazed at the strange things his grandparents said, some he never could figure out.

"That's an ole' saying, been around far back as I can remember. It means you really don't want to answer the question, because if you do, you'll probably lie."

"So, you don't want to lie to Momma?"

Poppa John smiled pondering his answer, "Well… you could say that, or you could say I didn't want to agree that your grandmother intends on spoiling y'all the whole weekend, like she said."

They both sat laughing as Violet brought her father a glass of lemonade. "What's so funny?"

"Oh nothing," he replied winking at his grandson.

The two girls walked into the living room with their bags. "As usual I ended up helping her finish," said Rose.

"That's what sisters do," smiled Poppa John getting up from the couch, "your momma and your Aunt Ruby helped each other all the time."

"And we still do," said Violet hugging her father at the front door. "Poppa, promise not to spoil them too much.

"Won't promise no such thing, if we had more grandchildren things might be different, maybe we wouldn't need to spoil them."

Violet smiled dearly at her father, "up to you, we'd have twelve children running around the house driving everybody crazy."

"Maybe," he kissed her on the cheek, "but since we only got three, we'll do what we please."

"Okay Poppa."

"Bye Momma."

"Have a good time," she replied kissing each of them as her father continued talking down the steps.

"…And you know we can't expect your sister to help with more grandchildren anytime soon, seeming as though she won't settle down long enough to find a decent fellow, Lord knows the ones she brought to the house were doozies."

"Don't worry. She'll meet someone."

"The meeting part's not the problem…" His words trailed off as he went down the driveway.

Waving to his mother with a big smile on his face Lil' Adam ran ahead of his grandfather and sat in the driver's seat. "See you Momma."

Violet watched as everyone piled into the old Buick. At least they did not have to crank it like the old Model "T" Ford. Everyone waved as Lil' Adam, beaming, slowly backed out the driveway. "Bye, have fun." Heading into the house, she noticed the time. "Adam should be home by now," she said feeling anxious.

* * *

As Lil' Adam was driving, he noticed an unfamiliar car quickly approaching him on the small road. The driver waved. "Hey, did you see that? Someone waved at me when they passed by."

"Son, pretty much everybody waves in the south. Not so much up north, got so many people and so many cars I reckon. Folks not as friendly up there either. Down here we like to show southern hospitality, so we wave."

"No, no, I don't mean that. I mean the driver of the car looked like Pops. Didn't you see who was driving the car that just passed?"

"No way was that him," said Rose looking up from her book.

"I did see a blue car but didn't notice who was driving, but I *know* it was not our father," said Lillie Mae staring out the window. "He's never getting a car, said he'd rather walk."

"It was him," her brother insisted. "You can't tell me it wasn't him."

"Not trying too," she argued. "But you know he doesn't have a car."

"Well, maybe it was him," said Rose siding with her brother. "Maybe he is driving his friend's car and plans to take Momma for a ride. But if you think he bought a car... you're dreaming."

"You'll see. That was Pops." The car swerved as he continued looking in the rear-view mirror.

"Son, focus on where you're headed. Your grandmother is excited to see all of us in one piece."

"Yes sir," he responded looking straight ahead. "I know that was him."

No one responded, breaking the silence, he turned on the radio and found "Deserie" by the Charts. Rose began singing along thinking of Juan, 'my darling, you know I love you so, don't know what you do to me, you make my heart feel so free'.

For Lil' Adam, the song reminded him of a girl at school, maybe he did need someone special, he thought, and soon he began humming along forgetting the blue car and the driver.

* * *

Pulling into the circular driveway, everyone was excited to see Grandma Mae who normally stood waiving on the porch, but this time she was not there. They all got out of the car, stretching, yawning, and wondering where she was.

"Mae," called Poppa John walking up the front steps, "now where is that woman?"

Their house, known as a 'shot-gun' house, was long and straight. Sunlight streamed into the front room, warm and inviting. In the center were two couches covered with plastic, facing each other, two reclining chairs so Grandma Mae and Poppa John could stretch out, or doze off, whichever came first. Four small tables with mix-match lamps and a large one in the center filled with family pictures and knick-knacks each with a story to tell. Blossoming plants hang throughout the room adding final touches of country beauty. Finally, over the fireplace hung a very large mirror surrounded by more family pictures, mostly of Rose, Lil' Adam and Lillie Mae.

The next room split, to the left, where the dining room held ten chairs tightly positioned around a large mahogany table glistening from a freshly waxed shine. Squeezed into the corner, was a china cabinet filled with dishes for special occasions only. On the wall was a very large painting of Jesus during the Last Supper, where His eyes appeared to follow you around the room. To the right, was Poppa John and Grandma Mae's bedroom, modestly furnished with a large dresser and mirror bordered by more pictures, a small table with an old-fashioned kerosene lantern, and a queen-sized bed neatly covered with a beautiful hand-made quilt.

The last room was the kitchen where a small light brown oak table and four matching chairs displayed the carpentry skills of Poppa John. In the corner was a new refrigerator, despite Grandma Mae's preference for the old one that needed large ice blocks inside to keep food cold. She did refuse to exchange her wood-burning stove for a gas range since it might, 'blow up the house'. Sunflower curtains brightened the room creating a welcoming country kitchen atmosphere. To the right was Ruby and Violet's old room, with twin beds covered with patchwork quilts made from scraps of their favorite clothes long outgrown, two dressers with mirrors on each side, two small tables and separate lamps adorned with white lace.

Off the back porch was the bathroom, added many years ago at the insistence of Violet and Ruby when all their friends received indoor plumbing. It only contained a small sink, bathtub, and a working toilet, a commodity Grandma Mae did not complain about.

Everyone headed for the kitchen expecting to see her preparing a big elaborate feast as always, but no Grandma Mae. There were signs of preparation on the table: chicken battered next to the cast iron skillet with a large clump of shortening in the center, okra chopped, corn shucked, tomatoes sliced, and biscuits perfectly shaped in a pan ready for the hot oven crackling in anticipation, but no Grandma Mae.

"Mae!" called Poppa John louder than before.

"Is she in the bathroom?" Lil' Adam asked heading out the door.

"You think someone came by and picked her up," said Rose.

"Maybe there was a problem at the Potato Patch," said Lillie Mae.

"Let's check out back," said Poppa John, "maybe she is in the barn".

Lillie Mae ran down the steps ahead of everyone else. Once she turned the corner, she stopped so quickly, Lil' Adam bumped into her. They both stood staring until Rose and Poppa John caught up to them.

"Mae!" he said frantically pushing ahead of his frozen grandchildren, worried.

"I'm right here," she answered sitting on the hay-covered floor feeding a small calf a bottle, as the calf's mother licked away blood streaked mucous. "Hello, come on in. Sorry dinner's not ready, but ole' Nellie had other plans."

For a while, they stood amazed watching the new mother and little calf. Finally, Grandma Mae attempted to stand as Lil' Adam helped her up. "Thank you, sweetheart, I'll finish up dinner while y'all get unpacked and washed up."

"Sounds good to me," added Poppa John as they all happily headed out the barn, leaving ole' Nellie licking her calf, now asleep nuzzled against his mother, full and content.

* * *

"That was a good meal," said Poppa John. "Don't think I could eat another bite. I'm full as a tick."

"You ain't never lied, but your belly's a heap bigger than what a tick could swallow."

Tightly squeezed around the small kitchen, the children enjoyed their grandparents' banter. It usually started with Poppa John saying something, followed by Grandma Mae responding with sarcasm mixed with ridicule, ending up being incredibly funny, often at the expense of their grandfather, who never seemed to mind if the joke was on him.

"Don't know what everyone is laughing at, this here is all muscle, thru and thru."

Grandma Mae walked over to him rubbing his stomach like a lamp in search of a genie. "Muscle, that belly hasn't seen muscle in …" She paused, her face portraying deep thought. "…I can't count how many years."

"It's in there," he said continuing to massage the area of their amusement, "just hard to see."

"Especially without your bifocals."

Everyone continued laughing as he stood up and began jiggling his stomach up and down, enjoying being the center of their heartfelt laughter. "Well, maybe it became a bit shaky over the years."

"Don't worry Grandpa, you can always be Santa Claus for the Christmas play," said Lillie Mae.

"Now that's a good idea," he grinned bouncing his shoulders up and down making his stomach shake more and more. "How does that story go, Ho, Ho, Ho… He shook when he laughed like a bowl full of jelly."

"You got that part right," said Grandma Mae ending the story and refocusing everyone. "Now let's get this kitchen cleaned up before it *is* Christmas."

The laugher slowly dissipated as they began the process of restoring the kitchen to its normal state, but no one seemed to mind, smiles stayed on their faces as they remembered Poppa John's Santa belly.

"John, why don't you and Lil' Adam chop up that ole' tree outback that fell the other day, could use some more firewood.

"But Mae, it's time for bed, and it's dark outside."

"Not that dark," she added removing her apron, folding it, and placing it neatly on the kitchen chair. "Just turn on the light and try not to chop off your foot."

"Grandma Mae," added Lil' Adam, "if you get a gas stove like we have, you wouldn't have to use the wood-burning one."

She answered in a softer gentler tone, "used wood for the stove, far back as I can recollect. I still can see granny standing by her potbelly stove cooking a whole meal with one skillet. Talking 'bout some good eating, I tell you! We'd all gather round to keep warm while she made cookies, the whole house smelled like love."

"Times are changing Grandma."

"Yes, they are. I wouldn't know what to do if I had a … what they call it, a 'gas range', reckon I'd be scared I'd blow up the house."

"We'd make sure it was safe," said Lillie Mae standing to reassure her grandmother.

"I know you would baby," as all three joined together for one big hug, "but granny to ole' to fool with some newfangled contraption. Probably burn up everything I cook. Then how would y'all get them good home cooked meals."

"You right, I don't want to mess up them meals," Lil' Adam said nestled in the group hug.

"Your grandmother is the best cook this side of the Mason Dixon line," they heard Poppa John say from the back porch.

"Ahh John," Grandma Mae said as a tear slowly rolled down her cheek. "Don't know what I'd do without you all."

For a moment, the children shared her joy and embrace until the sounds of crickets reminded them of the approaching darkness.

"Better come on son while we got a bit of light."

"Enough crying for today, Lil' Adam go on and help your grandpa," as she wiped her face with the back of her hand.

"Yes ma'am," Before closing the screen door, he turned to say to her, "I love you Grandma."

"I love you too baby," she smiled up at him, "now hurry along before it gets too dark and mind your Grandpa's foot."

7 SPOILED ICE CREAM

Although she knew her children would rather stay home, Violet enjoyed the private weekend, once a month with her husband; it was like a mini-honeymoon. She would prepare a nice candlelight dinner, and weather permitting they would cuddle on the porch swing looking at the stars sparkling in the moonlight.

Distracted by crackling gravel in the driveway, thinking it was her father returning, she walked to the kitchen door. "Now what, I tell you that girl always waiting 'til the last minute… bound to forget something. I hope they didn't drive all the way back here..." Before she could open the screen door, Adam quickly slipped inside blocking her view.

"Hey baby, looks like you in a hurry." He pulled her close to him and pressed his lips firmly against hers in a long welcome-home kiss. Violet smiled up at him relaxing in his arms, her thoughts erased as she enjoyed his embrace. "Waited all day for this," he whispered in her ear.

After a few moments, she regained her composure and attempted to look around his shoulder, but he continued to hold her closely. "I heard a car pull into the yard, thought Lillie Mae left something…"

"No, it wasn't Lillie Mae," he interrupted leading her away from the screen door. "Umm, something smells good. Let me light the candles."

"Adam, why you trying to change the subject… did someone give you a ride... drop you off... I heard a car drive up… but didn't hear one drive away?" She tried to turn and head back towards the door, but he was too fast, cutting her off each way she maneuvered, laughing heartedly at her futile attempts to get past him.

"Calm down woman! I tell you, there is no way to pull the wool over your eyes. I'll show you soon enough."

"Show me what," she squirmed unable to release herself.

"Now, now," he smiled slyly. "First let's enjoy this delicious meal I smell calling me from the stove, before it gets cold. I'm hungry. A bologna sandwich and apple won't hold a man but so long."

Violet could see the sincerity in his eyes and his desire for her to trust him. She knew he was up to something, but she did not want to spoil what he planned for the evening, so she allowed him to lead her towards the kitchen table.

"Thank you," he said breathing a sigh of relief.

"For the time being," she smiled in agreement wondering what he was up too.

* * *

"That was a good meal," said Adam leaning back in the chair rubbing his stomach. "I can't eat another bite."

"Well thank you," she answered standing to clear the table.

"C'mon over here before you start the dishes," he said pushing his chair back gesturing for her to sit on his knee. Automatically she sat down, giggling as he kissed her neck. "A good meal in my belly, a good woman in my arms, children gone for the weekend, house to ourselves, what more could a man ask for?"

"A clean kitchen," she responded attempting to get up.

"Can't it wait, let's sit on the porch for a minute, it's such a beautiful night." He pulled her closer. "The stars are bright. The moon is full. Ahh-wooo", he threw his head back and howled like a wolf.

"You so silly," laughed Violet enjoying his playfulness. "Okay, I'll sit on the porch under one condition, promise?"

"Pending the condition," he answered biting at her neck, "Ahh-wooo!"

"That you promise to help with the dishes."

"Oh, that's easy. I promise. Now let's hurry outside so the moonlight can shine on your beauty before I change into… Ahh-wooo."

She laughed loudly as he squeezed her, his head buried in the side of her neck. For a moment, she wondered if anyone heard them making so much noise. "Oh well," she thought happily.

On the porch swing, they rocked quietly for some time. "It's so beautiful," she said softly snuggling close to him. "Looks like a million stars twinkling in the sky."

"Only half as lovely as you," kissing her softly, his arm wrapped around her shoulder.

The swing squeaked rhythmically back and forth, as they sat looking at the moon and its celestial companions. Normally, one or the other would doze off, but tonight Adam could barely contain himself waiting for her to notice the surprise. Afraid she would fall asleep he stretched his arms out amidst a big yawn and said, "Such a beautiful night, I love you baby…"

Violet murmured, "Um-hum, I love you too…" her head resting on his shoulder, rocking… dozing…Suddenly, she put her foot down! The swing stopped, her eyebrows squinted together. "Whose car is that in the driveway," she asked suddenly as if awakening from a dream.

"What car?" he answered trying not to laugh.

"Adam John Williams Jr., don't you 'what car' me! You know *exactly* what I mean!" Violet stood up from the swing and walked down the stairs, hands on her hips. "I knew I heard a car in the driveway when you came, and I didn't hear a car leave. Then you tried to distract me, making me think I was crazy. I knew you were up to something."

"Ain't this a mighty fine car," he asked trying to wrap his arms around her.

"Yes," she said agitated, moving his arms away and walking down the steps to the passenger side of the car. "One of your friends let you drive it home?"

"Nope," he stood quietly watching her open the car door and look inside.

"Well who's car is it then?" she said, mentally scanning his list of friends, wondering who let him bring home such a nice car to sit in the driveway for hours.

"Yours," he said calmly walking to where she stood.

"It is a mighty fine car, lots of room in the back, *and* leather seats. Can you start it up?"

He reached in his pocket, took out the keys and obliged her request. He was content to watch her going from the front to the back of the car, full of excitement. He never felt prouder as a husband. All these years, she never complained as she walked practically a mile to catch a bus to work, never asking for a car to make life easier.

"Have you ever saw a dashboard like this before, it lights up so nice, such pretty colors." She pushed down on the horn. BONK! "Good sounding horn. Who's car?" She walked around to the back not really listening to her husband, completely preoccupied. "I like the lights on the back too, and the tires are so clean you can even tell how white they are in the moonlight. Whose car you say it was?"

"Yours."

"Yours, that's a strange name," walking around to the passenger side again and opening the door. "Where they from, another country? I like the way the windows roll up and down so easily, not like the ole' Model T. Ford Poppa had. You almost broke your arm trying to roll up the window. Who you say the car belongs too?" she continued focused entirely on the car instead of her husband's response.

"Violet Mae Williams," with both hands on her shoulder he gently turned her around to face him. "Listen to me… the … car …is …yours."

She looked at him in total disbelief thinking maybe she misunderstood what he was saying. Lifting her chin and looking directly in her eyes he continued, "This here is a 1950 Chevrolet Bel-Air Hard Top automobile, and it belongs to you."

Violet stood looking up at her husband, chills ran through her body, not knowing what to say. "You wouldn't try to fool me would you Adam?" she asked as tears began to form.

"No, baby I wouldn't try to fool you, I love you too much," pulling her close he wrapped his arms around her. For a moment, the world stopped rotating and it was only the two of them as tears rolled freely down her cheeks.

* * *

Finally sitting in the kitchen, calmer, she asked the questions she needed to ask. "When did you buy this… this Chevrolet Bel-Air Hard Top? How long have you planned to buy a car? Can we afford it? I can't believe it, Adam is it really ours?"

"Baby, calm down, I've been saving up for a while now." He sat across from her in the kitchen holding her no longer shaking hands. "You know how I feel about catching the bus and sitting in the back like a second-class citizen. We work as hard as the next fellow. Last Monday at work, Fred told me he saw a used Chevy down at Ben Franks Auto. Said Ben always gives colored folks a good deal. So, we stopped in after work and sho' nuf' he did treat me right. Told me the car belonged to a woman who had a colored driver. He asked me if I knew the driver. I said 'no' and he looked at me strange. You know how they think we know each other."

The two of them smiled realizing how often this happened. Violet, feeling more confident that he was not fooling her, fixed a glass of lemonade for the two of them as he finished telling the story.

"Thank you," he continued. "He said the car had thirty-thousand miles, in 'mint condition', and only cost eighteen-hundred dollars. When I told him I had cash, he looked at me like I was crazy."

"Oh my, Adam," her eyes questioning his decision, "that's a lot of money, can we afford it?"

"Don't you always say the Lord will make away."

"You right baby, you right." She nodded, convinced of his sincerity. Otherwise, he would not bring God into the conversation if he were joking. She reached over and kissed him, finally believing. "I'm so proud of you, thank you for making me so happy."

"Plus, I was tired of our children asking for a car." He dangled the keys in front of her face, "so here you go baby, our first family car, you want to take her for a spin?"

She stared at him and the keys.

"You CAN drive, can't you?"

"Of course, I can drive." She took the keys leading the way, hesitating before opening the door. "It's only… well I haven't drove for quite some time, and I'm not familiar with these newfangled cars. Do you mind driving this first time?"

"Of course, I don't mind." He began to speak with an uptown city accent. "It would be my *pleasure* Mrs. Williams, to chauffeur you around town, in this fine *automobile*." He bowed low before her, extended his hand and escorted her to the passenger side door.

"Thank you sir," she responded with the same dialect sitting in the front seat.

"Where too my lady?"

"Surprise me sir."

"My *pleasure*, my lady," he bowed once again kissing her gently on the hand and carefully closing the car door.

Once he was in the car, she scooted over very close to him. Thinking at first, she might be too close, but after he backed out the driveway and turned onto the road, he looked at her and smiled.

"Would you like to hear some music, my lady?"

"Yes sir, sounds lovely."

Searching through the radio stations he found, "Twinkle little star" by the Elegants. Now riding together everything seemed different, the stars twinkled brighter, the air smelled fresher, and the 'man in the moon' was no longer stationary from the porch swing but appeared to follow them smiling as they rode along. Violet took a deep breath inhaling the night air, her arm wrapped around the one she adored, "this is so perfect, honey, thank you."

Adam turned into a drive-in hamburger joint. It was a warm night with cars lined up for service. Soon after pulling into a parking spot, a girl on skates rolled over to take their order. "We'd like two vanilla ice cream cones please," he said apprehensively not knowing if they served colored people.

"Yes … sir," she replied chewing her gum between each word. "Two… vanilla… ice creams…"

"Thank you, ma'am," he tried to reply, but she sped away too quick to hear his gratitude.

Relieved to have service, the two of them watched in amazement as young people skated in and out of the restaurant with trays of hamburgers, fries, sodas, banana splits, and rolling from car to car with precision and accuracy. Soon their server rolled back carrying two ice cream cones wrapped in napkins. "Here … you go… sir…," she chewed happily. "That …will be …fifty-cents..."

He reached in his wallet and gave her a dollar bill. "Keep the change."

"Thank you, sir," she said this time without chewing. As she skated away, she looked back at him with a smile as if seeing him for the first time.

"That was nice of you dear, she seemed mighty happy."

"…and surprised," he added licking his ice cream before it started to melt. "I'm just glad to have good service without going to the back, or to the side or maybe no service at all."

"It's sad that people can be so cruel because of your skin color. Don't think about that right now," she said cheerfully scooting close to him. "Let's just enjoy our ice cream and celebrate our first family automobile."

"A mighty fine automobile, if I say so myself."

"You did a good job, I'm proud of you." After patting him on the back, she gave him a big kiss on the cheek.

"Thank you my dear," he answered in his uptown city accent.

They continued watching young people skate back and forth serving both colored and white customers. Once they finished their ice cream, Adam got out the car to put the napkins in the garbage a few cars down. As he was walking, he noticed a police officer sitting in his patrol car watching him the entire time. By the time he returned to the car, he appeared visibly shaken, his mood changed from jovial to gloomy.

"What's the matter honey?"

He stared straight ahead not responding to her question. Everything stood still inside, while outside business continued as usual, skaters rolling, customers laughing.

"Adam, what's wrong?" She pleaded nervously. He did not answer, his face expressionless, blank, she did not recognize him. "Adam you're scaring me! Please talk to me!"

As he started the car and began backing out, "nothing is wrong," was all he would say. He turned onto the highway continually looking in the rear-view mirror.

Silently they rode away, the radio turned off. She wondered if any song could pierce through the darkness that enveloped their Chevrolet Bel-Air Hard Top. What could have changed his demeanor? She sat in silence as he drove. The night no longer felt welcoming and friendly, but a dark and suspicious cover for monsters lurking behind the trees.

Once he turned down the highway leading home, his previously tense shoulders slowly began to lower as he relaxed, appearing to exhale. She wrapped her arm around his, squeezing softly. He looked at her and smiled, he was himself again.

"Honey, what happened back there?"

"Probably my imagination," he responded with a sigh of relief still glancing back. "It was just… no it was nothing. Forget it."

"No please tell me," Violet insisted. "You looked like you saw a ghost."

Seeing the concern in her eyes, he knew he needed to explain his behavior. "When I took the garbage, a police officer watched me every step of the way, like I did something wrong, looking at me with disgust, as if the sight of me made him sick. Shook me up, that's all."

"Well let's try and forget, we're almost home."

Quietness engulfed the car as they drove along the highway. They both tried to relax… Suddenly, bright flashing red lights expelled the darkness. Instinctively, they both tensed up, frightened, not from personal dealings with the police, but from the horrible stories they heard.

"Just calm down baby," Violet said nervously.

He took a big deep breath, staring straight-ahead, gripping the steering wheel tightly. Despite what she said, he could not 'stay calm'. His shoulders tensed more, his body stiffened, and his palms began to sweat.

The police officer slowly walked up to the car and shined a bright flashlight into the car blinding them. "Boy where you headed?" he inquired with a thick southern accent. They could not see his uniform or face, only a bright white light, but his tone was harsh and cold.

"We live over on Mulberry Road," he answered calmly to his surprise, wondering if this was the same police officer from the drive-in hamburger joint.

"Didn't ask where you lived, boy I asked you where you headed."

"We headed home sir," he responded respectively as possible his fingers gripping the steering wheel tighter.

"This here a mighty fine car boy," he added as the bright light temporarily left their faces to move along the exterior of the car. "What's a nigger doing with a car like this? Did you steal it?"

"No sir, this is my car," Adam responded, speaking very softly squeezing the steering wheel so tight the bones on his knuckles protruded under the skin. Violet squeezed his arm firmly, praying he maintain his composure.

"What kinda' car is this boy?"

"It's a 1950 Chevy Bel-Air, sir."

"Where's your license and registration?" said the police officer once again shining the bright flashlight into the car, intently watching

Adam, as he opened his wallet to remove his license and reaching in the glove compartment for the temporary vehicle registration from Ben Franks Auto.

"Hurry up boy! Can't believe a nigger got a car like this," he said sarcastically shaking his head as he unwillingly admired the car.

"Here you go sir."

Violet sat quietly holding her breath, maybe having a car caused more problems than they had before.

The officer snatched the license and registration from his hand. As he did this, Adam saw it was the same officer. When he examined the license, his eyes widened with recognition and his demeanor appeared to soften.

"Hey, are you the same Adam Williams that played for that colored team…the Kansas City Monarchs?"

Violet and Adam looked at each other with confusion, neither could believe the entirely different tone as the officer switched the light from the license to Adam's chest, instead of directly in his face.

"Yes sir," he answered bewildered when he noticed a smile.

"Sorry, I didn't recognize you. Boy you were one heck of a ballplayer, back what, nine, ten years ago. Me and the boys drove up to see most of your games." He continued as if they were old friends. "Boy, you sho' was good. Heck, you were even better than Jackie Robinson was! Your record was better, you had more homeruns, and your batting average was better. It was fun to watch you play. We knew for sure you would be the first hometown boy headed to the Major League. Until you blew out your knee, everybody hated that, pretty much ended everything for you."

Adam, not gripping the stirring wheel as tightly, stared at the officer who summed up his baseball career as if he wanted an autograph. Grateful he no longer called him 'nigger' yet saddened that he still referred to him as a 'boy'. Only now, 'boy' sounded more like an old friend, instead of someone inferior.

"My cousin Sammy used to live down the road from you. He always bragged how he played with you and the other boys over in that field off Highway 15 by the ole' Granger place …Willow Tree Field."

"Yeah, that's the place, I remember Sammy," Adam nodded with a slight smile. "Nothing could get past him at second base but a homerun."

"Yup, that was him. He won't believe I talked to you."

"Tell him I said hello."

"Will do sir, will do."

The police officer handed the license and registration back to Adam. Now they could clearly see his face. He was young, maybe in his mid-thirties, too young to be displaying the hatred they experienced earlier. His piercing blue eyes appeared genuinely friendly now, and a smile so broad they could see his teeth, a different person.

"Thank you," was all Adam could say as the officer returned his license and registration.

"Sorry to inconvenience you sir," he said politely lowering the flashlight.

"No inconvenience officer," he lied. The damage was done, they were not friends. He did not want any part of his schizophrenic behavior. The pain inside would not easily go away. All he could oblige him with was courtesy, like ole' man Jesse.

"Y'all have a goodnight," the police officer said tipping his hat to Violet. "Ma'am."

"Thank you officer," she replied looking back as he walked away.

The officer got into his squad car, made a U-turn, and drove into the darkness from whence he came. They sat frozen in their seats, not knowing what to say or do. Finally, starting the car, they headed home. No one spoke.

After pulling into the driveway, Adam sat staring out the front window, hands still gripping the steering wheel. "I'm sorry, I didn't mean for things to go that way. This was not what I planned." A single tear rolled slowly down his cheek.

"Please don't let what happened back there ruin our celebration." She gently touched his arm. The same arm she held tightly less than five minutes ago. "We're home now."

"I wanted to surprise you."

"Oh, you surprised me alright," she laughed lightening the mood. "Don't forget the car sat in the yard for a long time before I realized it was there…"

"…then you started to fall asleep," he shook his head smiling.

"Plus, I didn't believe you when you said it was our car. You had to turn me around and call me by my name for me to listen."

"I wish you could have seen your face when you finally heard me say it was our car. You looked shocked and happy all at the same time."

"I almost passed out."

"Thought our first drive would be to the hospital."

They both laughed, their mood uplifted.

"All I wanted to do was make you happy," he said looking her directly in the eyes.

Violet looked up at her husband no longer able to hold back tears. "Nothing could ever take that away."

"Let's start over," he kissed her as "There's a moon out tonight" by the Capris played softly on the radio. "I love you so much, thank you for always making me the happiest man in the world."

She laid her head on his shoulder peaceful and content. Once again, the stars twinkled, the moon smiled, and the night enveloped them, safely at home.

8 THE POTATO PATCH

Lil' Adam found it difficult sleeping with the crinkling sounds of plastic on the living room couch. At one point, he attempted to turn on his back, but the side of his face was stuck to the cushion. Early before sunrise, awakened by the delightful aromas of breakfast, he groggily walked into the kitchen rubbing his eyes feeling sleepless, "Good morning, Grandma Mae."

"You sleep good, baby?"

Watching her move quickly around the kitchen fixing biscuits, grits, bacon, sausage, and eggs, he started to tell her he would sleep much better if she removed the plastic from the couch, instead he politely said, "Yes ma'am."

"Get you some orange juice, breakfast almost ready."

Before he could sit down with the juice, she added, "Do you mind feeding the animals out back, your grandfather moving a bit slow this morning."

"Yes ma'am," he replied quickly taking a sip of orange juice before leaving. There was always plenty of work to do around the farm, the cows, chickens, and pigs needed water and food every day. He enjoyed helping, but appreciated Gus and Paul, farmhands who helped his grandparents complete everything through the week.

"And put lots of water in the trough," called Grandma Mae. "Gonna' be a hot one today."

"Yes ma'am."

She moved efficiently throughout the kitchen while pots bubbled, frying pans sizzled, and wood crackled in the potbelly stove from the hot fire. Her hands dusted with flour, she rolled the dough around until a soft mound formed, and skillfully shaped two pans of biscuits ready for the oven.

"Was that Lil' Adam I heard?" said Poppa John adjusting his overalls coming into the kitchen.

"I sent him off to tend to the animals, so you could sleep. He is such a fine well-mannered young man."

"He strong too, chopped that wood up last night like a champ, would take me four, five days, and Gus or Paul would take longer than that."

"I went in there to check on him last night, thought he needed a snack after all that work, but he'd already fell asleep, plum tuckered out."

"Good morning," said Lillie Mae walking slowly into the kitchen, "smells good in here."

"Thank you, sweetie. Can you set the table?" She rubbed butter on the golden biscuits hot from the oven, quickly placing them in a bowl on the table. "Tell Rose to gather up the eggs out the barn, we can take the extra ones to the store."

"Yes ma'am." Quietly, she peaked around the corner to watch her sister in the mirror and yelled. "Grandma Mae said get them eggs out the barn!"

Rose jumped. "You better stop yelling at me."

"And get out the mirror."

"Ugh," was her only response. Already dressed, she finished fixing her hair and went into the kitchen. "Good morning Grandma Mae," she said calmly hugging her grandmother and kissing her on the cheek.

"Good morning baby, you look so pretty this morning. All dressed up and ready to go, hate to have you get eggs. Tell Lillie Mae to bring them."

"I don't mind, back in a jiffy."

"Jiffy?"

"That means fast."

"Ohh," she said talking to herself. "Can't keep up with all the new words the chaps say, most of it don't make sense to me."

"What don't make sense," said Poppa John walking into the kitchen attempting to dry his hands on his overalls before his wife noticed.

"How yesterday they were chubby little babies, now they grow up in a 'jiffy'." She noticed the look of confusion on his face and gladly added. "That means fast John."

"You learn something new every day."

* * *

The Potato Patch was Grandma Mae's life-long dream. After Adam purchased the building, everyone worked together cleaning, painting, and stocking the shelves. Poppa John contributed money saved from his roadside fruit and vegetable stand to add a small kitchen in the back with a few tables and chairs for customers to enjoy Grandma Mae's cooking.

Located at a crossroad on the outskirts of town, things were difficult at first. The white customers, who patronized the previous owner Mr. Russell, would not come to a colored owned establishment. The colored customers, with very little cash, wanted to purchase items on credit, promising to pay when their crops sold. Grandma Mae did not give up hope. Before long, her warm smile and homemade apple pie shared freely with all her customers, softened the hearts of everyone, colored and white, enough to begin making a small business profit.

The William's children knew their duties. Rose helped in the kitchen. Lil' Adam took inventory, ordered supplies, and cleaned, while Lillie Mae, who felt she had the best job of all, waited on customers. Soon after arriving, breakfast was prepared, and if the breeze was right, the smell of bacon, biscuits, and fresh coffee, enticed customers for miles around. With only two small tables, a counter, and a few chairs, many mornings there was standing room only in the small restaurant.

During the crop-harvesting season, Poppa John allowed men to stand outside as they waited for local farmers to drive-by and select additional help each day. Most of the men stopped in for breakfast, "Morning Ms. Mae," they would say politely. Money or no money, she would always say, "Sit on down and eat son before you go off to a hard day's work."

This day, Rose looked up to see a young man standing at the counter. His clothes appeared worn but well-kept with carefully sown patches on the knees of his overalls. He looked familiar, but she could not place his face.

"Good morning Ms. Mae," he said smiling as he sneaked a quick glance over at Rose. "What you cook good?"

"Everything I cook *is* good son," she quickly responded while sprinkling grated cheese on her pan of scrambled eggs, not noticing the person speaking until she looked up. "Well I'll be, if it ain't Beau Henderson." Wiping her hands on her apron, she headed around the counter. "Come on here and give me a hug. How you been son, haven't seen you for quite a spell?"

"No ma'am," he responded glancing over at Rose again, distracted, until he received a large warm hug. "I mean, yes ma'am, I have been gone for quite a while."

"What can I get you son?"

"Nothing this morning ma'am, I came by to find work for today and stopped in to say hello."

"Well hello, it's good to see you."

"Thank you ma'am."

"Sound like you picked up a northern accent."

"Could be ma'am," he said shyly glancing over at Rose who was busy turning the sausages and stirring the grits, not appearing to notice him or their conversation. "I spent the last three years up at Howard University in Washington, D.C."

"Well I'll be, a college boy now," she said pulling him close for another hug, this time patting him on the back. "And stop calling me ma'am, been knowing you since you were in diapers, call me Grandma Mae."

"Yes ma'am, I mean, yes Grandma Mae ma'am."

"Rose, give the rest of the sausages to Beau while I see if we have more in the back."

"Yes ma'am," she reluctantly attempted a smile.

"I think I got some ham back there too, I hope you hungry."

Activity in the kitchen remained at a busy pace as breakfast customers sat down to eat as soon as an empty spot became available. There were no cash registers or menus, everyone left a quarter, fifty-cents, or whatever money they had on the table for payment.

Finally, Beau broke the silence, "How you been Ms. Rose?" he said timidly not looking her directly in the eyes.

"Been fine, thank you," she quickly responded hoping he would not say anymore.

"Your brother has gotten tall since I last saw him. He barely remembers me."

"I can't say I remember you either."

"You don't remember, I lived right down the road from Ms. Mae and Mr. John at the old Sam's farm." He sat down at the counter watching her move around the kitchen with the same efficiency as her grandmother.

"No, still don't remember," said Rose matter-of-factly sitting down a plate of grits, biscuits, eggs, and sausage in front of him before quickly returning to the stove.

"Remember I used to come over during the summer," he said leaving his plate to follow her behind the counter. "Your brother and I would play ball in the front yard and sometimes go swimming at the water hole."

"Okay," said Rose squinting her eyes as she walked back to the table to sit down a glass of orange juice with him right behind her. "I do vaguely remember Lil' Adam going swimming, but I don't remember you being there."

"Well maybe that's not a good example since you didn't come with us often, but your younger sister Lillie Mae always came. That girl could swim like a fish, never seen a girl swim like her."

"Okay, I do kinda' recollect … do you have a younger sister named Joyce Ann?"

"Yes! Yes, I do!"

"Beau?" said Rose squinting at him trying her best to place him in her memory.

"Yes! Yes! That's me!" said Beau enthusiastically letting out a sigh of relief. "You finally remember!"

"Well not exactly," she said nonchalantly walking back to the stove to take a batch of biscuits out the oven. "I remember Joyce Ann coming over to play with Lillie Mae. I don't remember you."

Dejected he sat down to eat breakfast. "How could she not remember me," he thought, "I had a crush on her all my life." Not hungry now, he moved his food around the plate.

Grandma Mae patted him on the back, "Beau, finish eating and get on out there before all the good jobs are gone." She cleared the empty tables, placing the coins in her apron pocket. "You need your belly full to work all day."

"Yes ma'am, I mean, Grandma Mae ma'am."

Rose regretted speaking to him harshly. "Now *he looks* like a lost puppy," she thought to herself. Determined to make up for her rudeness, she attempted to be nice. "How's Joyce Ann?"

"She is doing fine, Ms. Rose," said Beau appreciating her kindness. Feeling better, he began eating heartily nonstop, until he noticed her staring at him.

"You must be hungry."

"Sorry Ms. Rose, but your grandmother's cooking is so good. Don't get food like this at Howard."

"Can you call me Rose? Not Ms. Rose."

"Sorry, Ms...." He caught himself before continuing. "... Rose."

"Do you like it at Howard?"

"Oh yes," he said before finishing the last of his food and gulping down the orange juice in one swallow. "It's the best school anywhere. Are you thinking of going to college?"

"Don't really know yet, with the high cost and all."

"I know what you mean," he answered with a trace of disappointment in his voice. "I might have to take some time off myself to help Poppa pay for my next semester."

"I was sorry to hear your mother passed, fine woman," Grandma Mae said sadly placing her hand on his shoulder. "Your mother was a good friend of mine. Just as sweet as she could be, I know she mighty proud of you up in heaven."

"Thank you, wish I stayed home instead of going to school. Maybe things would have been different."

"Don't say that son, that's all she wanted was for her chaps to go to college."

"You right, Ms. Mae... I mean Grandma Mae."

"What happened with your Poppa?" said Grandma Mae sitting down two plates for the men at the next table. "I was asking John the other day how was Charlie, hadn't seen him since last winter. He normally stops by for a visit."

"They moved up to Buffalo with my Aunt Betty. Poppa got a job at a place called Bethlehem Steel. But you know Grandma Mae," he paused to smile with a distant look on his face. "It all worked out. Soon, Poppa will be making enough money to help me with school. He never could do that with what he made from the farm. Joyce Ann is going to an integrated school with white children and learning more than she ever did here. One day she wants to go to college too."

"I'm glad to hear that, God always has a way of working things out. Now go on and get out there so you can get some work."

"Yes ma'am!" Beau responded loudly, motivated by her encouragement.

"You're staying with your Uncle Jack while you home?"

"Yes ma'am."

"Stop by the house Sunday and get some dinner."

"Will do! Thank you, Ms. Mae, I mean Grandma Mae ma'am," happily Beau headed for the door quickly looking over his shoulder for one last glance at Rose.

"I'll see you Sunday," she laughed shaking her head at her granddaughter's indifference, watching as he crossed the road to stand with the other men. "That's a mighty fine young man. Don't you think Rose?"

"Yes ma'am."

Not bothering to look up, she continued washing dishes as the last of the breakfast customers slowly left the kitchen. She knew her grandmother had strong feelings towards Beau and would be more than happy if they were together, but to her he was just a country boy who moved to the city. Instead, her thoughts drifted towards Juan, a genuine city boy with curly hair, green eyes, and fancy clothes, not patched-up overalls looking for farm work. "Ahh," she sighed.

"He always liked you."

"Ma'am?" she replied squinting her eyes trying to act confused to avoid further conversation. "Who are you talking about?"

Not bothering to answer her granddaughter, she waved happily from the window. "See you Sunday Beau."

Rose watched as he returned the wave and climbed into the back of a farmer's truck along with several other men. She could see him smiling all the way from the kitchen. The thought of Sunday filled her with dread.

9 A NEW DRESS

Adam woke up early, eased out of bed, pulled the curtains to block as much sunlight as possible and left to prepare breakfast for his wife. Normally she was the one to deal with the hustle and bustle of getting everyone ready, fixing breakfast and lunch, then rushing them off before getting herself ready, but at least once a month, he enjoyed pampering her.

"Good morning beautiful," he said softly carrying a tray with breakfast and two red roses from the backyard.

"Ahh you're so sweet, thank you," she smiled. "What's the special occasion?"

"You are," he said sitting the tray on her lap kissing her gently on the lips. "I got so much to be thankful for, wonderful children, nice home, new car, and the most beautiful wife in the world. Since you always taken care of everyone, I thought you might enjoy going to town and buying yourself something nice."

"Just for me," her eyebrows squinted together trying to remember the last time she went shopping. "Don't know if I got a Saturday bus schedule?"

"What?" he looked at her strangely.

"Oh my goodness, I forgot, we have a car now. I don't have to worry about a bus schedule."

"It's a good feeling," he said sitting on the bed next to her.

"Yes, it is." Looking over her plate with a smile, "Umm, everything looks really good, toast, sausage, eggs, *and* grits. I didn't know you knew how to cook grits."

"Lots of stuff you don't know," he said tickling her on her side, delighted as she giggled. "Maybe I'll show you later." Laughing, they finished breakfast, enjoying each other's company and the time they had alone together.

* * *

After breakfast, Violet decided to call Ruby and invite her to go shopping. "Good morning." She stretched the phone over to the kitchen table with her feet casually placed on the chair. "You got anything planned for today?"

"Why you ask?"

Adam heard his sister-in-law's voice through the phone. He sat down in the chair and began to massage her feet.

"Ohh, that tickles," she giggled.

"What's going on," asked Ruby.

"Adam being silly is all," motioning for him to stop, but he continued despite her request. "Get dressed. I have a surprise for you,"

"Why I got to get dressed for the surprise?"

"Just be ready, I'll see you soon."

"Vee?" She stared at the phone. "I can't believe that girl hung up on me. What is she up too?"

She smiled to herself thinking about her sister who was more of a best friend than anyone she knew. Growing up, the two of them were inseparable, sharing secrets, whispering late at night until they heard Poppa loudly clearing his throat in the other room. Ruby was the protector, always making sure her younger sister was safe. No one dared tease Violet.

* * *

BANG, BANG, BANG. "What? Who can that be?" She rushed to the door while putting on her robe. "Can't get any sleep on my day off. First my sister wakes me up, now somebody banging on the door like they crazy, nobody sleeps late on Saturday's anymore?"

"Who is it!" she shouted pulling open the door.

"Morning Sis," smiled Violet, quickly kissing her on the cheek.

"What… Morning… How?" She stood at the door with her mouth open.

"Morning Ruby," smiled Adam walking in taking his hat off.

"What is going on here? How did you get her so fast? I just talked to you ten minutes ago."

"Told you I had a surprise," said Violet kissing her again on the cheek before sitting on the couch, "been waiting all night to tell you!"

"Do you want a cup of coffee?"

"What about the surprise?"

"I need help waking up first," she said through a yawn. "Y'all want some too?"

"No thank you," replied Adam from the couch. "When the last time you saw Fred?"

"Last night," called Ruby from the kitchen. "He tried to keep me out all night at that new joint on the bypass."

"The Honey Shack?" he said wishing she had never mentioned the place.

"Yeah, and it looks like that on the outside, a shack, honey."

"Ruby!" interjected Violet, "the surprise!"

Adam chuckled at her anxiousness to talk about the new car. "Hear that place is jumping on the weekends."

"You know it's true," she laughed pouring some hot water into a cup for coffee. "Why don't you come on out with us tonight, since the kids aren't home. It will be a blast and you can tell me all about the surprise. Fred can come by and pick you up, say around eight?"

"No," said Violet.

"No!" said Ruby, disappointed sipping her coffee. "Come on sis, you never go anywhere. What's your excuse? The kids ain't home, it'll be fun, like ole' times."

"I said no, we don't need Fred to pick us up."

"I thought you liked Fred?"

"I do."

"Then why you don't want him to pick you up?"

"Look out the window," said Violet frustrated shaking her head and waving her hand, no longer interested in surprising her.

Walking over she noticed the car in the driveway. "Lordy be, you finally got a car," she shouted and headed for the front door without hesitation.

"Ruby, you got on your housecoat and rollers in your head…the neighbors."

"They saw me in worse than this before. I have to get a closer look at this shiny new car."

By the time Violet and Adam got outside, Ruby was already sitting behind the steering wheel. "Sis, I love it! Is this a flip-top?"

"Well it's a hard top," she said happy to see her so excited. "But I think we can take the top off, right Adam."

"Yes," he said admiring the two sisters. "The only thing is you have to put the top in the trunk."

"Let's put the top down and go shopping."

"Ruby, it's cold out here."

"We can put on a sweater," she said motioning for her to sit in the passenger's seat. "There is this new colored shop that opened in town with fancy clothes like those in the movies, fashion stuff from New York City. Then we can stop for some lunch. Come on sis, let's go."

"Whoa' slowdown," said Adam smiling. "Don't you want to get dressed first?"

"Oh yeah," she said looking in the rearview mirror at her rollers. "It will only take a minute to get dressed, be right back." Before waiting for an answer, she hurried into the house.

"Adam, I hope you don't mind waiting?"

"No, I don't mind," he answered sitting in the driver's seat. "But I won't go shopping, that's for sure. You can drop me off at the Barber Shop. I'll sit with the fellows and get a haircut."

"I don't rightly know how long we'll be, seems like Ruby pretty much got everything planned."

"It's not a problem. Enjoy yourself, I don't mind one bit, spend the day with your sister. Get some of them fancy New York clothes."

"What about going to The Honey Shack?"

"Planned to take you there myself one day, but since Ruby brought it up first, maybe you'll feel more comfortable if she comes along. It's a pretty nice place."

"The name of the place doesn't sound nice," she said scooting over close to him.

"I'm sure you'll have fun, don't worry." He put his arm around her while they sat listening to "I only have eyes for you" by the Flamingos. "My love must be a kind of blind love. I can't see anyone but you."

She snuggled in his arms, "you always make me feel special."

"You are," he kissed her softly on the lips.

She smiled laying her head on his shoulder enjoying the moment. She felt protected and secure, her whole world moving around his orbit. "I love you so much."

"I know." He kissed her once again.

Suddenly the passenger door opened, and Ruby scooted in next to her. "You love birds ready to paint the town red?"

"That was fast."

"Didn't want you to change your mind, last time we went out was with Poppa's Model T Ford."

"I remember that ole' car."

"The only reason he let us go was because Big Adam promised to lookout for you."

"And you too," he added.

"The only reason he went," interrupted Violet squeezing his biceps, "was to crank it up. We needed somebody strong."

"Have to admit it was funny," laughed Ruby, "turning and turning to crank up that car until your arm felt like it would fall off."

"Then the crank would kick back nearly knocking you over. Still pains me to this day," laughed Violet rubbing her arm.

Adam smiled at the two of them reminiscing about old times and planning their activities for the day. However, he was concerned about taking Violet to The Honey Shack. His palms began to sweat. This was not the place for her, but somehow, he would have to control the situation, she deserved to have a fun night out, hopefully.

"Did you tell the kids about the car?"

"No not yet, we're surprising them at church tomorrow."

"Well you surprised me. I wondered who that was at my door so early in the morning. You better be glad I didn't have my knife."

"You still got that ole' thing."

"What ole' thing," laughed Ruby taking a long shiny knife out of her purse. "I got a new man in my life, and I ain't afraid to use it. Crazy folks everywhere, especially down at The Honey Shack."

"It ain't safe?" said Violet nervously.

"Just in case…"

"Just in case what!"

"Just in case somebody acts like a fool, especially since the place only…," she snapped her finger for emphasis, "that big. Anyway, you got Big Adam! You'll be safe."

"Adam, you ever been to this Honey Shack?"

"Maybe a couple times when it first opened," he lied, moving around uncomfortably as he drove.

"Don't recollect you telling me."

"At the time, wasn't nothing much to tell," he replied nervously avoiding her gaze, sitting up to look in the rear-view mirror, turning to watch passing traffic, any way but her way. "I know you don't like to go to places like that."

"Well tonight she does," interrupted Ruby hugging her sister. "It will be like old times, don't worry sis', you'll have fun."

Violet sat quietly thinking, a gnawing pain building in her stomach. She wanted to ask Adam more, but his evasive behavior prevented her from discussing matters further. Why was the thought of going to this place bothering her? She knew he enjoyed going to juke joints and drinking with friends, and that other women were attracted to her husband. She was not naïve but trusted him. Still the uneasiness in her stomach would not go away.

"Turn that up," said Ruby twisting in her seat singing "Let the good times roll" by Shirley Goodman and Leonard Lee in the background. "Come on baby while the thrill is on, come on baby let's have some fun. Come on baby let the good times roll, roll all night long."

Violet watched her sister snapping her fingers and purposely bumping her side each time she moved to the left. It did remind her of the fun they had together when they were younger, maybe she could enjoy herself, what would it hurt, she thought. "Okay, I'll go," smiled Violet dismissing her insecurities and moving closer to her husband as he drove to town.

* * *

Designed in a square, the Main Street of their small town included shops, restaurants, and a grassy area in the middle surrounded by park benches. In the center was a tall flagpole where the stars and stripes waved proudly. At every corner were garbage cans decorated red, white, and blue. The sidewalks were immaculately clean, and the streets were newly paved with bright yellow diagonal lines in front of the stores for parking. Standing on the curb watching his wife drive away, Adam wished he had given her a practice drive before she left. "At least there's not much traffic this morning," he said to himself before entering the barbershop.

"Morning Big Adam," said Willie who was cutting Fred's hair while others waited on the couch along the wall. The shop was full on Saturday mornings, everyone waiting patiently for a turn in the chair. Haircuts went quickly, and the barbershop was a source of the latest news and gossip.

"Mighty fine car you got."

"Thank you, only got it yesterday, runs like a charm."

"Didn't know you'd get it so fast, just dropped you off at the place yesterday," added Fred admiring his haircut in the mirror and handing Willie a dime.

"Man, you know I don't fool around, when I make up my mind, I do it. I saved up for a long time, and the price was right. No reason to wait around for somebody else to snatch up my good deal."

"I told you Mr. Frank would treat you right."

"He does," added one of the customers. "My brother got a used Ford, a few weeks ago, man it rides good, almost like new."

"It appears you got a car at the right time, folks boycotting the buses, because of what happened down in Montgomery, Alabama."

"What happened?" said the next customer sitting in the chair. "Close on the sides, light on the top."

"I didn't hear about a boycott," said another.

"Well in Montgomery, they locked up this woman named Rosa Parks," continued Willie. "She worked for some white folks down there and always took the bus home. This one day, she said she was thinking about that Emmett Till boy."

"Who is Emmett Till?" interrupted Fred.

"Don't you read the news," said Willie upset that everyone kept interrupting his story.

"I get all my news right here in the barbershop," said one customer.

"Fred can't read anyway," laughed another customer.

"You didn't see that article in *Jet Magazine*," asked Adam taking a seat on the couch.

"Told you he couldn't read."

"Hush man, your sister taught me last week in the back of my truck."

"Emmett Till," continued Adam taking a more serious tone, "was a fourteen-year-old boy, beaten to death down in Mississippi, so bad his own mother didn't recognize him, except for his father's ring, he still had on his finger after they pulled him out the river and shipped him back to Chicago in a wooden box. At the funeral, she had the casket open, so everyone could see his face, and they put the picture in the magazine."

"Um-hum," nodded one of the customers.

"Why was he way down there? Everybody knows you don't mess around in Mississippi."

"He was visiting some relatives in a small town called Money."

"There's a town called Money?"

"What happened that he got all beat up?"

"Emmett and his cousin went to the town store, fooling around like boys do, and apparently he whistled at a young white girl working there."

"That's where he messed up," interrupted Fred. "Nobody told him how things are in the south!"

"I'm sure somebody told him," continued Adam shaking his head, "but like most fourteen-year old's, he wasn't listening."

"Boys from up north come down here all the time and figure they can get any girl they want," added Willie.

"Maybe a colored girl, they love them city boys," said Fred. "But you a fool to try and mess with a white woman in the south, especially Mississippi." They all nodded in agreement.

"When the husband found out about a colored boy whistling at his wife, he got another fellow and snatched Emmett Till right out the bed in the middle of the night, while his grandfather begged them not to take him."

"Why he let them take the boy?"

"What choice he had," answered Willie.

"You right," said a customer nodding his head.

"Boy went missing for three days until they found him in the Tallahatchie River."

"Then shipped him back to Chicago in a wooden box," added another customer, shaking his head in disbelief. "Like a package."

"His face was so twisted, people fainted at the casket," said Willie.

"I saw the picture," added another customer. "It gave me the chills."

"And what happened to the men?"

"The all-white jury found them innocent of all charges."

"You know that don't surprise me one bit."

"Me either!" said a customer.

"Willie, what's all this got to do with the Rosa Parks lady?"

"Like I said when I was trying to finish my story," he said bluntly. "When she got on that bus she sat in the first row for coloreds, but when the white section became full, the driver asked her to give up her seat to a white passenger and move further back. She refused."

"Good for her," said one customer.

"Bet she got thrown in jail," said Fred.

"Sure did," said Willie matter-of-factly. "But she was part of a group called the NAACP…"

"The National Association for the Advancement of Colored People," said Fred proudly with a smirk. "I ain't stupid."

"…She was their secretary and they helped get her out of jail the next day."

"Hate to hear of a colored woman in jail," said Adam with a frown. "There's no telling what they'll do to them in a place like that."

"They beat the heck out of us when we in there," said a customer who had sat quietly in the barber's chair until that moment.

"And nobody cares either," said another customer.

"Well this fellow named Reverend Martin Luther King, said he cares, and is tired of colored folk getting treated any kind of way. They started this group called the SCLC…"

Everyone turned to look at Fred who was still admiring his haircut in the mirror…. "Why you staring at me? I don't know what that stands for."

"It stands for the Southern Christian Leadership Conference," continued Willie. "They put together the boycott down in Montgomery to protest how Rosa Parks was treated, and how we shouldn't ride the busses until we can sit where we want."

"You think it will make a difference?"

"Don't rightly know, but something has to be done."

"I been down in Montgomery," said a customer. "They got plenty busses all over the place loaded with colored folks. If they stop riding somebody will lose lots of money."

"Bet that gets their attention," said a customer.

"It would get my attention if everyone stopped coming to get their haircut."

"How they want people to get to work?" said the customer getting out the chair and handing Willie a couple coins.

"Thank you son," he said putting the money in a small box on the shelf. "They want people to walk or catch a ride. That's why I said Big Adam got his car on time."

"Reckon I did," he answered taking his turn in the barber's chair.

"This boycott sounds like a good idea," said Fred. "When we supposed to start?"

"Monday coming," answered Willie.

"That's soon," said a customer with a grimace. "I need to get up early. It's at least a five mile walk to the mill from my house."

"Whew! Hope somebody passes you on the way and gives you a ride."

"Me too," he replied with a worried look on his face.

"Man, it will be tough," said another customer, "but it's the only way to make things change."

"That's exactly what Reverend King was telling people down in Montgomery."

"I believe it," said Adam looking in the mirror satisfied with his haircut. "I'll talk to my wife, she has a couple of friends who work in town and can give them a ride. We can do this if we stick together and help each other."

"Wish someone was going my way," said the customer who worked at the mill. "But I'm headed cross town."

"Check with Johnnie on Lover's Lane Road," said Willie. "He drives a truck down past the mill, but he leaves mighty early."

"That's right!" his countenance lifted. "I see him leaving for work on my way to the bus. I can stop by his house today, thanks Willie. Take care."

"You too man."

* * *

Violet was glad the fashion shop was around the corner from the barbershop, since she did not want to admit she was nervous about driving. "How is this," she asked walking out of the dressing room turning for her sister to see.

"Like you somebody's grandmother," laughed Ruby, handing her a different dress. "Here try this."

She went back into the fitting room and soon came out wearing a red sparkling form-fitting dress, with no sleeves, a low-cut V-neck, and a hemline just above her knees.

"I think it's too tight."

"Girl you look good!" said Ruby walking around her sister examining her from head to toe. "I was thinking of that dress for myself, but you got all the right curves in all the right places."

"I can't wear this!"

"Why you can't?" she said with her hands on her hips.

"I'm a married woman."

"That's more reason to wear it."

"Where am I going to wear it? It's too tight and revealing."

"Wait until you see me in this," said Ruby holding up a white dress like the one her sister was wearing.

"Isn't that too small?"

"Come on sis, we just having fun," reassured Ruby. "You *do* want to have fun tonight, don't you?"

"Yes… But..."

"Look here's the plan. Bring your dress when you come over, so you can get ready at my house, and don't take your coat off until we get to 'The Honey Shack', then you can surprise Big Adam."

"He'll be surprised for sure." They both started to laugh.

"Don't be chicken," she quickly interrupted. "Now pay the lady so we can get out of here, I'm hungry."

"Ruby before we go, can I ask you something?"

"Of course, you my baby sister, you can ask me anything, anytime."

"Okay," she continued apprehensively. "I know Adam goes to that place sometimes on the weekend, and I'm sure women there are attracted to him, never mind!" She stopped not wanting to continue. She handed the dress to the cashier.

"That will be five dollars and forty-three cents ma'am."

Violet reached in her wallet and handed her six dollars. "Thank you very much."

Seeing the seriousness in her sister's eyes, Ruby did not want to push her, so she waited until they were in the car. "Violet whatever is on your mind, you can talk to me, no matter what."

"I feel so silly."

"Sis, please talk to me."

"Okay," she reluctantly turned to look directly into her eyes. "Have you ever seen Adam with someone at that place, The Honey Shack?"

"Where in the world did that come from?"

"Never mind Ruby, I told you it was silly," lowering her eyes.

"No don't feel that way," she lifted her sister's chin and saw the anguish in her face. "Big Adam *is* a good-looking man, you know that, and he's very friendly, you know that too. You also know that he loves you and the kids more than anything, don't you?"

"I know he loves us. But have you ever seen him with another woman at that place, being more than friendly?"

"No Violet," she lied, looking straight into her eyes. "I haven't."

"You wouldn't lie to me, would you?"

The last thing she wanted was to hurt her, but she had seen him with a woman named Carmen *many* times at The Honey Shack, and other places as well. She could never tell her that. Despite having spoken to him of her disapproval, he was a grown man. Her only consolation was his promise that Violet would never find out. She had no choice but to distort the truth.

"Would you lie to me?"

"Vee, of course I wouldn't lie to you," she lied again, hugging her closely desperately wanting to change the subject.

"Okay," smiled Violet feeling reassured, believing her sister.

"Let's go pick up that husband of yours and get some lunch. I'm starved!"

"I'm hungry too." She felt the need to discuss her concerns more, but her mother always said, 'what you don't know won't hurt you'. Turn the radio on Sis and see what's playing."

"That's my girl," she said gladly searching through the stations until she found "I wonder why" by Dion and the Belmonts. "When you're with me I'm sure you're always true, when I'm away I wonder what you do."

"How appropriate," Violet thought to herself as her mind filled with questions about their upcoming event. "I know he'll be true," she smiled confidently.

10 OLD FRIENDS

By ten in the morning, the Potato Patch was quiet. Farmers are no longer seeking extra help, so potential workers wander off. Rose and Grandma Mae begin preparing lunch. Occasionally a customer comes in to purchase some chewing tobacco, cigarettes, or a cold soda as the noon sun approaches. Lillie Mae keeps busy by sweeping the floor and straightening out items on the shelves, as Poppa John and Lil' Adam check supplies and pay monthly bills. *'Ding-A-Ling'*, rings the bell hanging from the front door as two customers enter.

"Good Morning Missy," said the man approaching the counter.

Lillie Mae looked up to a very tall man with blondish gray hair, matted from sweat beneath his brown Fedora, tilted slightly forward. His smile was warm and friendly, eyes sparkling with kindness. "Good afternoon sir."

"Annie say hello."

Wearing a pink ruffled party dress and white ribbons neatly tied around two blond ponytails, she squeezed her doll baby dressed in the same outfit, and shyly said, "Hello".

"Hello," said Lillie Mae, glad to see someone her age. "What can I get you?"

"Well," he paused, removing his hat to wipe the sweat from his forehead with a handkerchief neatly folded in his jacket pocket, "seems like it's going to be a hot one today, so I'll take your coldest orange soda."

"Yes sir," smiled Lillie Mae.

"Would you like anything Annie?"

"May I have some candy?"

"Okay, but only a little. I don't want your mother to say you get cavities when your grandfather comes to visit."

"I promise to brush soon as I get home," she said a large smile replacing her shyness. "How much can I get?"

"I'd say a dime's worth would be plenty." He reached into a small plastic coin carrier that opened when squeezed. "Here's a quarter. Will that be enough for a dime's worth of candy and the orange soda?"

"Yes sir, and you'll get five cents change back."

"You keep the five cents for some candy for you if you have permission from your parents."

"Thank you sir, that's mighty kind of you, I'll go ask my grandmother." Not allowed to accept things from strangers, she hurried over to the kitchen for approval. "Grandma Mae, this man and his daughter are buying some candy and a soda, and he wants to buy me some candy too."

Moments later, Grandma Mae entered wiping her hands on her apron. "Well I'll be," she said surprised, immediately walking over to hug the man. "Tom how you been, ain't seen you in almost twenty years."

"Mae!" he squeezed her tightly. "I can't believe it has been that long. Time sure does fly, but you still as beautiful as always."

"Oh Tom, you still the charmer," she grinned. "John! Come out here! You won't believe who the wind blew in."

"Who is it Mae?" yelled Poppa John from the back wondering what all the commotion was. Moments later he entered followed by Lil' Adam and Rose from the kitchen. "Well I'll be doggone, that you Tom?"

"You bet it is," he said reaching out his hand to his longtime friend.

"We can do better than that!" Poppa John stretched out his arms.

All the children stood with puzzled looks on their faces as the two men embraced each other. It was hard to believe twenty years passed by for the two of them, evidenced only by graying hair and protruding veins in their handshake.

"Rose, Lil' Adam, Lillie Mae, this is Tom Greene, a big-time lawyer from up north now, but him and your grandfather grew up together."

"Sure did," added Tom enthusiastically. "Our friendship started off under not to pleasant circumstances, but after that we were friends for life."

"I'll say."

"Well before you tell the story, I'll rustle up some lunch, anyone hungry besides me?"

All the children nodded in agreement with widely stretched eyes, including Annie looking up from behind her grandfather.

"And who do we have here?" said Poppa John.

"This here is my favorite granddaughter," said Tom proudly.

"I'm your only granddaughter Poppa," she quickly added.

"That is correct, but if I had a hundred more, you would still be my favorite."

"I knew she was your grandbaby soon as I saw her face. She's the spitting image of your daughter Suzanne, just as pretty as she can be."

"Y'all come on and have a seat at one of the tables," called Grandma Mae from the kitchen.

"Is this your place John?"

"Sure is, my son-in-law helped me to get this place when ole' man Russell died back three, four years ago, right Mae."

"Ten years ago," she shouted from the stove.

"I remember this place when we were kids. You fixed it up, I barely recognized it, adding a kitchen really makes a difference."

"Added that part for me," said Grandma Mae walking to the table. "Here's some nice cold glasses of iced tea while you listen to them tell how they got to be friends."

"Why you say it wasn't pleasant becoming friends," asked Lillie Mae sitting next to Annie. "Tell us what happened."

"I don't know how your grandpa tells a story," said Grandma Mae sitting the tea in front of Annie. "But when Poppa John tells a story, it takes a while."

"My Grandpa's the same ma'am," answered Annie and smiled at Lillie Mae who happily smiled back.

"Now Mae…"

"Go on and tell your story John while I fix lunch," she said cutting him off before hearing what he had to say. "We'll see who's done first."

"It doesn't seem like that long ago," he started with all eyes around the table focused on him. "I was nigh your age Lillie Mae, or maybe a bit younger, me and your Uncle Jessie was playing out in the woods some ways off from our farm. It was mighty hot, like today. Somehow, we came across a pond we never saw before. A tire swing hung down to climb and jump right into the water. We never thought about whose property we were on, and since nobody was around, we took off our clothes and jumped in."

"Is that the same pond we go to in the summer?"

"I believe it is," nodded Poppa John. "Well I tell you, we had ourselves a good ole' time, laughing and playing and swinging from that tire. Maybe an hour or so passed by and I looked up and saw two white boys standing on the side of the pond."

'What y'all niggas doing in this here pond?' he yelled.'

"John don't use that type of language around the children."

"That's what he said Mae. I ain't gon' lie, I want them to know the truth."

"Then what happened?" said Lillie Mae barely able to stand the suspense.

'You better get out now before we hang you up by a tree,' the other one yelled.'

"We didn't know what to do, no clothes on, too scared to move, shivering with fear."

"Wasn't nobody but Paulie and Frank, some kids from town who used to go down to the pond with me on really hot days," added Tom. "They always got me in trouble, probably dead and gone by now."

"Reckon they could be," said Poppa John. "Lord knows I didn't try to find out."

Tom continued, "Almost to the pond, I said to them, *'what's all this yelling?'* By this time, your grandfather and uncle had started getting out the pond and putting on their clothes. I recognized John from seeing him around town. He always seemed like a nice fellow, but back then, whites and coloreds were not friends. That never made sense to me. I yelled back at Paulie and Frank, *'This here is my pond, on my property, and if they want to swim here, they can!'* Let me tell you, they didn't like that one bit."

"Called Tom a *'nigger lover'* and other names not worth repeating, but Tom stood up to them."

"I was really pretty scared too," laughed Tom. "But the things they said made me realize I didn't want to be friends with them anyway. Actually, I was glad to be rid of them."

"And from then on whenever you saw Tom and John, accept at school, they were always together," added Grandma Mae from the kitchen.

"Town folk didn't like it much either, they called Tom names behind his back."

"Behind my back and to my face, but by then we were friends."

"The best of friends," added Poppa John.

"And we didn't care what anyone thought either."

"It did help that Tom's father, your grandfather Annie, was town sheriff," added Grandma Mae. "Nobody messed with Tom or John because Sheriff Green would lock you up before you could bat an eye!"

"And if Sheriff Green didn't get you, momma would," laughed Poppa John. "Paulie and Frank threatened to skin me alive if they caught me by myself, and one day I thought they would get a chance to do just that."

"What happened?" said Lillie Mae amazed.

"Tom was sick, so we were brave and went to the pond without him."

"Yes, I remember that," Tom added smiling at his friend. "I had a fever, could barely move around. Something was going around because I heard Pa say a lot of town folk were sick."

"And died," said Grandma Mae sitting fried chicken, biscuits, and corn on the table. "Rose bring some plates and napkins, everybody help yourself."

"Yes ma'am," said Rose moving quickly so she wouldn't miss the story."

"I lost my mother and two brothers," said Grandma Mae refilling each glass. "It was the typhoid fever, but folk started calling it 'Typhoid Mary' after this cook in New York who infected more than fifty people. That fever spread like wild fire, thousands of people died all 'cross the country."

Everyone began fixing their plates as the small kitchen area filled with murmurs of delight, while everyone eagerly awaited the remainder of the story.

"I knew Tom was home sick and I wanted to check on him, but momma said no, because she was scared I might catch the fever. It was such a hot day and we wanted to get a few minutes in the pond to cool off," he continued taking a bite of chicken and biscuit as everyone waited in suspense. "We headed down to the pond laughing and talking, not a care in the world. When we turned the last corner, there stood Paulie, Frank, and two other boys, standing at the edge of the pond."

"Were you scared?"

"Very scared," Poppa John quickly answered. "Soon as they saw us, one of them yelled, *'There them niggas go!'*, and another one yelled, *'we got you now boy, Tom ain't here to protect you!'* I looked at Jesse and yelled, *Run!* We ran as fast as we could without stopping or looking back. They chased us all the way home. Now, before we left, momma was home cooking in the back of the house, to this day I don't know how she knew we were in trouble, but when we turned that corner and you could see our house, she was standing on the porch with her shotgun! I never ran so fast in my life. Once we were on the porch, momma yelled, *'get behind me'*. They stopped dead in their tracks. She said, *'don't know why y'all after my boys and I don't rightly care, but if you don't get off my property, I'll blow your head off!'* She turned to us and said, *'get in the house!'* We didn't try to see what Paulie, Frank, and the other boys did; because when momma got her shotgun, you better do exactly what she said!"

Tom and Poppa John both began to laugh, not only from the remembrance of the story, but the look of shock on the children's faces.

"John, don't be scaring them like that," laughed Grandma Mae getting up from the table picking up some of the empty dishes, "don't pay your grandfathers' no mind."

"Mae, I'm telling the truth."

"The whole truth and nothing but the truth," laughed Tom. "I remember Mrs. Johnson came right over first thing the next morning. I was in bed, still not feeling well. I barely heard what she said to Pa, but I did hear that some boys chased her sons home. When I heard somebody was after John, I got up to put on my clothes and go after them myself! Momma stopped me. She said Pa was going to take care of the matter."

"And he did," interrupted Poppa John. "Don't know what he did, but we never had a problem from Paulie, Frank, or anyone else for that matter. Don't know if it was my momma or your poppa."

"I never could figure out why they had so much hate, never made sense to me... On a happier subject, I do remember the chicken soup your mother brought to the house that morning. Umm! Umm! It was good! Can Mae cook like that?"

"Sho' can!" said Poppa John loudly. "Put her to work in this here kitchen to prove it."

"Hush yo' mouth John," she replied with her hands on her hips. "Best way to a man's heart is thru his stomach."

Tom reached over and rubbed his friend's extended belly laughing, "And from the looks of things, looks like she got your heart *and* stomach." Everyone around the table laughed as Rose and Grandma Mae cleared the dishes.

"Tom, you and Annie come by this Sunday after church for dinner, having pig feet, black-eyed peas, okra, cornbread, and fried chicken, of course."

"Oh my. I'm only in town until Monday, but I don't want to miss a chance to taste some good home cooking. Annie would you like to stop by with Mr. John, Ms. Mae, and their grandchildren?"

"Yes grandpa," she smiled shyly.

"Well that settles it," said Grandma Mae before hearing Tom's answer. "Annie, you can bring some of your dollies. You and Lillie Mae will have a good time."

"Yes ma'am," she said politely looking over at Lillie Mae, delighted to have a playmate.

"Thank you for the fine lunch. You right John, she can cook, no wonder you have a few extra pounds."

"A few," nodded Grandma Mae.

"Just more to love Tom," he laughed rubbing his belly, "more to love."

"We'll see y'all Sunday around four o'clock."

"Sounds good," answered Tom taking Annie's hand. "Thank you again for lunch. See you Sunday."

They all stood on the front porch waving good-bye.

* * *

Things were a little slow afterwards. Grandma Mae and Rose were cleaning up the kitchen as the last of the dinner crowd finished eating. Only a few customers stopped in during this time, usually to pick up a chicken sandwich or purchase a slice of pie. Lil' Adam was still counting items on the shelves to place the monthly supply order. Poppa John sat in one of several wooden rockers on the porch smoking his pipe.

"Come sit with me Lillie Mae," he motioned for her to sit in the rocker beside him. Quietly they rocked as an occasional car or truck drove by.

Suddenly a car pulled up, quickly stopping within inches of hitting the porch. The driver was frantic, barely putting the car in park before jumping out.

"HELP ME! PLEASE!" he screamed. "My wife is having a baby! HELP ME!"

For an instant no one moved, only watched as the distraught man ran to the passenger's side trying to carry her out, her belly was so large she could barely move, and he could not completely lift her by himself.

Grandma Mae was the first to move into action. "Lillie Mae run, tell Rose to put on a pot of hot water."

"What you need a pot of water for?"

"Go on Chile' and listen to your grandmother," said Poppa John in a firm voice she was not used to hearing. "Come on son, let's help bring her in the back."

"Yes sir," replied a wide-eyed Lil' Adam, smart enough to know this was not a time for questions.

"I'll get some quilts and blankets for her to lie on," said Grandma Mae who appeared calm despite the chaos.

Before Lillie Mae could get in the kitchen, her grandmother pushed past her taking some towels from the cabinet. "Rose put on a large pot of water, once it boils put in these towels."

"Yes ma'am," she responded puzzled yet moving quickly, not understanding what was going on since she was in the kitchen listening to the radio before everything started.

"Lillie Mae, don't just stand there, help me clear some room over here, somebody having a baby."

"A Baby!" said Rose.

"Yes Chile'," she answered smiling to herself at the shock on her granddaughter's face. Calmly she pronounced each word. "Don't worry… I've done this before, many times… now get a big pot of water… on the stove to boil. And Lillie Mae, help your sister as best you can."

Motioning to the area on the kitchen floor spread with several quilts, "Put her here John!"

"Careful now," said the man drenched in perspiration, helping Poppa John and Lil' Adam lay his wife on the floor, her dress drenched in blood. The men stood watching and wondering what to do now as she lay there groaning in pain.

"You men go on the porch, I'll send for you when its time."

He touched his wife's hand, torn between leaving and staying, but ultimately glad someone else was taking charge, "Honey you'll be okay."

"Rose and Lillie Mae, y'all stay, I need your help."

Lil' Adam was the first to move, afraid to look back, relieved she did not ask him to stay. Happy to head to the porch, no *run* to the porch, he thought to himself. Glad to be with *the men*, to leave what appeared to be a woman's job, behind.

"I told her we shouldn't drive down south so close to the baby's time. She never listens," said the man heading out the kitchen wiping the sweat from his forehead. "Then we got lost."

"Calm down son," said Poppa John putting his hand on his shoulder. "You in good hands now, my wife Mae, been a midwife around these here parts for almost fifty years, learned from her mother and her mother's mother. Lost or not, the Lord helped you find the right place."

Lil' Adam paused briefly to look back at his grandmother. She was a fascinating woman, one who could assist delivering a cow one day and a baby the next. Amazed he watched her move proficiently, folding a towel to place under the woman's head, wiping the sweat from her forehead, holding her hand for reassurance, he could tell she did this before. For a moment he wanted to stay and stare uselessly like his sisters, but he hurried away to be with *the men*.

Taking a detour Poppa John left the two of them sitting on the porch for what seemed like an eternity. Periodically they would hear a loud moan from the kitchen, causing them to tense up simultaneously in the rocking chairs, frozen, not moving, nervous, and afraid to breathe. As the moaning dissipated, they slowly exhaled, relaxing for a moment until they heard more sounds of distress.

Finally, Poppa John opened the porch screen door carrying a bottle. "What's your name son," he asked glancing at his grandson before handing the man a small glass of whiskey. "Don't tell your grandmother you saw this."

"No sir," he responded with a look of shock on his face watching his grandfather drink. "Today is filled with things I never knew."

"Mae doesn't allow whiskey in the Potato Patch," he told the man. "But we not inside, we on the porch."

Despite his hands shaking uncontrollably, he took the glass and swallowed the contents in one gulp. His labored breathing appeared to slow as he relaxed, finally allowing the rocking chair to serve its purpose. The rhythmic squeaking sounds under his weight brought soothing calmness into the unstable situation.

"What's your name son, and where you from?" said Poppa John trying to distract him from the increasing volume of moans from inside, immediately refilling his glass.

"Thank you sir," said the man with a nod of approval. "My name is Sherman and my wife..." he paused to look uncomfortably towards the front. "Elaine and I are from New York."

"New York City?" said Lil' Adam excited, finally a subject that interested him. "I want to go there myself one day."

"No, we're from Buffalo, New York."

"Oh, don't believe I've heard tell of that part of New York."

"Me neither," added Lil' Adam disappointed.

"It's more west than New York City, not too far from Niagara Falls."

"I've heard of Niagara Falls, people go there for a honeymoon. Mae tried to get me to go up there...too cold for me, never been one to like cold weather."

"And lots of snow," he laughed sipping from his whiskey glass this time. For some reason, he felt comfortable with them. He was not a drinker or a person accustomed to socializing with strangers, but peace seemed to cover him as he relaxed on the porch.

"Snow, oh no!" laughed Poppa John. "I wouldn't know what to do with snow except make some ice cream."

"Or a snowman," laughed Lil' Adam.

"I was born there, so I guess I'm used to all the cold weather and doing things like sledding and ice-skating."

"Stop, you're making me cold," said Poppa John with a shiver, "your wife from there too?"

"No, she from around here. Well actually she was born here, but her mother and father moved to Buffalo when she was younger."

"For a job?"

"How'd you know?"

"I remember when folk started moving up north, lots a good paying factory jobs up there, nice homes. People fed up with the south."

"Maybe," he smiled nodding, "but whether it was Alabama, Mississippi, Georgia, or the Carolina's, they always spoke fondly of their hometown. I wonder why they moved in the first place if they loved it so much."

"Guess there's no place like home," smiled Poppa John loading his pipe with tobacco. "Do you smoke?"

"I got some cigarettes in the car if you don't mind."

"No son, go right ahead, I know how it is waiting for a baby."

They watched as he walked to the car, wearing dark brown corduroy trousers cuffed at the bottom, a tan striped sweater buttoned down the front, and black penny loafers. Fashionably dressed, thought Lil' Adam from what he saw in his sister's *Ebony* Magazines, maybe Buffalo was not as far from New York City after all.

Still parked dangerously close to the porch, it did not take long for him to locate his cigarettes. "You been through this quite a bit," he said attempting a smile while lighting his cigarette as the smoke rolled into his nose.

"Maybe not quite a bit," answered Poppa John taking a few puffs from his pipe. "Still something you don't get used too, harder for the women then for us men."

"You right, should I go and check on her?"

"If I know Mae, she'd rather you didn't. She'll only tell you to get back on the porch."

While he was talking, they heard a very loud scream from the kitchen. Refilling each glass, both men swallowed quickly.

"Don't know if I can take this much longer!" He took several puffs from his cigarette.

Poppa John patted him on the shoulder hoping to distract him with conversation. "How did you and your wife end up way down here from Buffalo?"

"My wife's grandmother has been ill for the last couple weeks. We wanted to visit her before the baby was born. The doctor said the baby wasn't due for a least another month, so it would be okay to travel."

"Um-hum, not surprised one bit, a baby knows better than the doctor when they are coming."

"I told Elaine I didn't want to take that chance with a fifteen-hour drive, but she wouldn't listen."

"Do they ever?"

"An hour from her grandmother's house, she said she felt something wet running down her leg."

"Um-hum, water broke."

"Nobody ever explained anything to me," his excitement growing as he retold the events. "I thought maybe she had to use the bathroom or something. I started looking for a gas station or somewhere to stop. Next thing I know, she started screaming about pressure she was feeling and wanting to push…"

"Um-hum, head moving down."

"I almost drove off the road," he continued taking several more puffs from his cigarette and discarding it off the porch. "Finally, I saw a hospital sign. When we got there, I helped Elaine out the car. Her clothes were wet, she was crying and moaning, but we made it, everything was going to work out after all."

"Um-hum, you thought," said Poppa John relighting his pipe with a nod as if he knew how the story was going to end.

"Got in the hospital, the lady behind the desk said lightly, comical almost, 'sorry no colored allowed at this hospital'. The hate I felt for her, the hospital, the entire south suddenly overwhelmed me, and I almost passed out on the floor!"

"Can't let hate eat at you son, been that way for a long time down here. The only hospital that takes coloreds is nearly fifty miles away."

"How did it get like that, this is America. In Buffalo, we might have cold weather and snow, but we can go to the hospital if we need too. Maybe they don't treat colored people as well as the white people, but at least they don't send you away."

"Most people around these parts have to take care of themselves best they can. Mae is a midwife, another woman down the road knows how to doctor on people for small things. And in real emergencies, we drive the fifty miles."

"That doesn't make any sense to me."

"What happened after they told you to leave," asked Lil' Adam anxious to know the outcome.

"They had to call security because I was demanding to see a doctor for my wife. They practically threw us out! I was ready to fight, but Elaine calmed me down."

"Good you did calm down son," said Poppa John. "I know a man always wants to defend his wife, especially with a baby on the way, but you got to know when the time is right. What would happen to her if they threw you in jail?"

"I can't imagine," agreed Sherman. "I helped her back to the car and we drove away."

Another loud moan came from the back, followed by a louder scream. The men all looked at one another, no one made a sound. Poppa John refilled his pipe, Sherman lit another cigarette, and Lil' Adam rocked gently in his chair wondering how a hospital could turn a pregnant woman away without helping her.

"I got back on the road and started driving. Not knowing where I was going, just driving. Elaine was in the back seat moaning and praying; 'Help me Jesus!' He paused to take another puff from his cigarette. They could see the tears building up in his eyes. They waited patiently for him to speak. "I just kept driving… lost!"

He stood up, finished his cigarette, and flicked the butt on the ground. "Before this, I wasn't a praying man. Elaine went to church, she asked me to go with her, but I never did, I never felt the need. While in the car, I listened to her call on Jesus, repeatedly. I have never been so scared in my life, I felt totally helpless, like I had failed my wife and my baby."

He stood there for a moment staring out into the darkness of the night, the sound of crickets echoed all around. "Driving frantically, I began to pray quietly to this Jesus my wife loved. Asking him to help us, we had no one to turn too, no one. I was lost."

Poppa John nodded as he rocked gently in his chair.

"Something told me to turn at the corner to the right. That's when I saw you and your grandchildren sitting on this here porch." Tears began rolling down his cheeks as he sobbed uncontrollably.

"Let it out son."

Sherman exhaled deeply, "I'm sorry."

"No need to be sorry son, nobody but the Lord that led you here. You not lost anymore."

Motionless, they quietly gazed at the moon and stars brightly shining. A comforting calmness passed over them, and over the Potato Patch, broken only by the loudest scream of them all…

Startled, all three men jumped. Poppa John grabbed Sherman who almost lost his footing and fell off the porch.

"Oh my God!" shouted Sherman running inside no longer able to contain himself. "Elaine! Here I come!" He arrived to see her smiling at him from the floor holding a tiny baby covered in blood with a bluish cord connected at the navel. Sherman fainted and hit the floor, BAMM!

"Guess he couldn't take anymore, not used to seeing a newborn baby straight out the womb."

"Me either," said Lil' Adam wondering why he did not faint too.

"Listen at you John, sounding like you know something," laughed Grandma Mae, wiping the baby with the cooled towels Rose had boiled earlier. "You forgot when Ruby was born you did the same thing, fell out straight on the floor, had a big knot upside your head for days."

"Reckon you right," rubbing his head as he warmly remembered the night his daughter was born, "took a week until the swelling went down, but it was the happiest day of my life."

"And Lil' Adam, I'm sure you are as strong as your sisters," she continued tying a string around the umbilical cord. "It's in your blood, cut this. Rose hand your brother them scissors."

"No way!" said Lil' Adam running out the kitchen with his hand over his mouth.

"Son, I guess you took after me," laughed Poppa John.

Sherman walked over to Elaine and kneeled beside her. The baby, wrapped in a dry white towel, sleeping peacefully. Smiling proudly, he kissed his wife on the cheek as tears streamed down both their faces.

"It's a girl," she said joyfully.

"She is so beautiful," gently touching his daughter's hands.

"And healthy," said Grandma Mae. "I suspect she weighs close to ten pounds."

"Thank you all so much, there's nothing I can give to repay you for saving my wife and baby's life."

"God already paid," said Poppa John, patting him on the back. "Just take care of your family son."

"I will, sir, with all my heart and strength."

"Now Elaine, I need you to give me one last push."

"Push," said Sherman alarmed and confused. "What's the matter? Isn't the pushing over?"

"They got to get out the afterbirth son, let's go back outside for a minute. You probably don't want to see that part either."

He obeyed without question, gently kissing his wife and daughter before following Poppa John back to the porch again.

"It won't be but a minute. We'll let you know, everything will be fine, the hard part is over."

Rose held the baby while Lillie Mae played with her little fingers, both oblivious to Elaine and their grandmother's efforts. With a few pushes, the afterbirth gushed onto the quilt and quickly cleaned up and discarded.

"You a strong woman, I'm mighty proud of you," she said gently squeezing her hand. "You did good."

"Thank you, Ms. Mae, don't know what we would have done without you and your family."

"It was the Lord that blessed you with this beautiful baby girl, nobody but the Lord."

* * *

As the day ended, everyone sat on the porch enjoying the quiet, reminiscing. After a while, Lillie Mae broke the silence with a question that bothered her earlier.

"Poppa John, when Grandma Hattie got that shotgun, where was Grandpa? Why didn't he get the shotgun?"

He sat for a few minutes taking several long puffs from his pipe. He never hurried. She waited patiently; knowing when he finally did answer, it would be in the form of a long an interesting story.

"Well, Lillie Mae," he said affectionately, pausing further to contemplate how much information to reveal. "Things are much different now than when I was a boy."

"When were you born, Poppa John?"

"I was born in 1898."

"That seems like such a long time ago."

"You remember when I told you your great grandfather was born a slave?"

"Yes sir, I remember."

"And how Master Luke, his owner, gave him land after they were set free?"

"That was after the Emancipation Proclamation in 1863," said Lil' Adam. "When President Lincoln freed the slaves."

"We learned that in school," said Lillie Mae knowingly.

"Did you learn that after the slaves were free across the south, nobody knew what to do?"

"Wasn't they happy to be free?"

"Being free didn't feed their families, and the only jobs they knew was what they'd been freed from... picking cotton and working in the fields, so Poppa stayed on with Mr. Luke to do some share cropping."

"What's share cropping?"

"That's when someone owns lots of crops, but they don't have anybody to tend to them. It's kind of funny if you think about it, they let the folks that used to be slaves live on the land and take care of the same fields they took care of when they were slaves."

"Only this time, paid," added Lil' Adam with a nod.

"That's right," he took another long puff. "Not a heap of money, barely enough to get by, but better than nothing, I suppose."

"Slaves used to do all that work for free?"

"Sho' did."

"That's why they called them slaves," said Lil' Adam somewhat sarcastically. "Free labor! That's why the south didn't want them freed, think of all the money they would lose."

"Poppa had a good head on his shoulder. Mr. Luke knew it and let him oversee the sharecroppers."

"Like an overseer?"

"The white folk in town didn't like that one bit!" He chewed on his pipe for a minute then took a few puffs, slowly blowing the smoke into the air.

"The next few years things seemed to be going good for colored folk, they got to vote, and helped elect President Ulysses S. Grant, a republican who promised to help colored people have better rights as citizens."

"That was because of the Fifteenth Amendment," said Lil' Adam.

"Glad to hear you learning the truth up at that school," he nodded his approval towards his grandson before continuing. "Momma said Poppa was so proud to register and vote. Colored folk were electing people all 'cross the country, but instead of it being a time to celebrate, they were being lynched."

"What is lynched?"

"You'll learn that next year," said Lil' Adam. "It's a term named after Judge Lynch out west in California during the gold rush," he paused once he noticed their confused looks. "People travelled there in search of gold, and if anyone did something wrong, like try to steal someone's gold, they were brought before Judge Lynch. If he found them guilty, they'd be hung before sunset."

"Whew! The same day," said Lillie Mae. "That doesn't sound right."

"Wasn't right," said Poppa John sadly. "Not only did they lynch out west, folks started lynching all over the south."

"The Emancipation Proclamation and the Fifteenth Amendment, gave rights to some that others were not ready for them to have."

"You right son, that's what happened to your great-grandfather, my Poppa," he said as a single tear rolled down his cheek. They all sat quietly as Lillie Mae softly squeezed her grandfather's hand. He took a few more puffs from his pipe. Slowly smoke floated up to the ceiling leaving the porch as a gentle wind pushed it higher.

"Don't know how it all happened," he continued. "One night the Sheriff came to get Poppa, I was only a small chap, your age. He told us the bank in town was robbed and a witness, one of the other white sharecroppers on Mr. Luke's land, said it was Pa'. All momma did was scream '*no! no! no*', begging them not to take him. He tried to tell them they had the wrong man. How he was home all week working, never left out. No one listened. No one cared either. All me and Jesse could do was stand and watch as they took Poppa out the house... we never saw him again."

Lillie Mae hugged her grandfather. "I'm so sorry," she said softly. She never saw him cry before, he was always laughing or the one laughed at, never sad.

"I'm all right baby. That was a long time ago. The Lord blessed me with a fine family and three of the best grandchildren in the world. These are tears of joy not sadness. That's why I'm expecting y'all to help make the world better, keep going to school and to college. Be a lawyer like Tom, helping people, or teaching people, like your Teachers at school. It's the only way colored folks can make things better."

"Yes sir," they all answered.

"You know the Lord always turns things around. We lost Poppa, but Grandma Hattie got a shotgun and had us learn to shoot it. She promised the next time someone came on her porch to take somebody away; it would be their last time."

Poppa John squeezed Lillie Mae's hand and smiled as he finished the story. "When your Uncle Jessie and I ran home that day, your Grandma Hattie saw us coming, and true to her word, she was on that porch with her shotgun. Those boys stopped dead in their tracks, like I said. She was a sight to see, bet it nearly scared them to death, big tall colored woman with a shotgun pointed at you."

"Would have scared me," laughed Grandma Mae walking out on the porch drying her hands on her apron. "Everybody knew Ms. Hattie didn't play, if you intended to come on her porch, you'd better come with a smile."

Everyone sat gently rocking and quietly reflecting on the events of the day and the trials of the past, as the sun slowly set to the west of the Potato Patch.

"It would have been nice to meet Grandma Hattie."

"Me too," said Lil' Adam walking over to hug his grandmother. "She sounds a lot like you."

"Thank you baby, that's a fine compliment."

Poppa John smiled, "I was getting a bit low, recollecting the pass and all, but Lil' Adam you right, Grandma Mae is a lot like your Grandma Hattie. They both strong God-fearing, hard-working women that love their children and grandchildren more than anything."

"And their husband," smiled Grandma Mae.

Poppa John sat quietly, not understanding why he was so emotional. Slowly he reached up and gently squeezed his wife's hand. "Don't know what I'd do without you."

"Me neither," she replied her heart full of love.

11 THE HONEY SHACK

"I hope we have a good time tonight," said Violet sitting on the edge of her sister's bed attempting to push back the gnawing uneasiness in her stomach. All through the night, she tried to understand why she felt such foreboding, as if at any moment she was about to step off a cliff into a dark abyss. "Maybe I shouldn't go. I don't want to mess up everyone's good time."

"You got to start thinking more positive," said Ruby puckering her lips in the mirror as she added additional lipstick. "I always have a good time, otherwise I stay home."

"Home sounds good, let's stay here, fix some popcorn, and dance to some songs on the radio like we used to do when…"

"Listen to yourself, stand up," she turned her around to face the full-length mirror. "You are a knockout, you're gorgeous. That dress fits you like a co-cola bottle. Why in the world would you want to stay home and eat popcorn? That doesn't sound boring to you?"

"No…"

"Stop, you been married too long. Come sit over here."

Ruby sat her in front of a vanity table with one large mirror in the center and two smaller ones on both sides. "Tell me what you see?"

"I see a mother with three children, fixing to go out with her sister and husband."

"Exactly… Boring… For tonight act like your sweetheart is coming to pick you up for a night on the town. You prepared yourself for weeks for this special occasion. All day your thoughts were about him, his smile, his smell, and his lips you long to kiss.

Tonight's the night all your dreams come true, and you'll be with the one you love."

Violet's shoulders dropped a bit. "Well if you put it that way, going on a date seems more interesting than popcorn, maybe even intriguing."

"That's my girl, no more excuses. Sit up straight," instructed Ruby, "shoulders back, chest out, stomach in." They both laughed as Violet robotically performed every command.

"First, let your hair down. It's pinned up like you ready to paint somebody's house, not paint the town." She began to loosen and brush her hair as it draped down over her shoulders. "Now isn't that better."

"Well yes," she answered timidly.

"Okay, what about makeup?"

"I don't normally wear any."

"Well since this isn't a *normal* night, let's see what we got." She began to look through her cases on the table. "Close your eyes."

"What you …."

"Shh, trust me."

Ruby drew a thin black line under her eyelid, added a touch of eye shadow, and a bit of mascara to her eyelashes. "Your skin is so pretty and brown. All I need to add is a little red blush for your cheeks."

"I don't want too much."

"Now for the lips," she continued ignoring her comments. "They have to be ruby red like me…. Okay, open your eyes."

"Umm," she smiled turning her head from side to side. "It looks very nice."

"Not your *normal*."

"Definitely not my *normal*."

"Here's the final touch." She opened the drawer and pulled out a pair of large silver hoop earrings. "Remember these?"

"It's been a long time since I wore any."

"And when you walk, move your head and hips in opposite directions, so they jingle, jangle…. Come on and practice with me."

Violet walked around the bedroom laughing and imitating her sister, swaying her hips from side to side as the earrings jingled. "I look like a puppet on a string."

"You look like a hip cat ready to swing."

"Thank you for always making me laugh."

"That's because I'm funny," she said hugging her tightly. "And I love to see you smile. Now, come on and put your jacket on, we don't want the guys to see our dresses until we get there."

"Oh right," she said hurrying to get ready as the horn blew. "They're here, they're here. I'm so excited, they're here."

"Vee," she said softly with raised eyebrows as she watched her walking in circles around the living room. "Maybe you are a bit *too* excited."

* * *

Soon they turned off the highway onto a small dirt road. Deeper they drove into the darkness, guided only by the front headlights maneuvering through the statuesque pine trees along the bumpy road. Only to arrive at a destination that fell short of anticipation, a small distressed wooden shed on the brink of collapse. "Is this The Honey Shack?" said Violet with a slight frown. "It really does look like a shack."

"It might look like a shack on the outside," said Ruby from the backseat. "But girl we gon' have some fun on the inside, right Fred?"

"You always do," he said wincing from the poke in the side. He had only dated Ruby for a couple months, but one thing he realized, wherever she went, she had a good time, and he enjoyed being around her. "Looks like a lot of people here tonight."

"That's why I'm parking way over here," added Adam. "Never know what might jump off in this place."

"Jump off?" said Violet her excitement replaced by anxiety. "Is it safe?"

"Vee, don't get your panties in a bunch, we got two big strong men to protect us. Let's go so we can get a good table."

For some reason her sister's words did not provide any emotional comfort. She could hear loud music and outbursts of laughter emanating from the tiny *leaning* wooden structure. Her shoulders tensed. "Have a good time in a place like this?"

"Baby don't worry, as long as I'm with you," said Adam taking her hand to help her out of the car, "you're safe."

Her mind racing with questions, she began to panic. What if they ended up separated from each other? What went on inside that made safety an issue? What if something did 'jump off'? Finally, taking a deep breath, she took his arm and allowed him to guide her into the dark abyss.

Once inside, she exhaled a breath of relief, it did look better. Red lanterns placed throughout the room provided a soft warm inviting glow. A long bar lined with wooden stools separated one side of the room. On the other side, small round tables scattered randomly, tightly seating four. To the side was a small area where several couples danced slowly to "Tears on my Pillow" by Little Anthony and the Imperials. Interestingly, the music was not as loud as it seemed from the outside.

"Big Adam, my Man," said the bartender loudly. "I haven't seen you in a month of Sunday's."

"Hey Nick," he quickly added. "This is my wife, Violet."

"How you do ma'am," reaching out to shake her hand. "Good to meet you."

"Same here," she responded with a smile feeling more relaxed.

"Mighty fine wife you got, no wonder you been keeping her away from here."

"Don't go getting any ideas."

"Ma'am I can tell you, Big Adam ain't the man he used to be," he laughed. "You got him spoiled eating all those home cooked meals. Good thing he's not playing ball anymore, or I could beat him to first base."

"See that's the dream you keep having, I told you to wake up," laughed Adam. "I'd be down the road and home in bed before you could squeeze from behind that counter."

"Watch out now," laughed Nick not minding being the blunt of jokes from his regular customers. "Ruby Mae, Ruby Mae, the girl of my dreams."

"Didn't you hear, dreaming is not good for you," she winked at him as she passed by the bar. "Send someone on over to set us up."

"Ohh, she still loves me."

Violet was surprised so many people knew Adam and Ruby. Apparently, they came to this place often, everyone treated them like they were famous. All the attention made her proud to be with them, as if she was famous too. Slowly her inhibitions began fading away.

"Baby, you look so nice tonight," Adam said calmly. "Let me help you with your coat."

"Thank you," she answered nervous to reveal the tight fitting red dress.

"Wow! I've never seen this dress before!"

"I got it today, you like it," blushed Violet, hesitantly twirling around.

"I love it," he said still smiling as he examined her from all angles.

"Ruby picked it out."

"Um-hum," he responded with a slight smirk on his face as he glanced over at his sister-in-law, "figures."

"What does that mean," interjected Ruby not appreciating his tone.

"Nothing, I like the dress, but I figured you picked it out, that's all."

"Um-hum," she responded rolling her eyes at him in fun, as Fred began to remove her coat, revealing an even tighter fitting white dress.

"Oh my!" was all Fred could manage.

Violet started to feel somewhat uncomfortable, since she could tell all eyes were on the two of them, and Ruby, making matters worse, adjusted the top of her dress revealing more cleavage than anyone thought possible.

"Them dresses legal," Nick called from behind the bar watching the women closely as they sat down. "Don't want to get raided up in here."

The jukebox began to play "So Fine" by the Fiestas. "My baby so dog-gone fine," one of the customers sang along with the song. "She loves me come rain or shine."

"The two of you look like fire and ice," said a man walking over to the table. "Which one can I take home with me?"

Adam stood up, towering over him, seriously staring for a few seconds before sitting back down, which possibly seemed more like an eternity to the man who posed the potentially deadly question.

"Sorry, sorry Big Adam. I, I didn't see you sitting there. I apologize, Ruby and Ms.... umm..."

Adam looked up from his seat with a scowl, intently.

"You have a goodnight ma'am," he said to Violet, quickly walking away.

Ruby could no longer contain herself and burst out laughing.

"Who was that," asked Violet feeling embarrassed for the man.

"An ole' friend," answered Adam in his normal calming voice. "He's just having fun."

"She sends cold chills up and down my spine," a customer continued to sing along with the music, laughing at the man sweating in his seat across the room. "Oh yeah, so fine."

"He doesn't look like he's having fun." Violet watched as he put on his hat to leave.

"What can I get everyone," asked the waitress.

"A double of the house special," said Ruby. "What you want Sis?"

"She'll take a co-cola," said Adam. "And I'll have a double house too."

"Me too," said Fred moving closer, hoping his date would notice.

"Sis, live it up." Ignoring his chair movement, Ruby reached over and squeezed her sister's cheeks as she did when they were younger. "Lord knows when you'll come back to The Honey Shack."

"The Lord ain't got anything to do with it," she answered beginning to feel out of place again. "I like to stay home with the kids most of the time, that's all."

"Nothing wrong with that," said Adam taking her hand. "Come on Vee. Let's see if you still got the moves."

"For sure I do," she replied happily jumping to her feet forgetting all her inhibitions once again. "Now that's something I can do."

"Girl you know I taught you everything you know," said Ruby standing up to join them, adjusting her tight-fitting dress. "Come on Fred."

All four of them squeezed onto the tiny dance floor. All attention focused on the sisters in the red and white shimmering dresses dancing, as "Tweedle Dee" by Lavern Baker, played merrily on the jukebox. "Mercy, mercy, puddin' and pie, you got something money can't buy," sang someone watching them as everyone clapped along to the music.

Adam, initially surprised by Violet's dancing and shaking her hips, took her by the hand, twirled her around and pulled her close, as they moved in rhythm to the song. As everyone sang, "I'm a lucky so and so, hubba hubba, honey dew, I'm gonna' keep my eyes on you."

"Sis look like you got some new moves," laughed Ruby as they headed back to their table.

"Rose taught me this new dance called *The Jive*."

"Oh yeah, I got that move, it goes like this," said Ruby shaking her body before sitting, getting the attention of many onlookers.

"I could barely keep up," said Adam pulling the chair out for his wife.

"Me either," said Fred arriving too late to pull the chair out for his date.

"Please," laughs Ruby. "No matter what dance you try to do, it always comes out two steps to the left and two steps to the right. I'm going to call you two-step Fred."

They all laughed despite his obvious embarrassment, although he never cared what Ruby called him, because she had a hold on him he could not shake loose.

"Here are your drinks," said the waitress balancing a tray of beverages.

"At last," said Ruby wiggling in her chair. "All that dancing made me thirsty."

"What's in the house special," asked Violet curiously sipping her cola.

"Hey Nick, what you put in this here brew?"

"All the things you like baby doll," he said pointing his finger at her, "and a little surprise to make you holler, Nick, Ohhh Nick!"

"There you go again. I got something for you," laughed Ruby as she walked over to the jukebox and announced. "Hey everyone, this song is dedicated to Nick the dreamer."

"Sh-Boom (Life could be a dream)" by the Chords began to play. He squeezed from behind the counter, bowed low and extended his hand to Ruby, who shimmied around him shaking more than believably possible. The crowd cheered and laughed as they danced. Nick moving more agilely than expected, twirling and dipping her to the music.

"I told y'all she loves me."

"Keep on dreaming," she responded kissing him on the cheek before taking her seat as everyone clapped.

"Let me taste your *house special*," asked Violet slowly sipping her sister's drink. "Oh my, that is strong!"

"Strong to last long," said Ruby snapping her fingers in the air as she twisted in her seat. "One of these will last you the whole night."

"With a headache the next morning, I'll stick with my drink. Adam might need me to drive home after the two of you finish with the 'double house special'."

"No, I'm good," he said leaning closer with his arm around her chair. "One is my limit. After that I'll be having a cola too."

"See the trick is, drink big swallows like this." Ruby turned her glass up and finished half of her drink, her body shivered from the strong content of alcohol. "Before the night is over, you don't even notice the taste."

"Because you wasted," laughed Violet.

"Remember this song?" said Adam taking Violet's hand to escort her to the dance area. "Rock me Baby" by B. B. King rolled smoothly from the jukebox speakers.

"Of course I do," she smiled.

"This song brings back some good ole' memories," pulling his wife very close to him. "You remember our first date?"

Blushing, she recalled the first time her father let them go to a party without Ruby as a chaperone. Her heart beat almost as fast as that very night. She could barely catch her breath. Ruby was right, this is a night to remember.

"Honey rock me all night long," he sang softly in her ear as they danced closely to the music. "Til' I want no more."

"Hey, I know you two married," said Ruby dancing next to them with Fred. "But this here is a public place, go on home to do all that."

"No, No, they fine," shouted Nick, "I just need to come over there and show Fred what you want."

"I know what she wants," laughed Fred as he twirled Ruby around and dipped her real low. Once back in his arms, he held her so close, he felt her heart beating as their bodies moved in rhythmic unity.

"Oh Yeah," said Ruby enjoying the moves. "Gone Big Daddy, show me what you got."

"And that's no dream," Fred said aloud for everyone to hear.

"You got her now boy!" someone yelled from a nearby table.

As everyone was dancing and having fun, Ruby saw Carmen come in the door turning her smile immediately into a frown. Without her sister noticing, she knew she had to intercept her before she tried to find Adam.

"Fred, act like you walking me to the table. I have to take care of something."

"Okay," he said as he watched Carmen stroll provocatively over to the bar.

Moving quickly, Ruby grabbed her firmly by the arm, "can I talk to you a minute?"

Startled, she jumped, "What you want?" She knew that Ruby had a reputation for being a no-nonsense woman, quick to fight, and quick to cut. She did not want to start any trouble with Adam regarding his sister-in-law.

"Look here," she said gripping her arm tighter and staring her sternly in the eyes.

"Ouch! That hurts!"

"Shut up," her eyes squinted in disgust. "I know you and Big Adam been messing around for a long time and it's not my business, but tonight he's here with his wife, my sister, and you better step off."

Carmen glanced over and saw him on the dance floor with someone she had never saw before, and when he looked her way, instantly she knew he was off limits.

"You hear me!" said Ruby shaking her. "Pay attention when I'm talking to you. And if you even look her way…"

"I'm grown," she answered snatching her arm from Ruby's grip. "I can…"

"I can slap the stew out of you, if you even look her way…," she grabbed her arm again even tighter than before. "…And if you do…You will have to deal with me!"

"Who you think you is," said Carmen loudly pulling away.

"Don't play with me girl," looking at her one last time with intent to kill, before heading back to the table without her sister noticing.

"Carmen," said Nick sitting a glass in front of her. "Got your first drink all set up for you."

"Thank you," she answered, smiling but noticeably shaken. "At least somebody knows how to treat a girl tonight."

"Ain't got nothing to do with that. Big Adam took care of this for you."

"Oh yeah," her expression changed to happiness as she wiggled on the barstool from side to side, looking around to see if he was watching her. "That's my man."

"Girly, let me give you a little advice," he said firmly placing his hand on top of hers. "Don't mess with Ruby when it comes to her sister. She is not playing with you."

Snatching her hand from under his, she tossed her long black hair off her shoulders and rolled her eyes, pretending not to listen.

"And Carmen," he said more firmly not wanting her to ignore him. "Don't be nobody's fool. The best thing for you to do is act like you don't even know him tonight. Big Adam is *not* going to leave his wife to come over here and be with you."

"I'll be the judge of that." She took her drink and walked seductively to the dance floor. "Ain't that a shame" by Fats Domino played in the background. "That's my song, Fred come dance with me."

Surprised he turned, wondering why she called him out. Glancing over at his date, he knew immediately that it would be best if he declined the invitation. "Girl you see I'm busy."

"Busy?" said Ruby shaking her head disapprovingly at him.

Soon Carmen found a willing partner, dancing very close while looking over at Adam, speaking loudly for everyone to hear. "Boy, you got the moves. Oh yeah! Oh Yeah! I like that. Boy, I like that."

"Who is that talking so loud?" said Violet turning to get a better look at the dance floor behind her.

"Some crazy hoot who had too much to drink," answered Ruby. "There is nothing worse than a woman who can't hold her liquor."

"She just got here," said Violet turning to get another look. "Why she keeps looking this way. Do you know her?"

"I've seen her around," said Adam without making eye contact with either woman.

"She looks familiar."

"Nick, send us another round," shouted Ruby hoping to change the subject.

"Will do, and make sure you save another dance for me."

"Her dance card's full," quickly answered Fred feeling assertive.

"Um, I like a strong man that knows what he wants."

"Well come on then let's hit the dance floor," he said taking her by the hand.

"Come on Sis."

"Okay, one last dance, it's getting late."

"Girl the night is young," laughed Ruby as they all headed to the dance floor.

The drinks were flowing, laughter and music filled the air as "Shake, Rattle, and Roll" by Big Joe Turner, played on the jukebox. Some of the patrons of The Honey Shack wanted Carmen to start trouble, but when they saw the sweetness and innocence of Big Adam's wife, dancing and laughing on the dance floor, everyone was happy she was enjoying herself. All except Carmen, who sat alone at a table fuming, attempting to stare a hole in the back of 'her man'. No one cared since the joint was jumping with music and merriment.

"Whew! We danced so long my hair is sweating out," said Violet as they left the dance floor.

"Umm," said Adam kissing her on the neck. "You know I like it when you all sweaty."

"Stop Adam," she giggled, "people watching."

"You my wife," he replied pulling her close to him at the table.

Frustrated, Carmen watched them kiss for as long as she could, drinking one drink after another as "Maybe" by The Chantels began to play. She knew he was married, but she still loved him. He was her man and she wasn't going to let him go, even if his wife did look like a Sunday school teacher.

"Save that kissing for when you get home," laughed Ruby. "You know Momma wants more grandchildren."

"Let's work on given them some more," said Fred as he tried to kiss Ruby on the cheek.

"Now here you go dreaming," she said looking at him as if he had two heads.

"He's right Sis, when are you settling down?"

"When I find somebody to settle down with," she answered, not liking the way the conversation was turning.

Sitting down a tray of drinks, Nick said in a sultry voice, "I told you, I'm your man."

"She knows who her man is," said Fred reaching in his pocket.

"I'll get that," said Adam handing Nick a five-dollar bill, with extra to cover Carmen's drinks, "and I'll settle who the best man is."

"Settle it then," said Ruby egging him on.

"Attention everybody," said Adam confidently standing up with his hands on his jacket lapel. "Who thinks I'm the best man in here tonight?" He took a bow as patrons began to laugh and clap, except for one person who rolled her eyes and looked away.

"You a big fine stud, I'll take you home," said one patron.

"I'll kiss them lips all night long," said another.

"Thank you, but I'm already taken. Ain't that right baby?"

"Adam," blushed Violet as he kissed her on the cheek, "you so crazy."

As the jukebox began to play "Hound Dog" by Willie Mae Thornton, Carmen stared at Adam with piercing eyes and yelled. "You ain't nothing but a hound dog, quit snooping 'round my door."

"Come on let's dance," said Ruby jumping to her feet pulling Fred along with her, hoping her sister didn't notice the snide remarks from the bar.

"No wonder you come here so much," she said finally enjoying herself along with everyone else except for one person sitting alone. Their eyes met. Violet froze; confused by the way she looked at her, as if she hated her.

"You okay?" said Adam feeling her body tense as he held her closely while they danced.

"Yes, yes, I'm fine," she answered not wanting to ruin everyone's good time. She tried to finish the dance but could not avoid the woman's stares.

"Let's take a break," said Ruby looking at her reflection in her compact. "Or I'll need to find a straightening comb if I don't stop all this sweating. Nick gimme' something to wipe my face."

"Trying to tell you it's not hot," he said handing her some napkins. "That's my love heating up the joint. I'll be over around four a.m. to put out the fire."

"He never stops," said Fred feeling insecure.

"Don't worry," reassured Ruby putting her hand on his knee, "you my guy."

"For always?"

"For now," she answered kissing him on the cheek, more concerned with her sister and Carmen who was watching her every move. It was only a matter of time before something happened.

"Yeah Ruby, it's time to start a family like your sister?" said Adam trying to help his friend.

"Don't *you* start!"

"Oh my!" said Violet startled by her thoughts. "What time is it?"

"It's almost twelve," answered Adam. "What's the matter?"

"The kids," she said anxiously. "I want to get up early enough to surprise them at church tomorrow."

"That's my sister," laughed Ruby. "Out on a Saturday night with good drinks, good music, and good-looking men, and her mind is on church."

"As yours should be," she quickly interrupted.

"Sis, let's have one more dance, this here is a fun song." Drinking the last of her drink, she danced over to Fred while "Don't you just know it" by Huey Smith and the Clowns played, and mostly everyone squeezed on the dance floor.

* * *

"I'm exhausted, it's past my bedtime," said Violet wiping her face.

"Come on, stay a little longer Sis, the party is just getting started."

"Maybe next time," said Violet as Adam helped her with her coat.

"Next time?" said Ruby.

"Next time?" said Adam.

Violet smiled at them both. "I really enjoyed myself. Now that we have our own car, maybe we can do this again. You don't mind, do you?"

"Of course not," lied Ruby looking at Adam.

"Of course not," he replied uneasily, knowing the chances of avoiding potential problems next time might not happen as positively as this time.

"It reminds me when we were kids and Poppa finally bought a radio. We would be in our room listening to big band songs by Count Basie and Duke Ellington, dancing and dancing until he'd shout, 'turn that music off before I throw that thing out the window'."

"You don't mind do you Adam," asked Violet softly noticing a distant look in his eyes.

"Oh no," he said quickly focusing on the conversation. "Long as I'm with you, I'm happy."

"Don't blame you man," added a patron at the next table. "They both some good-looking chicks, no disrespect Big Adam."

"Fire and Ice!" yelled Nick from behind the bar.

"Ruby you coming?" said Violet.

"No," answered Ruby giving her sister a hug. "I got a few more moves in me before the night is done."

"How you getting home?"

"Don't worry, we'll squeeze in with somebody heading our way."

"You sure?"

"Yes Sis," Ruby kissed her on the cheek. "Tell momma I'll be over tomorrow, haven't been to Sunday dinner since I started my job at the mill."

"Okay," she answered feeling much better since she would see her tomorrow. "She'll be glad to see you."

"Can I come too?" said Fred.

"We'll see," laughed Ruby.

Adam and Violet waved good-bye. Other patrons acknowledged their departure with friendly waves as well. Except for one person who frowned and turned her back as they passed by while the music played, "There goes my baby" by Ben E. King and The Drifters.

They walked out into the darkness of the parking lot now filled with cars. "I really did have a nice time," said Violet looking up at Adam before getting in the car.

"I'm glad you did," he said kissing her gently on the lips.

As she heard the music playing from the crowded little wooden structure, a feeling of sadness came over her, attempting to wipe away the happiness she felt earlier. Driving away, she started to turn on the radio, but decided to ask a question that bothered her most of the night. "Adam, do you know that girl from The Honey Shack?"

"What girl?" he answered knowing exactly who she meant.

"The one that kept talking loud and staring at us?" she said with her eyes squinted, irritated with his response.

"Baby, many people in the place were talking, why you think some woman was staring at us?"

"Cause every time I looked her way, she was looking my way."

"Maybe she thought you were staring at her."

"Adam," said Violet frustrated by his evasive answers. "Do you know her?"

"I know most of the people that hang out there."

"You *know* what I mean," she said ready to cry.

"I know you my wife and I know I love you more than any woman on this earth, and I know I am not interested in anybody else except you. Now scoot on over here so I can kiss your sweet lips."

"But you're driving."

"So," said Adam reaching down to give her a long kiss as he drove through the dark forest.

"Adam, you better watch the road."

"Baby, I'm the best driver you'll ever know."

"You're the best driver and the best man."

"And the best lover," he said squeezing her around the waist.

"Oh Adam," giggled Violet warmly, completely forgetting the woman and the question.

He turned on the radio, glad to hear the distraction of "Sea of Love" by Phil Phillips playing softly. She looked up at him trying to remember what had previously upset her, but he pulled her closer, kissing her gently on the lips once again, her mind clear and her heart full of love.

12 GOING TO CHURCH

Sunday morning moved quickly for the Johnson family, starting with the classic breakfast of bacon, eggs, sausage, grits, and homemade biscuits, enjoyed by everyone. Clean-up time was always important. Grandma Mae hated coming home to a sink full of dirty dishes. Then it was off to church.

Pilgrim Baptist, a small one-story red brick building nestled in the southern pines, with beautiful stained-glass windows, and a large white cross for a steeple. Inside, were ten long wooden benches on each side, separated by a narrow aisle, with barely enough room for the choir members to march down before service began. The pulpit, elevated slightly above the congregation, included the Pastor's larger chair and two chairs for visiting clergy. One-step elevated the platform, on one side an area for choir members, on the other, a large black piano in the corner beneath a large picture of Jesus with outstretched hands.

Sunday school started promptly at nine o'clock, the children's class gathered near the back, and the adults near the front. Approximately forty-five minutes later a bell rang, the church bustled with movement as parishioners headed for their favorite church seats, socializing briefly, or going outside for a few minutes of fresh air. The Johnson grandchildren, headed straight for their designated spot behind the deacon's wives, who sat directly behind the deacons. Poppa John anchored the end of the aisle, followed by Lillie Mae, Rose, and Lil' Adam all sitting quietly until service started. Promptly at ten, the choir members marched down the center aisle singing,

"We're marching to Zion" by Issac Watts and Robert Lowry, followed by the Pastor and any visiting clergy. Grandma Mae always sat in front for a direct view of everyone on the third row in case anyone fell asleep or became distracted with chatter.

Once in place, the choir began singing their opening song, as stragglers quickly found seats. However, this Sunday they watched their grandmother's eyes stretch wide in disbelief as Violet and Adam walked down the aisle to sit next to Poppa John. Beaming with joy, she sang extra loudly.

"How did you get here?" Lil' Adam whispered to his parents sitting past Rose and Lillie Mae.

"It's a surprise," answered his mother.

"We got a car, I knew it, I told you I saw Pops driving past us the other day," he boasted proudly to his sisters. "What kind of car is it?"

"Shh," said an elderly woman sitting behind the family.

Lil' Adam looked up to see Grandma Mae with her finger to her mouth and a stern frown on her face. He knew he was in trouble for violating the rule of no talking in church. The punishment dealt immediately after service with either ear pulling or cheek squeezing. He mouthed the word "sorry" hoping to defray the penalty. Responding with a nod and a smile, she was more pleased seeing her baby girl in service than his minor infraction.

"My church family," the Pastor continued with a slow southern drawl that made it difficult to stay awake. "Let not your hearts be troubled down here on earth. Jesus went to prepare a place for us up yonder in heaven. Things are rough down here…"

"Amen, Pastor, Amen," responded church members.

"But it's only for a moment, this earth is not our home, one day we'll be in a better place."

"Thank you Jesus."

"If we look around down here, we might get discouraged. Luke 21:28 tells us, 'and when these things begin to come to pass, then look up, and lift up your heads; your redemption draws nigh'. Let me tell you, don't look down, look up."

"Amen, Pastor, Amen."

"…I stopped by to tell you some good news this Sunday morning. If you have accepted Jesus as Lord and Savior, then shout Hallelujah, you saved. Look up; I'll see you up in heaven."

"Yes sir, Pastor, yes sir."

"If you *haven't* accepted Jesus," he paused sternly looking around the sanctuary. "Then you not saved, and I came to warn you that hell will be your home."

"Oh Lord, preach Pastor preach."

"That's some bad news especially the way things are down here, Jim Crow laws, colored only signs everywhere, separate schools, poll taxes, can't afford to vote, sitting in the back of the bus, and in the back of the courtroom. It's not looking good for us colored folks down here. Sometimes it feels like hell now."

"You right Pastor."

"Wouldn't it be awful sad to have hell now and hell later, that's like double hell."

"Yes Lord, help us today."

"Search your heart my sisters and brothers. Do you know Jesus? Do you know Him for yourself? Momma can't know Him for you, Poppa can't know Him for you, you must know Him for yourself. It's not too late my son. It's not too late my daughter. Come and know Jesus for yourself."

"Amen Pastor, Amen."

"What a friend we have in Jesus," the Pastor began to sing, joined by the choir with, 'all our sins and grief to bear,' as he walked to the front raising his arms for the congregation to stand. "Come on down my son, come on down my daughter."

"What a privilege to carry…"

"The doors of the church are open to anyone who doesn't know Jesus in the pardon of their sins."

"Everything to God in prayer…"

"Don't wait too late to say 'Yes' to Jesus, instead of double hell, you can have heaven in your reach."

Soon a young man walked from the back of the church. Grandma Mae's face lit up with a bright smile as she watched Beau slowly walk down to the front, briefly turning to glance over at Rose.

"Praise the Lord!" exclaimed the Pastor with his arms opened wide to embrace him. "God bless you my son, you're making the right choice. God bless you."

The church continued to sing as the Pastor spoke with Beau until the chorus ended and he raised his hand to speak. "My church family we have here Beau Henderson, who recently moved back home from up north. He has decided to accept Jesus Christ back into his life."

"Hallelujah! Hallelujah!" everyone shouted.

"He'll be baptized immediately after the deacons prepare the baptismal pool, let's all welcome Mr. Henderson." The pianist softly continued playing "What a Friend we have in Jesus", as movement once again commenced throughout the church.

"Mom can I go out and look at the car?" anxiously asked Lil' Adam.

"What car," whispered Violet?

"I know you drove here. I saw Pops Friday on his way home."

"Wait until service is finished," she whispered.

"It is finished," he persisted.

"Listen to your mother boy, we still got the baptism," added his grandfather.

"Do we have a car," he stared at his father barely able to contain his excitement.

"Yes son."

"Adam… why you tell him?"

"I knew it!" Lil' Adam said loudly as others turned to look at him.

"Boy, we still in church," said Grandma Mae walking up to them.

"Hi Momma."

"Hi Baby," she said happily hugging them both.

"Son, I see you finally went and got an auto-MO-bile," smiled Poppa John.

"Yes sir," he answered.

"Guess it was time."

"Rose, go on up and shake Beau's hand before the baptism."

"He saw me already."

"Go on Chile'," she insisted, motioning for her to hurry.

"Who is he," asked Violet.

"You remember, that's Charlie Henderson's boy Beau, they lived down the road, 'til his mother passed, came by the Potato Patch yesterday, thin as a rail. He's trying to fine work while he off from school for the summer."

"Momma can I go out and look at the car," interrupted Lil' Adam.

"…Staying with his uncle," she smiled as her granddaughter shook Beau's hand in the front of the church. "But he loves him some Rose, been sweet on her ever since they were kids."

"Momma, please can I go out and look at the car."

"Now I remember him, he always said he came to visit Lil' Adam but ended up spending all his time running after Rose trying to get her attention."

"That's him," she said shaking her head looking at Beau's wide grin, "still the same way."

"Momma Please!"

"Boy leave your mother be, can't you see we are talking, wait 'til the baptism's over, now hush!"

"Wade in the water," the church began to sing as Beau walked behind the choir stand, where they kept a small pool of water filled for such an occasion. Everyone sang as the Pastor submerged him backwards into the shallow water, "wade in the water, children, wade in the water, God gon' trouble the water." Soon the baptism was over, and everyone began leaving for home or socializing outside the church.

"That was a fine service. John invite Beau over for dinner once he's all dried off."

"Mae, I want to look at the new family auto-MO-bile."

"Go on now John," she insisted, "plenty of time to see a car."

Seeing how disappointed he looked, Violet kissed her father on the cheek, "We'll wait for you out front, Poppa."

"Pops, where the keys?"

"Hold on son," laughed his father dangling the keys. "You don't even know which car it is."

"Bet I do," he said grabbing them and running ahead of everyone.

"That boy is excited to have a new family car," laughed Grandma Mae, "or as your Poppa say 'auto-MO-bile'."

"Men-folk like anything they can drive, whether its trucks, cars, tractors, remember that ole' Model T Ford you had to crank to start. Reckon we had a boat they'd want to drive that."

"I'd like to drive a boat myself," added Adam. "Maybe we'll get that next."

"Can we," said Lillie Mae.

"Adam, please don't get her started."

"Grandma Mae you'd come ride in the boat with us, wouldn't you?"

"Chile', don't include me in that, won't see me in no boat, too much water, not getting in more water than I can drink."

They all laughed as they headed towards the car, which wasn't hard to locate with Lil' Adam sitting in the front seat, and his head hanging out the window yelling, "Hurry up, gonna' give everyone a ride in my new car."

"Momma, how is it Lil' Adam's car. It's the family car?"

"Please don't start with that whining."

"This car is the coolest," beamed Lil' Adam blowing the horn. "Man, don't that horn sound boss."

"It's my turn. Let me sit there," said Lillie Mae opening the driver side door.

"Get outta' here girl," he said pulling the door closed. "You can't drive anyway."

"I didn't say I wanted to *drive no way*," she mocked him. "All I want to do is sit behind the steering wheel like you, Dad can I get a turn?"

"Let your sister get a turn in the front seat."

"Ahh man, she always gets what she wants."

"Naah, naah", she said sticking her tongue out at him as he got out of the car.

"Lillie Mae if you keep acting like that you can get out right now," scolded Violet.

"Yes ma'am," she answered pretending to be gloomy. Two seconds later, she was bouncing up and down on the front seat, blowing the horn, and making faces at her brother, who finally walked away in disgust.

"This is a fine auto-MO-bile," said Poppa John looking in through the passenger's side.

"John, where you come from," exclaimed Grandma Mae startled by his sudden appearance. "Is Beau coming to dinner?"

"He said he's coming," he answered not looking her way. "Son, you did a good job."

"Thank you. Guess we got it in time, especially with the boycott coming and all."

"What boycott?" said Lillie Mae still in the front seat.

"Stay in your place Chile', that's grown folks business," said Grandma Mae walking around to the passenger's side. "Think I'll be riding home with y'all, scoot on over here baby, I got to get home and start my dinner."

"I'll drive," said Poppa John jumping into the driver's seat. "Here Adam take my keys, you can take the truck, me and the children will drive on home."

"Yes sir," smiled Adam, "glad to oblige".

"You don't mind do you son?" said Grandma Mae more politely.

"No ma'am, don't mind at all. Right proud to have you drive our new car, many times as I drove yours."

"Well then, we'll see y'all at the house, directly. Violet you might as well get dinner started for your mother, we might make a few stops on the way."

"Poppa John can I get a turn to drive too?" said Lil' Adam.

"Sure son."

"What?" said Grandma Mae looking at her grandson, then her husband, "I don't want to be diddly-dabbing all around town, who's fixing dinner?"

"Don't worry, I'll take care of dinner Momma, enjoy yourself," said Violet reaching into the car to kiss her on the cheek.

"Thank you baby," answered Poppa John. "Get in Rose."

As they drove away, Violet and Adam could here Grandma Mae fussing, "John, this is a fine auto-MO-bile and all, but I won't be out all-day joy riding while you and Lil' Adam take turns driving across the country… company coming!"

"Ahh Mae, we know company coming, can't we enjoy the ride before they come?"

"Can we get some ice-cream?" asked Lillie Mae.

"Sure can."

"Can I drive home after that?" asked Lil' Adam.

"Oh Lord, no telling when we'll get home," said Grandma Mae putting her hand to her forehead and shaking her head.

"Maybe I should go help with dinner," added Rose who was not interested in driving, joyriding, or ice cream.

"Thank you baby, at least someone else is thinking 'bout dinner, John stop the car."

Violet and Adam stood waving, wondering why the car suddenly stopped. After a few seconds Rose opened the back door, got out the car, briefly waved, and started walking towards them.

"Baby, is everything all right?"

"Yes ma'am. Just thought I'd ride with you and help get dinner started, since company coming."

"That is very kind of you, sweetheart."

"Yes it is," Adam added giving her a hug, "especially since I want to know who that young man was that smiled at you on his way to the baptism?"

"Now Adam," said Violet sliding to the middle of the front seat. "Let Rose be. She a beautiful young lady ready to graduate high school, maybe on her way to college..."

"And my job is to make sure she does that."

Rose climbed in the truck next to her mother looking out the window as they drove away, angry with herself for not staying in the shiny new family car, at least the focus was not on her.

"What's his name?" he continued despite his wife poking him in the side. "Nothing wrong with a father asking his daughter a couple questions regarding a gentleman suitor."

"Gentleman suitor?" said Rose shocked, wondering where he got that idea, ready to jump out of the car and walk the rest of the way.

"Adam, all he did was look at your daughter on his way to give his life to the Lord, which is more important. Besides, he is a nice young man, in college, and they've been friends since they were chaps."

"How come I haven't seen him before?"

"Probably because we weren't there to see who they were playing with."

"Oh."

"Anyway, momma invited him to dinner."

"She has?" sighed Rose.

"Good! I'll get to talk to him myself."

"No you won't," she quickly responded. "They are friends. Rose will tell us if there is anything else we need to know, won't have you embarrassing her that way."

"Thank you momma," she said softly.

"We'll see," he answered making sure to get in the last word.

13 THE ROUND TABLE

"Momma, Momma, guess what," said Lillie Mae running into the kitchen.

"Hold on baby," said Violet wiping her flour-covered hands on her apron. "Calm down."

"Poppa John let me drive the new car!"

"What!" said Adam looking up from the kitchen table not excited at all. "Vee…honey…"

"Don't worry dear. I'm – I'm sure she doesn't mean it that way."

"I got to drive our new family car. Isn't that the coolest?"

"What is she talking about?" Violet turned calmly to her mother trying to get an answer before Adam passed out.

"Sorry it took so long. You know your Poppa had to stop everywhere," she said patiently handing Rose a small container of ice cream. "Here baby, I didn't want you to miss out."

"Thank you, umm, strawberry, my favorite."

"Don't eat a lot now, get a small taste and save some for later. It's almost dinner time."

"Yes ma'am."

"Stopped to pick up a few groceries, sure is a mighty fine auto-MO-bile you got Adam. That trunk in the back has plenty room."

Adam sat quietly, confused, not knowing if he should be angry or happy or break something.

"Did you let Lillie Mae drive the car?" insisted Violet.

"Only from the mailbox to the house," answered Poppa John walking in with another bag of groceries. "She did good for her first time behind the wheel."

"I told you," beamed Lillie Mae trying to get a taste of ice cream.

"Didn't you get some," Rose asked, turning to avoid her sister's spoon.

"That was two hours ago, I'm hungry. Is dinner ready?"

"Poppa," Violet tried to get the conversation focused back on the original topic. "Lillie Mae isn't old enough to be driving, she's only twelve."

"Only twelve," he answered matter-of-factly getting his pipe ready to light. "By the time you were twelve you drove the tractor all over the farm."

"Don't light that thing in here," said Grandma Mae putting the groceries away. "Lillie Mae, see what is keeping Beau and your brother with the rest of the groceries."

"Beau?" said Rose immediately feeling sick on the stomach, handing over her ice cream. "Here you can have this."

"Thanks," said Lillie Mae, happily taking the container and heading for the front porch.

"The rest of the groceries?" said Violet looking over at Adam who had his head resting on his chin, staring out the kitchen window.

"After we got the ice cream, we were in town already, might as well pick up a few things. It didn't make no sense for Beau to walk, since we pass his house on the way home."

"Here you go," said Lil' Adam with the last of the bags.

"Hello Ms. Violet, Mr. Williams," said Beau respectfully. "How are you Ms. Rose?"

"Don't call me that?" said Rose walking out the kitchen.

"Now Rose, be nice."

"That's all right Ms. Mae ma'am. She always says that when I call her Ms. Rose."

"Okay then," she replied affectionately. "Y'all get washed up, dinner almost ready."

"Yes ma'am," said both boys as they left the kitchen.

Adam finally spoke while the women were getting dinner prepared. "Ms. Mae, does Beau like Rose?"

"Oh yes," she answered waving her hand at him and shaking her head. "Boy adored that Chile' since they were younger than Lillie Mae…"

Violet looked over at her husband with an 'I told you so' look.

"…followed behind Rose like a puppy, still she paid him no mind."

"Reckon I'll go have a talk with him."

"Adam," said Violet cautiously. "I don't think –"

"Now Violet," interrupted Grandma Mae. "If Adam wants to talk to Beau, that's fine. Rose is his daughter and he has a right to know how a young man feels. Although John already talked to him, guess it won't do no harm to talk some more."

"Momma, sit down and rest your feet. I'll get everything finished."

"Thank you Baby, my feet are *killing* me."

"Your shoes too tight?" said Violet as she started the last pan of fried chicken.

"Not used to wearing them so long," she said sitting at the kitchen table rubbing her foot.

"Seems like a whole lot going on today."

"More than usual, I'd say. That reminds me Adam, before you talk to Beau, can you add the extra section to the dining room table?

"Yes ma'am," he said relieved to leave the kitchen.

"Vee, I forgot to tell you, Tom and his grandbaby are coming over for dinner too."

"How's he doing, haven't seen him in years?"

"He stopped by Saturday, John was so glad to see him."

"And he has a grandbaby?"

"She's a sweet girl, same age as Lillie Mae. They hit it off fine soon as they met."

"Maybe they'll be friends like Poppa and Mr. Tom."

"That would be mighty nice."

"Momma, Grandma Mae!" shouted Lillie Mae running into the kitchen. "Here comes Aunt Ruby, and she has a gentleman friend with her."

"Let me go out here and see who she brought home this time."

"If you see Rose, tell her to come and help set the table please."

"Okay honey." Before she could reach the dining room, her daughter was standing there with a tall, nicely dressed, nervous looking man behind her. "Hi Baby, how you been?"

"Good Momma," said Ruby giving her a hug and kiss on the cheek. "I'd like you to meet Fred, a good friend of mine."

"How you do, Mrs. Johnson," he said reaching out his hand. "Glad to finally meet you."

"Same here," said Grandma Mae shaking his hand. "Have a seat son. I got to find some comfortable shoes."

"Yes ma'am."

"I'll go help Violet in the kitchen."

"Ruby don't leave your company standing there. Mind your manners. Let him go out back with John and the other men folk."

"Yes ma'am."

"Well, don't just stand there, walk him around back, and tell Rose to come set the table."

"Yes ma'am," said Ruby, respectful of her mother even as an adult.

Smiling, Fred realized he never saw her listen to anyone's request. She seemed almost kind, respectful even. Maybe he had her pegged all wrong.

"Come on Fred," she snapped in her regular tone.

"Maybe not," he thought.

"Lillie Mae, why you back in that room hot as it is," asked her grandmother.

"Changing my clothes ma'am."

"That sounds like a good idea, believe I'll do the same."

"It's too hot for a dress," she said barefooted, putting on shorts and a shirt with the sleeves cut out.

Grandma Mae squinted, quickly trying to pull a cotton print dress over her head. "Is that Tom's car pulling in the driveway?"

Before long, she was greeting him on the porch. "Hey Tom."

"How is everyone doing this fine Sunday afternoon," he said kindly tipping his hat, professionally dressed in a suit and tie.

"Fine, but today is a hot one."

"You can say that again," wiping the sweat from his brow, "John around back?"

"I see you remember your friend well," laughed Grandma Mae.

"He always did like to stay around back until dinner was ready."

"Scared I'd ask him to do something," she shook her head. "How you Miss Annie?"

"Fine ma'am," she answered shyly, wearing a frilly yellow dress with white ankle socks and carrying a brown paper bag.

Before he left, Tom noticed the uneasiness on his granddaughter's face. "Annie, you'll be fine with Ms. Mae and her granddaughter, they're like family."

"That's right baby," she said coming down the stairs and hugging her close to her bosom. "And call me 'Grandma Mae', like everyone else."

"I brought my baby dolls," she smiled holding up the paper bag.

"Great," said Lillie Mae running down the porch steps to take her hand. "Come on, let's go get my dolls and they can all meet each other."

"That sounds like fun," she answered happily waving to her grandfather as they ran in the house.

"Lillie Mae see if you can find something cool for her to put on, don't want her pretty dress soiled. Do you mine Tom?"

"Oh no, go right ahead. Last thing I want is my daughter upset that Annie's new dress has a stain or something."

"When you get around back, tell John, dinner is ready in ten minutes."

"Will do," he answered, walking along the side of the house to the backyard.

Heading towards the kitchen, Grandma Mae called to her daughters, "Y'all need any help?"

"No thank you, everything's taken care of," answered Violet.

"Then I'm going in here and rest my feet."

"That sounds good," said Ruby, helping to set the table. "Vee, how many places you think we'll need?"

"Many as will fit, every time I turn around, somebody else is coming to dinner."

The two sisters laughed while setting the round table with the "good" china, only used for special occasions. Soon Grandma Mae went to the back porch and called everyone for dinner. She watched them pass the bathroom, heading directly to the dining room and quickly added, "I know I might have to remind the young ones to wash their hands, but I *know* I don't have to remind the older ones."

"Don't mind you reminding me," laughed Tom making a detour into the bathroom. "Cause the older I get, the more I forget."

"You right," laughed Poppa John. "That is why you need a wife, Mae always telling me something I forgot, or something I lost."

"That's because you can't recollect nothing, and you'd lose your head if it wasn't attached to your body.

Once in the dining room, she directed everyone where to sit. "Tom, you and John can sit at that end of the table, and Miss Annie you can sit next to your grandpa."

"Can I sit next to Annie?" said Lillie Mae.

"Of course," she answered patting them both simultaneously on the back and noticing each one of them carrying a baby doll. "Lay the babies on your lap."

"Shouldn't they put the dolls away until after dinner?" said Violet.

"No, they'll be fine, it's good practice, when you and Ruby were babies, I could feed one and nurse the other, at the same time."

"And still eat dinner," added Poppa John with an impressive nod.

"Momma," said Ruby looking around embarrassed. "Nobody wants to hear that, company's here."

"It's true. I could even use the bathroom holding the two of you, but at least I *had* children."

"Momma," Ruby interrupted. "Please just say the blessing."

"Rose, you and your aunt with no children, sit here."

"Now Mae."

"Okay John," she answered. "Violet, you Adam and Lil' Adam sit down by your Poppa, at the head of the table, I'll sit down here, next to Beau and Rose."

"Mae, say the blessing."

"Let's all stand and hold hands," she paused waiting for everyone. "Dear heavenly Father, thank you for this food my daughters prepared. May it be good to eat and filling to our bodies. Thank you for our good friends spending time with us, and Miss Annie, and my grandchildren. And may I have many, many more."

"Amen," said Ruby prematurely closing her mother's prayer.

"Amen," everybody else responded.

"But I wasn't finished..."

"Mae, the food smells good and we ready to eat," said Poppa John, motioning to everyone around the table to sit down. "Dig in and help yourself everybody."

"I'm so hungry I could eat my shoe," said Lil' Adam.

"Well I wouldn't want you to do that son," laughed Grandma Mae, "I'll talk about more grandchildren later."

"Momma Please," said Ruby reaching for the corn.

"Have to talk one day."

"We will, just not *this* day."

For a time, no one spoke as the aromas of the southern cooked meal of fried chicken, pig feet, cornbread, collard greens, fatback, okra, and corn, filled the air as everyone delighted in the food and time together.

"Um-hum Vee," said Adam pinching her thigh under the table. "You cooked all this, girl I didn't know you had it in you."

"Somebody please tell this man that I know how to cook!"

"I can vouch for that son," interrupted Poppa John. "Both my girls can cook, and my grandbaby too."

"Thank you," said Rose smiling from the other end of the table across from Beau.

"You mean to tell me you have good food like this all the time?"

"All the time," answered Grandma Mae. "I am mighty proud of my girls. They sure can cook."

"Mae's the best cook on this side of the Mason-Dixon Line, reason I married her."

"Don't know if that's the reason, but I know you were thin when I last saw you," laughed Tom.

"I suspect I got a bit rounder over the years. Good eating will do that to you my friend."

"I know what you mean," added Adam rubbing his stomach as everyone laughed in agreement.

"Grandma Mae, can we go out on the porch with our dolls after dinner," asked Lillie Mae. Even though her mother and father were present, she knew the protocol – her grandmother was boss.

"Yes baby, for a bit. Y'all got school tomorrow, so it won't be long before its time to go."

"Yes Ma'am," they both replied.

"Tom, are you still living in Philadelphia? Will Annie be able to get back to school in time?"

"I still live in Philadelphia, but Annie moved down her with her mother over the summer, she'll be going to Newberry Middle."

"That school is right down the road from our house," said Lillie Mae excited as the two girls headed towards the front porch with their doll babies, laughing and talking as if they knew each other for years. "Maybe you'll be able to come over for a visit."

"What grade is Lillie Mae in?" said Tom.

"She's in the sixth grade at Forrest Middle School," said Violet.

"Isn't that school all the way across town, wouldn't Newberry be closer?"

"It would be closer," interrupted Adam matter-of-factly, "but Newberry is for whites only."

"I'm surprised that hasn't changed," he continued with a confused look. "Have you heard of *Brown vs. Board of Education*?"

"Awhile back, some of the fellows at the barber shop said there was a law to get rid of separate schools for colored and whites."

"Actually," continued Tom. "The case went all the way to the Supreme Court. In May of 1954, they ruled that it was unconstitutional for schools to separate based on race, and that separate schools were not equally educating students."

"The schools here are still separate," said Poppa John pulling out his pipe.

"Now John…" said Grandma Mae looking his way with an eye of disapproval. "I know you not 'bout to light that thing in here."

Tom responded reading the look on his friends' face, "I'll go with you."

"Grandma Mae, can I go too?" said Lil' Adam.

"Yes baby, everybody finished anyhow, us women folk might as well start cleaning up. Beau you want a plate for later to take home?"

"Yes ma'am," he smiled glancing over at Rose. "I'd greatly appreciate that."

"Okay, then go on out there with the men folk, unless you intend on helping with the dishes."

"No ma'am, I mean yes ma'am. I, I mean yes Grandma Mae ma'am."

"Chile' just gone outside," she laughed waving her hand at him.

After he left, all the women laughed at his stammering infatuation. Except Rose, who stood up, rolled her eyes, and walked to the kitchen, without looking their way.

Shaking her head after they left, Grandma Mae chuckled, "Umh-umh-umh, that boys got a hankering for your daughter."

"Right now, she likes music more than anything," said Violet gathering up some plates to take in the kitchen.

"Give her time, she'll find a fellow," said Ruby right behind her sister.

"You sound like the pot calling the kettle black," added Grandma Mae with sarcasm.

"Momma, don't start on me."

"I didn't say anything."

"But I know what you meant."

"You both need to stop," said Violet standing between the two of them. "Momma, Ruby is fine, she got a nice apartment, and a good job."

"It's not natural for a woman to be living alone, one day she with this fellow, then one day she with that fellow, ain't natural."

"Momma, I love you and I know you want me to be married and have more grandchildren. I'm not ready." Sitting down her plates, she walked over to her mother and gave her a hug. "But when I do find the right fellow, you'll be the first to know."

"I want you to be safe, being all alone and such," she said rubbing her daughter on the back as tears rolled down her cheeks. "We worry about you, that's all."

"I'll be fine."

"Momma," reassured Violet with a smile patting her mother on the back as she walked past her. "Nobody messes with Ruby. Last night everybody jumped in line at The Honey Shack when she came in the door."

"The what kinda' shack?"

"The Honey Shack."

"Oh Lord! I heard bad things go on in that place," she responded shaking her head with a look of concern. "Can't believe you went there…"

"I couldn't believe it either. But Ruby asked me to go, so we went…"

"We?"

"Adam and I went with Ruby and Fred…"

"Like a double-date?"

"Momma, please let me tell the rest of the story."

"I'm listening," she smiled. "Chile', I'm glad you finally went somewhere, but the Honey Shack?"

"It wasn't as bad as people said. Ruby walked in the place like she owned the joint, and nobody messes with her, been that way since we were chaps."

"You right," Grandma Mae nodded in agreement. "Still can't say I like you down at that Shack place. But I do remember that one time, you came home crying, said some girl laughed at your dress. Ruby found out and high-tailed out the house before I could catch her. All she said when she came back was, 'she won't bother you no more'."

All four women laughed while they worked together cleaning off the table and washing the dishes. Rose smiled the most, since she loved to hear stories of her mother and aunt when they were younger.

"You should have seen Vee in this little skin tight red dress I picked out for her, had all the guys looking her way."

"Hush yo' mouth," said Grandma Mae with her hands on her hips. "Where was her husband?"

"Yes, where was *her husband*?" said Rose wondering what exactly was going on and how her father let her go to a place like that.

"You know he was there," continued Ruby.

Not accepting her aunt's explanation, she turned to her mother, "Momma, why did you go there?"

"Baby, don't let your aunt worry you," said Violet seeing the concern in her daughter's eyes. "You know your father won't let much go on. And anyway, she is leaving out the part where she took off her coat and had on this white dress, that I still can't figure out how she got it to zip up."

They continued laughing as Ruby danced around the kitchen swaying her hips and singing, "That is why I love you so" by Jackie Wilson, playing on the radio.

"I love that song," said Rose dancing with her Aunt as they both moved from side to side, twisting each other, partner style.

"And when you kiss me with your ruby red lips, it thrills me so, I turn a back over flip." Ruby motioned to her mother, "come on Momma and dance with us."

"No Chile', you can go on and dance around here until the kitchen finished. I'm going to rest my feet in some Epsom salt out on the porch."

"Don't go Momma, I want to show you a new dance Vee did last night, so you can show Poppa when you listen to the radio."

"Stop playing, my stepping days are over," waved Grandma Mae without even looking back.

"Poppa," she yelled out the kitchen window. "Momma said you can't cut a rug no more."

"Girl, don't let her fool you," he replied standing up to move around in a circle as if he was dancing with a partner. "I might have married her for her cooking, but she married me for my smooth moves."

"I didn't know you could dance," said Lil' Adam, his head tilted up, sitting under the shade tree in the backyard.

"Boy, back in the twenties, I was a dancing fool. We had a talent show every year at the end of school. I would practice two, three times a week. I was always dancing. I won first place three years in a row."

"John was an excellent dancer," said Tom. "I went over to the school all the time to watch him practice. All the fellows were jealous because all the girls came to watch too."

"Did you go to the same school Mr. Tom?"

"We wanted too," he answered as his smile changed to sadness.

Poppa John added, "back then was pretty much as it is now. I went to the Colored School and he went to the White School, but that didn't stop Tom from coming around."

"Every chance I got, I would come to John's practices, and any other event going on at his school."

"Because of a certain girl Tom fancied," he added with a wink towards all the other men sitting under the tree.

"Sally Ann Rogers," quickly interjected Tom with a smile on his face, "the girl of my dreams."

"Only problem… she was the colored girl of your dreams."

"I guess it wasn't meant to be, back then," said Tom lowering his head.

"Things still haven't changed. Coloreds and Whites are still frowned on if they are together."

"And interracial marriages are illegal in all the southern states," said Tom. "But the law can't change the heart."

"You right about that," said Poppa John lighting his pipe.

"We tried to keep it a secret as much as we could. I'd give her rides to and from town if she needed, mostly at night."

"Nobody figured it out," asked Adam.

"It's hard to keep stuff like that a secret in a small town like this." Poppa John looked at his son-in-law suspiciously. "What's done in the dark, always comes to the light."

Overwhelmed with guilt, Adam quickly looked away, afraid he knew, afraid his own eyes would betray him. His palms began to sweat. He sat frozen, wanting to leave, but had nowhere to go. Could he know? Could anyone know… his secret?

Tom continued softly telling the story of how he had to give up his beloved Sally Ann Rogers. "My secret came to light, actually it was already in the light, but I did not know."

Remembering one night that changed everything. Tom attempted to excuse himself from the table as normal. His mother didn't mind, she knew he wanted to spend time with friends. But this night, his father got up from the table and followed me to the car.

'Son where you headed?'

'Nowhere special, just out to get some air.'

'Air on the front porch not good enough for you?'

'Reckon it is,' I answered, but I walked over to my car anyway still planning to leave.

Before I could get in the car, Poppa blocked me from opening the door, looked me straight in the eyes and said, 'Son I know you been seeing that colored girl around town.'

I froze, my heart stopped beating. I was shocked, not so much that he knew, but choosing to call her 'that colored girl', and he said it with such hatred and disgust.

Poppa continued, 'son you know I don't have nothing against colored people. Heck, I know your best friend is colored. I like John, he your friend, but people talk when your friend is a colored girl. Can't say I blame you though, she's a mighty-fine looking girl, colored or not. Son, don't think you the first white boy with a hankering after a colored girl? I had me a couple colored girls I fancied when I was your age. My Poppa told me never to take them around where nobody could see us, take them back in the woods or behind the barn. I reckon I should have explained those things to you, since you were driving this colored girl around town in front of everybody, you should know better! But it's too late now, the ladies at your mother's ice cream social, that meet every Tuesday, brought it up right in the middle of their little get together, almost broke her heart.'

'How long she knew?'

'Few weeks now.'

'She never said a word.'

'And she won't. Son, white women don't want to know stuff like that. It embarrasses them. They gentle creatures. This has gone on since colored people came to this country from Africa, or wherever they came from, back when they were slaves. Just do your business quietly son. Don't take her out in the public.'

It scared me that my father approved of a promiscuous relationship if nobody knew. 'It's not like that,' I tried to tell him. 'I love her and plan to marry her!'

He slapped me hard across the face. 'Boy watch your mouth! Your mother would drop dead if she heard you even say such a thing. Go on and pester her every now and then but be careful not to make any colored babies. You don't have to marry her.'

'I want to marry her,' I tried to explain to him. 'Things have changed, it's not like it used to be.'

'Things haven't changed one bit. Your momma said she wants you to stop seeing that colored girl, and that's that.'

'You're lying, momma didn't say that, and I won't stop seeing her.'

He slapped me again. 'Boy, I won't have you talking that way to me. Now I tried to reason with you and allow you to see the colored girl quietly. But if you insist on seeing her anyway, embarrassing your mother, and being the talk of the town, then we don't have any choice.'

'No choice?'

'What kind of example are we setting with a colored girl sitting up in the front seat, all close to you, driving around town for everybody to see? Son I am the sheriff of this town. Therefore, you give us no choice but to send you off to school in Philadelphia and stay with your uncle George. He's already agreed to let you take an internship in his law office before school starts.'

'And if I refuse?'

'We are trying to do what's best for you,' he said calmer. 'I know you enjoy being with the colored girl.'

'Her name is Sally Ann.'

'What kind of reputation will you have with little colored babies running around all over town? You think you can still be a lawyer. What about your mother and the humiliation she will suffer from her friends at the ice cream social club, the sheriff's wife with little bastard children, nigger children.'

'How could you say that?' I screamed and slammed the car door walking back towards the house. I never heard my father use that word. It struck me

like a solid punch to the stomach. 'My best friend is colored! I can have a colored friend, but I can't marry a colored girl!'

'Tom, wait, I'm sorry. I didn't mean to say that.' He tried to reach out to me, but I pulled away. 'John is a good boy, and his father was a good man, who was hanged by an angry hateful mob that didn't care that he was a good man. All they saw was his color. All they saw was hate. And if I wasn't the sheriff, what do you think would happen to you, with your colored... your girlfriend.'

I turned to look at him and saw the anguish in his eyes, tears streaming down my face.

'I'm sorry, I wish things were different son,' he said sorrowfully. 'But as a lawyer, maybe you could do something to help them change.'

I knew he was right. I could not change the problem if I stayed here. My father embraced me as tears fell from both our eyes.

'I promise you I will help make a change.'

'I believe you son.'

I went into the house and kissed my mother who had been standing at the window, listening and watching. She smiled softly. We did not say anything to each other. I headed upstairs to bed.

'Becky, he became a man tonight.'

'I know Frank. I know.'

'Maybe I did the right thing by leaving; maybe not, only time will tell. All I felt at that moment was a broken heart. I never saw Sally Ann Rogers after that night.'

"Who found out Tom?" said Poppa John shaking him on the shoulder to get his attention, "Tom?"

"Yes... Yes," he answered shaking his head as he focused back on the men sitting under the shade tree. "I was remembering how upset Poppa was."

"Told you, 'what's done in the dark always comes to the light'."

Silence encompassed the backyard. Faintly you could hear "I'm thru with love" by Dinah Washington, floating through the air from the kitchen. Poppa John blew a big puff of smoke in the air. Everybody watched it float up towards the shade tree, slowly disappearing into the branches and out of sight. Tom became even sadder as the song continued, "... for I must have you or no one, that's why I'm thru' with love..."

"Mae always says God will work it out somehow, might not be the way we want, but it works out all the same."

"Thanks John," said Tom fighting back tears trying to smile. "You always knew how to make me feel better."

"Story didn't end all bad. You went away and became a big-time lawyer, like you said."

"That doesn't make up for Sally Ann Rogers."

"But maybe you can help make a difference," added Beau who had been silent up until now.

"That's just what my father said," a smile beginning to emerge on his face.

"And you have," continued Poppa John. "Didn't you tell me you helped with the colored children wanting to go to the white school?"

"I did!" he answered proudly lifting his head.

"Is that the *Brown vs. Board of Education* lawsuit, you mentioned earlier that went all the way to the Supreme Court?"

"You heard of it son?"

"Yes sir, from my last semester at Howard," said Beau enthusiastically. It was a great legal battle that will change schools throughout America, eventually."

"Humh, when is that happening?" said Poppa John.

"Schools haven't changed where we live," added Lil' Adam shaking his head.

"Why is that Tom?"

"The lawyers for Brown won the case," he answered. "Now the individual states, mostly southern states, need to enforce the law. And rumor has it, that Thurgood Marshall, the lead attorney for the case, is a nominee for the Supreme Court."

"Colored man on the highest court in the land," laughed Poppa John. "Hope I live to see that."

"You might," continued Tom. "Mr. Marshall is a powerful and eloquent speaker, better than any I've heard, colored or white. One aspect of his case presented expert testimonies of the detrimental affect colored children suffer because of segregation that couldn't be disputed by the defendants."

"Tom, say that so regular folk understand."

"Separate schools make colored children feel inferior."

"I could have told you that, reckon I should be a lawyer too."

Everyone laughed, lightening up the conversation, lifting a solemn cloud that had settled. While they heard "Yakety Yak" by the

Coasters from the kitchen as Ruby yelled, "if you don't scrub that kitchen floor, you ain't gon' rock and roll no more."

"That's my girl," said Fred without thinking.

"Mine too," said Poppa John looking over at him seriously.

"Ahh, yes sir," he added apologetically.

"Y'all better get on in here. These chaps got school in the morning," called Grandma Mae from the kitchen window.

"I didn't realize it was so late," said Adam rubbing his knees as he walked around to reduce the stiffness.

"Your knees still bother you son?"

"From time to time," he replied.

"I got some ointment Mae made up. I rub it on my knees and back when they get to aching. I'll get you some."

"Thank you," hopeful all was well between them.

"No telling what she put in it, but it works. I warn you, it smells something awful."

"Smell won't bother me, especially if it works."

"You want a ride Beau?" said Tom dusting off his hat.

"It won't be out your way sir?"

"No, pass right by Jack's on my way. You can tell me your summation of the Brown case, sure to put Annie to sleep before we get home. Her mother will be awful mad at me anyway for keeping her out so late on a school night, so at least I can say she took a nap in the car."

"Thank you sir."

"Go ahead, I'll meet you out front."

"What's the matter Tom?" asked Poppa John.

"Well, I wanted to ask you something," he said tracing the rim of his hat with his fingers. "Never mind!"

"Tom! You my oldest and best friend, just because you moved away you think I don't know you after all these years… You want to ask how Sally Ann Rogers is doing after all this time."

"You know me well my friend," he smiled, almost blushing, without looking up as he continued to rub the rim of his hat. "I was wondering what happened to her since I left. Didn't want you to think my asking would be inappropriate."

"Tom you know Sally Ann's my first cousin. We all grew up together. I knew how you felt and how she felt from the beginning, nothing is wrong with that."

"It's only after all these years my feelings for her have never changed."

"Tom, time doesn't change feelings."

"Pa made me leave without saying anything to her. I did not say good-bye. I know she has probably hated me all these years." Tears began to fill his eyes.

"It's not your fault how things happened back then. She understood the rules that coloreds and whites could never be together, especially since your Pa was the sheriff."

"Did she ever ask about me?" said Tom with a glimmer of hope in his voice.

"Ask 'bout you!" he answered with a slight grin on his face, holding his friend in suspense. "That's all she ever did was, ask 'bout you. After a while I got tired of her asking."

"What did she say John?" He was almost jumping with renewed excitement. "After all these years, what did she say?" Anxiously he waited for his friend to continue, thinking. Did she ask because she cared or because she never wanted to see him again? A feeling of dread suddenly came over him. On the other hand, did she ask because she wanted to avoid him if he ever returned home? His mind raced through all the possibilities.

"Know you trying to catch up an all," yelled Grandma Mae from the back porch. "But these chaps got school tomorrow."

"Mae, we'll be in directly," answered Poppa John waving his hand towards the kitchen, slightly raising his voice.

"John, please, what did she say?"

"I'll tell you this," he answered focusing back on his friend who was literally shaking him for an answer. "She never stopped loving you either."

"How you know?" he gasped, barely breathing, barely believing something so wonderful could be possible.

"Did she marry?" was all he managed to say through tears now rolling freely down his face.

"Nope, never did," answered Poppa John enjoying the renewed hope in his eyes, reminding him of when they were boys. "But I knew she wouldn't, although everybody told her to forget you. She even had some decent suitors, but deep in her heart, I guess she always hoped…"

"Hoped what John?" said Tom holding on to every word.

"Crazy as it sounds," he paused. "She always hoped the two of you would be together one day."

Tom sat down on a large tree stump, deep in thought, no words to express his feelings. His tears continued, not of sadness or dread, but of happiness and hope. "I feel as if a door in my life that was closed has been reopened. I can breathe again, dream again, and hope again."

"A couple years back when your Elle passed, she wanted so much to be with you and help you thru your hurt."

"John do you think she'll see me?"

"These chaps got to get home," called Grandma Mae louder and more forceful, "takes almost an hour to get to town."

"Here we come Mae," answered Poppa John walking towards the kitchen. "Come on Tom, before Mae has a fit. I will talk to Sally Ann. She usually stops by once or twice a week. You sure you want to see her?"

"With all my heart John, I do," he said wiping the tears from his eyes. "I know I got married when I graduated Law School. Even though it was more of an arranged marriage to please my mother, I grew to love Elle. I thank God for our daughter and my granddaughter. But after she passed away, and I hate to admit even before she passed, not a day went by that I didn't think of Sally Ann Rogers."

"Tom things still haven't changed since you left."

"I don't care John. Things might never change. All I know is, if there is even a small chance that she would see me, the whole town can know. I don't care anymore. The whole world can know."

"Are you leaving Tuesday?"

"Ohh," said Tom letting out a long sigh his shoulders dropped in frustration. "I can't postpone the case I'm working on, it has already been held over for a week to bring Annie home, and get her settled into school. Is there any way she might see me tomorrow night?"

"Tom, her seeing you tomorrow then leaving the next day, might rip her apart, that's not fair to her."

"You right John. I can't do that to her or to myself." Tom walked away, his shoulders slumped, his heart aching. He longed to speak to his beloved Sally Ann Rogers, but it would be too painful to leave her again. After all these years was what his father said coming true, they would never be together. As he headed up the porch steps, he took a deep breath. Outwardly, he could force a smile on his face, but inside his heart lamented over a love long lost.

"Wait!" said Poppa John walking quickly to catch up with his best friend. "When are you coming back home?"

"Christmas," said Tom wondering hopefully what was on his friend's mind. "Ever since Annie was born we spend Christmas together."

"I do the same with my grand's."

"You think by then…." Tom paused.

"I think," said Poppa John placing his hand on his friends' shoulder. "By then, I can talk with Sally Ann. That way she can figure out what she wants to do, nearly killed her the last time you left, wouldn't want to break her heart again."

"I want to see her, but you right, I'll wait. The last thing I want is to hurt her again. This time she can make the choice. Whatever it is, I'll respect her decision, but that's such a long time away."

"Don't worry ole' friend, Christmas will be here before you know."

"Thanks John," his heart lifting with anticipation. "I haven't been this excited about Christmas coming since we were kids."

"It's about time you two came in here, been out there like two ole' biddies for hours."

"Now Mae," answered Poppa John reaching his arm around her waist and kissing her on the cheek. "We had some catching up to do. That's all."

"Thank you so much Mae for having us over for dinner. I am going to miss cooking like this when I go back to Philadelphia."

"Well then, I guess you should move back home," she smiled handing him a plate wrapped and ready to go.

"Maybe I will," he smiled looking over at his friend. "Maybe I will."

14 MY TURN TO DRIVE

"Hurry up back there, you hear me," she said hurriedly putting an apple and a bologna sandwich into each small paper bag. "I let you sleep a bit later since I'm taking you to school."

"Yes ma'am," she heard echoing from the bedrooms.

This morning was special, not only was it the first day of the boycott, but Violet had to drive the children to school, then pick up Carrie Mae and Irene, her friends who normally rode the bus. She felt nervous looking outside at the sparkling car in the driveway washed daily by either her husband or son. Surely, they would notice the slightest scratch.

"Fred's pulling up in the driveway."

"Here I come," answered Adam, taking his lunch and kissing her softly on the lips. "Take your time driving. And don't worry; you were always a good driver."

"Thank you. I will see you tonight." She smiled as she watched him walk towards the car, waving before he got in. Her heart swooned with love as she thought of how he always knew how to comfort her.

"Momma can I drive?" said Lil' Adam, grabbing a lunch.

"He just wants to show off in front of his friends," said Lillie Mae with her hands on her hips.

"Chile' you something else," laughed Violet at the sight of her youngest daughter. "How do you know what goes on with your brother? He's in high school."

"Momma you know I don't pay any attention to that girl," he said, more focused on looking out the window. "Here comes Juan and his sister. Can we give them a ride?"

"Rose would like that because she LOVES JUAN," taunted Lillie Mae.

Grabbing her lunch and rolling her eyes in complete disgust, Rose walked past her sister towards the back porch. "Momma, I'll wait for you outside."

"Here they come now," said Lil' Adam. "Can they ride with us?"

"Okay, it will give me a chance to talk to… what's her name?" She turned to her daughter who had a look of panic on her face. "…about the smoking thing at school."

"Momma *please* don't say anything. We just got to be friends."

"Good then, maybe you'll learn how it feels if someone brings up *your* business."

"Ha, ha, ha," laughed Lil' Adam as he headed out the door to greet his friends. "Juan, come on, we got a ride this morning."

"I got front," said Lillie Mae running to the car forgetting what her mother said.

"Ain't no more room in the front."

"Rose would you like to sit in the back with us," asked Juan holding the car door open.

"No thank you, I'll sit in the front," said Rose politely trying not to blush, but inside she screamed, 'He is SOOO Cute'.

"Why do I have to get in the back… MOMMA."

"Chile' don't start it's too early in the morning, get in the front and shut your mouth or walk."

"Yes ma'am," she said respectfully to her mother as she stuck her tongue out at her brother.

"You must be Juan," said Violet reaching her hand out to him.

"Yes ma'am," he answered quickly grabbing her hand, "pleased to finally meet you, thank you for giving us a ride.

"Pleased to meet you too, and your sister?" No wonder Rose likes him, she thought. He is a very attractive young man, tall, green eyes, wavy hair, northern accent, well dressed, manners, outwardly he appears to be very nice, but his sister was already on the wrong foot.

"My name is Juanita ma'am, pleased to meet you," she said with a smile.

Initially the road to school was very quiet. Lillie Mae appeared to have stopped breathing, afraid any minute her mother would bring up the 'smoking thing'. Rose, sitting next to Juan, did not want to confirm her inner turmoil and tried her best not to look his way. So as always, the neutral sibling broke the silence.

"Let's listen to some sounds," said Lil' Adam proudly driving down the highway to school. Soon, "I love you so" by the Chantels, played on the radio, everyone moved their heads gently side to side to the music, accept Rose whose heart was beating so fast, she thought someone would notice. From the side of her eye, she could see Juan looking at her, then he spoke.

"Rose, do you like this song?"

She could not believe he asked her that, panicking she stuttered, "ahh, ahh." Scratching her head, hoping to avoid eye contact, she attempted again to answer. "Ahh, yes I do."

She could feel the heat forming on her face. Bravely she looked at him; he had a sly smile on his face. Then, he did the most *unspeakable* thing.... He winked. She thought she was going to die. "Just stop the car and let me out," she screamed inside, wondering how she was going to make it all the way to school.

"Mom, I could drop you off at Mr. Gist's then pick you up after school," said Lil' Adam, turning to her with his most charming smile.

"Boy don't try your father's smile on me," she laughed. "I think this car got you dreaming like the Bartender at The Honey Shack."

"You went to The Honey Shack?" He turned to look at her, his eyes squinted in disbelief.

"That place is the most, only the coolest cats hang out there," said Juan from the backseat.

"I heard that too, but not my Momma!"

"Are you saying I'm not a cool cat?" smiled Violet enjoying putting her son on the spot.

"Oh, you definitely a cool cat," he answered diplomatically. "Just that I never heard you say you went."

"I never went before, your Aunt Ruby asked us to go last weekend."

"Did you have fun?" said Lillie Mae happy the subject was far from smoking.

"Of course," she smiled briefly recalling her visit. "Everywhere with your Aunt Ruby is fun. She supposed to stop by this weekend Rose, so you can show her the Jitterbug."

"Why they call it the Jitterbug," asked Lillie Mae.

"Way back when we were growing up, if you drank something really strong that made you shake, we'd say 'you got the jitters'," answered Violet wiggling her shoulders as if she was cold. "Then in the thirties Cab Calloway, a big band leader, put out a song, *The Call of the Jitterbugs*, and folk would jump and shake to the music, just having fun, and he said 'y'all look like jitterbugs'. I guess after that, everybody started saying it too. Really there's no such thing as a jitterbug."

"Up in Chicago we call it the West Coast Swing," added Juan confidently. "It's a little different than the Jitterbug, but not much."

"Come over Friday around six o'clock and show us?" said Violet surprising herself. Normally she was not assertive, but ever since The Honey Shack, she felt more vibrant and ready to try new things.

"Yes ma'am," he answered enthusiastically looking directly at Rose when he spoke. "I'd love to come over."

Rose let out a deep sigh rolling her eyes, "Mom-maa."

"Don't worry honey, you won't be alone, the whole family will be there."

She gasped, her mouth open in astonishment, "and that makes it better."

Arriving at school, Lil' Adam made one last attempt before getting out the car, "Are you sure you don't want me to drop you off? In case you don't feel comfortable driving."

She shook her head smiling as he kissed her on the cheek, "Go on now." Scooting over behind the steering wheel, she watched them as they climbed out the car. "I can't pick you up after school, but some chicken is in the icebox for dinner. I'll be home as soon as I drop everyone off."

"Can Margie and Naomi come over too on Friday?"

"That's fine baby, I got to go," said Violet waving quickly. "Lillie Mae, you best behave yourself, I didn't forget what happened."

"Yes ma'am," she said sadly walking away with Juanita who had a confused look on her face. "The smoking thing…"

"Oh," she knew immediately what she was referring too. "Did you get a whippin'?"

"No, but it was close, did you?"

"No, but my dad yelled so much I got a headache?"

"My dad said how bad smoking was for you, stinky breath, stinky clothes, and yellow teeth. Can't figure out why anyone does it?"

"Me either."

"It's not worth a whipping. I'm not doing it anymore."

"Me either."

That settled the two girls ran across the field to school with only a few minutes before the bell rang, happy their smoking days were over.

"Rose," said Juan catching up to her and gently putting his hand on her shoulder. "You don't mind me coming over, do you?"

"Ahh, no, why you say that."

"You seemed a bit frosted when your mother asked me."

Trying not to look him directly in the eye, she ignored his question. "There goes Margie and Naomi. I'll see you in class."

"Okay, I'll…" he started to speak but she ran away before he could finish.

"Juan, what's the matter?" said Lil' Adam walking up to him with other classmates.

"I don't think your sister wants me to come over?"

"I told you, she's just shy, but I have to warn you, my Aunt Ruby…she is not shy."

"Oh," said Juan puzzled.

"Don't sweat it. Let's get to class before the bell rings."

"Okay."

He watched as Rose and her two friends walked up the steps to class, constantly turning to look back at him, none of them appeared to be shy. He felt confused, but he really liked her, and if he could get her family to like him Friday night, it might be just what he needed to break the ice. "Wait up!"

"Rose, did he ride with you this morning," giggled Margie. "Did you hold hands in the backseat?"

"Nooo, stop, he'll hear you," she whispered nearly panicking. "Can you both come over Friday night? My Mom and Aunt are doing some kinda' get together?"

"Will Juan be there?" asked Naomi.

"Yes, he will," she looked around to see how far away he was from them. "Please, please, I need you both to come, if you don't, there's no telling what my Aunt will do or say if she thinks we're a couple."

"A couple," said Margie, her eyebrows raised as she elbowed Naomi. "Whew! You move fast girl."

"She in Love."

"I am not, can you come?"

"Sure, we'll come," said Margie puckering up her lips and twisting her hips. "But first chance I get, I want a slow, slow dance with that Chicago fire."

They all laughed as the bell rang and they headed into school. Rose felt much better knowing her two best friends would be there. She wanted to see Juan, but not surrounded by family members asking a million embarrassing questions. Just the thought of it made her dizzy. "The more friends I can get to come, the merrier, or should I say, the safer."

* * *

Violet felt nervous, driving made her uncomfortable, so much to think about and watch out for. Riding the bus gave her time to reflect on her responsibilities for the day. Now she had to add, taking her children to school, picking up riders, and taking them home in the dark. What if she scraped up against another car, or ran through a puddle of mud? Ironically, parking in front of the Gist home, she scraped the tires on the curb.

"Oh my goodness," panicking she jumped out the car. Standing there inspecting the tires for damage, she heard someone call her name.

"Violet is that you?" she looked up to see Mr. Gist running towards her. "Is everything okay? Are you hurt?"

"No, Mr. Gist, everything is fine," she answered wondering where he came from so quickly. "I hit the curb when I parked. I haven't drove in so long, seems like I'm a bit rusty."

"This is your car?" he responded jovially putting his hand on her shoulder. "I'm so relieved. I saw you bending down by the tires and I thought someone ran into you. Thank God. I thought you were hurt."

"Oh no sir, everything is fine."

"This is very nice," he answered preoccupied, walking around to examine further.

"Thank you sir, Adam surprised me with it last weekend."

"Don't mean to meddle, but wouldn't it be better for him to drive, since the railroad is nearly thirty miles from your house. Hate to see the car sitting here all day."

"He insisted on me driving so I could pick up my friends who work in town. Normally we catch the bus but since the boycott and all..."

"The boycott?"

"Yes sir. Colored folks are not riding the bus until we can sit where we want, didn't you hear?"

"No, but I do agree if you pay to ride the bus, you should be able to sit where you want. Pull into the driveway, there is plenty of room, I won't have you parking on the street like a stranger, you are part of the family."

"I appreciate that, but it seems fine here. I know I'm close enough to the curb."

"I insist," he said opening the car door for her. "Besides, we don't want any mishaps to this beautiful car while it's parked on the street. It'll be safer in the driveway."

"Well if you insist," said Violet hesitantly. "Probably would be safer in the driveway?"

"I'm sure," he smiled.

"Well hop on in I'll give you a ride up to the house," she said happy to drive him for a change.

"That sounds nice."

As Violet pulled into the driveway, she saw Carl Jr. standing in the doorway still in his pajamas, with a wide grin on his face. She could barely get out of the car before he was embracing her.

"Ms. Vee, Ms. Vee," he said excitedly. "Is this your car?"

"Do you like it?"

"Oh yes! Can we go for a ride?"

"Don't you have to get ready for school first young man?" asked Mr. Gist checking his watch for his son and himself.

"Then can we go for a ride Ms. Vee?"

"Let's get dressed for school first like your poppa said. After that, I'll rustle up some breakfast, and maybe a ride."

"Promise?" he said with warm hopeful eyes.

"Yes, I promise," she answered ruffling his hair as they headed into the kitchen.

"Yippee! Yippee!" He jumped up and down.

"Carl, run on upstairs and get ready. I want to talk to Ms. Vee before I leave."

His expression changed instantly from happiness to fear. "Yes sir," he answered slowly walking up the stairs.

"What's the matter?" said Violet wondering if something happened over the weekend. "Is something wrong with Lizabeth?"

"No, she is fine. I just need to talk to you."

"Yes sir," she answered as a feeling of dread came over her as well.

He sat at the kitchen table his hand on his forehead. "It's Daisy."

"Yes," she sat down next to him. "What is it?"

"She hasn't got any better since Frank died," he began as tears began to form. "Somehow she holds things together while you are here through the week. On the weekends, she becomes very despondent, sitting by the upstairs window staring at the driveway as if she is expecting someone. Now she is sitting so long, she's soiling her clothes."

"Oh Lord." Violet took his hands. "I'm so sorry Mr. Gist."

"The doctor's want to have her committed."

"Oh no!"

"The children need her with them, but not like this. I don't know what to do." No longer able to hold back the tears, he began to weep uncontrollably.

Violet pulled him close to her with his head lying on her shoulder. "There, there Mr. Gist, don't worry" she said patting him softly on the back. "The Lord will help us figure out something."

Carl Jr. ran into the kitchen crying, "Please don't leave Ms. Vee! Please don't leave!"

"Nobody's leaving around here, come here baby," she said calmly pulling him towards her.

His eyes swollen, tears rolling down his red cheeks, "Poppa said he wanted to talk to you."

"Carl Jr.," she answered focusing totally on him. "I'll always be here for you no matter what. Your poppa is concerned that your mother needs help to feel better."

"Yes son," added Mr. Gist kneeling in front of his son so they were face to face. "Ms. Vee will always be with us. But your mother can't take care of you and your sister like she wants too."

"Ms. Vee can't you come stay with us?"

"I wish I could sweetheart, but I got to take care of my family too."

"They can stay here. We got plenty of room," he added feeling better since that would solve all their problems.

"Carl, I know that sounds like a good idea, but we can't impose on Ms. Vee. She has her own family."

"What if I get somebody to stay on the weekends?"

"Somebody like you?" he said with an attempt to smile.

"Maybe not just like me, but somebody that can take good care of you and your sister. How is that?"

"That might be a good solution," said Mr. Gist hopefully. "Do you know anybody?"

"I might," she pondered. "A friend of Rose finished school last year and has not found a job. If you'd like, I could ask her."

"Did she ever do this kind of work before?"

"She has four younger brothers she helps to take care of, and she has a good head on her shoulder. Besides the money would help them out, her poppa lost his hand in a crazy accident down at the mill. Probably wouldn't have died, but the colored hospital is so far away, he didn't make it in time."

"Why he couldn't go to the hospital right in town?" said Carl Jr. glad to offer a suggestion. "It's not far."

"Oh baby, don't concern yourself with that. You already late for school, come on and eat your breakfast."

"Look at the time!" said Mr. Gist examining his watch. "I think he already missed his bus. Can you drop him off? I promised to get to the office early. I have a meeting this morning."

Before Violet could answer, he kissed Carl Jr. on the cheek and headed out the door.

"You didn't eat breakfast," she called to him.

"Don't have time."

She ran to the door, "Here's your briefcase?"

"Thank you, I need that."

"Yippee! Now I get to ride in your new car."

Violet smiled as she hurried to fix breakfast. "Carl Jr. I need your help to run upstairs and get your sister."

"She's sleep," he answered indifferently not wanting to get up from the table.

"With all this commotion going on, she's not likely sleep." Turning the sausages in the pan and grabbing a bowl to mix the pancakes, she wiped her brow as beads of sweat began to form. "Wish I had enough hands to check on her myself and cook breakfast."

"I'll go check on her," he said seeing her frustration.

"Come here baby." Violet stopped cooking, wiped her hands on her apron, and knelt in front of him. "I am so proud of you for being my little helper."

"I love you Ms. Vee," he said hugging her tightly around the neck.

"I love you too. Now run on up there and get Lizabeth."

"Yes ma'am," he answered happily disappearing up the stairs, glad to help.

"Poor Chile'," she whispered. "His poppa too busy and his momma don't even know what's going on. Wish I could take them both home."

A few moments later Carl Jr. came downstairs holding his little sister. "Here she is Ms. Vee. She wasn't sleep, just like you said, but Momma still sleep."

She took her and immediately began kissing her on the cheeks. "Good morning baby doll." Elizabeth giggled with delight. "While you eat your pancakes and sausage, I'll wash her off and change her, so we can take you to school."

"Yummy! My favorite, pancakes and sausage," he said rubbing his stomach as she sat his plate in front of him. "Ms. Vee, will the new person cook like you?"

"We'll see," she said ruffling his hair. "Get finished. I don't want you to miss school."

"Yes ma'am," he answered digging into his plate as if he had not eaten for days.

Carrying the baby, Violet stopped in the room to check on Ms. Daisy. "Good morning ma'am?"

A gentle breeze flowed through the open window, circulating a smell of urine throughout the room. Ms. Daisy, still in her nightgown, lay in a fetal position clinging to a pillow. The bed covers, partially on the floor, appeared soiled.

"Good morning," she continued gently stroking her forehead, "you all right sweetheart."

"Umm-hum," she mumbled, squinting up at her. "Vee is that you?"

"Yes ma'am, I came to check on you before I take Carl Jr. to school."

"Umm-hum," she stirred briefly before appearing to drift back to sleep.

"Lizabeth say morning."

"Mor-ning," she managed to say pointing to her mother.

"Ms. Daisy, when we get back I'll get your breakfast and get things cleaned up."

"Um-hum," she mumbled rolling over.

"My sweet Lizabeth, let's get you washed up and a clean diaper. Your brother about to miss the whole day of school, by the time we get there it will be lunchtime. I'm sure he'll be fine with that."

Immediately, she washed her in the bathroom sink, wrapped her in a towel, and laid her in her crib as she kicked and laughed while Violet sang her a song:

My lil' sweetie lying in the bed
Just can't wait to be fed
Here's a lil' powder for your tummy
Tickle, tickle, tickle, you so funny

After brushing her hair, she put her on a yellow dress with white flowers. "My, my, you look so pretty. You're such a happy baby," said Violet as they headed downstairs.

"Ms. Vee, I'm already to go, and I drank all my juice."

"I see you did, without me telling you."

"Umm-hum," he answered the same as his mother.

"Remember I told you to say, 'yes ma'am' or 'yes Ms. Vee'."

"Yes Ms. Vee," he smiled.

"Here you go Lizabeth, eat this." Violet handed her a flapjack wrapped around a sausage. "Carl Jr. run upstairs and get your sister a bib, we don't want her to mess up her dress, now do we?"

Filling a bottle with milk, she headed out the backdoor holding Elizabeth, who merrily ate her rolled up breakfast, followed by Carl Jr. carrying a bib in his hands. "Good thing we got the car."

"Can I sit in the front?"

"Why is it everybody likes to sit in the front?"

"I like to see where I'm going."

"I guess that is as good an answer as any. Squeeze in here real close, I'll drive with one hand on the wheel and one hand on Lizabeth."

"You can do that Ms. Vee?"

"Chile' I've been driving before you were born."

"Can you teach me how to drive Ms. Vee?"

"Let's get you to school first. We can figure out the rest some other time. Now look back and see if the road is clear."

"It's clear Ms. Vee," he looked back up and down the street. "I love your new car."

"I'm glad you do. I love it too."

On the way, Violet saw colored people walking along the road. She wished she had time to give them a ride. The busses she saw were almost empty, with maybe one or two riders in the front. She knew they were not colored riders. "Maybe the boycott will work," she thought to herself.

"Run on in," she said reaching over to open the passenger's car door. "Don't seem like you late, other children running in too."

"There's Bobby. He is in my class."

Carl Jr. jumped out the car and ran to catch up with his friend.

"Bye Ms. Vee," he turned to say before entering the building.

"Bye baby," she waved back as the door closed behind him and she turned her focus to Elizabeth, who had remnants of flapjack and sausage grease smeared on her face. "Let's get you home."

"Mom-ma," she smiled pointing out the window.

* * *

Pulling in the driveway Violet saw two cars, one was Mr. Gist's and the other looked very expensive. "Looks like we have company." She picked up the smiling baby and quickly wiped her face with her apron.

"Violet, please have a seat," sighed Mr. Gist, looking up from the table with puffy eyes and disheveled hair. "Dr. Reynolds from the Psychiatric Institute is upstairs."

"Sir, is there a problem?"

"No, everything is …," he paused and put his head down. "No, I need to be honest at least to myself, I can't lie anymore. I have to talk to someone… Remember this morning I had to rush to work…"

She nodded. "You had a meeting."

"Yes, I was meeting with Dr. Reynolds. And after I explained what was going on with Daisy, he wanted to come immediately to evaluate her."

"Yes sir," answered Violet picking up a baby doll for Elizabeth.

"Unfortunately, the doctor has decided to admit her right away. His initial diagnosis is severe depression."

"Oh Lord, does Ms. Daisy know they are taking her away?"

"No, we both tried to explain it to her, but she just sits and stares out the window like she did the entire weekend."

"I know it sounds mighty bad Mr. Gist," she said placing her hand on top of his. "But she needs help."

"Don't know how I'm going to explain it to Carl Jr. and my poor baby." He picked up Elizabeth and gently kissed her on the cheek as tears began to fall. "She doesn't have any idea what is happening with her mother."

"That's because she is such a happy baby, hardly ever cries, just as sweet as she can be. Carl Jr., he the same way, both wonderful chaps. I pray Ms. Daisy gets better so she can see all she has."

"Dr. Reynolds thinks with medicine and therapy, shouldn't be more than a few weeks before she can come back home. I just have to make arrangements for the children, probably take them up to Boston with my mother."

"They don't need arrangements. You said it would only be a few weeks. They can stay with us until Ms. Daisy comes home. We have plenty room."

"Oh no Violet, I can't inconvenience you and your family like that."

"Them babies is my family, I love them like my own, been with them since they were born. Besides, if they went to Boston, Carl Jr. would change schools in the middle of the year and make new friends. My son has an extra bed in his room, and we can put Lizabeth's crib in the room with my girls."

"Seems like an awful lot to ask Violet."

"That's what we do when we family."

"What will Adam say?"

"He loves children," said Violet waving her hand, "been pestering me to have more, this will be right down his alley."

"Only for a few weeks. Any longer than that, I'll see if my mother can stay here until school is out for the year."

"And I'll have Rose's friend come spend some time with the children. If they get along, she might be able to help with them when Ms. Daisy comes home on the weekends when I'm not here."

"I'd like to meet her," he said feeling better after Violet helped sort out matters.

"Well this Friday we planned to have a small dance party, it'll be a good time to meet her."

"A party Vee, we *are* being an inconvenience. And I don't know if the children are up to that now."

"I understand," she continued once again pressing her hand on his. "But maybe it'll be good for the two of them to have some fun. Lord knows they been through enough heartache and pain."

"Excuse me Mr. Gist," said a tall man wearing a white Physician's jacket. "Sorry to interrupt you."

"No, no, how can I help you," he answered moving his hand away from Violet and standing up with Elizabeth.

"Dr. Reynolds has finished examining your wife, and he wanted me to advise you that a car will be arriving shortly to take her to *the Institute*."

"Thank you," he answered. "I'll take Elizabeth upstairs to see Daisy. I should have let Carl Jr. stay home from school, so he could say good-bye to his mother."

The bedroom, eerily quiet, was dark despite the morning sun trickling through the slightly opened curtain. The air stale from the odor of urine that left a tickle in the back of the throat. Ms. Daisy sat motionless in the exact spot from earlier. Her hair uncombed and tangled like a bird's nest, her lips cracked and dry, her skin pale and withered, her eyes vacant, unaware of their presence.

As they stood there, the baby reached out smiling, "mom-ma". Her mother did not respond. Violet felt her heart breaking with sorrow.

"Daisy, Carl and Elizabeth are here to say good-bye," said Dr. Reynolds talking very slowly. "Do you understand?"

She did not respond even when he gently tapped her on the shoulder. The doctor nodded, and the assistant gently stood her up, firmly secured her in a white jacket that wrapped crisscross in front of her and tied around her waist. With the task completed, he sat her in the chair by the cluttered desk.

"Honey, we are here, and we love you," said Mr. Gist stooping directly in front of her with Elizabeth, hoping she would focus on them. "Soon as I can, I'm going to bring Carl Jr. to see you."

"The car is here sir."

"Daisy, you are going away, but don't worry," he tried to sound strong. Finally, unable to fight back tears, he began weeping loudly, which caused Elizabeth to cry as well.

"I'll take her," said Violet rubbing her on the back and rocking her.

The doctor placed his hand on Mr. Gist's shoulder. "Once you arrive at *The Institute*, stop in the office to complete some paperwork."

"Yes, yes I will." He stood, mentally not connecting the words, turning towards the window, allowing his tears to fall quietly.

Kneeling on the floor in front of her, Violet spoke loudly as one would speak to a partially deaf person. "Ms. Daisy, don't worry about the children, we'll take care of them. You just get better and come back to us soon. Lizabeth, kiss your mother on the cheek."

Violet tilted her over as she kissed her mother. "Mom-ma", she said reaching for her again. Briefly, Daisy's eyes moved quickly from left to right as if trying to focus on her daughter.

"Daisy, Daisy, can you hear me?" shouted Mr. Gist shaking her as she sat in the tightly wrapped jacket, but her eyes became empty once again as she gazed beyond him.

"Sorry Carl," said Dr. Reynolds motioning the orderlies to take her to the car. "Don't forget to stop in the office."

As they led his wife quietly out the bedroom, Mr. Gist sat on the bed crying. From Violet's arm's, Elizabeth looked from one adult to the other, not understanding why everyone was crying.

"Da-Da," she said reaching out to her father.

"Elizabeth, my sweet little baby," he cried holding her close to his chest, rocking back and forth on the bed, gently rubbing her head.

Violet sat down next to him, patting his back, began to sing:

Pass me not oh gentle Savior, hear my humble cry.
While on others thou art calling, do not pass me by.
Oh Savior, Savior hear my humble cry.
While on others thou art calling, do not pass me by.

15 FIVE IS ENOUGH

The days went by pleasantly. The William's family easily settled into a routine that included two additional children. After dropping off the children at school, Violet found it enjoyable to clean her own home and prepare dinner for her own family. She found herself singing throughout the day while Elizabeth played in the corner. Maybe Adam was right, one more child, or two would fit perfectly into their family dynamics.

In the afternoons, she sat patiently in a long line of mostly colored drivers, waiting for Carl Jr. who soon ran out of the building laughing and talking to friends before getting in the car. "Ms. Vee, can I get a ride everyday instead of riding that ole' hot bus?"

"We'll see," she said affectionately.

"My friend Bobby didn't believe me when I said this was your car. He said, 'colored people can't have cars like this unless they are driving white people', what does that mean Ms. Vee?"

"It means your friend Bobby doesn't know what he is talking about. Remember we said that sometimes people say mean things. We can't stop them, but long as your heart," she reached over and put her hand on his chest, "is full of love and not hate, the good Lord will bless you."

"Yes Ms. Vee," he answered looking up at her wanting to make sense of why others treated her differently, not really understanding the Lord she always spoke of.

"Now how was your day?"

"It was fantastic," he began enthusiastically. "I got to be first in the recess line. We went outside to the playground and guess what Ms. Vee?"

"Yes baby," she smiled glancing over at him attentively.

"I got to pick my team for the kickball game – I had sooo much fun – then in class I got all my arithmetic right – at the end of the day I got to erase the blackboard," he paused to catch his breath, "all by myself."

"Sounds like you had a busy day. Did you eat your vegetables at lunch time?"

"Yes Ms. Vee, they had carrots and green beans. They were not as good as the ones you fix, but I ate them anyway."

"That's good."

"Can we have fried chicken for dinner tonight?"

"Carl Jr., we had fried chicken yesterday and the day before. Can we try meatloaf?"

"Okay then," he smiled shrugging his shoulders. "Hi Elizabeth, do you want some meatloaf for dinner or fried chicken?"

She looked up and smiled but stayed focused on the two small baby dolls Lillie Mae gave her to play with.

"Ms. Vee, can we stay with you and Mr. Adam forever?"

"No sweetheart," she smiled at him concerned that he asked that question, but glad he felt at home with them. "You have your own family and it's a good family too. Your mother and father love you very much. Soon you will all be back together."

"Poppa works all the time and Momma hasn't been the same since Frank died. She doesn't love me and Elizabeth anymore."

"That's not true sweetheart," Violet looked over to see the tears forming in his eyes and knew she had to pull over to respond properly. Seeing an area near a clearing of pine trees, she drove onto the grass. The sun beamed down intensely, causing droplets of sweat to form on her forehead from the short walk to the passenger's side. Opening the door, she reached in to hug them both at the same time.

"I know for a fact that your mother loves you very, very much."

"Not since Frank died."

"Please don't cry," she said wiping his face with her apron. "Or I'll cry."

"If she loves us, then why did she go the hospital?"

"What did your Poppa tell you?" said Violet cautiously not wanting to confuse him more.

"He said she wasn't feeling well and needed to go away. Was it my fault Ms. Vee? I tried to make her feel better."

"You did a great job taking care of your mother." Violet pulled him close to her. "You are so strong."

"But she still had to go away?"

"Not because of you sweetheart, she was still sad about Frank."

"Aren't we enough Ms. Vee," his voice cracking.

"Oh yes, the two of you are more than enough. Your mother loves you and your sister with all her heart, and as soon as she gets better, she will come home, and everything will be like before. You watch and see."

"Poppa said Frank was up in heaven watching over us, same as Grandpa."

"Yes he is," she said hugging him. "Now let's hurry home to get the fried chicken started."

"You said we are having meatloaf."

"I know, but one more day of fried chicken won't hurt us," she touched her finger in the dimple of his chin. "But just for you."

"Yippee," he said with a big smile. "And biscuits too."

"Biscuits too."

"I can eat that every day Ms. Vee."

"I see you can," laughed Violet as she got back in the car.

"Thank you Ms. Vee."

"Why are you thanking me?"

"I don't know, just thank you."

"You're welcome."

As she turned down the road home, she saw her children walking with some friends. Lil' Adam was throwing a football back and forth to another boy on the other side of the road. Lillie Mae was playing tag with the same little girl that rode with them in the mornings. Rose appeared to be slowly walking, holding hands with Juan. When she blew the horn, everyone froze, and Rose immediately let go of his hand, staring at her mother as if she saw a ghost.

"Y'all want a ride," said Violet sticking her head out the window.

"Hey momma," said Lil' Adam running across the road to give his mother a kiss on the cheek, unconcerned that the dropped football rolled into the woods.

"I got front."

"Hi Lillie Mae," said Carl Jr. shyly hoping she would not be mad he was in the front.

"Hi Carl," she said picking up Elizabeth holding the baby dolls.

"Baby," she said pointing at the dolls.

"Yes, remember this is Mae-Mae and this is Lulu."

"Lulu," she said proudly.

"You are a smart baby."

"Mom what are you doing here?" said Rose opening the door to get in the backseat.

"Will we see you tonight, Juan?" said Violet ignoring her question.

"Yes ma'am," he answered excited to meet more of the family. "Lil' Adam told me to come by, but Rose wasn't sure if you were still having it."

"We're still having it," said Violet glancing back at Rose. "Don't you want to walk with your friends?"

"No ma'am, we have lots to get ready," she answered slamming the door, quietly adding with a touch of mockery, "since we still having it."

"Rose watch this," said Lillie Mae holding up one of her dolls. "Lizabeth, who is this?"

"Lulu," she smiled pointing at the doll.

"I taught her that."

"That is wonderful," she said sarcastically, reaching for Elizabeth who happily climbed into the back seat with her.

"Lulu," she said lifting the baby.

"Carl, you have a good day at school," asked Rose, ignoring Juan standing at the window."

"Yes ma'am," he said enjoying all the excitement with the William's family.

"You don't have to call her ma'am, that's for old folks," said Lillie Mae.

"He's only showing his manners," said Violet frowning at her daughter. "You can say ma'am as much as you please."

Carl Jr. sat happily between the two of them thinking how completely different this family was from his own. "Ms. Vee, why are we having a party tonight?"

"Just for fun," she smiled at him briefly then turned back to the car window. "Juan, we'll see you tonight around six o'clock."

"Yes ma'am," he replied and waved at Rose in the back seat who was too preoccupied with bouncing the baby up and down to notice him still standing there.

"See you later Mom," called Lil' Adam.

"Come straight home now, hear."

"Yes ma'am," he answered jumping to catch the football in midair.

Lillie Mae taunted her sister as they drove away, "your boyfriend still waving at you."

"He's not my boyfriend," answered Rose rolling her eyes.

"Your boyfriend… your boyfriend… bye Juan."

"Momma, please tell her to stop saying that, bad enough he's coming over tonight with Dad *and* Aunt Ruby."

"I can't wait, this will be good," taunted Lillie Mae, making up a song as she bounced up and down in the front seat. "Your boyfriend's coming over tonight…"

"Sit still Chile', I'm trying to drive."

"Your boyfriend's coming over tonight."

"Momma Please," pleaded Rose.

"Lillie Mae stop bouncing and teasing your sister."

She turned towards the back and stuck out her tongue.

Carl Jr. sat quietly surprised she didn't get in trouble, maybe Ms. Vee didn't see her. And, they are having a party tonight, 'just for fun'. I love this family. I think I'll stay forever.

* * *

Carl hurried to open the car door for his mother, conservatively dressed for a woman in her seventies, in a golden colored dress with matching hat and a white laced shawl. Thinking she was lonely after his father passed away years ago, he offered for her to move in with him and the family, but she insisted the hot southern sun was too much for her to bear.

"Where are the children?" said Mrs. Gist sternly looking in the back seat after he put the bags in the car. "You didn't bring them to the airport to greet their *grandmother*!"

"Mother, your plane arrived at eleven o'clock in the morning, I didn't want to take Carl Jr. out of school, Violet is picking him…"

"Doesn't the bus bring him home," she interrupted rudely.

"Yes, normally it does," he answered taking a deep breath trying to remain calm. "But the children are staying with Violet and her family since Daisy has been in..."

"I know you didn't leave my grandbabies at that negra's house?"

"Mother please, Violet has been with Carl Jr. and Elizabeth since they were born. And with Daisy in the hospital…"

"Ohh is that supposed to be an excuse for leaving them with that… that… *family.* Lord only knows what goes on in their house, with my grandchildren. How could you!"

"Mother," he said more firmly. "I didn't just *leave* Carl Jr. and Elizabeth, Violet thought it was a good idea…"

"And YOU agreed!" she said taking a deep breath. "I am appalled! We see who oversees this family."

"Mother," he said trying to gain his composure and remain patient. "I 'agreed' because I was sleeping at the hospital during the night and running back and forth from the office checking on Daisy's progress during the day. Who was going to watch the children?"

He looked at his mother next to him, arms folded, neck stretched forward, and her head tilted sideways. He thought she would be more concerned for his welfare, how he barely ate or slept.

"Fine, now I am here," she waved her hands dismissing his statement. "Just take me to my grandchildren immediately. They'll be staying at the house with me tonight!"

"Mother," expelling all the air from his lungs in one breath.

"Don't mother me!" she said unsympathetically. "I want my grandchildren home tonight!"

"Yes Mother," he answered calmly starting the car and slowly driving towards home. Growing up he recalled his mother's stubbornness and how his father tried to sway her opinions, until he eventually stopped trying, knowing she was completely in charge and he could never win the argument.

"And you can tell that negra' gal we no longer need her services!"

Trying to remember if he asked her to come, or did she invite herself, he drove silently towards home feeling like a child, understanding the defeat his father endured year after year. Normally Daisy's sunny personality brought light to their dreadful encounters, but for now, he would have to endure his mother alone.

"And don't drive so fast, you know I get motion sickness!"

"Yes Mother."

16 DANCING THE NIGHT AWAY

Carl Jr. thought tonight was the most exciting night ever and could hardly wait for the party to begin. "I can't remember the last time there was a party at my house. When I turned eight, we did not have a party. When Elizabeth turned two, we did not have a party. No one even comes to visit us, and tonight we are having a party 'just for fun'. I love this family. Can I stay forever?"

"Once your mother gets home," she said ruffling his hair as he sat at the dinner table. "I'll make a big batch of biscuits and fried chicken and have ourselves a party. And I promise we can all dance the night away."

"Thank you, Ms. Vee, I will love that."

"Okay then, run along and play while I finish cooking."

Lillie Mae and Elizabeth were already on the living room floor playing with baby dolls, along with Patricia Ann, who was interested in a job with the Gist family on the weekends. Soon, Carl Jr. sat next to them with some Tonka trucks. Lil' Adam and Juan engaged in a game of checkers on the coffee table.

Sadly, Rose fretted in her room since Naomi did not want to come, when she found out Margie went to the picture show. Everyone was going to have a good time but her, she thought. She remembered the first day of school when she envied the other girls who appeared to be enjoying themselves. A backup friend would be the cat's meow. "Mom-ma," she shouted looking out the window from her room, "here comes Aunt Ruby."

Everyone looked to see her walking up the front pathway wearing high heel shoes, her hips moving vivaciously from side to side, stopping only to wave at her ride. Lil' Adam looked at Juan with an 'I told you so' expression. Juan nodded his approval thinking, "she's a knock-out". Smiling, Carl Jr. spoke aloud, "she's beautiful". Patricia Ann and Elizabeth played quietly in the corner not noticing the new attraction.

Violet wiped the sweat off her brow as she turned over the third batch of fried chicken, thinking how much work the dance party was turning out to be. "Is she by herself?"

"Yes ma'am."

"Hi Aunt Ruby," said Rose, opening the door before she had time to knock.

"Hi baby," she replied giving her a hug and kiss on the cheek. "Where's your mother?"

"In the kitchen, cooking."

"Hi Ms. Ruby," smiled Carl Jr. as he ran and squeezed her around the waist.

"Oh my," she responded a bit off balance from the strong hug. "This can't be Carl Jr. Have you grown since I last saw you?"

"Yes ma'am," he said smiling as she twirled him around.

"And you are so handsome. Can I get a dance with you tonight?"

His eyes stretched wide, "Yes ma'am, you sure can."

"Hi Aunt Ruby," said Lil' Adam looking up from his checkers game.

"Hey Bean," she said taking off her coat and handing it to Lillie Mae. "Here you go baby."

Casually dressed, she wore a black shirt tied at the waist with the sleeves folded to the elbows, and snugly fitting leopard print Capri pants. Immediately her gaze turned to Juan, "Who do we have here? I know you didn't come here to play checkers, fine a-looking boy as you."

Juan, completely caught off guard by her feisty mannerisms and fashionable dress, was unable to focus anyway on the game. Smiling to himself, he remembered Lil' Adam saying his aunt was not shy, that definitely was an understatement, as he watched her switching over to the record player.

"How are you Ruby," entered Violet wiping her hands on her flour stained apron, kissing her sister on the cheek. "Have you met everyone?"

"Not that dreamboat over there *acting* like he's playing checkers."

"Momma," panicked Rose. She knew her aunt was beginning to meddle with her comment about 'acting', it was going to be worse than she thought.

"This is Juan a friend of Lil' Adam, and Patricia Ann a friend of Rose's."

"Why the sounds not playing," she continued barely noticing the introductions. Looking through the selection of records, she quickly found "Finger Poppin' Time" by Hank Ballard and the Midnighters. Right away, she began dancing around the living room snapping her fingers.

"I thought this was supposed to be a dance party, everybody just sitting around here like ole' people… let me see some finger poppin', come on Carl Jr."

He gladly jumped up and began dancing with Ruby, attempting to mimic her hip gyrations the best he could, while trying to snap his fingers. It ended up being SNAP, move hip to the left, SNAP, move hip to the right. "Look at me Ms. Vee."

"Get it baby," she said clapping along to the music, while he danced with a serious look of concentration on his face, trying to keep up. Even Elizabeth and Patricia Ann were clapping their hands.

"Oh yeah! Its finger poppin' time, I feel so good and that's a real good sign," sang Ruby as she twisted around the living room floor, holding his hand with her left hand and snapping her fingers with her right hand.

"Come on Ms. Vee and dance with us."

"Okay," said Violet snapping her fingers and dancing with the two of them. "Come on everybody, let's dance."

Lillie Mae joined in with Carl Jr., and Rose motioned for Patricia Ann, who gladly got up carrying the baby in her arms as they danced in the group. The Gist children fit in perfectly with the Williams' family, enjoying the music and the fun. Carl Jr. thought to himself, "I love this family. I think I'll stay forever."

"You boys better come on, less you scared the women folk will show you up," said Ruby shaking her hips as she twisted low to the floor.

"We have to finish our game," said Lil' Adam waving his hand. "I'm trying to concentrate."

"What's your friend name?"

"My name's Juan ma'am," he answered standing up. "Sorry man, I can't focus on the game."

"Here comes Bobby, here comes Sue," laughed Ruby twisting in front of him. "Come on here boy and show me what you can do."

"Boss Cat," he jumped up ready to dance not bothering to look back.

Lil' Adam shrugged his shoulders, disappointed with his friend, "Man let's finish the game."

"Come on son," said Violet motioning for him to join them.

Just as he stood up, the song ended.

"Ahh to bad," he said getting ready to sit back down.

"Don't you move," said Ruby putting another record on the player. "We just got started."

The faster paced song, "Speedo" by the Cadillac's, began playing as everyone danced without inhibitions, shaking and twisting, and moving all around the living room enjoying each other's company. Eventually the focus turned to Lil' Adam and Juan, trying to outperform each other, and ended up putting on a show for everyone. Rose stood clapping impressed by Juan and her brother's dance movements.

"Whew!" said Violet rubbing the sweat from her forehead. "That was too fast for me."

"I'm thirsty Ms. Vee," said Carl Jr. his face cherry red.

"Me too," said Ruby reaching her hand out to shake his hand. "Baby you the best eight-year-old dance partner I ever had."

"Thank you," he said proudly shaking her hand. "I didn't even know I could dance."

"I tell you I could barely keep up with you," said Ruby walking over to put another record on the player. "Vee, fix me something to drink."

"You might as well come on and eat," she answered, motioning to everyone before heading towards the kitchen.

"Fried chicken Ms. Vee," his eyes shining with anticipation.

"Again!" asked Lillie Mae. "We had fried chicken for a week!"

"It's Carl Jr.'s favorite."

Walking over to the table, she sat down with her arms folded. "Does anyone care what *my* favorite is?"

"That's not how we treat company."

"Carl Jr. is not company, he's family."

"You right," said Violet attempting a compromise. "What other favorites do you like baby?"

"Umm, let me think," he said putting his finger to his temple enjoying the attention. "I like meatloaf."

"Meatloaf it is," she said with a wink.

"Do you like meatloaf Lillie Mae?" he whispered softly wanting her to be happy as well.

"Yes, I like meatloaf," she whispered back. "I like fried chicken everyday too. I was only teasing you."

"Oh," he nodded, thinking, "I love this family. I think I'll stay forever."

Before long, Violet sat a plate of fried chicken, green beans, mashed potatoes, gravy, and biscuits on the table and a smaller plate for Elizabeth. "Patricia Ann, I can feed her while you get something to eat."

"Thank you Mrs. Williams, I can feed her, I'll get something later."

"She loves fried chicken like her brother. I let her feed herself for a bit, then I feed her, else she will play with her food and make a mess everywhere. Mash up the string beans and try to slip them in between her chewing on the drumstick."

"Yes ma'am," she answered respectfully.

"She likes you," smiled Violet, encouraged to see the two of them getting along so well. Patricia Ann was a natural. She gave all her attention to Elizabeth who enjoyed every minute.

"I hope Mr. Gist likes me, I really would like to have the job."

"I'm sure he will." Violet watched her patiently feeding green beans on an imaginary airplane landing in the baby's mouth.

The two of them were getting to know each other very well. Every morning after Carl Jr. went to school, Patricia Ann was with Elizabeth, playing, reading, feeding her and changing her, giving Violet time to do many things around the house she had neglected. She would make a great addition to the Gist family on the weekends and maybe permanently.

Ruby putting her hands on her hips, turned her attention to the young man standing in front of her. "You got some good moves, umm, what's your name again?"

"Juan ma'am," he answered putting out his hand.

"My sister is the ma'am, call me Ruby."

Rose, worried what her aunt would say or do next. She hurried to look for another record in hopes of distracting any questions. Glancing at Juan, she saw him calmly sitting on the couch watching her. His leg crossed squarely over his knee at the ankle, with one arm stretched out on the couch, as if he were waiting for her to sit next to him, and a smile on his face that was confident she would.

"Juan," shouted Ruby, snapping her fingers to get his attention. She could see his focus was on Rose and her intentions were to find out as much as she could about him. "Where you from?"

"Oh," he said startled a bit. "I'm from here now, Ms. Ruby, but I used to live in Chicago."

"Chicago, the windy city, I've been there awhile back."

"Ruby, you know you ain't been to Chicago," called Violet from the kitchen. "Come on in here and let them chaps be."

"No wonder you move like that," she continued ignoring her sister. "You know how to do that Chicago Jive?"

"Yes ma'am."

"There you go with ma'am again, folk don't say ma'am from Chicago."

"Sorry Ms. Ruby, just that my poppa's from here and he said it's proper to say ma'am. I have been saying it since I could remember."

"Ruby stop telling that Chile' what to say."

"Who you here with Lil' Adam or Rose..."

Panic struck Rose like a lightning bolt. If she could, she would climb into the wall and blend in with the other pictures, accept her expression would not be of happiness but of extreme embarrassment. "Momma, did you call Aunt Ruby for dinner?"

"Ruby," Violet said sternly. "Get in here girl."

"Here I come," she said waving her hand at the kitchen. "Rose put on that 'boogie' song, so we can watch Juan do that Chicago Jive."

"What if he doesn't want too," she asked, shocked at her request.

"I don't mind Rose," he said softly.

"Ohh... aren't you the sweet one," said Ruby squeezing his cheeks with both hands.

Somehow, despite complete embarrassment, she found "Choo Choo Ch'Boogie" by Louis Jordan and His Tympany Five. Then without hesitation, Juan stood and began moving to the beat like a professional dancer with steps they never saw before. At one point, his body mimicked a train rolling along to the rhythm of the song. Everyone came into the living room watching in amazement at his abilities. Ruby snapped her fingers as she moved from side to side totally entertained. Midway through the song Juan grabbed her by the hand and twirled her into the movements of the song. Dancing and laughing they sang along, "take me right back to the track, Jack."

"Oh yeah I like this," she said flowing rhythmically as if they had been dancing together for years. "You good boy... you good!"

"You pretty hip for somebody's aunt," he panted once the song ended slightly out of breath.

"You saying I'm old."

"No ma'am, I'm just saying..." he hesitated. "You sure you never danced the Chicago Jive before."

"Baby, I'm a natural at everything," she answered with a wink that surprised Juan.

Rose cheeks turned beet red, she never felt so embarrassed in her life.

"Boy, you sho' can dance," said Violet patting him on the back.

"Teach me," said Lillie Mae trying to imitate some of his steps.

"Why bother girl, you're not going anywhere to dance," said Lil' Adam never missing a turn to aggravate her.

"You don't know where I'm going."

"Yes I do."

"Mom – maa," she whined.

"Lillie Mae if you start with that, you're heading straight for bed."

Lil' Adam motioned to Carl Jr. on the way into the kitchen. "Come on let's get some more fried chicken."

"Save some food for somebody else," called Violet. "Lord knows the two of you can eat more chickens then I can afford."

Carl Jr. hurried back into the kitchen to get a second helping, saying to himself, "I love this family. I think I'll stay forever."

"I see y'all still dancing up a storm in here. Ruby, I thought you wanted something to drink." She went over and sat next to her sister who had flopped on the couch totally out of breath.

"I do, but I couldn't let that young buck show me up."

"Oh my gracious," said Rose with her hand over her forehead.

Violet, noticing her daughter's distress, pushed off Ruby's knee to assist getting up from the couch. "Come on girl, because if you want something to eat, better get in here, before Lil' Adam and Carl Jr. eat up everything in the house." She headed back into the kitchen followed by Patricia Ann, carrying Elizabeth still chewing on a drumstick.

"Here I come," said Ruby smiling as she put one last record on the player. "Here is something you two can dance too."

"In the still of the night" by The Five Satins began to play. Ruby winked at Juan and smiled at Rose, before leaving for the kitchen.

For a moment, they both sat looking at each other, both uncomfortable, yet glad they were finally alone. The music played, "… I held you tight because I love you so, promise I'll never let you go… in the still of the night."

Standing, Juan made the first move, reaching his hand out to her. "Do you know how to slow drag?"

"Probably not the way you can," answered Rose feeling the heat of her face flare up again. Her heart beating so fast she thought for sure she would pass out.

"It's okay, I'll show you."

Careful not to move too fast, he stepped directly in front of her almost face to face, their lips inches away from touching. Slowly he placed his right hand near the middle of her back. "You can put your hands around my neck or my waist if you like."

Feeling the warm breath of his words on her face, she responded quickly, "Okay." She placed her hands around his neck, her fingers locked together tightly.

Putting his left hand around her waist, he gently pulled her even closer. "Just relax and feel the rhythm of the music."

"Ohh," she mumbled caught off guard by his embrace. Never having danced like this before, she felt almost breathless, her body moving together with his, floating on a cloud to the music.

"You okay," he asked moving slowly still holding her close.

"Um-hum, I, I'm okay."

As the music continued to play, "I remember that night in May the stars were bright above..." They danced entangled together as one. Juan moved her with ease to the beat of the music, inhaling the fragrance of her neck as he gently caressed her back with his fingertips. She moved naturally in response to his lead, unsure of her feelings, uncomfortable with his body pressing tightly against hers, but not wanting to stop. The song continued, in slow motion as they moved in cadence from left to right.

"Do you like the song," he asked his voice sultry against her ear, almost a whisper.

"Yes, it is one of my favorites."

"Am I holding you too close?"

"No," she lied. So close, she could not tell if she felt his heartbeat or hers. So close, the warmth of his breath heated her neck. She felt weak in her knees. Did he know how he was making her feel? Was he doing this on purpose? She could not tell, nor did she have the courage to ask. He was so close, she felt...

"WHAT is going on in here," said Adam with the voice of a roaring lion.

"Ahh – Ahh," said Rose immediately jumping out of Juan's grasp.

"What's the matter," said Violet running from the kitchen followed by Ruby, Lillie Mae, and Lil' Adam, still chewing with a drumstick in his hand.

"My daughter's in here doing some god-forsaken dance with..." He paused to stare at him, with the intensity of a homeowner catching a burglar red-handed in the act of stealing his most precious items. "Who are you? No, don't tell me, you're Juan."

"Ahh, yes sir," his voiced quivered, wondering how he knew his name.

"Adam, calm down," said Ruby going over to remove the record scratching repeatedly at the end of the song.

"Ruby this is my daughter," he shouted.

"And she ain't a baby; besides, I saw you dance that way."

He stared at her as if she had revealed a secret, speechless. Violet immediately noticed the tension between the two of them. Her sister's statement creating questions she had to address at another time. Squinting at Adam in frustration, she shook her head and went back to the kitchen. "Come eat. Time out for dancing anyway, we need to put these children in the bed."

Carl Jr. looked up from the kitchen table when he heard the word 'bed'. He was not ready to go, there was too much excitement. For the first time he thought about home, and despite loving this new family, he thought about his own.

* * *

"Excuse me," said Mr. Gist at the doorway to the living room. "Was I interrupting something?"

"Mr. Gist," said Violet wondering how long he was standing there. "No, no, please come on in, we were just..."

"Da – da," said Elizabeth smiling and reaching for her father.

"Lizzy," he answered taking her into his arms as he wondered who all these people were. For a moment, all the negative things his mother said came to mind. Did he know them well enough to entrust his children to them, especially if others were in their home he did not know.

"Poppa, Poppa," said Carl Jr. running to him with his mouth and hands greasy from fried chicken.

"There's my boy," he said picking him up and holding both children in his arms. "I've missed you both so much."

Everyone stood awkwardly watching the small family reunion. Mr. Gist felt something he had never felt before at the Williams' home, out-of-place. All he could think of was his mother's negativity. Was she right about them? In his heart, he knew she was wrong and pushed any doubt in his mind away.

"Umm," said Violet noticing the bewildered look on his face. "You remember my sister Ruby."

"Yes, oh yes," he said reaching out his hand. "Your face looks familiar. You and Violet closely resemble one another."

"Except I'm the good-looking one," said Ruby smiling seductively as she watched his face turn a bashful shade of red.

"Ruby," said Violet sternly squinting her eyes at her and shaking her head. "And this is Patricia Ann, Rose's friend. She has been helping me with Carl Jr. and Lizabeth."

"Hello," he said pleasantly. Impressed by her smile, he lost sight of his other concerns. "Is it Patricia…Ann?"

"Please sir, call me Patty," she said politely reaching out her hand.

"Only if you don't call me sir," he smiled putting down Carl Jr. to shake her hand.

"Come on in the kitchen, we got plenty to eat."

"Juan show us that Jive dance you were doing earlier," said Ruby heading over to the record player as tension in the room began to ease.

"I'm not sure ma'am if now is a good time."

"You all right," she replied placing "At the hop" by Danny and the Juniors on the record player.

With everyone else leaving, he felt somewhat better, but right before Adam entered the kitchen, he turned and gave him the meanest stare. Chills ran down Juan's spine as he grabbed the couch to prevent from falling.

"Kid, you all right?"

"Ahh yes ma'am, I'm all right… I think," he answered wondering if he should leave. Before he could decide, she grabbed his hand and whirled him around. Shocked and almost knocked off balance, he began dancing, fearing he had no choice. 'Let's go to the hop', played on an on as he danced unconsciously wondering what he had gotten himself into.

* * *

"How is Ms. Daisy?" said Violet, fixing the two men a plate while the music played from the living room.

"Much better, much better, I'm not really hungry Vee."

"When's the last time you ate?" she asked placing large plates of food in front of them.

"Grabbed a bite this morning in the hospital cafeteria…"

"After all that time, you hungry, you just don't know it."

"I'll help you eat it," smiled Carl Jr. standing next to his father eyeing the fried chicken.

"Carl Jr.," she said firmly but lovingly, "you gonna' turn into a chicken pretty soon."

"This chicken is good honey," said Adam licking his fingers. "No wonder Carl Jr. wants more."

"Thank you, but he can't have any more to eat tonight, poor Chile' will bust. And it's time for bed."

"Vee, I came to pick them up," said Mr. Gist taking a few bites of food.

"Poppa I want to stay, I love being here with Ms. Vee and everybody."

"I'm sorry son, but your grandmother came all the way from Boston this morning. She wants to stay at the house and take care of you and your sister until your mother gets better."

"Can't we stay here? We had a party and I was dancing and …" he added stretching his eyes with excitement.

"Now Carl Jr.," interrupted Violet from the kitchen sink. "I'm sure your grandmother misses you both something awful, she hasn't seen you since last year."

"She ain't no fun," he sulked.

"Son, please don't say ain't."

"She isn't no fun."

"Miss Patty, I would like you to come Monday with Violet. That is, if you are still interested in the position."

"Yes sir, I'm still interested, and maybe I can find some fun things to do for the children next week. I can bring some games from home I play with my younger brothers, if you like."

"Would that help you feel better son?"

"Yes sir, I guess so," still wishing he could stay.

"Miss Patty, I do have to warn you, my mother was brought up in the old South. Her ways are a bit antiquated."

"Sir?" said Patty confused.

Violet, who had met his mother on numerous occasions explained. "She can be a bit difficult at times, but she means well."

"I just wanted to apologize beforehand. I know she can be very harsh," he continued putting his head down slightly. "She won't be staying too long Miss Patty, only until my wife returns. My mother says she doesn't need any help, but I appreciate all the assistance you both can provide."

Violet sat at the table finally with a small plate of her own. "Monday morning I'll fix her some hot biscuits with a bit of honey. That will surely take her mind off anything else. She'll be fine."

"Can you fix me some too," asked Adam reaching under the table to squeeze her leg.

"Me too," said Carl Jr.

"What am I going to do with you two?"

"Would you like me to get them ready to leave, sir, I mean, Mr. Gist," asked Patty.

"Yes, thank you," he smiled pleased with her initiative.

"There's a small suitcase in the closet by the bathroom, you can ask Lillie Mae to show you."

"Yes ma'am."

"I appreciate all your help and prayers for me and my family."

"We enjoyed having them. It's going to be lonesome around here..."

"Been telling you it's time we had another one," interrupted Adam, reaching under the table to squeeze her leg again, but anticipating his actions, she jumped up too quickly.

"Adam, we have company."

"Don't mind me," said Mr. Gist putting on his hat to leave. "I recall the times me and Daisy would play around like that, seems like such a long, long time ago."

"Those times will come again, Mr. Gist. Wait on the Lord, that's all."

"Hope it won't be too long," he answered sadly.

"Here they are, Mr. Gist, packed up and ready to go," said Patty carrying the baby in one arm, the suitcase in the other with Carl Jr. standing right beside her.

"That was fast. I am impressed with how you handle everything, and the children seem so comfortable with you."

"Thank you, Mr. Gist, sir."

"I told you she is a fine girl and will be a lot of help around the house," said Violet taking Elizabeth, who immediately laid her head on her shoulder. "She is so tired, bless her heart."

"Ms. Vee can we stay just one more day," pleaded Carl Jr. "We have so much fun here."

"I promise," she said kneeling in front of him. "We'll have some fun next week. And I might even take you to school one or two days."

"That's good Ms. Vee," he said reluctantly knowing it would not be the same without the entire William's family, who were always dancing, singing, and laughing. That is what he called fun. Sadly, he had to admit the party was over.

"Look, I fixed your favorite to take with you."

Seeing the brown paper bag his eyes stretched with excitement, "Fried Chicken!"

"Yes Carl Jr., fried chicken." She hugged him close to her. "Now you behave for your grandmother and help with your sister. I'll be there on Monday."

"Yes ma'am," he smiled taking the bag. "Come on Miss Patty, I can show you my army soldier men. Poppa, she's a girl, but she knows how to play Army."

"Is that right," smiled Mr. Gist looking at her with approval.

"Yes sir, I have four brothers I look after. They keep me pretty busy, and you got to know how to play Army, if you have brothers."

"I'm sure they will miss having you around."

"They say they won't, but they probably will."

"I'll carry that," he said reaching for the suitcase.

"Thank you sir."

"I can give you a ride home," he said hesitantly, "unless you were staying. I wouldn't want you to miss the party."

"I don't mind a ride, sir."

"I'll call your mother and let her know Mr. Gist is dropping you off," said Violet.

"Maybe if it's not too late I can get to meet her."

"It's not too late. She's probably still trying to get my brothers settled down and into bed."

"Well let's get going. Thank you Vee and Adam, I don't know what I would have done without your help."

"Anytime Carl," said Adam patting him softly on the back.

"Thank you, Mrs. Williams," said Patty carrying Elizabeth fast asleep.

"You're welcome."

"I like that name. Can I call you Patricia Ann?" said Carl Jr. as they headed towards the door.

"Miss Patty will be just fine," said Mr. Gist holding the door open.

"Can I sit in the front seat?"

"Okay son," he said feeling much better than when he first arrived.

"Bye Ms. Vee," yelled Carl Jr. from the window as they were backing out the driveway.

"Bye baby," she waved from the back porch with Adam standing next to her. "Be good."

"I will Ms. Vee. See you Monday."

She heard his voice trailing off as they drove away. "It seems like Patricia Ann will fit in well with the Gist family.

"Um-hum," he answered focusing his attention on her. "Now let's go work on them children, don't want you to get lonesome." He leaned down to kiss her softly as the moon shined romantically in the background, rubbing his fingers through her hair.

"You know we got company," she said sweetly which only increased his desire to kiss her more.

"You do," said Ruby standing at the back door watching them, "won't be any working on *children* tonight."

Startled, Violet stepped back from her husband to fix her hair. "Girl, how long you been standing there?"

"Long enough to know you two are the out kissing-ness couple I know."

"I hear tell Fred wouldn't mind a little more kissing from you, maybe make some children of your own," said Adam sarcastically.

"Don't know where you heard tell of that, sounds like nonsense to me."

"Now, now you two," said Violet always the mediator. "Best get on in the house and take care of the children we got before we make some more."

"That reminds me," he said opening the screen door for her. "I need to talk to that Juan boy and find out why he was groping my daughter."

"Adam, please don't embarrass Rose," she said, frustrated with him once again. "He was not groping, they were dancing, and I was in the kitchen."

"Then you don't know. Vee, I'm a man. I know what I saw. Let me handle this."

The three of them headed into the living room expecting to see more unsupervised slow dancing, instead, Lil' Adam and Juan had resumed their checkers game, Rose was reading a copy of Ebony magazine, and Lillie Mae was playing with her baby dolls.

"See what I tell you," said Violet poking him in the side.

"Fine," he answered with a slight scowl on his face.

"Come on Juan, and show my sister that swing dance," said Ruby heading towards the record player.

Juan looked up from his game hesitantly glancing at Adam whose stare made it perfectly clear that a swing dance, or any dance, was not a good idea. Beads of perspiration began forming on his head.

Seeing his hesitation, Ruby tried to console him. "The party is not over yet, there's still more time for dancing, ain't no need to worry Juan."

"He better worry," Adam said harshly, his eyes never breaking contact with Juan who slowly looked at the floor. "Come on the porch a minute."

"Adam, let them have fun," said Violet seeing the discomfort on Juan's face and even worse on her daughter's face.

"Vee, let me handle this," he said heading towards the porch. "Lil' Adam you come too."

"Huh," he turned to his mother confused.

"Go on baby, you know how your father is when he gets his mind set on something."

"Yes ma'am." Lil' Adam quickly stood up from the checkers game wondering why he had to go on the porch, it should be Rose not him.

Juan stood up slowly to go with his friend, making one last attempt at salvation. "I'm sorry if I caused a problem, Mrs. Williams. I didn't mean any harm."

"Son, don't let my husband scare you," she said patting him on the back as he walked to the door. "He'll give you the 'no talking to my daughter speech' that's all. All you have to do is agree with him, nod your head up and down, and say 'yes sir Mr. Williams sir', and you'll be fine."

Now Juan was more terrified than before. Heading to the porch, he kept thinking of her advice – 'nod, agree, say yes sir', or was it 'agree, say yes sir, then nod'. He could not remember the order, but why even try, because as soon as Mr. Williams started talking, he would likely pass out.

Both boys stood on the front porch behind Adam, his back to them while he stared out into the darkness, with one hand on the banister and the other on his side, near his belt. Even as teenagers, the thought of him removing his belt increased their anxiety one hundredfold, sweat began to form on both their foreheads, neither dared to speak, each stood quietly waiting for what seemed like forever.

Finally, he turned and roared, "Concerning my daughter, what are your intentions?"

They both jumped as his thunderous voice shook the foundation of the porch. Only the crickets appeared to know the answer, as one responded nearby, while another replied from afar. The boys stood in silence, their thoughts carried away by the night.

"I said…" This time standing directly in front of Juan, "concerning my daughter, what are your intentions?"

"Uhhh, w-what, uhhh, excuse me sir?" stuttered Juan, finally able to speak as his knees knocked together.

"You can't hear boy?"

"Uhhh, yes sir Mr. Williams sir," he remembered to nod. "I can hear."

"Then what are your intentions with my daughter?"

"Umm… umm." No matter how hard he concentrated on what to say, understandable words would not come out of his mouth. He looked over at Lil' Adam hoping for some type of support, but he gave none.

"Um, friends… Mr. Williams, sir."

"Friends," said Adam laughing heartily for a moment easing their anxiety. "Friends don't dance that close. I don't dance that close with my wife. Do you intend on my daughter being your wife, boy!"

"No, no sir," sweat pouring down his face alarmed at the mention of marriage. "I mean, not at this time, sir."

"Then what were your intentions dancing that close?"

"I'm sorry sir. I didn't mean any harm," he nodded trying to recall the earlier advice. "That is how we dance in Chicago, Mr. Williams, sir."

"This isn't Chicago." Adam turned to his son like a drill sergeant. "And where were you when he was dancing all close with your sister?"

"I was in the kitchen sir," he answered quickly to make it known that he had not witnessed the travesty in question.

"And you think that makes…"

"Why are you upsetting these boys?" interrupted Violet, poking her head out the screen door staring intently at her husband.

"We'll be in directly," he answered in a kind gentle voice, meeting her gaze with a smile.

"Adam, I told you, they were only having fun. The boy already apologized to me in the house and probably to you by now. Let them come in, it's getting late."

She looked over at both boys standing rigidly as soldiers. She smiled sweetly letting them know she was on their side. They hoped she would say something further in their defense. Before leaving, she turned to give a firm look towards her husband, before quietly closing the screen door.

"Adam," he continued, turning towards his son, loudly enough that both boys jumped. "You know I don't mess around when it comes to my daughters and my wife."

"Yes sir," he replied, not used to hearing his father call him by name.

"Next time either one of your sister's dance with anybody, you *better* stay in the room, or you will answer to me!"

"Yes sir."

"And as for you, Juan Nesbitt…"

Juan's eyes stretched. How does he know my last name? His panic increased, beads of sweat formed on his forehead once again.

Adam smiled slyly, "You're Leon Nesbitt's son, heard he was back in town and with all the stuff going on around the house about Rose and some new kid, I figured it was you. I have known your father since high school. Vee knows him too. He did the same thing with her. When you get home, ask him to tell you the time he tried to slow dance with my wife."

"Your wife, sir?" said Juan confused.

"Yes," laughed Adam patting him on the back as if the last fifteen minutes never occurred. "She wasn't my wife back then, but she was my girl. Almost messed up our relationship, but that's in the past. Tonight, Juan Nesbitt, I'm letting you slide."

"Sir?" he said timidly, thinking Mr. Williams was joking, and would later pounce on him with more accusations of marriage and questions of intentions.

"This one time," he smiled squeezing Juan's shoulder enough to cause slight discomfort but not pain. "On account of two things, one, I know your father and two, my wife gave me the 'eye' … twice."

"What's the 'eye'?" said Lil' Adam confident that with the mention of his mother, the storm had passed over.

"The 'eye' is what a woman gives you when she doesn't like what you are doing. And if you want to stay on her *good side*, it's best you don't keep doing what she doesn't like you doing."

Both boys were glad to hear of a subject that completely baffled them at this age… women. Neither of them had a girlfriend, so they greatly appreciated any advice regarding such a complicated subject. They listened intently.

Now that he had their undivided attention, without fear, he sat on the banister, folded his arms, and tilted his head to the side, shrewdly, like a lion explaining to his cubs. "See women got this special look they give, almost the same look you'd give a two-year-old about to burn their fingers on the stove, and you shout STOP."

"Ohh," they nodded in agreement, both picturing the image in their minds, "that look."

"Now I got to get on in this house and fix things by bedtime. Here is the number one rule with a woman, never even *attempt* to go to bed until you fix things up."

"Why not," they both asked hanging on his every word.

"A woman doesn't just let things go. If we had a disagreement…" Adam pointed at Juan who began nodding in agreement. "We could settle things quickly and move on."

"Yes sir."

"Women, on the other hand, let things fester on the inside. If she is mad with you on Monday and you don't fix it by Tuesday, she surely won't let you get any rest on Wednesday. Then by Thursday, you think she forgot entirely and the next thing you know on Friday, you walk in the door from work, happy to be home with your family, and she knocks you in the head with a frying pan…BAMM! … for something that happened on Sunday."

Both boys jumped, as they pictured the image in their heads.

"Adam," called Violet from the kitchen using the same tone she used with the boys earlier. "It's getting late."

"All right," he smiled turning to the boys. "She sounds real sweet now, maybe I still have a chance to fix things."

"Well goodnight," said Juan turning and heading down the front steps.

"Where are you going son?"

Juan looked up and smiled; glad he called him 'son' instead of 'boy'. "I'm going home."

"You can't now."

Juan looked at him confused once again.

"Come on back up here. If you go home now, my wife will think I ran you off, and I won't be able to fix things."

Both boys looked at him not making the connection.

"Remember the 'eye'?"

They still looked confused.

"You two need help," he laughed at their innocence and lack of knowledge regarding women. "She *gave* me the 'eye' when I first came home for causing a commotion when we had company, that's not hospitable. Mind you," he squeezed Juan's shoulder again. "Slow dancing so close with my daughter was wrong, and you won't do it again will you?"

"No sir."

"For me to fix the 'eye', we *all* have to go back in the house to show that everything is all worked out."

"Yes sir," he answered, glad to return inside.

"And that slow dancing thing, won't happen again," he said squeezing his shoulder this time causing discomfort.

"No sir," he said swallowing down the building anxiety and the pain. "It won't happen again sir."

"We'll start over proper," he said patting him heartedly on the back. "Welcome to my home son. Come on in."

Soon as they walked into the house, Adam started snapping his fingers and tilting his head from side to side to the music, as "Twilight Time" by The Platters played softly in the background. Juan and Lil' Adam looked at each other amazed at this instant transformation.

"Watch, I'll show you how to dance with a lady. Are you paying attention?"

"Yes sir," they both nodded impressed.

He took his wife's hand, kissed it gently, twirled her around and began dancing to the slow-paced song. "Watch... my hand is on her waist and her hand is on my shoulder, as I gently lead her around the room. *And* there is room enough between us, in case I want too..." He dipped her down low to the floor, "make a special move."

Violet beamed with delight as he led her smoothly around the living room, reminding her of when they were younger attending dances in high school. He was such a charmer, then and now, always satisfying her completely.

"Then you sing softly in her ear, 'Deep in the dark your kiss will thrill me like days of old, lighting the spark of love that fills me with dreams untold. Each day I pray for evening just to be with you, together at last at twilight time'... Continuing to dance around the room the atmosphere filled with love and romance. "Then you close with the finale," he dipped her once again, low to the floor.

Once the dance was over, Lillie Mae clapped, happy to see her parents enjoying themselves. Rose, impressed with her father's charm and knowledge of the song, hoped one day she would marry someone like him. And Lil' Adam and Juan stood in agreement understanding all he told them about 'fixing things'.

"Your Pops is good."

Breaking the mood, Ruby waving her hand at them. "You dance like my grandparents."

"In my house, this is how we dance. You got that Juan."

"Yes sir," he answered quickly glancing over at Rose who turned her head away immediately.

"Okay you made your point," agreed Ruby. "I guess it is my twilight time to get on home."

"And me to get the kitchen cleaned up," said Violet fixing her hair and rearranging her apron. "That's enough dancing tonight, time for bed."

"There's no school tomorrow," whined Lillie Mae. "Can't we stay up late?"

"It is late, just because there is no school doesn't mean you can stay up all night," she responded picking up glasses off the coffee table. "You *can* stay up to help with the dishes."

"Never mind," she answered sadly walking over to hug her Aunt Ruby. "Goodnight."

"Ahh, look at that face," she said hugging her tightly. "Goodnight baby."

"Mom, I'll help with the dishes," said Rose glad to leave the room, not bothering to look back.

"The night is still young Vee," said Ruby hanging up the phone. "Fred's on his way. Come on and go with us to The Honey Shack, the girls can finish the dishes."

"No, my shack days are over for now," answered Violet, rubbing her back. "I haven't got over my aches and pains from the last time I went."

"If you went more regular, you wouldn't have aches and pains." Ruby stood up moving her hips from left to right in a slight circular motion while snapping her fingers. "You can't get exercise like this, cooking and cleaning."

"Go on girl," laughed her sister.

"Thank you, Mrs. Williams, for inviting me," smiled Juan hoping he would see Rose before he left.

"I'll drop him off," said Adam kissing her on the cheek. "I won't be long, so I can take care of my unfinished business."

"I'll be waiting," she winked.

"Oh yeah, now that's the good 'eye', y'all boys see that."

"Adam, you need to stop filling their heads with all that how to treat a woman stuff," she smiled shaking her head as they headed down the driveway.

Soon Fred pulled into the driveway and Ruby waved good-bye, making one last request for her sister to come along. "Sis, it's not too late."

"No, thank you," smiled Violet, waving good-bye.

Coming on the porch, Rose stood next to her mother. "Momma, why didn't you go with them to The Honey Shack?"

Violet put her arm around her shoulder, as they watched the glowing yellow flickers of lightening bugs in the darkness, thinking of an appropriate illustration to make it easier to understand.

"I had a good time when I went, but some things you experience, once is enough…like red velvet cake. It tastes sooo good when you have it *sometime*, but if you had it *all the time…*"

"You wouldn't enjoy it as much."

"Yes baby," she smiled marveling at her wisdom.

"Poppa and Aunt Ruby like to go all the time."

Violet stood quietly for a moment, "I guess some people like *a lot* of red velvet cake."

17 AULD LANG SYNE

Juan did not live far from the Williams family. Soon they turned into his yard, the tires crackling on the gravel driveway. From a distance, you could see a light in the front of the small house. As they came close, a dog ran alongside the car barking until the car stopped, and Juan got out. "Timmy, quiet down. You can get out. He just likes to bark, especially at night."

"You sure he won't bite," asked Lil' Adam feeling uncomfortable.

Before Juan could persuade him further, the porch light came on illuminating a large man whose frame filled the doorway, wearing a plaid shirt partially tucked in under his hanging belly on one side, and loose on the other side. You could see he was chewing, nonstop, on what appeared to be a very large turkey bone.

"Juan, that you?"

"Yeah Pa, Mr. Williams dropped me off.

"Big Adam Williams?"

"Hey Leon." Adam stuck his hand out the car window before opening the door, but the warning barks of Timmy changed his mind.

"Juan take the dog around back." He waddled off the porch still holding the half-eaten drumstick, peering into the open car window. "Big Adam that you?"

Once the dog was out of sight, he got out the car, towering a foot over the round man determined to finish his meal. "Yup," he smiled reaching out his hand. "It's me."

"Excuse me," he said rubbing his free hand on his wrinkled clothes before shaking his hand. "Almost finished this here turkey leg, you want to come on in for dinner, got plenty."

"Uhhh, no thank you, we stopped by to drop your boy off."

"How you been Big Adam, ain't seen you in… nearly twenty years?"

"Been doing well and you?"

"Good, good, that your son? Juan talks about him all the time. How you," Leon asked looking in the car from the driver's side.

He answered quickly, "Fine sir," not wanting to prolong any conversations but it seemed Mr. Nesbitt was not ready for them to leave.

"This is a mighty fine automobile Big Adam. I always wanted a new car like this." He continued to examine every inch, rubbing his fingertips along the finish with one hand and sucking on the turkey bone with the other.

Adam finally ended the examination. "Okay then," he said getting into the car. "Maybe we'll stop by sometime and let you give her a spin."

"Her? You didn't name her yet?" he asked excitedly throwing the turkey bone to the side of the house where Timmy immediately grabbed it and ran around back.

"Uhhh, no."

"Last car we had, called her ole' Bessie, 1938 Plymouth. Then we lucked up on an abandoned ole' rusted truck and fixed it up. It ran good for about ten years or so. That was ole'… I can't seem to remember the name we gave that truck, but I think it was ole'…"

"We'll be seeing you Leon," interrupted Adam, starting the car, his feeling of cordiality over.

"Okay then," he said not minding he did not finish his story. "Stop on by anytime. I'm here every day, been waiting to hear from the mill, put in for a job, ain't heard from them yet. You still down at the railroad?"

"Um-hum," he nodded disinterested.

Leon moved closer to the window as his belly pushed into the car. "Maybe you can put in a word for me. I know I put on a couple pounds," he said slapping his jiggling stomach. "But some solid muscle under here, I'm still strong as an ox. Do you think you could, I mean, put in a word?"

"I'll ask around and let you know," he said dryly as he slowly began backing out the driveway.

"Thank you Big Adam, thank you. Stop by anytime. I'm here every day, been fixing the back porch since last..."

As his voice trailed away, Lil' Adam saw Juan walk around to the front of the house, the headlights reflecting the relief on his face that no one mentioned the slow-dancing episode. "See you on Monday Juan. Come by the house so you can catch a ride."

"Oh, how is Violet?" said Leon trying to catch up to the moving car to hear a response.

"She's fine," he said as he put the car into drive and little by little started down the highway.

"Tell her I said howdy," he shouted his voice trailing off as they drove away.

"Sure," he answered too soft for him to hear.

After driving for a few minutes, Lil' Adam asked, "will you tell Momma he said 'howdy'."

"Probably not."

"I thought you said you used to be friends?"

"Did I say friends?" He paused to negatively shake his head. "Back in high school, the girls liked me because of baseball and they liked Leon because of his dancing."

"He could dance," he said finding it hard to believe from his current physique.

"He was pretty good. But the main girl we both liked was your mother."

"Momma?" The conversation was growing more interesting as he tried to picture his mother having two gentlemen suitors.

"Yes son, your mother," he nodded matter-of-factly. "She has always been very good-looking, but it was more than that, account of she was sooo sweet too, always smiling, I couldn't think of anything but her, I barely made it outta' high school."

The night air blowing softly in the window, Adam sat reminiscing as they drove along, while "A Thousand Miles Away" by The Heartbeats played softly in the background. "And she liked me too. Your grandfather not so much at first. Always said I was coming by too much and eating too much. No disrespect, but I really didn't care, I knew your mom was the girl for me."

"Everything was going good, she was my girl and I was her man. Then Leon decided he wanted her for his girl too. Fellows told me he was carrying a torch for her, in her face when I wasn't around. I never said anything until the night of the Sweet Heart dance."

"They had them back then?"

"Yes, we did, I'm not that old," he said sarcastically glancing over at him with a smile. "At the dance we were all having fun, taking turns dancing with this one then that one. I was mostly dancing with Vee. Next thing I know, Leon walked up to us and asked her to dance to a slow song, 'Gee baby, ain't I good to you', by The King Cole Trio."

"You still remember the song?"

"Yes, I do." Shaking his head remembering the frustration long past, he continued the story. "For a minute I was caught off guard. Then, I remember thinking he had some nerve dancing with my girl to a song that talked about buying fur coats and diamond rings… Plus they were dancing very close, too close for me. I tried to ignore it at first, until he whispered something in her ear. To this day, I don't know what he said, but I know he looked over at me all suspicious-looking, like he was daring me to do something."

"I stood there for a while watching, sipping on a Coca-Cola, trying my best to act like their dancing wasn't bothering me, but I was about to blow a fuse. Every now and then, one of my fellows would walk up to me, ready to bust his chops if I wanted them too, but no I stayed calm and gave them the nod that everything was cool."

"Then he pulled your mother *real, real* close like I saw Juan tonight with your sister. And quicker than a fox can grab a chicken in a hen house, I walked up to him and punched him dead smack in the jaw."

"Like crazy," said Lil' Adam nodding his head in agreement. "Did they kick you out the dance?"

"Yup, sho' did."

"Did Mom leave too?"

He nodded smiling to himself, "and she never said a word about getting put out the dance."

"What happened with you and Mr. Leon?"

"First time I spoke to him since then was tonight by the car."

"Wonder what he said in her ear?"

"Wish I knew. Guess it don't rightly matter now."

"Guess it don't."

* * *

Shortly after getting into bed, Lil' Adam heard a soft tapping on the door and knew immediately that it was his mother. Every night she would sit on his bed as they went over the events of the day. He could never share this with his friends, who thought talking to your mother meant you were a 'sissy', but he didn't care.

"Baby, you sleep?"

"No, come on in."

She sat quietly on his bed admiring his neatly organized room. In the corner was a small desk with a pile of comic books, G.I. Joe men lined up ready for battle. Underneath were two boxes filled with Tonka trucks and other toys saved over the years.

He sat up in the bed as she fluffed up his pillow to make him comfortable. She sat quietly waiting, never initiating conversation, always allowing him to bring up a topic. "I didn't know Juan's father used to like you in High School?"

"Where'd you get that from?" she laughed.

"Pop told me how he punched him in the face because he was dancing to close to you."

"Juan's father?"

"Yes, he called him Leon, so I guess his name is Leon Nesbitt."

"I *knew* that boy looked familiar," she said sitting at the foot of the bed grinning and shaking her head. "Your father brought up the Sweetheart's Dance?"

"Pretty much, especially the punching part and how you had to leave."

"Your father was so jealous, he didn't want me dancing with nobody really, but then Leon started dancing close and…"

"Whispered something in your ear," laughed Lil' Adam enjoying the time with his mother.

Violet smiled shaking her head, finding it hard to believe Adam still held on to such old memories. "He told you that too?"

"He said he wish he knew what Mr. Nesbitt whispered in your ear."

"Get some rest." She kissed him on the forehead before leaving.

"What did he say," asked Lil' Adam.

At the door she turned with a mysterious smile as if she had unfinished business to take care of herself. "Goodnight son, get some rest."

"Goodnight," he smiled too tired to protest the unanswered question.

* * *

Violet climbed slowly into bed not wanting to awake her husband, but he was not sleep.

"Lil' Adam told you about Leon," he said snuggling up close behind her as soon as her head touched the pillow.

"Yes somewhat," she answered relaxing in his embrace. "But he did say you wished you knew what Leon Nesbitt asked me years ago at our Sweetheart's Dance.

"What did he ask you," he said kissing her on the neck as if it really did not matter.

"It's not important what he asked but what I answered."

"And what was that?"

"I said 'I'm already somebody's girl."

He paused for a moment in the darkness pleased with her answer. Without saying a word, he gently turned her towards him as the glow of the moonlight radiated on her smiling face. He kissed her passionately, no longer sleepy.

.

18 ROAD TRIP

Normally the Williams family took the train once a year to visit Adam's parents in Kansas City, but with a new car, it seemed like a good time for their first family road trip. Early before dawn while everyone slept, Violet began preparing fried chicken, biscuits, and a big gallon jar of lemonade for the long drive. After packing the lunch, she began cooking breakfast, filling the house with the aroma of bacon, sausage, eggs, and hot coffee.

Adam, first in the kitchen fully dressed and ready to go, snuck up behind her at the stove. "Umm," he said squeezing her around the waist and kissing her on the neck. "There's no need trying to sleep around here, food smells good, you smell good, don't know what to eat first." He began nibbling her ear as she giggled.

"Oh Adam, you're so sweet," she smiled, stopping for a moment to return his affection. "But we got a long day ahead of us, we need to be getting them children out of bed."

"Y'all better come eat," he shouted towards the back then returned to her other ear.

"I could have done that."

One by one, the children came in rubbing their eyes, automatically taking their place at the kitchen table, as their mother sat a prepared plate in front of them.

"I can't remember ever getting up this early," said Lil' Adam the first to be seated.

"Me either," said Rose yawning, rollers still in her hair.

"It's dark outside," said Lillie Mae in her nightgown. "Why we up so early? I heard a rooster crow."

"You'll be fine," said Adam excited and ready to go. "It will be daylight pretty soon and by the time the sun gets hot, we will almost be there. Hurry up and get done with breakfast so we can hit the road."

"But it's dark outside," whined Lillie Mae.

Adam took a sip of his coffee. "Won't be dark long, now get moving. Vee, I'm not eating too much, might get sleepy on the road."

"I'm already sleepy," said Lillie Mae putting her head down and pretending to snore.

"Chile', finish your breakfast," said Violet sitting down with her plate. "Once you wash up and put your clothes on, you can go back to sleep in the car."

"Pops you know the way?" said Lil' Adam.

"Been going up to Kansas City some way or another long before now, pretty much know the way in my sleep."

"Don't mention sleep," whined Lillie Mae.

"How long does it take," said Rose with a yawn.

"Long enough to get there," interjected Violet. "Too early for questions, eat your breakfast. The sooner we leave, the sooner we get there."

Once she finished eating, she quickly washed the dishes and carefully reached in the drawer when no one was looking, took out a map and slipped it in her purse. She purchased it the day before at the gas station just in case he really didn't, 'know the way in his sleep', like he always claimed. Before she could turn around, he came through the kitchen with suitcases for the trunk and stopped to kiss her on the cheek, "Great day for a road trip."

Violet laughed as he headed out the door. He was more excited than she was, especially since he was a momma's boy. Her in-laws were always nice to her, maybe her father-in-law more than her mother-in-law. For her, going to Kansas City was more work than a vacation, and when she returned, she was exhausted. Taking a deep breath and releasing a final sigh, she grabbed the bag with the chicken and biscuits and headed out the door, double-checking to make sure she had the map.

Adam stuffed all the suitcases in the trunk with room to spare. Having his own automobile was a wonderful experience, better than catching the train, and especially better than catching the bus, stopping at every small town in America. "Hey Vee, maybe you should sit the lunch in the front, won't stand a chance in the back with your son."

Before she could reply, she watched her youngest daughter struggling down the steps carrying both bedroom pillows and three large baby dolls. "Chile', where are you going with all that?"

"There's no room for that," said Lil' Adam snatching the pillows and running towards the house.

"Momma, tell him to give me back my stuff," she whined. "I want to be comfortable."

"We all do," added her father as he closed the trunk. "And thank God, we have a large enough car, but there is no room for you to stretch out with baby dolls and pillows."

"Just for my head.... Please Daddy." She gave him her most pitiful look that never failed.

"Chile', go back in the house and get a small pillow off the couch!" said her mother foiling her plot for sympathy, "and only one baby doll."

"But they are a family, they go everywhere together."

"Sorry baby girl, not this time, your mother has spoken."

"Yes sir," she answered obediently returning up the stairs.

* * *

It was not long before they were driving on the highway, admiring the colorful array of fall foliage majestically displayed in the Appalachian Mountains, as the sun slowly began to rise, appropriately listening to "Kansas City" by Little Willie Littlefield, enjoying the music and the ride.

"I'm hungry," said Lil' Adam sitting in the middle of the backseat, so his sisters could have window views. "What's to eat?"

"Smells like chicken and biscuits," said Lillie Mae.

"I know you not hungry," said Violet turning around to look at her children. "We barely left home."

"Can't much blame them," said Adam with a smile, "chicken smells so good, I wanted some for the last thirty, forty miles."

Violet reached into the bag and sat two pieces of chicken and a biscuit on a napkin next to her, so he could eat and drive, and gave the same to her son in the back. She always cooked enough for everyone to have several pieces, not wanting to stop on the road, since some places denied access to them at their establishments.

"I want some," said Lillie Mae with her baby doll on her lap and a small pillow propped against the window.

"Rose, what about you?"

"No thank you," she smiled turning only briefly from the window. "I'll wait until lunchtime."

"Hope there's some left," laughed Lil' Adam, his mouth full of food.

"I won't let you eat everything," said Violet shaking her head sitting aside a piece of chicken and a biscuit for Rose, just in case he tried.

"I have to use the bathroom," said Lillie Mae after drinking two cups of lemonade.

"Figures," said her mother shaking her head.

"It's time we stopped anyway so I can stretch my knees," said Adam. "Maybe I'll see a gas station, might as well fill-up too."

Violet's stomach churned with a sudden feeling of dread as he turned off the highway and they drove for what seemed like miles away from the exit. "The sign said the gas station was this way, shouldn't we have gotten to it by now?"

He did not respond, not wanting to alarm anyone with his anxiety. He kept driving down the road with no other traffic or homes anywhere. "Maybe that was not a good exit."

"I need to use the bathroom," said Lillie Mae this time more frantically wiggling in her seat.

"Here it is, here it is," said her father pulling towards the gray weather worn service station.

"I don't know Adam, it looks kind of rundown," said Violet.

"We don't have much of a choice."

Once he drove up next to the only gas pump a bell sounded, Ding, Ding. A few moments later, a man appeared in overalls with no shirt, rubbing his eyes as if just waking up. Immediately Adam got out the car shielding the view of his family.

"Ain't seen no niggas' around these parts in a long time. You lost boy?" The pale man with dirty ruffled hair and an unshaven face, barely in his twenties, squinted up at Adam towering over him in height and weight.

Violet's heart sank when she heard the young man's cruel hate-filled statement. How could he talk that way? He did not know them. She began to pray for her husband and the stranger.

Sitting quietly in the backseat the children were shocked. This strange person used the "word" forbidden in their home. And they never encountered anyone calling their father a 'boy', since no one they knew would be crazy enough to do that.

"Only want some gas sir, then we'll be on our way," he answered calmly.

"But momma…" Lillie Mae whispered shaking in her seat.

"Hush Chile', now is not the time," she whispered looking back. Her eyes, full of fear, as the man began to walk around the car.

"Did you steal this here car boy?" he said near the gas pump with a cigarette hanging out of his mouth.

Adam winced at the word 'boy' but remained calm, not smiling, yet not appearing to be angry, expressionless. "No sir," was his only response, as he stood adjacent to the pump blocking the view of the occupants while the man began to put gas in the car.

Finally, the gas pump clicked. "That'll be eighteen dollars and fifty-cents boy," he said coldly taking the twenty-dollar bill without any more comments.

"Keep the change."

He stood there without enough manners to say 'thank-you'. As they drove away, the gas station faded in the rear-view mirror, but the experience would last forever, no one spoke.

Finally, Adam pulled over on the side of the road in a wooded area, "If anyone needs to go to the bathroom, now's the time."

The William's children looked from one to another, then to their parents, not understanding, since there was no bathroom in sight.

"Vee, you and the girls go first, me and Lil' Adam will keep an eye out, haven't seen any cars pass by for quite some time."

She reached over and kissed her husband on the lips, "I'll holler if we need you." Grabbing some napkins out the lunch bag, the three of them walked quickly into the woods soon out of sight behind some trees.

Adam sat thinking more of his wife's kiss than the experience at the gas station. He stared into the woods waiting for the slightest sign of trouble, ready to defend his family to the death if necessary.

* * *

Following the road signs, Lil' Adam saw an approaching one of interest, 'Welcome to Little Rock Arkansas'. "That's the place where the colored students wanted to go to a white high school and the Governor had the National Guard block them from attending. Until President Eisenhower called in the Army to protect them to they could enter in the building."

"I watched it at the barber shop," added Adam shaking his head. "I couldn't believe it, the Army lined up in front of the building, clearing a path for the nine students to walk up the steps as white's yelled holding signs that they would not go to school with Negroes."

"They had protection on the outside," said Violet sadly. "I can't imagine what was going on in the inside?"

"Worse then what I went through at the gas station."

"Do you think one day things will be better? When we will get to go places, like stores and gas stations, even to school, and just learn together and be friends," asked Lillie Mae.

"I hope so baby."

Before long, they were off the highway onto a well-kept street lined with trees. A light coating of snow covered the grass, something they rarely saw in the south. The redbrick homes were very similar: close to the curb, small front yard, narrow driveway with four steps leading to a porch barely large enough for two chairs. Adam's parents moved there to be close to him when he played for the Kansas City Monarchs. Initially they were the only colored family in the area, accepted only because of their son's notoriety, but as the years passed, the neighborhood slowly integrated and whites began moving away.

"We made it," said Adam with a sigh of relief turning into the driveway behind his father's Pontiac.

"Thank you Jesus," said Violet with an even longer sigh. Turning, she saw her mother-in-law running down the stairs without a coat or hat. Feeling a slight twinge of dread, she wished the two of them were closer, but only visiting once a year, made building a relationship difficult.

"My babies," she yelled, followed by Grandpa with her coat in his hands. With both grandfathers named John, the children called Violet's father Poppa John, and Adam's father Grandpa.

Adam jumped out the car not minding the cold, "Momma!"

Mrs. Williams, dressed in a long-sleeved dress with an apron tied around her waist, was less than five-feet tall. Her son standing well over six-feet, bent down to kiss her on the cheek. "Hi baby," she smiled, "you look good."

"Thanks Momma, you are too," he smiled reaching his longs arms around her round portly body.

"Grandma, grandma," called the children running to her for hugs and kisses. She happily obliged speaking to each one individually, asking about their trip and saying how much she missed them from last year.

Lil' Adam managed to scrape up enough snow to form a small ball and hit Lillie Mae in the back of the head. "Oww, that's cold," she pouted.

Violet got out of the car carrying two bags full of used paper towels, empty cups, and foil wrapped remnants of biscuits and chicken bones. "Hello," she nodded, her hands were too full to wave."

"Y'all help your mother get stuff out the car. How you been baby?"

"Fine ma'am," she answered walking over to give her mother-in-law a hug and kiss. One thing she knew for sure, the Williams family loved to hug and kiss, surely the reason Adam was so affectionate, so she did not complain.

Grandpa was patiently trying to put his wife's arm into her coat, but she kept moving to hug everyone. He was tall like his son and very handsome, with only a little gray on his temples. "Hold still Deena."

"Oh stop," she said shaking her arm out the only sleeve he managed to get on, "we only out here for a minute."

"Hi Poppa," said Adam hugging his father. "How you like my new car?"

"This here is a fine automobile son," he said walking around to have a closer look. "Did you have a good trip?"

Before he could answer, Lillie Mae ran over to hug her grandfather, "Hi Grandpa."

"Hi baby, look at you," he said standing back. "Last time you were here you came up to my knees, now you tall as me."

"Oh Grandpa, you always say that," she laughed hugging him again as her expression changed to a more serious face. "On the way here, this man called Poppa mean names."

"Oh my," said Grandma. "Come on in so we can talk, it's getting chilly out here."

"I'm hungry too," she added.

"Good! I got plenty of food."

"She's not really hungry Mrs. Williams," said Violet following behind as they headed in the house. "They were eating the whole time."

"Nonsense, they hungry, I been cooking all day, got all their favorites."

Violet looked at her husband for support, but all he did was tilt his head, hunch his shoulders, raise his eyebrows, then leaped up all four stairs to open the door for his mother. "No support there," she thought.

"Vee, you're looking well," said Grandpa, taking the garbage bags from her as the two of them walked up the stairs together. He was always extra kind to her, which helped, since Adam and his mother focused exclusively on each other, often excluding her from their conversations.

The living room was cozy and warm from the crackling fire glowing in the fireplace. A newspaper lay open on one side of the couch next to knitting needles and a partially finished blue scarf. "Go on in and wash your hands while I get the table ready for dinner."

"Yes ma'am," they all said enthusiastically especially Adam. He enjoyed his wife and her mother's cooking, but there was nothing like his own mother's cooking. He quickly jumped ahead of his children to be the first in the bathroom.

"You need help Mrs. Williams," asked Violet walking directly into the kitchen knowing the answer in advance.

"Thanks Violet," she said looking up at her from the stove. "You can wash your hands off in the sink and set the table if you don't mind."

"No ma'am, I don't mind." She spread the red tablecloth on the large dining room table and put seven settings of plates, forks, spoons, knives, and napkins at each chair. Soon her husband and three children raced from the bathroom as if they were starving, with

Adam playfully blocking the door to the kitchen. Everyone laughed as they all tried to squeeze through. If she did not know any better, she thought, it would be hard to distinguish the parent from the child.

"Daddy's cheating, he's not letting us in," whined Lillie Mae.

"Whoa! We all can't fit in here no way," laughed Grandma. "Have a seat at the dining room table while your mother brings the food in."

Violet began bringing in bowls and platters filled with barbecue chicken and ribs, macaroni and cheese, collard greens, buttered rice, cornbread, and for dessert, pound cake, apple pie, and ice tea. She wondered who was going to eat all this food, until she looked at her husband, so excited he could barely contain himself.

"Umh-umh finger licking good," said Adam rubbing his hands together.

"I can't wait to eat," said Lil' Adam.

"Me either," said Lillie Mae twisting in her seat.

Violet felt a small twinge of jealousy as she took her place at the opposite end of the table. She could not remember the last time they were this excited to eat dinner, all accept for Rose, who looked at her mother sympathetically.

"Let's say the grace before your father gets started," laughed Grandma. "There won't be any stopping him after that."

"You got that right," he responded looking around at every item wondering what to select first. "Pa, I see you been busy on the grill."

"Son, you know how your mother is, she wants her barbecue from the grill, snow or not. Right proud of how they turned out, can't wait to dig in myself, like you said, finger licking good."

Adam reached over to sneak a pinch off a rib bone. POP! Grandma slapped his hand as if he were a two-year-old again. "Wait until we say grace," she smiled. "You act like you haven't eaten in months."

Violet looked over at her husband shaking her head, he had lost all his senses. She wished she were closer, so she could pop him herself. She continued to stare at him hoping he would look her way, but he would not… such a momma's boy.

"Grandma everything looks so good," said Rose leaning forward attempting to block her mothers' intense gaze towards her father.

"And smells good too," said Lillie Mae.

"Um-hum," nodded Lil' Adam.

"Thank you," she nodded stretching out her arms to hold hands. "John, say grace before your son loses his mind."

"Lose something," mumbled Violet under her breath, frustrated with her husband.

"You say something Violet?"

"Everything does look good Mrs. Williams."

"Thank you … John."

"Dear heavenly Father," he started on queue. "Thank you for allowing my daughter, grandchildren, and son to visit us once again, this time in their very first family car, a truly fine car…"

"John!" interrupted Grandma.

"And thank you for this WONDERFUL meal my wife has prepared over the last week, with me cooking outside on the grill in FREEZING cold weather…"

"John!"

"In Jesus name we pray. Amen."

"Amen, let's eat," added Adam digging into the platter of ribs without waiting for anyone else to begin.

In a matter of minutes, everyone's plates were overflowing with food. All you could hear were sounds of chewing, crunching, and sucking, mixed in with plenty 'umms' and 'ahhs'. When no one could eat another bite, Adam was the first to speak. "Poppa those ribs were so good they melted off the bones right down my throat, didn't even have to chew."

"Thank you son."

"And let me tell you momma," he said reaching over to kiss her on the cheek. "You put your foot in the *entire* meal."

"Thank you, I'm glad you're enjoying it."

"Grandma, that still sounds crazy that putting your foot in the food means the food is good, sounds more like it would be bad," said Lillie Mae. She never would have spoken out at the dinner table at Grandma Mae's house, who believed children should be 'seen and not heard'. However, her father's mother encouraged them to always 'speak your mind' whenever they wanted to say something.

This time Grandma knitted her brows together before speaking, deep in thought. Lillie Mae suddenly became nervous, maybe the rules changed, and she spoke out of turn, meddling in 'grown folks' business, as Grandma Mae often told her.

"Baby, now that you mention it… that sure does sound crazy." She began to laugh as everyone around the table laughed also. When Grandma laughed, her round body shook up and down as happiness filled the dining room, even Violet joined in with laughter. Unfortunately, her happiness was short-lived since she had to do what she always did at her in-laws after a meal… clean up.

In the beginning years of her marriage, it bothered her that no one seemed to notice her frowns while she went back and forth between the kitchen and dining room. They were all too busy laughing and talking… all the time. As the children grew, sometimes Rose would attempt to help, but Grandma would always gesture for her to sit back down so she could hear the rest of a story or ask her a question to hear her point of view.

"Let's go in the living room, so we can stretch out, I'm about to bust."

"Me too Grandma," said Lil' Adam.

"You barely ate much, when your daddy was your age he could eat three, four times that much."

"Thank God I played a lot of ball and got plenty exercise."

"Or we would call you 'fat daddy'," laughed Lillie Mae.

"I wouldn't have been your daddy because your momma would not have looked my way." On his way to the living room, he playfully reached his arms around his wife's waist from behind, kissing her on the neck, while she cleaned off the table. "Would you baby?"

"Stop now, you see I got work to do."

"Don't get too tired, I have a surprise to show you in my room once the children are in bed."

"I know about your surprises," she laughed, enjoying his attention. "I'm not going anywhere near you tonight. I'm in the room with the girls and you're in the room with your son."

Squeezing her tighter, he nibbled gently on her neck, "I'm telling you it's a surprise you never heard of."

"Go on boy," she pulled away with a stack of dishes.

"Tonight," he said blowing her a kiss and winking his eye.

From the living room, he heard his mother, "Adam, on your way, look in the chifforobe in my pink housecoat pocket and get my snuff and my spit cup from under the kitchen sink." This was her favorite pastime after dinner, dipping snuff. Soon he handed her a small red tin filled with fine brown powder. She took a few pinches and placed the contents inside her bottom lip. Everyone found a comfortable area in the living room to stretch out, accept for Violet who headed straight for the kitchen.

"Grandma what's that you always putting in your mouth?"

"Snuff, kind of like tobacco, but you don't put it in a pipe, instead you place the powder in here." She pulled her bottom lip revealing a brown paste-like substance in her mouth. "Don't rightly know when I even started. I reckon I saw my mother dipping when I was your age, and when she wasn't looking I'd sneak and try it. After a while I liked it so much, been dipping ever since."

"Since you were twelve?"

"Don't get any ideas Lillie Mae," said Adam sitting in the middle of the couch with both arms outstretched above his daughters. "Your mother hears you mention dipping snuff and she'll tan your hide."

"Not in this house," Grandma quickly interjected with a strange laugh that suggested the statement was more serious than funny. She patted a tiny spot next to her on the recliner, "now come tell me what happened on the road that got my baby upset."

Getting up from the couch, she snuggled up close to her grandmother with barely enough room for them both. "Grandma you so cuddly," she said trying to squeeze her arms around her but not able to completely reach.

"I know baby, men like cuddly women. Tried to get your daddy to marry that cuddly girl from town, what was her name John?"

"She wasn't cuddly, she was fat," interjected Adam.

"What's wrong with fat?"

"Deena," said Grandpa sitting up in his recliner opposite his wife, turning to her in disbelief. "He married a fine girl. And you weren't 'cuddly' when I married you. You were nearly the same size Vee is now. You got 'cuddly' over the years."

Grandma quieted down as everybody laughed, "Maybe a small bit." Then everyone really started to laugh, because they all knew she had gotten quite large over the years. "Maybe it was that extra taste of apple pie."

"With ice cream on top," added Grandpa as they continued laughing.

For an instant Violet wondered what was so funny in the other room, but the piles of dishes and dirty pots and pans quickly turned her focus to the work at hand.

"Grandma, why white people hate us," asked Lillie Mae once the laughter stopped. "Is it only because we're colored?"

"Ahh baby is that what was bothering you," she said pulling her real close as her expression changed from happiness to sadness. "I always prayed my grandchildren wouldn't know anything about that type of mess. That's what it is to me, just plain ole' mess, one man hating another man because of the color of his skin, nothing but mess!"

"The man at the gas station kept calling Daddy, 'boy', and the other word that is even worse," she continued as a tear formed in her eye.

"Don't cry baby," she said with love but firmly. "Don't let other folk's hatred make you feel sad. I'll tell you like my mother told me, 'they can say what they want, long as they don't hit you'."

Lillie Mae squinted up at her grandmother trying to understand what she meant, "else what?"

"Else I would squeeze the life out of him with my bare hands," said Adam sitting up from the couch.

"That's why you wouldn't let me use the bathroom there?"

"I knew I couldn't stay in that place much longer."

"Baby your father was trying to keep you safe."

"But we had to use the bathroom outside."

"I didn't tell you all the times your grandfather made me use the bathroom in the woods…"

Everyone smiled anticipating the rest of the story, forgetting about the man at the gas station, as warmth and family closeness replaced sadness and anger.

"Let me tell you," said Grandma squeezing Lillie Mae affectionately. "We came down to visit you for Easter this one year and it was pretty cold outside. Remember that time John?"

"Sure do. Wasn't snow still on the ground before we left?"

"I don't remember that, but it was too cold to be using the bathroom outside," she smiled as Lillie Mae laid her head on her shoulder.

"Grandma are there signs on bathrooms here separating people?" said Lil' Adam laying on the floor with a pillow from the couch.

"Oh no baby, we don't have 'Whites only' signs up here, but the further south you go is when the problems start. And, if a bathroom has a 'Colored only' sign, you better off going in the woods. This particular time, your grandfather tried to make me use the bathroom ten times before we left the house, since he tries to drive all the way South without stopping."

"I stop for gas," interrupted Grandpa.

"This one time," she continued after looking over at him with a smirk shaking her head. "My stomach started rumbling and growling something awful."

"And we didn't need gas."

"And I couldn't wait until we did."

"Then she nagged and nagged a thousand times, for nearly fifty miles."

"It wasn't that far," she put her head back and sighed. "Who is telling the story anyway?"

"Tell your side."

"Finally, when I almost you-know-what in my clothes, he pulled over on the side of the road, the closest tree was a half-mile into the woods."

"Now Deena, it wasn't that far."

"Was to me, stomach cramping and gurgling, and you want me to walk a half-mile into the woods… by myself."

"By yourself," asked Adam concerned, hoping she really was exaggerating.

"By myself," she answered matter-of-factly, as if Grandpa would get in trouble because she told on him.

"Son," he replied, pointing in his defense. "She had to walk far as from here to that coffee table."

"And I'm out there in the cold, stomach bubbling, wide open country, miles from nowhere, trying to get behind a tree before another car drives by and gets an eye full of my hinder parts. Suddenly, I heard something moving in the woods like footsteps coming right at me. I tried to hurry up and wipe myself without falling over, but I couldn't move fast enough…. It kept coming closer and closer and closer."

Grandma paused as everyone held their breath anticipating what would happen next. For a few seconds, the only sound was the quiet rumbling of pots and pans from the kitchen. "Then, I yelled out, JOHN ADAM, as loud as I could."

"She practically gave me a heart attack. I ran fast as I could through the trees tripping and stumbling, scared to death. Thought for sure something had plum taken her into the woods, and I'd never see your grandmother again."

"Whatever it was, the sound stopped, don't know if it was from me hollering or your grandfather flying through the woods like a bat outta' hell…"

"Momma," said Adam shaking his head surprised at his mother's use of words.

"I'm telling the truth son."

"What was in the woods Grandma?" said Lillie Mae entrenched in the story.

"Believe it was a grizzly bear," she nodded. "I thought I saw something large, black, and hairy behind the trees."

"There are no grizzly bears in those woods."

"We weren't in the woods, we were in the mountains."

"Deena, it still wasn't a grizzly bear."

"Oh hush," said Grandma waving her hand reaching for her spit cup.

Adam smiled watching his parents bicker back and forth same as they did when he was growing up. The good thing was that before the night was over they would be hugging.

"Which way you come son?" said Grandpa John changing the subject pushing his recliner back elevating his feet.

"We took mostly Highway-60, to 13, to Highway-7," he said proudly.

"See that's why you had problems. When you travel the highways, you stay mostly in the south until you get on Highway-7 heading north, always had problems when I went that way."

"I hated that way," said Grandma reaching over for her spit cup.

"Now when we come down to visit, we take Interstate-70 across to Interstate-64, for as long as we can, before we head South on Interstate-75, lot faster and many clean welcoming bathrooms along the way."

"Everything's all cleaned up, Mrs. Williams," said Violet squeezing on the couch next to her husband, exhausted from the long drive and having to clean the kitchen, where it seemed every dish and pot in the house needed washing. It was going to be a long four days, she thought to herself.

Adam pulled her close to him and kissed her on the cheek. He knew how tired she was, yet she never hesitated to help. He knew his mother loved to cook, but never liked to clean-up afterwards, which always fell to him and his father, now her.

"You so sweet," said Grandma.

"Yes, she is," said Adam squeezing her on the hip, out of everyone's sight, only his father noticed.

"I reckon you all must be tired," he said winking at his son.

"Yes sir, it was a long trip," said Adam, stretching his arms and pretending to yawn.

"Well settle in, so you can get some rest," said Grandma rocking back and forth attempting to roll out the chair. "Got a big day of cooking ahead, I know the men folk will be watching that television and all them football games."

"Yes ma'am," said Lil' Adam enthusiastically, jumping up to help his grandmother out the chair. Aside from the hugs and kisses, all the food, and the funny stories, watching television was the best thing about going to visit their grandparents in Kansas City.

"Hear the Cleveland Browns are playing tomorrow," said Grandpa sitting up almost as excited as his grandson was. "Got that new boy… named Jim Brown, I think."

"Yes sir, voted MVP last year," answered Lil' Adam with pride, always ready to talk about sports.

"MV what?" said Grandma wanting to be involved in all conversations.

"MVP, Grandma," he said respectfully. "That stands for Most Valuable Player.

"Colored boy?" she looked impressed.

"Came out of Syracuse University, up there in New York," joined in Adam, feeling revived as well.

"Colored boy … in football," said Grandpa nodding. "Not many of them in sports."

"One day there will be more."

"I believe you baby."

"But I tell you, that boy can run," continued Grandpa. "Did you ever see him play?"

"No, only heard it on the radio," said Lil' Adam putting his head down. "On account of we don't…"

"Have a television," interrupted Lillie Mae fully awake as well. "Grandma can you believe we don't have a television yet…"

"Lillie Mae," her mother sighed.

"Grandma," she continued giving her a big squeeze. "We are the only people in the neighborhood without a television." Her intentions were not to aggravate her mother, but she knew if she was going to make a pitch for a television, now was the time.

"Lillie Mae, we already talked…" started Violet.

"The whole neighborhood?" interrupted Grandma. One thing she prided herself on, and her grandchildren knew it, was being first, first to buy a house in an all-white area of town, first in the family to buy a new car, and first in the family to buy a television.

"The WHOLE neighborhood," she added thickly pouring on the emotion.

"Umh, umh, umh," Grandma said shaking her head in disbelief.

"I begged and begged them to get us one, begged and begged."

"We can't have our baby begging for a television, can we John?"

"Seems like Violet has talked …"

"I won't have my baby begging," she interrupted not bothering to hear what he had to say, hugging her granddaughter tightly. "Don't worry. We'll see what we can do."

"Thank you Grandma," said Lillie Mae kissing her on the cheek.

"Me too," said Lil' Adam kissing her on the other side.

Rose who had been listening all along kept her eyes closed, pretending to be sleep, not wanting to be part of the television controversy. Besides, she agreed with her mother and Grandma Mae, that television was a waste of time, aside from dance shows of course.

Violet stared intently at her baby girl hoping she would look her way, but she would not. "Soon as I get my hands on her," she said to herself.

Adam felt her body tense up, and gently rubbed her arm. He knew the game Lillie Mae was playing, having played it many times himself as a child. However, he also knew his wife despised manipulation of any type.

"Honey you got the suitcases in the room," she asked trying to sound as pleasant as possible.

"Um-hum," he answered calmly still rubbing her arm knowing he had lots to fix before bedtime.

"We best be getting to bed," she said wiggling away from him and standing to leave. "We had a long day."

"You go on then," said Grandma sadly indifferent. "I'm going to fix some hot chocolate with marshmallows…anybody want some?"

"Yes Grandma," all three grandchildren said in unison.

"And I baked a fresh batch of chocolate chip cookies this morning to go with it. I'll warm them up, so they'll be nice and hot."

"Yummy," said Lillie Mae as she followed her grandmother into the kitchen, not daring to look her mothers' way.

"Come on Lil' Adam and Rose, I want to hear everything that's going on back home, school, church, family, everything."

Violet watched as all three children followed by her father-in-law head for the kitchen leaving the two of them alone. She sat wondering could they really want hot chocolate and cookies, after eating such a large meal a couple hours ago. Faintly she heard her mother-in-law, "You got a boyfriend yet Rose?"

"No ma'am."

"She does too," shouted Lillie Mae.

"She forgot I told her to mind her own business," said Violet completely frustrated.

"Come on," said Adam taking her hand and leading her out the room. "We got thirty minutes before hot chocolate time is over."

"What?" she whispered.

"Remember I told you I had a surprise to show you." He looked at her slyly, leading her into his old room, quietly closing the door behind them.

"Adam don't try anything funny with me… I am *not* in the mood."

"Shh," he whispered putting his finger to his lips.

In the distance, they heard laughter and muffled sounds from the kitchen. Once inside the room, he passionately kissed her. She melted in his arms like a young girl slipping away for a secret kiss.

"This is the surprise… I knew you didn't have a surprise."

"You did, huh," he said trying to kiss her again, but she stopped him this time.

"I'm going to get them chaps so they can go to bed," she said pushing away from him. "They'll be up all-night eating cookies and drinking chocolate. Then tomorrow they'll be sick."

"Look at this before you go," he said reaching in his pocket pulling out a small black box. "Happy Anniversary sweetheart."

Forgetting all her prior frustrations, she took the small black box. "Adam our anniversary isn't for weeks."

"I know sometimes it gets a bit tough for you, with my mother and all the cleaning you have to do. It's supposed to be a vacation, but you do more work here then you do at home. I wanted to let you know how much I appreciate you."

"Oh baby," she said quickly kissing him and opening the small black box containing a thin gold necklace with a sparkling cross pendant. "Adam it's beautiful." She turned around and lifted her long black hair for him to place it around her neck.

"I love it," she said admiring how it shined on her neck from the mirror's reflection. "Thank you."

"You're welcome," smiling he turned the lights out. "Now where were we, time is running out." He picked her up in his strong arms, carried her over to his boyhood twin bed, gently laid her down, and kissed her once again, this time she offered no resistance.

* * *

"I am so full Grandma," said Lillie Mae rubbing her stomach as they walked into the living room. Her mother and father were sitting on the couch looking very happy, but not sleepy.

"You ready for bed," asked Violet very pleasantly.

"Yes ma'am," she answered, confused at her mother's change in attitude. She knew from the angry glances her mother gave her before going to have cocoa, that she was in trouble, but now all seemed forgiven. She smiled as she sat cozily next to her mother.

"Is that a new necklace," asked Rose.

"Yes, your father gave it to me when you were in the kitchen."

Adam smiled proudly as everyone came to look at the golden necklace. Grandpa looked proudly over at his son, as their eyes met, they both nodded knowing he had resolved all previous frustrations.

* * *

As the women prepared Thanksgiving dinner, the men sat in the living room enjoying every minute of the televised football game. Amidst the shouts of "Run Boy Run", Violet would come in from the kitchen to see them jumping up cheering for Jim Brown. Maybe she had to admit that television was not completely bad. Her husband, son, and father-in-law appeared completely engulfed in the excitement of the Cleveland Browns.

"Vee, Vee, come watch," said Adam pulling her to sit on his lap. "That boy can *run.*"

"I told you," said Grandpa enjoying every minute of the game. "Last week he ran over three hundred yards against The Washington Redskins."

They all watched Jim Brown number thirty-two, weave in and out of the other players who futilely attempted to grab him. He was too fast and woefully the other team's score fell far behind. A touchdown was eventually going to happen, because even when another player managed to tackle him, it took three or four other players to drag him down.

"Dinner will be ready in thirty minutes," said Grandma mixing up a bowl of cornbread with no interest in football. "That game best be over by then."

"We'll be in directly Deena," not taking his eyes off the game.

Violet kissed her husband on the cheek, knowing it was her time. "See you baby." Before leaving, she rubbed the top of her son's head and began to sing, "hi-ho-hi-ho it's off to work I go." No one noticed. Once she was in the kitchen she heard, "Run Boy Run," followed by, "TOUCHDOWN!"

* * *

After dinner, everyone sat around looking as stuffed as the Thanksgiving turkey used to look. Grandma coerced the entire family to consume excessive amounts of turkey, dressing, rabbit, rice, gravy, potato salad, rolls, fried chicken, turnip greens, candied yams, lemonade, iced tea, followed by coconut cake, pound cake, apple pie, and ice cream, almost to the point of regurgitation.

"I can't eat another bite," moaned Lillie Mae leaning back rubbing her stomach.

"I know baby," answered her mother, sympathetically, but unable to overrule her mother-in-law's persistence for everyone to 'have some more', almost to the point of gluttony.

Normally once their stomachs had settled the entire family would go roller-skating, but this year they found themselves wobbling into the living room, turning on the television to watch "The

Honeymooners". A new family tradition was beginning. As the evening progressed, sounds of snoring replaced sounds of laughter.

Violet was the first one to awaken from the food-induced slumber with Adam's head on her lap, sound asleep. She looked around to see her mother-in-law in her favorite chair, feet stretched out, snoring. Her father-in-law, separated from his wife by a small coffee table to hold glasses, cups, newspapers, and other items needed for their television viewing pleasure, snoring also. Her children, all comfortable on the floor with pillows, were sound asleep. "Momma said that picture box wasn't good for nothing," she said loudly, easing slowly from under her husband's head as he turned to get comfortable without her. "I reckon it is good for something…putting everybody to sleep."

Walking into the kitchen, she sighed heavily, looking around at all the dirty dishes, pots and pans, remembering what her mother-in-law said right after dinner, 'let's watch one show until our food settles, then we will clean the kitchen'.

"I guess one show turned to two shows, now the picture box is watching everybody except me." Shaking her head, she began the process of tackling the aftermath of their Thanksgiving feast. Her only entertainment was the sounds of laughter from the television.

When Violet was drying the last pot, exhausted, her mother-in-law walked slowly into the kitchen. "Baby why didn't you say something, I could have helped you clean up everything. I feel so bad, you been working in this kitchen ever since you got here."

"Oh, no ma'am, I'm fine," she lied.

"You sure?"

"Yes ma'am."

"Well goodnight. I'm going to get these babies into bed, so they can get some rest, least I can do."

"Babies… Rest…," Violet thought to herself, "must not be talking to me." She grabbed the broom and quietly began sweeping, too tired to complain. The kitchen sparkled as she turned off the light and headed to bed. Lying next to her husband, she felt more like the maid than ever before.

"I've been waiting on you to come to bed," he snuggled next to her.

She wanted to be honest about how tired she was, and how much work she had done since they got there, but before she could gather the exact words to say, she heard him softly snoring.

"Goodnight," she sighed kissing him on the cheek.

* * *

Morning found Violet washing the same dishes, pots and pans she washed the previous day and the day before that. "Why in the world is this kitchen always such a mess?" she said aloud. Unfortunately, no one was present to hear her complaints, since her mother-in-law insisted everyone watch an episode of "The Red Skelton Show" right after breakfast.

"Momma, you're missing it," said Lillie Mae running into the kitchen excited. "It is sooo funny. Hurry up before it goes off."

Before Violet could answer, her daughter returned to the living room to join the laughter of the others already in progress. "There is no way we are getting a picture box, television, … whatever you call it, we not."

Violet hurriedly finished drying the last of the pots and quickly swept the floor, determined to get her family off the couch and back on track with their after-Thanksgiving roller-skating tradition. As she entered the living room, her in-laws once again were sitting in their favorite loungers, fast asleep. Her family sat absorbed, watching what appeared to be a courtroom scenario.

"Come on over here baby," Adam patted an empty spot on the couch. "We're watching Perry Mason, "the case of the restless redhead."

"I don't care," she exclaimed walking over to the television turning all the knobs at the bottom, one made the picture roll up and down, the other made it roll faster and faster.

"Momma why you do that?" said Lillie Mae loud enough to wake up her grandparents.

"What's going on?" said Grandma wiping the droll from the side of her mouth.

"No more picture shows," she answered frustrated as she kept turning knobs until she finally found the one to turn off the television. "There!"

"Now we'll never know who it was," said Lillie Mae disappointed.

"Never know who?" said Grandma, her eyes fluttering as she attempted to wake up.

"Nothing Mrs. Williams, we're all getting ready to go roller-skating." Violet stood her ground, ready to defend her actions against the television even if no one would stand with her.

"Thought you'd be gone by now," she said surprising her daughter-in-law. She pushed the footrest down and began rocking her large frame toward the end of the chair. "Get on out of here and have some fun. Didn't know it was so late, time for me to start lunch… Baby help me up."

Father and son jumped up simultaneously. One on each side. "Momma, what would you do without us?"

"I don't know baby, struggle by myself or wake up your father." She shook her husband on the foot, "John Adam wake up, are you going with my babies roller-skating?"

"What, what," he responded quickly pushing the footrest down.

"I said," she put her right hand on her hip and tilted head to the right appearing frustrated. "Are you going roller-skating?"

"Yes, yes of course," he answered standing up without assistance, his shirt twisted around from his long nap.

"First fix your britches," said Grandma walking over to straighten his clothes, attempting to rub out some of the wrinkles with her hand. "Don't want you looking like an ole' timey farmer."

"Yes dear," he smiled. After thirty-five years of marriage, he learned to say as little as possible and allow her to do to him whatever she pleased.

"Momma he's good," his son intervened, wondering if he would allow his wife to do that when he was older, he hoped not. "We're just going skating for a bit. Violet thinks we watched enough television."

She frowned at him for blaming her.

"Oh nonsense," said Grandma carrying her large frame into the kitchen. "You only making up for the shows you didn't see, since you don't have a television. Go on and have some fun, I'll have something special fixed by the time you get back."

Violet stood frozen for an instant as a flash of dread came over her at the thought of washing… cleaning… sweeping…everything again.

"You all right baby?" her husband asked gently putting her arms into her coat since she appeared in a trance.

"Yes," she shook herself back to reality. "I need some fresh air."

"Well let's get going. Pa you driving?"

"Son, I thought you'd never ask."

* * *

"Did you have a good time skating?" said Grandma standing at the front door dispensing hugs and kisses to everyone.

"Sure did," answered her son, first in line to enjoy his mother's hug. "And you know I had the best moves on the floor."

Next came Lil' Adam, nudging his father out of the way, "but none of them can skate like me."

"Don't know how you didn't trip over your feet, staring at them girls," said Lillie Mae.

"They were staring at me," he responded after plopping on the couch.

Rose smiled quietly, accepting her hug and kiss as they both came in the house, ahead of Grandpa and Violet not quite up the front steps before the door closed.

"The girls staring at my baby," said Grandma walking over to her grandson pinching his cheeks. "That's because you so handsome, like your father was."

"What you mean was?" laughed Adam taking a seat next to his son.

"He had the girls staring at him too Mrs. Williams," said Violet hanging up her coat and sitting next to her husband.

"Sure he did, always has, don't let that get you all riled up."

"Oh, she gets all riled up, all the time," he said tickling her and kissing her on the neck. "But I keep her so happy and full of loving…"

"Adam!" said Violet feeling her face blush.

"That's my boy," laughed Grandpa.

"Like you know," said Grandma with a smirk.

He walked over to her, put his long arms around her, and kissed her on the neck. "In all these years, never heard you complain."

"Go on now you ole' geezer," giggling like none of her grandchildren heard before. "Get washed up, I got something special to eat."

Suddenly Violet felt a flash of dread as everyone else smiled happily.

By the time they returned, Grandma had sat on the table, a large bowl of fried okra and corn, a platter of cheeseburgers with sliced tomatoes and onions sitting next to it, and individual bottles of orange soda.

"Grandma I love you," said Lillie Mae squeezing her tightly. "Everything is my favorite."

"Mine too," added Lil' Adam.

"Hold on, I got one more thing…"

Soon she came back with a paper towel lined plate of homemade fried potatoes. "Be careful, they hot out the frying pan."

"Frying pan?" repeated Violet grimacing as she thought of how many pots and pans it took to make this huge lunch full of 'favorites', but no one noticed her discomfort.

"Pass the burgers."

"Pass the potatoes, never seen none made like this," said Adam taking a big scoop and loading in onto his already full plate.

"We stopped down at the diner one Saturday for a hamburger and the girl asked if we wanted to try 'wedges'. We never heard of them before, but we tried them. I figured I'd make some with your burgers, see how you like them, with my special touches of course."

"They are the best, I love them Grandma," said Lillie Mae and everyone else agreed through murmurs and nods.

"These here taste a heap better than the ones at the diner," said Grandpa winking at his wife.

"You know I had to spice them up a bit."

"That's why I married you."

"Oh John," she said walking over and giving him a hug, followed by a kiss on the lips. The grandchildren froze in their seats, jaws hanging open with food, witnessing their open displays of affection.

"I figure why go to a place and pay for food when they act like they don't want you there anyway, just stay home and cook it yourself."

"At least they don't tell you to go around the back," said Lil' Adam thinking of his father as he took a big bite of his double-decker hamburger.

"That makes me feel sad Grandma, like I am nobody," added Lillie Mae.

Everyone was quiet for a moment as they stopped eating long enough to see the hurt in each other's eyes, having all felt the pain she spoke of at one time or another.

"I know baby," she said reaching over to squeeze her close. "I thought things would be better by now."

"Aren't they better here, in the North?" she asked hopefully. "I didn't see any signs like we have at home."

"We don't have signs you can see, but the hearts of people still need to change, even here."

"Now, now," said Grandpa sitting opposite Lillie Mae and patting her on the arm. "This is our family Thanksgiving weekend, no need to get into how to change the north and the south. Son, pass me some of that okra and corn while it's still hot."

Everyone's focus returned to the prepared meal as they started their second and third helpings, accept for Violet who wondered why her husband seemed so happy when eating his mother's food. Later, once they were finally in bed, after all the television shows on the family's part and all the cleaning on her part, she had a chance to ask him what had bothered her since they arrived.

"Adam, do you like my cooking?"

"You know I do," he answered holding her in the darkness.

"Best in the world?"

"In the whole *wide* world."

"Better than your mother's?"

Realizing where she was heading with her questions, he pulled her closer. "Different than my mother's… but I dig your desserts the most."

She smiled to herself amused by his attempts to make her feel better. "You didn't have dessert tonight."

"You the dessert," he whispered biting her gently on the shoulder. "Umm, now that's sweet."

She relaxed deeper into his embrace forgetting her jealous feelings and insecurities. She resisted mentioning that his constant accolades regarding his mother's cooking made her feel inferior about her own cooking. And how no one seemed to notice her struggle to maintain an immaculately clean kitchen while they sat watching hours and hours of television, nor did anyone offer to help, except Rose, once. She had every right to start a fight, but she didn't, and chose instead to rest in the arms of the man who had the ability to redirect her thoughts and change her mind regarding any anxieties she had, or thought she had. Besides, they were going home tomorrow, maybe next year she would take up the fight. For now, she preferred to focus on her job as a wife, the most rewarding of all. "Adam that tickles," she whispered as he nibbled on her earlobe.

* * *

The way home was less eventful, thanks to Grandpa giving his son directions for the interstate that had nicer bathrooms and friendlier gas stations. "And son, if you can't see the gas station as soon as you exit, don't bother looking, just get back on the interstate and take the next exit." The men loaded up the car with suitcases ready to say their good-byes. Everyone was sad to leave but happy to go.

"No need to stop for food," said Grandma coming to the door with two shoeboxes filled with fried chicken and bologna sandwiches. "Adam, stop every now and then so the children can get a cold soda."

"Yes momma," he kissed her and received the tightest hug. "I love you."

"Oh baby, I love you too, don't make me cry."

"Thank you, Mrs. Williams," said Violet kissing her mother-in-law on the cheek wondering when she had time to fry chicken, but glad she didn't have to clean. She sat the boxes on the floor in front of her, although no one could possibly be hungry after stuffing themselves with hotcakes, sausages, eggs, and orange juice.

"Good-bye Grandma," the children echoed as they received their final hugs and kisses.

"Here baby," she rushed over to the car to wrap the blue scarf she knitted around Adam's neck. "This will help you stay warm."

"Thanks Momma," he said admiring his scarf. "When did you have time to make this?"

"Was almost finished when you came," she kissed him on the cheek. "And take this coffee to help you stay awake."

"Vee can drive if I need help."

Violet looked up from the front seat, thankful her husband had spoken up for her and grateful to be finally going home.

"Have a good trip, son," he said patting him on the back as they embraced.

"Thanks Pa, take care of Momma."

"Always do," he smiled.

"I'm going to be sending a surprise," said Grandma waving as they drove away.

"What does she mean Adam?"

"I have no idea," he answered focusing his attention on the long drive home.

"Maybe it's a television," chimed Lillie Mae from the backseat.

"My goodness, I hope not."

"Didn't you like the television shows?"

"I was too busy in the kitchen," she answered with a touch of sarcasm.

19 RUN RUN RUDOLPH

Life finally returned to normal for the William's household as they prepared for the upcoming Christmas holiday with cleaning, decorating, baking, and preparations for a family get together. "White Christmas" by Clyde McPhatter and the Drifters played in the background, as Adam and the children decorated the tree singing along. "I.. I.. I.. I'm dreaming of a White Christmas just like the ones I used to know," sang Lil Adam to the higher part and Adam singing the lower part, "And may all your Christmas-ses' be white," ending with Lillie Mae singing the last part, "jingle bells jingle bells jingle all the way." They all joined together to sing, "ouuu."

Amidst their singing, Violet heard someone knocking on the door. "Who could that be? Rose make sure that last batch doesn't burn. I would never hear the last of it if we brought over burnt cookies for dinner."

"I won't Momma. I will mix up an extra batch of oatmeal raisin cookies. Grandma Mae wants to take some to the store."

"That's fine." Wiping her floured hands on her apron, she passed her husband and two other children still singing. "Did y'all hear somebody knocking at the door?"

"No ma'am, but there's a big Montgomery Ward truck outside," said Lillie Mae hanging a red shiny ball on the tree.

"Then why didn't you get the door."

The person banged on the door harder and harder, finally overshadowing the music.

"I'll get the door," said Adam snatching the door open with a frown.

"Are you Adam Williams Jr.," he asked timidly.

"Yes I am."

"Sign here please."

Once Adam signed on the clipboard, the man turned without a word and walked back to the truck. A few minutes later, he returned with a large box on a cart. Everyone squeezed in the doorframe to watch him hoist the large package, step-by-step-by-step up to the top of the stairs, then wheeled the box over to the door, slid it off the cart, and walked away. They all stood staring at each other wondering what was in the box, as the man backed the truck out the driveway and never looked back. No one commented on his rude behavior, everyone was too excited.

"Let's see what's in the box," said Lillie Mae breaking the silence. "I bet you I know what it is."

The two men lifted the box into the living room and everyone joined in ripping the cardboard away to reveal a … television.

Lillie Mae jumped up and down, "I knew it."

"Oh no," said Violet letting out a large sigh and shaking her head.

"Just in time for football," said Adam.

"And the fight," said Lil' Adam. "Can I invite Juan over to watch it?"

"Oh no," said Rose running out the room. "The cookies are burning!"

"She's not worried about cookies, but about Juan coming over."

"Lillie Mae, what I tell you about meddling in other folk's business," said Violet turning her attention back to the television.

"Plug it up Daddy," said Lillie Mae, completely ignoring her mother. "Plug it up, this is the best gift ever."

"Where you want it Vee?"

"Adam, you know how I feel. I don't want anything to do with this here picture box."

"Television," said Lillie Mae dusting it off with a tissue. "It's so pretty and new."

"Don't correct me Chile'," her mother said sternly.

"Yes ma'am," she said quickly not wanting to upset her mother on this special day.

"I'm not going to let this, this *THING*, from your mother, upset our holidays!"

"I know baby," said Adam embracing her in his arms. "She didn't mean any harm."

"It will do harm," reluctantly lying her head on his chest.

"We won't let it." He rocked her slightly in his arms, then twirled her around as "Santa Baby" by Eartha Kitt, played in the background.

As the song ended, she felt somewhat better. "Promise?"

"Promise, no harm will be done," he said kissing her on top of the head. "Now where do you want me to put it?"

"Put it here Daddy, put it here," said Lillie Mae satisfied her father had solved the problem of having a television.

"No, no, by the window," said Lil' Adam moving a chair to make room.

"The tree is by the window," she said waving her hand at his apparently bad choice. "Over here is better."

"No over here is better."

"There is no plug over there," she said sticking out her tongue.

"The sun will block the picture over there."

"Here we go," said Violet.

"Don't worry sweetheart, we'll work it out," reassured Adam still holding her while there two youngest argued where the television should go. "Okay, okay, that's enough you two. Once we finish the tree we'll figure out a place for the box, I mean television."

Lillie Mae looked up from the floor, attempting a smile for her mother.

"Tree first," said Violet not giving in to her daughter sympathy seeking looks. "And I mean it." She returned to the kitchen confident her husband would work things out.

"Is this good Daddy?"

"That looks like a good place. But let's finish the tree first like your mother said."

"Okay," she answered willing to make the compromise. "At least we finally have one."

The wonderful aroma of cookies, cakes, and pies filled the house. Each Christmas the family came together for a holiday feast. Violet and Rose were responsible for the desserts, Ruby brought her famous macaroni and cheese, and Grandma Mae prepared the meats, vegetables, and breads.

While baking commenced in the kitchen, the other family members finished decorating the tree. Normally there were arguments about where to position the ornaments or how to hang the garland, with Adam intervening to make the final decision. This year, Christmas songs played softly, no arguing, no bickering, no intervening, nothing. "It's awfully quiet in there. We better go check on them!"

As they entered the living room, the first thing they noticed was the tree. All the decorations were on, but you could tell it was a rush job. Violet started to voice her disapproval but quickly realized no one would be concerned, because they all sat intensely watching two women on television attempting to wrap chocolate balls on a slow rolling conveyor belt.

"Mom, its *I Love Lucy*," said Lillie Mae smiling and patting an empty spot on the couch next her. "Come sit down."

Violet hesitated. "You know I don't like this television." But the longer she watched the more she found herself laughing, as the ladies frantically ate more and more chocolate balls while the machine went faster and faster.

"What are they doing?" said Rose squeezing in next to her mother on the couch as the rest of the family laughed hysterically.

Now the machine rolled along at high-speed, but the women were determined not to let any chocolate balls pass without wrapping each one first, an almost impossible feat. They began stuffing chocolate balls in their baker's hat, down their blouses, and in their mouths.

The phone rang several times before anyone noticed, so busy laughing to the point of tears. Lillie Mae finally jumped up just in time.

"Hello, yes, we love it," she shouted not allowing her grandmother an opportunity to say much. "We're watching *I Love Lucy*, it is SOOO funny. You are watching it too… Okay I will tell them… Thank you so much for the television… It is the best Christmas present ever… Good-bye Grandma, I love you." Before hanging up, she quickly put the phone back to her ear, "kiss Grandpa for me."

"Grandma wanted to know if we got the television. I told her we loved it and we were watching *I Love Lucy*."

"We heard you," said Lil' Adam annoyed he couldn't hear the television, vying for more room on the couch as she sat down next to him. "Move over!"

"You move over," she responded poking him in the side.

"No, you move over!"

"That's it show's over," said Violet walking over to the television turning all the knobs.

"I'll get it," said Adam jumping up.

"See what you did," said Lil' Adam.

"You mean what you did," said Lillie Mae elbowing him again.

"That's enough from both of you. Your brother and I have to get a haircut anyway before it gets too crowded."

"Can you drop me off at the record store," asked Rose.

"I wanted to see a movie," said Lillie Mae.

"That's why I don't like this… this… thing! We all have something we could be doing besides sitting in front of it … doing nothing." Violet stood as each one of them looked at her as if they had no idea why she was frustrated.

"Forget it," she said shaking her head walking out the room.

Before anyone could say a word, she came back with her hat on tilted slightly to the side, her purse on her forearm, and the car keys in her hand. "I am on my way to town to check on the Gist's. If you want to sit here and watch that… television, you go ahead."

With that, she put on her coat from the hallway closet and headed out the front door. As if a bell had sounded, they raced around intent on not being the last one out the house. Adam was first to grab his hat and coat out the closet immediately running out the front door. Followed one-step behind was Lil' Adam. Rose ran to her room, grabbed her purse, hat, and coat only a few seconds after her brother.

"Hey!" said Lillie Mae standing in the middle of the living room watching them leave one-by-one. "Wait for me!"

Instead of grabbing her coat and hat like the others, she ran to the window. Looking out she saw Lil' Adam jumping in the back seat. Rose ran down the steps putting her coat on before getting in the car and closing the door. Her mother started the car.

Lillie Mae panicked. She grabbed her coat… no hat. She ran to her room… no purse. "Oh well, no money anyway," she thought as she locked the door, ran down the steps with her coat in her hand as the car was pulling out the driveway.

"Hey," she ran yelling. "Wait for me." The car stopped.

As she approached the car, all she could hear was everyone's laughter. "Leave her Momma, Leave her," shouted Lil' Adam.

Lillie Mae started to cry, "Would you leave me?"

"No baby," her mother chuckled lightly getting out the driver's seat to let her sit in the front. "I wouldn't leave you."

"But I would," laughed Lil' Adam pushing her head down from the backseat.

"And I wouldn't let him," said her father wiping a tear from her face and kissing her on the cheek.

Riding down the road towards town, "A Lover's Question" by Clyde McPhatter, stirred their thoughts. For Violet, she was not able to shake the uneasiness in her stomach since The Honey Shack. Looking over at her husband, who turned to smile at her, she wondered if she should worry when they were apart. Adam thought about the words to the song also, determined to stay away from 'his lover' despite all the messages she sent his friends that she wanted to see him. And Rose wondered if Juan felt the same way she felt, since neither of them had spoken after the 'slow dance'.

"That's one of the records I want to buy," she said out loud.

"Drop us off at the barber shop first," said her brother. I know how you are when it comes to records."

"How am I, know-it-all?" said Rose irritated.

"SLOW!"

"Rose can you go with me to the Gist house? Patricia Ann will be there, and afterwards we'll see about your records?"

"Is that all you think about?" said Lil' Adam, enjoying an opportunity to aggravate his sister.

"And the lover's question she wants to ask Juan," added Lillie Mae from the front seat, immediately followed by a POP on the cheek from her mother.

"He'll probably be at the barbershop," said Lil' Adam moving over to elbow his sister, who immediately pushed him back, hard.

"Forget it," she sulked, staring out the window longing to run away.

"Leave your sister alone," said Adam turning to wink at his daughter. "Baby go with your mother, you'll get your records."

Rose felt much better as her father got out the car, feeling she had his support. She wanted to find out how Juan felt, but not if it meant embarrassment from dozens of men standing around gossiping in a barbershop.

"That looks like Mr. Leon's car. Rose come on in and say hello," said Lil' Adam taking a hit in the back of the head from his father.

She rolled her eyes and scooted to the middle of the backseat away from the window. Lillie Mae turned wanting to further aggravate her sister, but the look on her mothers' face warned her not too.

* * *

"Ms. Vee! Ms. Vee!" shouted Carl Jr. running down the driveway to meet them. "My mother's coming home today, Ms. Vee! She's finally coming home!"

Violet picked him up and squeezed him tightly. "I know, I know, are you happy?"

"Yes," he answered hugging her around the neck. "I am sooo happy I could just bust. Hi Lillie Mae, hi Rose, my mother's coming home today."

Lillie Mae thought to herself, "I heard you the first ten times." One glance from her mother made her quickly change her mind before speaking her true thoughts aloud. "That is crazy."

He stared at her confused by her choice of words.

"That means she is happy for you," said Rose ruffling his hair. "I am too."

"Crazy," he said looking forward to using this new word as much as possible.

"Hi Mrs. Williams, Hi Rose, Lillie Mae," said Patricia Ann standing at the kitchen screen door holding Elizabeth, dressed neatly in a blue dress with a white apron around her waist, her hair tied up in a ponytail with a white ribbon. "Come on in, I'm fixing some lunch."

"Lillie Mae, you want to see my new train set Miss Patty helped me put together. It is crazy!"

"Crazy?" asked Patricia Ann.

"Lillie Mae taught him a new word," said Rose shaking her head.

"Come on," he continued taking her hand pulling her. "It goes all around my room. I love it. It is so crazy!"

She smiled as Carl Jr. led her up the stairs, despite his chattering non-stop, she enjoyed his company, maybe a younger brother was better than an older one.

"Don't be long, lunch is almost ready."

"Seems like you are getting on pretty good," said Violet taking a seat at the kitchen table followed by Rose.

"Yes ma'am," said Patricia Ann, sitting the baby on a pallet in the corner of the kitchen surrounded with toys like Violet taught her. "The children are wonderful, no problem at all. They are like my brothers, only they mind better."

"I am very happy for you," said Violet noticing the clean kitchen.

"And Carl, I mean Mr. Gist," she smiled, practically blushing. "He treats me like I was part of the family."

"You call him Carl?" she asked with a concerned look on her face.

"No ma'am, I don't… most of the time, but he wants me too." Patricia Ann avoided Violet's eyes and began slicing a large ham.

"I think it'd be best if you call him Mr. Gist."

"Yes ma'am."

"How is Mrs. Gist?" said Violet instinctively getting the bread and mayonnaise to help make the sandwiches.

"Ms. Daisy's coming home this afternoon."

"No, I mean *the* Mrs. Gist," said Violet with a smile, "the mother".

"Ohh her," she said sadly. "She stays upstairs in her room most of the time not saying much to me at all, except to call me negra' gal. Carl… Mr. Gist has asked her not to call me that many times, but she doesn't listen."

"Never has."

"The other day, Carl Jr. asked me why she calls me that. It broke my heart that he heard her. All I could say was 'I don't know'. I must have looked sad since he hugged me around the waist and said, 'I know your name is Miss Patty."

"Oh, that's so sweet," said Rose.

"Made me cry."

"Would make me cry too," said Violet slicing some tomatoes. "That boy is so sweet."

"Yes ma'am, he is. Are you staying for lunch?" she asked wondering why Violet was making so many sandwiches.

"No, Mr. Williams and Lil' Adam are waiting at the barbershop. I only stopped by to see how you were getting on since Ms. Daisy is coming home today, and to see if you needed help fixing dinner."

"Mr. Gist said he was taking the whole family to dinner," she said adding sugar to the freshly made lemonade. "He asked me if I would like to come, but I said no."

"That's good, they need some time together alone as a family."

"Yes ma'am."

Her sad tone worried Violet. She knew when she went home every day, Patricia Ann stayed because she said Mr. Gist wanted her to help put the children in bed. "Have you stayed every night and on the weekends too?"

"Yes ma'am."

"When was the last time you went home?" said Rose seeing her mother's concerns.

"Maybe a month ago," she answered looking up as if she could barely remember. "But I'm going home tonight after I help Ms. Daisy and the children get dressed for dinner."

"I know your mother will be glad to see you," said Violet putting her hand on the young girl's shoulder. "The Gist's are like family to me as well, but they are *not* your family."

"I know ma'am," she answered as tears formed in her eyes. "I gucss I got too attachcd."

"Don't cry, it's easy to get attached, they are wonderful people."

"But I need to be here for the children and Carl."

"I know the children and Mr. Gist need you, but Ms. Daisy will be here. This is her family baby. Let's see how she does her first week home."

"Yes ma'am, I will," she attempted a smile.

"Set the table for the children while I take this tray upstairs to Mrs. Gist."

"Do you want me to go with you?"

"Don't worry, I can handle her," smiled Violet with a wink.

"Ms. Vee, come look at my train," said Carl Jr. as she reached the top of the stairs holding the tray. "Isn't it crazy?"

"Yes it sure is crazy," smiled Violet. "Wash your hands for lunch."

"Yes ma'am. Come on Lillie Mae."

Her eyes pleaded with her mother. "Is it time to go?"

Carl Jr. pulled her into the bathroom. "We got some yellow soap and some white soap, which one do you want?"

"The yellow," she said reluctantly, already tired of her new little brother.

"That's my favorite too. The white one smells like flowers or something, but the yellow one smells like nothing. I don't want to smell like flowers, do you Lillie Mae?"

Violet knocked on the door to Mrs. Gist's room.

"Who that!" said an angry voice.

"Good afternoon," said Violet pleasantly as she entered the room.

"That you negra' gal?"

"No, Mrs. Gist, it's not Patricia Ann, it's me Violet."

"Umh, what you want," she said bitterly sitting in a plush armchair next to green ceiling-to-floor draperies, pulled to the side allowing sunlight to flow freely into the room. In the corner a small dresser filled with bracelets, necklaces, and other cosmetic jewelry sat directly across from a large queen-sized bed, neatly made, covered with a white laced quilt and several decorative pillows. Dressed in a long black skirt with a tan shirt and ivory brooch around the collar, she frowned when she saw Violet with the lunch tray, despite being hungry.

"I came to bring you something to eat and see if you need anything before Mr. Gist comes home with Ms. Daisy."

"Umh, you need to teach that other negra' gal to come see if I need anything too," she said walking over to the small table near the bed. "Used to be a time when a negra' would come and ask what you needed… all day long if need be. This here gal brings the food two, three times a day and runs off, like I want to bite her or something."

"Mrs. Gist, maybe she doesn't like being called negra' gal when her name is Patricia Ann."

"Umh, I can't remember that."

"What can I get for you?"

"I need a pen and some paper to write my friend and tell her I'm coming home."

"Yes ma'am. Did you enjoy your stay?"

"Loved everything except that scaredy-cat negra' gal."

"Ma'am?" said Violet as if she did not hear her.

"When are you coming back to work?"

"I'll be here Monday morning ma'am."

"What you doing here today? Isn't today Saturday?"

"Yes ma'am, it is," she said placing a napkin on her lap. "I came by to make sure everything goes well when Ms. Daisy comes home."

"You the kinda' gal we used to have around here when I came up. What's your name?"

"Ms. Violet ma'am."

"Umh, that other gal is not like you, sneaking around all times of the night. She thinks I don't know what she is doing?"

"Yes ma'am," she answered wondering the same thing.

"Tell her she needs to check on me too."

"Yes ma'am, I will do that," said Violet with a smile. "Enjoy your lunch Mrs. Gist."

"Umh," was her only response.

Violet returned promptly with the pen and paper. "Here you go Mrs. Gist. I also brought you a couple books from the library."

"Umh, you a well-trained…gal, don't see them like you anymore…have to take you back to Boston with me."

"No ma'am, I'm fine here."

"How is it all you …," she hesitated. "All you colored gals want to be around Carl so much."

"Mr. Gist and Ms. Daisy treat us like we part of the family, not like servants."

"Umh," she said ignoring Violet's comments.

"Tell that… other colored gal to bring me up some more lemonade."

"Yes ma'am."

Violet came downstairs smiling as she entered the kitchen. The children, including Lillie Mae and Rose, were sitting at the table eating lunch.

"You're smiling, did it go well with Mrs. Gist," asked Patricia Ann.

"Best laugh than cry," she shrugged. "The bad news is she wants you to bring her some more lemonade. The good news is now she calls you colored gal instead of negra' gal."

"Well I guess coming from her, that's an improvement," she smiled getting up to take the lemonade.

"One more thing, it might help if you go in her room from time to time to see if she needs anything." Violet sat down to continue feeding Elizabeth. "She is from the old times when colored people waited on white people hand and foot."

"That sounds crazy like slavery," said Lillie Mae looking up from her sandwich.

"Slavery wasn't crazy, like good, was it Ms. Vee?" said Carl Jr.

"No baby, it was crazy like bad, not good at all, but don't mind yourself with that, eat your lunch."

"If anyone ever treats you like that Ms. Vee," he continued looking up at her with eyes filled with anger and sincerity.

"I know baby," she interrupted touched by his loyalty.

"And you too Ms. Patty."

"Thank you, Carl Jr.," she said kissing him on the cheek before leaving the room with the lemonade.

"I like Ms. Patty."

"She likes you too baby," said Violet trying to get Elizabeth to eat her vegetables. "Here comes the airplane full of peas."

"Zoom, zoom," she giggled as she opened her mouth.

Patricia Ann ran into the kitchen practically out of breath, "what you do to Mrs. Gist, she was almost nice to me."

"If you be nice to her, she'll be nice to you... sooner or later..."

All three girls and Carl Jr., looked at her in disbelief.

"Ms. Vee can you stay with us today," asked Carl Jr., as they were getting ready to leave.

"Not today baby, but I'll see you Monday bright and early."

As the girls were getting in the car, Violet pulled Patricia Ann to the side to speak with her without the children hearing. "I know Mr. Gist is a very kind man and he treats you very well, but remember he has a wife and family. We don't want anything to jeopardize their relationship, especially with Ms. Daisy coming home today."

Patricia Ann stood looking uncomfortable with her head slightly lowered. "Yes ma'am".

"Now if you cannot handle yourself properly with this family, maybe we should try and find you another one."

"No ma'am, that won't be necessary."

"Very well then," she replied hugging her before turning to leave. "And if you need a ride tonight, give us a call and we'll make sure you get home. You need to spend time with your own family for a while."

"Yes ma'am."

"Bye Ms. Vee," said Carl Jr., waving merrily from the porch as they drove away.

While driving, "Lonely Teardrops" by Jackie Wilson played softly in the background. The words from the song, 'just give me another chance for our romance', caused both Rose and Violet to look at each other.

"Momma, do you think Patricia Ann likes Mr. Gist?"

"I believe she does," answering sadly. "I spoke to her briefly and I hope she understands, otherwise she will have many lonely teardrops herself."

"Who Momma," asked Lillie Mae looking up from playing with her baby dolls in the backseat.

"Keep minding your own business," she smiled looking back at her daughter. "I need to focus anyway on getting to this barbershop."

Finally, she saw the road to town next to a ten-foot tall plastic Santa waving merrily in front of a sleigh filled with beautifully decorated presents, pulled by reindeer with white lights draped over their antlers and red garland around their necks. On top of every light pole in town were large decorative candles on one-side, and candy canes on the other, connected by silver strands of garland crossing throughout the street. The town bustled with activity as people greeted each other with smiles and well wishes, stopping only to admire the shop windows framed with green garland and filled with displays of wooden toy soldiers, miniature mangers, golden angels, and beautifully decorated Christmas trees. In the center of the town square stood a fifty-foot blue spruce, decorated with every type of ornament imaginable, and topped with a large white star that lit up at night. Around the base of the tree were red, green, and white poinsettias, handed out to residents, on a first-come basis, after the New Year. The busses were still empty of passengers, but no one seemed to matter.

Turning down the street leading to the colored section of town, Violet became nervous as she noticed several cars parked around the barbershop. "Rose, go check and see if your father is ready."

"Can't you blow the horn?"

"She's scared Juan will be in there."

"Go on Rose."

"Can't Lillie Mae go, please? She'll be glad to see who is in the barbershop, she so nosey."

"I am not."

"Is too," said Rose rolling her eyes.

"Please girls... Let's all go," said Violet quietly praying that Juan's father was not there.

The barbershop, crowded with men waiting for haircuts or standing around enjoying conversations, had only two barber chairs, Lil' Adam was in one and Juan was in the other.

"Hey baby," said Adam walking over with a fresh haircut looking extremely handsome. "You're back sooner than I thought."

"Your haircut looks good," she said nervously not used to being around so many men.

"Thanks," he said kissing her on the cheek. "I wanted to look nice for Christmas dinner."

"Daddy you always look nice," said Lillie Mae not embarrassed by all the men looking their way.

"What you know 'bout looking nice," he laughed squeezing her cheeks.

"You do look good," Violet blushed.

"Well I need to get haircuts more often," he smiled reaching around pinching her on the backside.

"Adam!" she jumped causing others to turn and notice them more. "We are in public."

"Violet?" said a voice from the waiting area. "Is that you?"

She watched as a very large man with a huge belly hanging over his pants started walking towards her. She wanted to run out the door, but it was too late, he recognized her, and she recognized him. She threw a quick disappointed look at Rose, who immediately felt guilty.

No wonder her mother did not want to come in, "Sorry Momma," she mouthed.

"Violet it's me Leon," he said moving quickly towards her with outstretched arms.

Adam stepped directly in front of her, causing Leon to step back, settling for a handshake instead of a hug.

"Leon?" said Violet acting as if she did not recognize him from when she first walked in the barbershop, a logical assumption since he changed so much from high school.

"I know, I know," he smiled slightly embarrassed holding his stomach. "I did put on a couple pounds."

"Only a couple," she said trying to sound as positive as she could. "How have you been?"

"Aside from eating too much, been doing good, real good," he said only able to see her partially since her husband still stood between them intensely staring. "Trying to find a job… Big Adam did you hear anything down at the railroad?"

"No not yet," he said dryly.

"You must be Rose?" he said starting to put his hand out but noticed the stares of her father intensify. "Juan said he was in your same grade. You sure is pretty, the spitting image of your mother when she was in high school."

"Thank you, sir."

"Call me Leon."

"No she won't." Adam abruptly interrupted stepping closer to him, almost face to face. Without shifting his gaze away, he added, "I'll see y'all in the car as soon as Lil' Adam gets done."

"Okay, good to see you Leon," she said nervously, glad to leave as her husband opened the door.

"You too Violet, Ms. Rose, and… I didn't catch your other daughter's name…"

"And you won't!" said Adam closing the door in his face.

"Who was that?" said Lillie Mae as they hurried to the car as her father went back inside the barbershop.

"I think that was Juan's father," added Rose getting into the backseat.

"Whew, I know you glad Juan don't look nothing like his father, but he might one day."

Rose sighed as she shook her head at her sister. "Momma, you liked him in high school?"

"Not really. He liked me, but your father made sure nothing ever came of it."

"I'm glad you picked Daddy, I couldn't imagine him being my father."

"Lillie Mae get in the car Chile', he didn't look like he does now back then." Violet smiled slightly, "as I recall he was rather handsome, pretty much like Juan looks now."

"Eww! Rose what if Juan looks like that in the future," said Lillie Mae elbowing her sister.

"Leave me alone," said Rose turning to look out the window away from the barbershop. Her thoughts turned to Juan who was waving at her before her father pushed them out the door. "He still is the cutest guy I know and the best dancer… I think he might look like his mother… I hope anyway," she thought to herself ignoring her sister who continued chattering on and on about how Juan would look like his father when he was older.

"Didn't mean no harm, Big Adam," said Leon as he walked behind him.

"You good," he replied handing two dollars to the barber as Lil' Adam got out of the chair wondering what he missed.

"See you in a couple weeks Willie."

"Have a spot waiting on you."

"Pops, can Juan come over to watch the fight?"

"Check with your mother," he said turning towards the front door.

"She'll say yes," Lil' Adam said to his friend sitting in the barber chair. "Come over around five."

"Make that six," added his father. "I'll be home by then."

"Y'all got one of them picture boxes," asked Leon following behind Adam. "I sure would love to see that fight. They say Sugar Ray been talking a lot of stuff with the rematch and all. What's that fellow's name he supposed to be fighting?" Adam continued walking out the door without acknowledging Leon's question, leaving him standing there looking confused.

"You think Mr. Leon's coming over to see the fight?"

"If he does, I'll probably end up punching him in the mouth again for some reason or another."

The mood home lifted as "Run Rudolph Run" by Chuck Berry played in the background and thoughts turned to Christmas, Santa Claus, presents, and family. Before long, they were all snapping their fingers and singing, 'run run Rudolph, Santa's got to make it to town, Santa make him hurry tell him he can take the freeway down'.

20 HOME FOR THE HOLIDAYS

Grandma Mae enjoyed having family and friends over for Christmas. She spent many days decorating the living room, hanging stockings on the fireplace labeled for each grandchild, wrapping presents tied with colorful ribbon, and draping shiny silver garland on every available space despite Poppa John's complaints.

"Mae it's just too much, every time I come in the living room I feel I'm lost in a silver jungle."

"It's never too much for Christmas. Gon' out back and cut me a nice pine tree, make sure it's nice and full without any gaps between the branches, and shake it really good I don't want any critters trying to catch a ride."

"Yes Mae," he answered reluctantly grabbing his coat and hat reminded that all of this was for the grandchildren. Soon he returned dragging a seven-foot evergreen into the living room and placing it in a wooden tree stand he made years ago.

"That's a nice one John."

"You say that every year Mae."

"Well I guess that's cause' you find a good tree every year," she said kissing him on the cheek. "Once I fill it up with my extra garland, candy canes, and angel on top, it will be the best tree ever."

* * *

"Merry Christmas Momma," said Violet followed by the rest of the family carrying food and presents. Everyone greeted one another with hugs and kisses as the fire crackled in the background. "The house looks lovely."

"See you started up the fire Mr. Johnson," said Adam rubbing his hands together.

"Yup it's getting chilly out here, radio say it might snow."

"Hasn't done that in years."

"Nope," he replied dryly noticing his daughter coming back in with another box. "Look like you brought a bakery, all the cakes, pies, and cookies, really smell good Vee."

"Thank you, and I know they taste good too, all the sampling we did."

"That's the best part," he laughed cheerfully.

The house quickly filled with activity, final touches made to meat and side dishes in the kitchen, and the dining room table was neatly decorated with red and green hand-made tablemats and a white embroidered snowflake in the center.

"Momma you did a beautiful job with the table settings."

"Just a little something I pulled together."

"Here comes Anna, Mr. Tom, *and Beau*," said Lillie Mae smiling at Rose.

"Grandma Mae, you invited him?" said Rose in obvious discomfort.

"Oh Chile' hush, ain't nothing wrong with Beau. He'll be a lawyer one day, watch and see. And a good catch, somebody ought to grab."

"Momma you sound like you like him," laughed Violet as she began setting the table.

"I do! If I was ten, twenty…" she paused as her daughter looked at her. "Okay, forty years younger, I'd be smiling in his face."

"No, you wouldn't," said Poppa John squeezing her around the waist and kissing her on the cheek. "Because your eyes would be on me."

"Go on John, I ain't stuttin' you," she laughed pushing him away. "Get the door you see we got company coming."

After he left the room, Grandma Mae spoke softly to Violet. "How you and Adam doing?"

Caught completely off guard, a sharp pain ran down her spine. Her mother had never asked about her marriage, they were always so happy together. Anxiety overwhelmed her and all she could say was, "What do you mean?"

Interrupting their conversations, Tom walked in the room hugging them both. "Merry Christmas, everything smells delicious, I can't wait to eat."

"Same to you Tom," replied Grandma Mae, happy for the diversion, mad with herself for bringing up Adam to her daughter as John had told her not to do. "Where's Annie?"

"Once she saw Lillie Mae, they took off together with their new dolls."

"Merry Christmas Mrs. Johnson," said Beau politely. "And you to Mrs. Williams."

"Merry Christmas baby," said Grandma Mae smiling sweetly. "Come on over here and give me a hug."

"Yes ma'am. I mean Grandma Mae ma'am."

"Chile' call me what you like," she said hugging him and patting him on the back.

Violet laughed shaking her head as she placed more plates on the dining room table, still thinking of her mother's question.

"Merry Christmas everyone," said Ruby walking into the living room with a bottle of wine, followed by Fred struggling to carry the casserole dish and several boxes of presents.

"Hello everyone," he nodded.

"Hey sis, Merry Christmas," she said kissing Violet on the cheek. "Does Momma need help in the kitchen?"

"No, I mean maybe," she said shrugging her shoulder not focusing on her sister or her date.

"What's the matter," asked Ruby.

"Nothing, nothing," she said walking into her mother's bedroom.

Ruby followed her still carrying the bottle of wine. Violet was almost in tears as she sat on the bed. "If you don't tell me what is going on, nobody in here will have a Merry Christmas. Did someone hurt you?"

"No, no I'm fine."

"Vee, I can see you not fine."

"It's just… Momma asked how Adam and I were."

"So..."

"So, she never asked me that before."

"Is that a reason to be upset?"

"Do you know if something is going on with Adam," she asked as tears began to fall.

Ruby sat next to her on the bed squeezing her sister's hand knowing exactly what she was referring too. They barely escaped her finding out at The Honey Shack. All she could do was act confused and say, "Going on?"

"Is he seeing someone?"

"Why are you two in my room with a bottle of wine and we haven't had dinner?" said Grandma Mae. "And Vee, why you crying?"

"You asked me how Adam and I were doing and… and…" she resumed crying.

"Baby, baby, don't cry," said her mother sitting down putting her arm around her shoulder. "Are you pregnant?"

Violet turned to her mother with a smile slowly coming across her face. "Yes, how did you know?"

She laughed, shook her head pulling her daughter to her bosom. "I'm your mother, and I know nothing but a baby in your stomach will get you all upset and worried about a man."

"Vee, that's wonderful, I'm so happy," said Ruby hugging them both, thankful their conversation shifted away from her husband's infidelity. "Is that what all this crying is for?"

"I guess so," smiled Violet as her mother wiped the tears away with her apron. "I wanted to surprise everyone at dinner with the big announcement."

"You can still do that. We'll act surprised," she smiled looking at Ruby. "Now when is it your turn."

"I'm glad you said that since I was making an announcement too," she laughed standing up rubbing her stomach.

"Chile', you better not have an announcement until you married. Now put that wine down and get my macaroni and cheese from Fred, standing in the middle of the living room afraid to move until you tell him."

After their mother left, Violet whispered, "Ruby are you pregnant too?"

"Not that I know of," she laughed looking in the mirror at her tightly fitting dress. "If I was, I wouldn't have any clothes to wear. I barely could fit this."

"Well, neither of us will fit in our clothes after eating all the food Momma fixed."

"Least you have an excuse," she said hugging her sister as they joined the others.

The men, gathered by the fireplace, discussed the upcoming fight between Sugar Ray Robinson and Gene Fullmer. However two had their minds on other topics. Beau, looking towards the dining room hoping to catch a glimpse of Rose, and Tom, looking towards the front door expecting another guest.

"Y'all, come on," said Grandma Mae counting the chairs making sure there were enough places for everyone. Beau was first into the dining room, hoping to get a seat next to Rose.

"Looks like a car coming up the road," said Poppa John mainly to Tom who immediately left the room.

"Where's he going," asked Grandma Mae.

"He had to run outside, no need to wait."

She smiled, happy for Tom as everyone found places around the table. After Poppa John gave the blessing, filled platters and stuffed plates circulated the dining room table as holiday cheer filled the Johnson home.

"Aunt Ruby you put your foot in this macaroni and cheese," said Lillie Mae getting a second helping.

"Chile' who taught you that?" she laughed.

"Your foot, her foot, and my foot," said Adam rubbing his flat stomach rippling through his tight fitting cotton shirt as he winked at Violet who giggled despite herself.

Confused, Annie looked at Lillie Mae before taking another bite, not wanting anymore if someone put their foot in the food.

"It's okay," she whispered. "It's just a saying, I'll tell you later."

Tom felt kind of foolish standing on the porch waiting for the car door to open. After all it had been over thirty years since he last saw her, thoughts flooded his mind. "Would she recognize him? His hair was thinning. He had gained a few pounds, maybe more than a few pounds. Would she notice?" His heart pounded in his chest as the car door opened and she stepped out…

"Sally Ann!" he called, amazed at her unchanging beauty, and throwing the learned restraint of being a lawyer to the wind as he ran to the girl of his dreams.

"Tom," she answered not having time to catch her breath before he pulled her close to him and kissed her passionately. Time stood still as they embraced each other, neither wanting to let go.

"I'm sorry, I shouldn't have kissed you," he said after their lips separated.

"No, please don't apologize. I waited all my life for this moment."

"Can you forgive me? My father…"

She placed her finger to his lips stopping him from speaking. "I love you and that is all that matters."

He could not believe his ears. Did she say she loved me? This had to be a dream. Here she was before him, her beauty more exquisite than he remembered. Her eyes warm and inviting, full of love for him. Her body firm and strong against his, her lips slightly parted… inviting… He kissed her again.

"Leave with me Sally Ann, today," he said gazing into her eyes never wanting this moment to end. "I would die if I lost you again."

"Tom, my sweet Tom," she said gently touching his face. "You never lost me. I've been here all the time."

Tears rolled down his face, never in his life was he happier. He stood afraid to move, barely breathing. "I think I am going to pass out."

"You two lovebirds best come on in and get something to eat," said Poppa John from the porch.

"I can't let you go," he whispered his arms wrapped around her. "One more kiss."

"Tom, I'm not going anywhere," she said taking his hand.

"You can lead me to the ends of the earth, long as we are together." He felt himself floating towards the house.

* * *

"Everyone, especially Annie," announced Tom beaming like the noonday sun. "This is my dear, *dear* friend Sally Ann Rogers."

"Hello," she smiled shyly. "It's been quite a few years since I last saw everyone."

"Time stands still for good friends," said Grandma Mae getting up to hug Sally Ann. "You know you always welcome. Have a seat, we got plenty of food. And best save some room for dessert, Violet and Rose made some pies and cakes that could win first prize at the county fair!"

"And I helped," grinned Lillie Mae.

"To lick the spoons," said Lil' Adam with a smirk.

"That's the best part," laughed Poppa John. "Sometimes I like the batter more than the cake."

"Next time I make a cake Poppa, I'll save the spoons for you," laughed Rose as everyone joined in the festive atmosphere.

Soon Grandma Mae began replacing the savory foods with desserts, a pound cake, a two-layer coconut cake, a three-layer red velvet cake, and a sweet potato pie. Everyone's eyes stretched wondering how they could possibly eat everything and be able to walk out the dining room without assistance. "And if you still have room after that, there's an apple pie and a blackberry cobbler on the kitchen table, and vanilla ice cream in the box."

"Oh no," said Ruby holding her stomach in, "only a bit of room in my dress, as it is."

"Well go in my room and put on a dress that fits," said Grandma Mae heading back towards the kitchen. "Don't make no sense; dress so tight can't even breathe."

"You like my dress, don't you baby."

Fred sat frozen with a look of disbelief. "Don't ask me that… here," he whispered.

Grandma Mae came back from the kitchen holding a pitcher and Poppa John started smiling, "um-um homemade wine!"

"For the grown folk only," she added looking at Annie and Lillie Mae while pouring a small amount of wine in everyone else's glass, accept Violet.

"That's not fair," she pouted. "When will I be old enough?"

"Never," said Adam shaking his head amused at her antics.

Once everyone received either lemonade or wine, Poppa John stood up. "One of our family traditions is to take turns saying why we are thankful from the oldest to the youngest."

Lifting his glass, "I'll start us off, to my good friend Tom and my cousin Sally Ann for finding each other after many, *many* years, may you be as happy as I am with my wife." He reached over and kissed Grandma Mae on the cheek. "I love you Mae."

Not much for showing affection, she stood and shook her head. "It's my turn, to my family and friends, may our dinner table grow more and more each year."

"I guess I'm next," said Tom proudly standing up. "To my wonderful granddaughter Annie, whom I love dearly and to Ms. Sally Ann Rogers whose beautiful smile, has made me a very happy man."

"Thank you," blushed Sally Ann as he kissed her on the cheek.

"You all have been so kind," she stood lifting her glass looking around at everyone's smiling faces, finally resting back on Tom who quietly put his arm around her waist. "My dear Tom, may our future erase our past," she said softly her eyes filling with tears.

Tom squeezed her closer, fighting back his own tears. "I love you," he whispered in her ear.

"That's so sweet," said Ruby. "I'll go next!" Standing up, she pressed out the wrinkles in her tight dress, as everyone waited patiently. "To my family and friends, I pray the New Year brings *new* life."

"Ruby!" said Violet gently elbowing her sister.

"I'll go next," said Adam not noticing his sister-in-law or wife. "To my family, you mean everything to me. And to my wife Vee, the sweetest, kindest woman in the world, more beautiful today than the day we married."

"Thank you, Adam," she said as he kissed her on the cheek. "I have more of an announcement..." She paused, standing, as everyone looked towards her in anticipation. "Momma figured it out, somehow, and Ruby almost gave it away…"

"You're having a baby!" burst out Poppa John.

"Yes, I am," she answered to warm smiles and clapping from her family as her husband picked her up and swirled her around almost knocking over the dining room table.

"Lord have mercy," he shouted with excitement. "Girl when were you going to tell me."

"I was waiting until New Year's Eve but..."

"Congratulations," said Tom and Sally Ann both hugging the happy expectant mother.

"Yippee! That's the best Christmas present ever," said Lillie Mae leaning over to hug her mother around the waist.

"I hope it's a boy," said Lil' Adam walking over to kiss his mother on the cheek.

"Not like you," his sister quickly responded, poking him in the side.

"And definitely not a crybaby girl like you."

"I ain't a crybaby."

"Is too!"

"Is not!"

"That's enough!" interrupted Adam carefully pulling the chair out for his wife to sit back down.

"I am happy for you," said Poppa John kissing her on the cheek. "You always have been a good mother and I thank you for another grandchild."

Grandma Mae kissed her daughter. "Now if we can just get that sister of yours…"

"Get me to do what," said Ruby standing with her hands on her hips. "Have a baby, I can do that."

"Not without a husband," said Grandma Mae shaking her head and standing with her hands on her hips mocking her daughter. "I won't have you setting bad examples for my grandbabies."

"Now Mae, we got company," added Poppa John as he went back to his seat.

"Don't 'now' me," she said taking some empty plates into the kitchen.

"Momma I'm grown," said Ruby following behind her with more dishes.

"Baby," said Adam, gently touching Violet's hand after she gathered plates from the table. "Can I talk to you a minute on the porch?"

"Is the toast over?" said Poppa John. "Come on Tom, we might as well go have a smoke."

"I'll be right out, ole' friend," he said smiling without taking his eyes off Sally Ann.

"Poppa John, can me and Annie go play with our dolls?"

"I would if I was you before your grandmother asks you to help clean up. "Lil' Adam, you and Beau come help me get some wood and fix this fire up?"

On the porch, Adam looking deep into his wife's eyes kissed both her hands gently. "You love babies so much now we are having another one."

She smiled up at him. "We're not as young as we use to be."

"Speak for yourself," he laughed pulling her close to him. "Honey I have ten more babies in me waiting to come out."

He gently rubbed her back kissing her softly. "I love you."

"I love you too," she smiled squeezing him tightly.

Poppa John stood at the door watching his youngest daughter. He enjoyed seeing her so happy. "I won't let anything take that away," he thought to himself.

"Poppa," said Violet a bit startled to see him standing in the doorway, quickly smoothing out her dress and fixing her hair.

"You look so beautiful Vee," he said kissing her on the cheek. "I remember when you were a chap you couldn't get enough of your dolls, wasn't near as fancy as Lillie Mae's, but you played with them night and day. Well, I guess Mae will have to make a new batch of baby dolls."

"That would be nice," she smiled. "I'll go help out in the kitchen."

"That's fine baby," he said focusing more on his son-in-law as he took out his pipe.

"It's getting chilly," said Adam feeling strangely uneasy as he turned to head inside.

"Can I have a word son," he said walking towards the porch rocker.

"Yes sir," he answered an aching knot forming in his stomach.

Poppa John did not rush. He slowly packed his pipe with tobacco: *tap, tap, tap.* Once filled, he struck a wooden match on the bottom of his boot and puffed. Smoke slowly floated towards the ceiling, disturbed only by an occasional breeze from the night air.

As Adam stood waiting, small beads of sweat gathered on his forehead despite the outside chill. Maybe he wanted to congratulate him privately, but deep down, he knew that was not the case. A storm raged within, his stomach turned. Finally, 'the dark was coming to the light'.

"Vee mighty happy with the baby coming and all," he spoke slowly, taking a long puff from his pipe. "That's my baby girl and I enjoy seeing her happy."

"Yes sir, she mighty happy," he answered with a sigh of relief thinking his father-in-law wanted to share in his happiness. "I'm happy too."

"Don't rightly care if *you* happy," he said coldly, "because you got a funny way of showing it."

Adam froze, realizing his tone was not congratulatory, now he felt like the scolded one afraid to move, watching his father-in-law, stone faced, rocking back and forth, slowly, emotionless. "He knew!" The words shouted in his mind. His heart raced, sweat flowed freely from his forehead. "He knew!"

Seeing the panic on his son-in-law's face, Poppa John took his time before speaking. "I knew for quite some time now, town to small *not* to know that sort of stuff."

Adam collapsed in the chair next to his father-in-law, head down. "I don't want to hurt Vee. The last thing I ever wanted to do was hurt her."

"Told you what's done in the dark always comes to the light. At first when I heard folk talking, I didn't believe what they said, didn't want too. Mae told me 'believe half of what you see and none of what you hear'. I let it go then, but tried to mention it to you awhile back, under the tree…"

"Yes sir," Adam nodded, remembering the time.

"… but folk kept talking, saying you down at this Shack place… Then when Mae said you took my baby down there, I knew I had to talk to you. Boy is you crazy? I know Vee suspects something, but would never say anything to you, it would break her heart. I pray she never finds out, but surely she will with that Carmen woman sash-shaying all around town."

Adam's eyes stretched in fear, *shocked* he knew her name. His stomach growled and churned as he rushed over to the edge of the porch anticipating the departure of his Christmas feast previously enjoyed.

Poppa John looked over at him while rocking slowly uncaring, as his wife's efforts to prepare a wonderful family meal jettisoned off the side of the porch. "Son," he said with a hint of sarcasm. "It's time you stop going to that shack, ain't no place for a family man."

Looking up wiping his mouth, shame gripping his heart like a vice. "Couldn't live if I hurt Vee, I won't go anymore sir."

"Now you won't," he grumbled with a tone of neither belief nor disbelief, as the rocking chair creaked back and forth. "I loved you like a son and you betrayed me, you betrayed Mae, your children, and my daughter."

"John is everything all right?" said Tom walking onto the porch. "Mae had me bring your jacket."

"Thanks Tom, can't take that cold night chill like I used too."

"Chill," laughed Tom. "This is a winter treat for folks from the North. Give me a pillow, I could sleep right here on the porch, happy as a lark."

Adam gathered himself and turned to leave, unnoticed by the two friends, never more embarrassed in his life. Caught; he knew that would happen eventually, but the thought of Vee finding out, now, in her condition, devastated him more than accusations, even if they were true. He closed the door preparing for what was to come next.

"Congratulations are in order, my ole' friend," said Tom patting him on the back.

"Oh yes, yes," he smiled still distracted but not wanting to dampen his friend's happiness. "Everything is wonderful. How are you and Sally Ann, any good news?"

"Better than what I could ever dream," he said delighted to discuss his favorite subject. "Sally Ann wants to take things slow, can't rightly blame her for that, but I'd marry her today if she'd have me, even if I had to take her North to make that happen."

"Yes, it's still illegal for colored and white to get married here."

"I know soon things will be different John, I've been working with the courts trying to get the laws changed. We live in the United States of America. People should be able to marry whoever they choose."

"Should be," said Poppa John filling his pipe. "But that will take time."

"You're right, I know," said Tom saddened for a moment. "But I will never give up. And I will never give up my Sally Ann Rogers again for nobody… ever again!"

"I'm glad to hear that."

"Sally Ann!" said Tom startled jumping up from the rocker wondering how much she heard.

"John, thank you for inviting me over," she smiled.

He laid his pipe down and stood to hug her, "on your way home?"

"Yes, I'm in charge of getting things organized for the New Year's Eve watch night dinner at church, you and Mae planning on coming?"

"Believe I heard tell of it?"

"Can I come?" said Tom helping her with her coat.

"Of course, if you like," she blushed and started down the steps towards her car. "Hope to see you and Mae, John."

"I'm sure you will," he smiled as he watched the two of them walk down the driveway. Tom put his arm around her like old times. "They always did make a good couple," he said softly as he headed in the house. "I hope things turn out better."

Tom escorted her to the car door. "What time should I pick you up?"

"You sure you want to do this?"

He lifted her chin slightly until their lips were practically touching. "Why don't we make this New Year's Eve watch night dinner a wedding service."

"Tom" she smiled coyly. "Are you asking me to marry you?"

"Yes, would you like me to get on my knee," he asked taking her hand and bending one knee to the ground, without hesitation. "Sally Ann Rogers will you take me, Tom Greene, to be your lawfully wedded husband?"

"Tom get up," she laughed taking his hand. "You still the joker I knew in high school."

"Thanks," he said struggling to stand back up. "I got a few more aches and pains physically, but mentally I'm still the same."

"*Times* haven't changed from high school."

"Neither have my feelings toward you."

He took her hand and looked deeply into her eyes. "I married once to please my parents and a society that said whites should marry whites and colored should marry colored. When my wife died instead of sorrow, I felt freedom… that sounds terrible. I've never said this to anyone."

"Tom," she said gently caressing his cheek.

"I know I have a few more wrinkles and a lot less hair."

"You're still as handsome as high school."

"And you're more beautiful now than ever before."

Tom tenderly held her face in his hands as they both gazed into each other's eyes. The cold night air swirling around them, unnoticed. "Sally Ann Rogers… Sally Ann Rogers, for many years I've longed to say your name and to kiss your lips."

"Then what's stopping you?"

Without hesitation, Tom took her in his arms as they lovingly kissed, and for one moment in time, all was right with the world, and it did not matter what color they were, or where they lived, only that they loved each other dearly.

* * *

Retiring to the living room, everyone sat comfortably around the fireplace. Lillie Mae and Annie were contently playing with their new Christmas dolls, while Rose looked through a copy of Ebony magazine. Grandma Mae, Violet, and Ruby sat chattering happily thinking of baby names, and baby clothes, and baby furniture, while Adam sat next to his wife trying to act interested but his mind was far, far away. Lil' Adam and Beau, returning from outside with some freshly chopped firewood, dropped the pile on the floor, awakening Poppa John from his nap.

"Ms. Mae… I mean Grandma Mae. Can I have a slice of apple pie?"

"Of course you can, told you to make yourself at home, your mother was my best friend in the world. I love you like I loved her."

"Yes ma'am, I mean Grandma Mae ma'am".

"Rose get Beau some pie and a big scoop of that ice cream."

Frustrated, Rose wondered why she always had to be the one to do something for Beau. All she wanted was to sit quietly with her magazine. When she looked up, she saw all eyes were on her, waiting to see her response. Smiling pleasantly, she answered her grandmother, "yes ma'am."

"Me too," said Lil' Adam putting the last piece of wood on the pile.

"You can get some later," said Grandma Mae sternly. "Wake up your grandfather and tell him he's got company… and stop all that snoring."

"Yes ma'am," said Lil' Adam unable to assist his sister. "Sorry."

"You tried," she said heading towards the kitchen only to find Beau happily awaiting her seated at the table. Getting a bowl and spoon, he watched her every move, "You're staring Beau," she said matter-of-factly.

"Oh, I'm sorry, it's just…" he paused not ready to express his feelings towards her outwardly. "Don't you want some pie?"

"I don't eat pie. Do you want vanilla or chocolate?"

"Which one do you like?"

"I don't eat ice cream."

"Well," he said not discouraged by her indifference. "Most people eat vanilla with apple pie. What do you think of chocolate with apple pie?"

"I don't know," she said gazing awkwardly into the open freezer.

"Chocolate then," he said happily.

She took out the chocolate ice cream and put two large scoops on top of his apple pie without looking at him, then plopped the bowl down on the table.

Immediately he took his spoon and combined some apple pie and ice cream together without taking his eyes off her, "Umm, this is good."

"Thank you," she said briefly glancing at him before turning to leave the kitchen.

Before she could pass by him, he gently took her hand, "please don't go."

Her initial instinct was to snatch her hand away, but his eyes were so gentle and caring, almost pleading with her to stay.

"Please," he said softly.

She sat down trying to remember why he frustrated her so, was it her grandmother's obvious matchmaking or his constantly following behind her like a lost puppy. For some reason, looking in his eyes, she no longer could remember her irritations.

"Rose," he said focused on her entirely as if no one else mattered, still holding her hand at the table. "I wanted to talk to you about something that is on my mind."

"Oh no, someone help me!" she thought panic-stricken. "He's going to ask me to marry him!"

"...I'm so excited, Mr. Tom was able to get me a full scholarship to Temple University in Philadelphia, Pennsylvania."

"Oh," she said feeling stupid.

"Long as I keep my grades up," he continued.

"I'm sure you will," she said back to her matter-of-fact tone as she patted the top of his hand with her other free hand.

"Thank you, I appreciate your confidence."

"Beau, you're like a brother to me, we've been around each other long as I can remember. You were always smart. Congratulations. Don't worry, you'll do fine."

"Rose," he said now with both his hands gently squeezing hers. "I don't want to be like a brother to you."

She quickly moved her hands, pretending to be confused. "What do you mean?"

"Don't you know how I've felt all these years." He reached to hold her hands again, but she stood up.

"Do you want some more pie?" she asked quickly taking his plate to the stove without looking back at him.

"Rose, please," he said walking over to stand closely behind her with his hands on her shoulders. "I'm leaving in January. Can I write to you while I'm away?"

"Yes of course," she answered pulling away from him to cut another piece of pie.

"Not as a brother Rose," he paused. "I can't believe I'm struggling with what to say. I'm going away to be a lawyer, speaking publicly should not be a problem for me."

She turned to look at him, how sweet he was, struggling with what to say. Her demeanor softened. "Say what you need to say," she whispered kindly.

Without hesitation, he blurted everything out, "Rose, I love you and want you to be my girl…" he stopped from the shocked expression on her face. "Okay, that was too much."

"Yeah," she smiled enjoying his nervousness, unable to hide her softening feelings towards him.

"See that," he said touching her cheek gently as she finally looked at him. "I love your smile, seems like all my life I have tried to get you to look at me and smile, but you're always trying to get away from me, to avoid me. Am I so repulsive?"

Rose touched her finger to his lips. "Don't," she said compassionately. "There is nothing wrong with you."

He stepped closer to her and this time she did not back away. "Can I kiss you Rose?"

Stomping into the kitchen, Lillie Mae shouted, "Grandma Mae said for you to fix me and Annie some pie and ice cream! … Why you jump?"

Annie giggled.

"I'm telling!"

"Telling what?" said Rose moving over to the cabinet to get two saucers. "Nothing to tell, and if you make up something, I'll make the rest of the year miserable for you."

"There's only seven days left," she answered sticking out her tongue.

"And they will be the worst seven days of your life," she said squinting her eyes with a voice Lillie Mae dared not cross. "Now sit down!"

Beau smiled as he watched the younger sister ease quietly into her chair without another word. He sat next to her offering a kind glimpse to finish his second helping of pie enjoying the family moment.

"Annie," said Rose back to her sweet voice. "Would you like chocolate or vanilla ice cream with your apple pie?"

"Vanilla," she answered happily.

"I'll take some vanilla too, this time. If you don't mind," said Beau holding up his saucer.

"I don't mind," said Rose with a quick glance and smile towards him.

"Ohh, I'm telling!"

"Telling what?" said Lil' Adam as he headed towards the cabinet to get a saucer.

"Don't ask," laughed Rose shaking her head. "You know how your sister is."

"Lillie Mae, you in here messing in your sister's business again," said Violet walking into the now crowded kitchen.

"No ma'am."

"You and Annie were supposed to get some pie and ice cream then high tale it back."

Ruby pushed past everyone to get a bowl out the cabinet. "Why should they hurry back, so they can fall asleep with all the other ole' folks?"

"I'm not old," said Violet looking over at her sister cutting a big piece of cake.

"I know, you were dozing off because you're pregnant."

"Girl hush and get your cake," she laughed waving her hand.

"I'm getting a piece to go. I have to find a livelier bunch of folk."

"The Honey Shack?" said Lil' Adam from his seat at the table.

"You want to go?"

"No," interrupted Violet.

"Beau what about you?" said Ruby with a smile and a wink towards him. "Rose can come too."

From the opposite side of the kitchen Violet could see their embarrassment, "girl leave them chaps alone. You are as bad as Lillie Mae meddling in other folk's business."

"Then you come on and go with me."

"Please, I won't bother even answering that."

"Annie, are you ready to go?" said Tom in the doorway.

"Not really," she answered wondering if everyone here was always so interesting and different.

"Beau, do you want a ride to town?"

"Yes sir," he said standing up to take his plate to the sink.

"I'll get that," said Rose gently touching his hand.

"Thank you," he said and for a moment, time stood still and only the two of them were in the kitchen, their eyes locked together in affection.

"Well let's go," Tom smiled breaking the silence, reminded of his younger days with Sally Ann.

"Beau I packed you a bag for the road," said Grandma Mae squeezing through the kitchen. "When are you leaving for school?"

"Not until next week," he answered watching Rose's every move but this time she did not turn away and smiled back at him.

"The Potato Patch is closed until after New Year's, so take this food anyway, and stop by next week, every day if you like. Rose will be here showing me how to use my new sewing machine."

"I'll surely come by then ma'am, I mean Grandma Mae ma'am."

"Thank you Mae, for having us over," said Tom.

She smiled handing him a bag. "I wrapped up a whole pie for you."

"I'm sure to have sweet dreams tonight."

"Bet you'll have sweet dreams anyway," said Ruby slyly with a wink.

"Ruby," said Violet shaking her head. "What won't you say?"

"No, it's okay," added Tom. "I'm not ashamed any longer to let others know I enjoy the company of someone of a different color."

"Me either Poppa," said Annie standing up to hug him around the waist.

"And if Sally Ann would have me, I'd marry her tonight."

"In the south?" said Ruby.

"On the moon if I could."

"Be more likely."

"Ruby," said Grandma Mae firmly as she turned kindly towards Tom. "Don't worry, things will change around here one day, the good Lord will see to that."

"Amen Momma," said Violet.

"Amen," smiled Tom nodding confidently in agreement.

* * *

With Christmas dinner over, the children sent home with full stomachs and happy hearts, Grandma Mae and Poppa John sat enjoying a quiet moment in front of the fireplace, as flames danced across glowing logs.

"That Tom sure does love him some Sally Ann," he said stirring the fire as the wood crackled, the charred embers glowed red hot in the background.

"Sure does. He said in the kitchen he'd marry her if she'd have him, you think she would?"

"I believe she would."

When he sat down, he moved closer to his wife. He never was much of a hugger or a kisser, nor was she, which made things all the better, but on this holiday night, he felt different. Maybe it was the new baby on the way, or maybe it was all the love in the air from Tom and Sally Ann, or the growing romance between Rose and Beau, something was different. Slowly he put his arm over the shoulder of his wife of forty-five years, unsure of how she would respond.

She looked at him half smiling, instinctively wanting to ask him what was wrong with him, or tell him to move his arm, but instead she cuddled even closer, softly resting her head on his shoulder.

He was surprised.

For a long time, they both sat cuddled together as the flames slowly dwindled and the ashen logs warmed the room, cozy.

21 ONE LUMP OR TWO

When Juan and Leon showed up to watch the fight between Sugar Ray Robinson and Gene Fullmer, it was very awkward for everyone, but as normal, Violet remained hospitable and Adam tried his best to suppress his feelings of annoyance to accommodate her wellbeing. Tensions did subside somewhat, when Poppa John arrived.

"What time does the fight start?" he said standing at the door holding a covered cake plate. "Your mother sent over this coconut cake, I told her nobody ate cake at a fight."

"Thanks Poppa," said Violet taking the plate. "I'm glad you came."

"I can't wait to see the fight, never saw one like this before. Wouldn't miss it, your mother might not like the picture box, but I sure do."

"Then why don't you get one?" she said taking his coat.

"Mae said she'd bust it with a hammer if I tried to bring one in the house. And I been with that woman long enough to know, she might do just that, not about to take any chances."

They both laughed as they headed into the living room.

"What have Momma and Rose been doing for the past couple days?"

"They've been fiddling with that sewing machine every day. At first, she tried to act like she wasn't going to like it, and said sewing by hand was better, until Rose showed her how easy it was to use, now she happy as a lark. I tell you," he chuckled. "They cut up everything they could get their hands on for some quilt they're making. And she said if you got any clothes you don't want, send them by me."

The men sat on the edge of the couch waiting for the fight to start, but also for easy access to a feast of chicken, biscuits, popcorn, pretzels, and lemonade. One person could not stop eating from the time he entered the William's home…Leon. Adam sat on the opposite couch, feeling sick to his stomach as he watched him continuously chewing …nonstop.

"You made it just in time," said Lil' Adam going over to hug his grandfather.

"They only talking right now," said Adam waving his hand to greet his father-in-law, barely turning his head away from the commentators and keeping Leon in his peripheral vision.

"Vee you got plenty to eat."

"I got some string beans, mashed potatoes and gravy too, if you'd rather have that," she said poking her head out from the kitchen. "Didn't think nobody wanted dinner while the fight is going on."

"I'll take a plate," replied her father taking a seat next to Lil' Adam.

Before he could get comfortable, Leon jumped up from the adjacent couch, his hand outstretched. "How you do Mr. Johnson. You probably don't remember me. I was almost your son-in-law."

"Almost?" he replied, a puzzled look on his face.

"Well not actually almost, but …," he tried to clarify his statement until Adam turned completely around from the television to stare at him.

Violet entered the room carrying a plate of food and a glass of iced tea, just in time. "Poppa, you remember Leon Nesbitt, Ms. Fannie Mae's son. I went to high school with him."

"Can't say I do," he said shaking his hand anyway, "especially the 'almost son-in-law' part."

"Pay him no mind," she said throwing an angry look at Leon as she handed her father his plate.

"I don't," said Adam low enough that only she heard him.

"Poppa can I get you anything else?"

"No, no this is plenty," he said with a nod. "Who's fighting tonight?"

"Sugar Ray Robinson against Gene Fullmer," said Adam gazing intently at Leon helping himself to his third piece of chicken and fourth biscuit. "It's their second time fighting, Fullmer beat Sugar Ray the first time and took the title. I heard it on the radio. Couldn't figure out how all three judges called it unanimous? Sugar Ray's gonna' get revenge tonight."

"I never heard of either of them," said Poppa John noticing his son-in-law's agitation with the almost son-in-law. "Back in my day, Jack Johnson was the man. He was the first colored heavyweight champion, beat anybody crazy enough to get in the ring, white folk didn't like him."

"On account he had a white wife," said Violet pulling a chair next to her husband's side of the couch, handing him a small plate from the kitchen.

Agreeing with his daughter, Poppa John continued. "They pretty much ran him outta' town. He spent a year in prison for violating Jim Crow laws about coloreds and whites being together."

Adam feeling better after Violet fixed him his own special plate of food and sat next to him, joined in the conversation. "Well back in my day, the champ was Joe Louis, best colored fighter in the world."

"Oh yeah," said Leon stuffing his mouth with popcorn from one hand and reaching for a piece of pound cake with the other. "Now I heard of Joe Louis."

Juan slumped deeper into the couch wishing he had never came, especially when he found out Rose wasn't going to be home.

"Didn't we used to listen to some of his fights on the radio?" Violet put her arm around Adam's arm as they watched Leon eating and talking with a mouth full of everything. She knew it was difficult for her husband to be hospitable in this situation, but at least he was trying.

"Sure did," he said calmed by her touch.

Everyone sat watching as the two fighters stood in separate corners of the boxing ring with their team, trying to stay loosened up as the announcer introduced former boxing champions to the audience. One of them was Joe Lewis, who walked into the ring wearing a suit and tie.

"He looks spiffy," said Violet.

"Look at that nigga's hair," laughed Leon pieces of chicken flying out his mouth.

"That's it!" exclaimed Adam jumping up from the couch pointing towards the door. "Get out my house!"

"What's the matter," he asked his mouth hanging open with pieces of chicken mixed with popcorn in full display.

Violet quick to her feet moved in front of her husband, "Adam, Adam hold on, let me talk to you in the kitchen."

"Vee, I need to handle this!" Furious, he gazed intensely at Leon while cradling his left fist with his right hand.

"Adam please," she said softly.

"Lord help me…," he said letting out a long sigh as he closed his eyes for a few moments, his body shaking. Finally, he turned and headed towards the kitchen.

"Leon!" she turned to him sternly. "We *never* use that word in this house."

"I'm, I'm sorry," he stuttered.

"You better be," she paused to catch her breath. "For Juan's sake, I will see if my husband might let you stay without knocking you upside your head. If you know how to pray, you should start now!"

Leon stared blankly at her scared to chew the remaining chunks of food in his mouth. Juan sank lower in the couch wishing he could disappear.

"What happened?" said Lillie Mae intercepting her mother on her way to the kitchen holding a baby doll in each hand.

"Get in there and speak to your grandfather," she snapped.

"But, what's the matter?" Not used to seeing her mother upset.

"Go on now."

"Nobody ever tells me what's going on."

"Come her baby, sit next to me," said Poppa John putting his arm around her and kissing her on the cheek. "Nothing is going on, everything's fine."

"Then why momma mad?"

"Nobody gets mad but dogs, let's watch the fight."

"I thought there would be *two* fights for a minute," said Lil' Adam nervously.

"Me too," said Leon finally taking a large swallow of lemonade.

"Won't be nothing of the sort," Poppa John added confidently. "Vee knows how to handle her husband, but if I was you 'almost son-in-law'… I'd think twice before I say anything else."

"Yes sir," he answered his head hanging low.

"Why, what happened?" sighed Lillie Mae frustrated looking from person to person. "I miss everything."

* * *

"Vee, he cruisin' for a bruisin', dip stick," said Adam, agitated, pacing back and forth in the kitchen, finally pouring himself a small glass of gin. "I can't take anymore... he's eating up all the food... digging in the popcorn with both hands... practically ate a whole cake, and he keeps on watching every move you make. Vee, he got to go!"

"Baby, I understand you upset," she said soothingly, taking her apron and hanging it behind the door. "But Leon is our guest. Maybe life has not been kind to him. We have each other, to care for and love, he has no one to lead him or guide him. Let's set an example of kindness for him."

Adam listened. Slowly his anger diminished as he watched her turn, pressing her dress out with her hands over a perfectly flat stomach even after three children and one on the way. His eyes moved to her hips expanding slightly as she bent down to pick up her fallen hair tie. Walking over to her, he smoothed her hair back with his hand, forgetting Leon and anyone else for the moment. "You are so beautiful! What did I do to deserve you?"

She smiled up at him, wondering how after all these years he was still able to make her blush. "I'll let you know later," she answered stepping closer to him and placing her arms around his neck, without another word tiptoed to kiss him affectionately.

"Every time I come here, the two of you making out like you still in high school," said Ruby startling them as she walked in from the living room. "No wonder you pregnant, kissing like *that*."

They both smiled. Violet slightly embarrassed. Adam completely satisfied with her analogy.

"I'm gonna' call you Mother Hubbard."

"Mother Hubbard?" he asked swallowing the last of his gin.

"You know the nursery rhyme we used to read to the kids. 'There was an ole' lady who lived in a shoe. She had so many children she didn't know what to do'."

"Oh, we know what to do," he laughed reaching over to pinch her on the backside as she giggled with delight.

"I saw that," said Ruby handing him a brown paper bag.

"Thanks," smiled Adam pulling out a bottle of gin, opening it, and happily refilling his glass. "You right on time."

"Pour me one," she said hanging her coat behind the door.

"You need to eat first, I'll fix you something," said Violet watching her husband pour a second glass of gin.

"Thanks, ain't y'all watching the fight, Poppa said it's about to start."

"Ready to start, I almost forgot," gasped Adam gulping down a third glass of gin and quickly leaving the kitchen.

"Almost forgot?" said Ruby puzzled.

"Yeah, we had a problem with Leon."

"Leon?" said Ruby taken aback. "Leon Nesbitt?"

"Yes," said Violet making a small dinner plate for her sister. "Didn't you see him in the living room when you came?"

"That fat cat on the couch stuffing his face with popcorn… Eww, what happened to him? He used to be a *fine* honey."

"Not anymore."

"Didn't he have a hankering after you?"

"I reckon," she said reluctantly.

"And Big Adam let him in the house?"

"Not directly," she whispered watching the door to avoid anyone overhearing. "Lil' Adam invited Juan and Leon came too."

"No wonder that poor child sitting in the living room looking like he fixing to die. What was the problem?"

"Nothing," she said nervously wanting to change the subject. "Let's get in there before the fight starts. Is Fred coming?"

"He in there," she answered taking her plate and grabbing the bottle of gin. "Sis, bring some glasses when you come and make some more popcorn! Cause there's no way I'm eating from the bowl Leon's stuffing his face with."

"Me either," laughed Violet.

Ruby sat her plate on the coffee table and squeezed between Poppa John and Lillie Mae.

"Where's mine," asked Fred.

"I thought you were eating the stuff on the table?" she answered eating a big spoonful of mashed potatoes not waiting for his response. "When's the fight starting?"

"Go in the kitchen Fred, Vee will fix you a plate," said Adam pouring himself another drink. "Mr. Johnson, you want a drink?"

"Nooo son, I gave that up long time ago… being a family man and all."

Normally Adam would have felt a twinge of guilt, but after four shots of gin and one-step away from punching Leon in the mouth, he didn't think twice about his father-in-law's comment.

"Never seen this Sugar Ray fellow," said Ruby taking a bite of chicken trying to divert her brother-in-law's attention as he poured another drink. "Joe Louis was my man."

"You missed him wave to the crowd earlier. He was a heavy weight," said Adam, shivering from another straight shot of gin. "Sugar Ray is a middle weight."

"What does that mean," asked Lillie Mae with her head resting comfortably on Poppa John's arm.

"The bigger men fight in one group called heavy-weights, and the lighter men fight in another group, middle-weights," said Lil' Adam matter-of-factly, always glad to explain something to his sister.

"Yeah, yeah, I get it," she said shaking her head at him. "Large, medium, do they have a small-weight group?"

"Feather-weight," he added confidently.

"I don't know what weight group this Sugar Ray in, but I know one thing… his hair looking better than mine," said Ruby as everyone joined in with her laughter, reducing the tension in the room.

Feeling relaxed enough to take a handful of popcorn, Leon thought to himself, "that's what I said," but dared not speak his thoughts aloud again.

"Here's fresh popcorn," said Violet sitting a large bowl in the middle of the coffee table and picking up the other bowl. "Here Leon you can finish this one."

"Thank you Vee," he answered hesitantly smiling up at her. "This popcorn sho' is good."

"I thought you said they were ready to start," she said ignoring him and sitting back in her chair next to Adam. "I'm glad I didn't miss Sugar Ray."

"How did he get that name," asked Lillie Mae taking a handful of the fresh popcorn.

Never missing an opportunity to wiggle her hips, Ruby stood up twisting from side to side, "Sugar Ray sounds sweet as me". Everyone laughed as she danced around the living room imitating a boxer throwing punches, at Fred first then at Leon, who jumped with nervousness, causing everyone to laugh more.

"Chile' sit down," said Poppa John smiling and shaking his head. "Make me wonder if you ever be ready for a chap when you act like one yourself most of the time."

"I'm ready to make…"

"Ruby!" interrupted Violet. "Your drinks are cut off!"

"Fine then," she sulked squeezing into a spot on the couch, this time next to Fred. "You don't mind do you baby?"

"Nope, sho' don't," he smiled as she scooted closer to him.

"Vee, your sister is crazy," said Adam, his speech slurred.

Violet handed him a glass of tea, "Drink this."

Lil' Adam looked at his father strangely, then answered the almost forgotten question. "When he first started boxing somebody said he was 'sweet as sugar' and he got the name 'Sugar', but his real name is Walker Smith Jr."

"Then why don't they call him Sugar Walker?" said Lillie Mae finally interested in what her brother was saying.

"Well, when he first started boxing at fifteen, he didn't want his mother to find out, so he used the name of a retired boxer Ray Robinson, and the name stuck."

"Sugar Walker, didn't sound right anyway," said Lillie Mae.

"You right, that name is not as sweet as Sugar Ray," said Ruby about to refill her glass with gin, but Violet poured in iced tea instead. She looked up at her sister but did not protest. "And who the other guy?"

"Gene Fullmer, they call him the Cyclone from Utah," said Adam soberly as Violet sat next to him rubbing his back.

"That makes sense, plenty of cyclones in Utah they say," nodded Poppa John.

"Pops, Sugar Ray will take the title from him, you watch."

"Shouldn't have got it in the first place," frowned Adam.

As the fight started, the two men began a sparring dance around the ring sizing up each other. Punch for punch, round for round, neither displaying a clear advantage. Shouts from the audience came of low blows and rabbit punches, but the fight continued round after round. Cheers rang out when Sugar Ray landed a blow, in contrast to moans when Fullmer landed one.

"This is a slow-moving fight," said Ruby throwing fake punches at Fred, who sat unfazed without turning away from the television, only moving his head to see around her fist in his face. "I like action."

"How you put up with her?" said Violet shaking her head in sisterly frustration.

"Because he is madly in love with me," she responded kissing him on the cheek, "right baby?"

"Yes madly," he answered leaning forward to avoid her.

"Sugar Ray's moving all around the ring, looks like the Cyclone is getting tired of chasing him," said Adam pouring another shot of gin despite his wife's stares.

"Used to be fighters didn't move all around like that," said Poppa John. "They'd stand toe-to-toe, bare hands, knuckles only, slugging it out until someone fell down."

"And got they brains knocked out," said Violet wincing at the thought.

"Blood all over the place!" he continued proudly. "Once saw a boy plum near got his eye knocked out, it was hanging on the top of his cheek."

"Eww Poppa," exclaimed Violet covering her mouth as she left the room.

"You okay baby," said Adam without taking his eyes off the boxing match.

"Sorry Vee," said Poppa John sincerely. "Forgot you having a baby, I reckon you don't want to hear talk of blood and eyes falling out."

"She having a baby?" said Leon before he could catch himself.

Everyone froze as stillness gripped the room. In the background, a bell rang, and the announcer's voice rang out, "round number five coming up." Yet no one looked at the television, all eyes were on Leon.

"Ahh, congratulation Big Adam," he said finally making his best attempt at a smile.

Now all eyes turned to Adam as a potential fight overshadowed the actual fight in the background. Lillie Mae looked up from playing with her baby dolls wondering why everyone was staring at her father. She waited uneasily.

Adam turned instantly ready to pummel Leon the same way Sugar Ray was doing to his opponent. He stood, angry, fist in hand, ready. Before advancing towards the unwanted houseguest, he glimpsed the face of his youngest daughter looking up at him, and the gentle touch of his wife's hand landed quickly on his shoulder. He paused, for what seemed like minutes to everyone watching and replied, "Thank you."

"Whew!" sighs of relief filled the room especially from Leon who had braced himself for a punch.

"Anyone want some cake and ice cream?" said Violet outwardly trying to display cheerfulness, yet inwardly just as relieved as everyone else.

"I do!" said Juan jumping up from the couch anxious to leave the living room, not caring any longer for the fight.

"Me too," said Lillie Mae quickly following behind them.

"What kinda' cake is it?" said Lil' Adam for once glad to follow his sister.

"Coconut," said Violet taking saucers from the cabinet. "I am glad someone is eating this ice cream, been in the freezer since last week."

"It's a knock out!" yelled Fred amidst cheers from the living room.

* * *

"You can turn the radio on," said Grandma Mae peaking around the corner from the dining room where she sat cutting out squares from old clothes, now happy to make her first sewing machine made quilt. "Y'all been sitting there an hour, ain't said one word."

"Yes ma'am," answered Rose respectfully. Quickly glancing at Beau while cutting quilt pieces, she noticed how nicely dressed he was in his Temple University sweater, white shirt, new style dungarees, and penny loafers, maybe he was not the 'country bumpkin' she previously envisioned. Still she wondered why he did not leave, especially after ignoring him the entire time. He continued to sit on the couch smiling obediently, like a well-trained puppy. She sighed, turned the radio on, and sat back on the opposite side of the couch away from him.

For Beau, this was the first opportunity he had to spend with her since Christmas. He was content to sit and watch her all day. Unfortunately, her eyes continually avoided his. He thought they made a connection last week, but maybe not. He longed to talk to her and say how he felt but he lacked courage or was it a fear of rejection.

"We belong together" by Robert Carr and Johnny Mitchell began to play on the radio, then he encouraged himself to speak to her.

"Rose, what are you making?"

"A quilt for my grandmother," she replied nonchalantly.

"Can I sit next to you?"

She shrugged her shoulders, "if you want too."

He nervously scooted over on the couch as close to her as possible. "Rose," he said softly touching her hand, surprised she did not pull away. "As far back as I can remember, I have had strong feelings for you, but you never seem to notice me, why is that?"

She shrugged her shoulders again, "I told you I have always thought of you like a brother."

"Is there a chance," he paused. "Could you ever think of me as something else?"

"Something else, like what?"

"Do you remember that night in the kitchen after Christmas dinner?"

"Yes, I do."

"I felt we were close to… Or maybe you were going to allow me to…" he struggled with his words and put his head down, frustrated with himself.

She lifted his chin up to see her eyes, "kiss me?" She said softly.

"Yes," he shouted with enthusiasm.

"Y'all all right in there," called Grandma Mae without getting up.

"We are ma'am, I mean Grandma Mae ma'am."

Rose shook her head softly smiling at him, "you are so sweet".

"Sweet enough for you to take this pin and be my girl?" He held in his hands a small gold pin in the shape of an owl with a red letter "T" on it. "Rose, I know you think of me as a brother, but please can you give me a chance as… as a boyfriend?"

"Beau, I don't know…I…"

"Rose," he gently interrupted. "Take this pin as a symbol of my love for you. All I ask is that you think of me fondly when I am away. Can you do that Rose?"

"Yes," she smiled. "I can do that."

He placed the pin on her shirt and took her hands in his as the lyrics continued, 'You're mine my baby and you'll always be. I love you so much. I swear by everything, everything I own, I'll always, always love you.' This time he was not nervous, the song said everything he felt, he reached over and gently kissed her on the lips and she returned the kiss. Her first kiss.

* * *

The two boys ran back into the living room expecting to see Leon on the floor, instead everyone stood watching Sugar Ray congratulated by others in the ring as the crowd roared with excitement. "Ladies and Gentlemen, the time one minute and twenty-seven seconds of the 5th round, winner by a knock-out and the new middle-weight champion of the world.

"I missed it," said Lil' Adam frustrated. "For ice cream and cake."

"Yeah you did son," said Adam patting him on the back. "But it was a good fight and that punch Sugar Ray landed was crazy!"

"Sho' was," said Poppa John, heading towards the closet for his coat. "I better go on home and check on the womenfolk."

Surrounded by trainers, reporters, and friends, the Announcer asked, "Can you tell me how that punch was setup?"

"Before I say anything," interrupted Sugar Ray. "…Fans of mine from the bottom of my heart, it was your prayers that enabled me to be successful tonight. This victory belongs to you and your faith in me and your faith in God. I thank you…"

"Now I like that," said Violet proudly as she began removing the empty trays, platters, and glasses, then kissing her father on the cheek. "Tell Momma I'll be over early in the morning to pick up Rose."

"Will do," he nodded, kissing each grandchild on the cheek. "Ruby behave yourself."

"Poppa you know I always do," she smiled hugging him tightly.

"I guess we're heading home too," said Leon timidly. "Thank you Big Adam for having us over."

"You're welcome," said Violet with a gentle smile, ignoring her husband who didn't respond nor look up from the television. "Take care of your father Juan."

"Yes ma'am, I will."

"I'll wrap you up some cake since you didn't get to eat yours in the kitchen."

"Thank you," he said politely.

"I'll take some too," added Leon.

"I'm not surprised," she smiled.

"It was goo-ood."

"Thank you," she said shaking her head wondering how the years changed him so much from high school.

As everyone said their good-byes and the women began to clean up, Fred pulled Adam to the side. "I got a message for you," he whispered.

"What do you mean?" Adam frowned, leading him to the front door away from everyone else.

"Your friend," he looked around to make sure no one was listening. "Told me, and I mean *told* me, like a threat, to tell you if you don't come by the Shack tonight, she's coming by your house. Man, I think she's serious."

"Yeah, okay," he said nervously. "I promised I wasn't going to that place anymore."

"I'm not trying to get in your business, but I'd hate to see Violet heartbroken if Carmen comes here starting stuff, not to mention what Ruby would do."

"Yeah man, you right, I can't have that either."

"Why y'all in the corner cackling like two old hens," said Ruby getting her coat. "Let's go Fred, I can't stay out long, I got to work in the morning."

* * *

Adam sat in the kitchen as Violet finished the dishes, torn, longing to tell her of his infidelity, yet hoping he could fix the situation without her ever finding out. He reached for the bottle of gin to pour another drink.

"Honey, isn't it too late for another drink?" she said lightly touching his hand. "What's the matter? This is not like you. Is something bothering you? Are you still upset about Leon?"

"No, no, I'm fine," he smiled handing the bottle to her, watching as she quickly placed it in the cabinet. "I have to make a run and take care of something."

"Adam," she said sadly, her heart sinking deeply, immediately tears came to her eyes. "Why baby, it's so late?"

He stood lifting her chin, "Sweetheart, I got myself in a mess…"

She started to say something, but he touched her lips. "Let me finish. Vee, you know I love you with all my heart, don't you?"

"I do," she said attempting a smile.

He held her closely, "Then just trust me, I promise, later, I will tell you everything. For now, know I love you no matter what."

She rested in his arms fearing what was coming next, not wanting him to leave, barely able to breathe, barely able to comprehend what was going on, only knowing in her heart that something was drastically wrong.

* * *

Adam walked into The Honey Shack as "He's Gone" by the Chantels played on the jukebox, several couples danced slowly on the dance floor. Carmen sat drinking as she had done every night for the last few weeks, listening to sad songs that echoed how she felt inside, "…come back to me and I'll never let you go, I'm sorry for what I have done, believe me you are the only one…" Despite the late hour, patrons filled most of the tables.

When he noticed her at the bar with her head down, nervousness came over him and for an instant, he felt something tell him to turn around and go home. Before he could decide, she saw him, and her face lit up with hope and desire.

"I knew you'd come," she smiled squeezing him tightly, her head on his chest, but he did not respond. "What is wrong? I missed you so."

"Look," he sighed, taking her by the shoulders moving her away. "You told Fred you wanted to see me, or you would come to my house. Carmen, you know I can't allow that."

"But I'm sorry, for anything I have done or said, Adam please forgive me," she pleaded and tried to embrace him once again, but he stepped back. "Don't do this Adam, I love you."

"And I am sorry about that," he shook his head. "I really cared for you too."

"Cared for me too," she looked at him questioning his words, raising her voice for everyone to hear. "After all these years, all this time, that's all you can say, is you cared for me too."

"Big Adam, you good," asked Nick offering him a drink.

"Yeah, I'm fine," he waved trying to smile. "No thanks, I'm not drinking. I did not come to stay."

"I understand man."

Adam turned and walked away, leaving Carmen standing in the middle of the floor as everyone looked on.

"Don't you walk away from me," she shouted.

The night air cold upon his face, his heart ached. "This was harder than I thought," he said to himself. He started the car, glad at least everything was over. He could move on with his life and new baby. He sighed, relieved to go home.

Suddenly, he saw Carmen stumbling down the steps of The Honey Shack, leaving the door open. Her coat half-pulled on her shoulders, purse dangling, walking wobbly towards the car. "Big Adam, *get* out of that car right now!"

He turned the car engine off, took a deep breath, and complied with her request, not wanting to attract more attention. He spoke calmly, "Carmen it's over, I'm sorry but I'm going home now, please leave me alone."

"I won't, I'm not, going to leave you alone," she responded angrily, tears and makeup streaming down her face. "I can't leave you alone, I'm having a baby."

He froze, stunned, unable to respond, sitting in the car, one hand on the steering wheel, the other slowly rubbing his head. He shouted. "What… what are you saying? Are you crazy? Are you lying? Is this some trick to get me back in your life?"

He sat in the car not knowing what to do. Words of the past haunting him, *'what's done in the dark always comes to the light'*. Emotions flooded his heart, anger at himself, hatred for her. How did he get himself in this situation? Nothing made sense. He should not be here. Finally turning on the ignition he said, "I can't take this."

"Don't you drive away from me Adam Williams!" she screamed reaching into her purse, pulling out a small handgun, placing it to her head. "If you leave, I will do it, so help me."

"Where did you get that? Have you lost your mind completely?" He got out the car with the engine running. "Give me that."

"Not until you talk to me," her hand shaking nervously, her finger on the trigger.

"Okay, okay," he sighed more nervous than afraid. "Get in the car."

* * *

"Hi sis, sorry to wake you," said Violet anxiously on the phone.

"Vee is that you," she asked confused. "What's wrong, you sound like you were crying? Is something wrong?"

"No, not that I know of," she hesitated. "It's just that Adam left here an hour ago… Ruby, I'm afraid… Something's not right…"

"Sis, don't cry. Fred and I will be over to find out what is going on. Okay?"

Through her tears, she replied, "Yes."

"Everything is going to be fine, don't cry, I'll be there soon."

After hanging up the phone, Ruby screamed, "Adam, if you hurt my sister, I'll kill you myself," not caring that she startled Fred lying next to her.

* * *

"I must be dreaming, no… this is a nightmare," Adam said shaking his head not believing the events of this night as he drove into the darkness. "You're *pregnant*?"

"Yes I am." She attempted to touch his arm, but he snatched away. "I want us to be a family."

He turned towards her as if she were a stranger, his eyebrows knit together in anger and confusion. "I have a family and I have a wife. You knew that all along."

"But I thought you would leave her."

"I never told you that."

"Now that I am having a baby…"

"Nothing will change," he interrupted driving faster than the speed limit allowed. "I will not leave my wife!"

"And all this time you made a fool of me." She sat quietly, her head turned towards the window as tears dripped onto her shoulder. "I am so stupid, thinking you would be happy that we are having a baby and we would be together as a family…so *stupid*."

Silence filled the car speeding along the highway. No music played. Deeper and deeper into darkness they drove. The earth stood still. Time stopped. Brokenhearted, she reached into her purse and once again pulled out the small handgun.

"Carmen, what are you doing!" he shouted angrily. "Don't play with that thing. Put it away!"

"No," she said calmly with a distant look in her eyes. "You said it was over, and now you're right."

She lifted the gun towards him. The car swerved as he tried to grab the gun away from her… driving… wrestling... anger… frustration… sadness… She pulled the trigger.

* * *

"Ruby, Fred, come on in," said Violet pulling open the door frantically. "The phone is ringing."

"Vee calm down, I'll get the phone," she said turning to Fred. "Sit with her."

"What's going on in here," asked Lil' Adam coming from the backroom. Followed by Lillie Mae in her pajamas, "Momma what's wrong?"

"Hello…No this is her sister…Yes sir…I understand…Yes we have a way…Thank you."

"Ruby what is it, tell me," she screamed shaking her sister, tears streaming down her face. "Something is wrong, I know it, please tell me."

"Sis," she hesitated, swallowing she tried to continue. "There has been an accident."

Immediately Violet fell to the floor, sobbing, "Oh Lord Jesus, help me."

"Vee," continued Ruby kneeling to hold her sister in her arms, rocking back and forth. "Adam is… he is in serious condition in the hospital."

"What happened Ruby?"

"They didn't say much. We'll find out when we get there."

"I knew something was wrong," Violet continued to cry uncontrollably.

"We can get through this. I promise it will be all right. I am here with you. Vee, can you be strong for the children and the baby?"

"Yes," she said taking deep breaths. "I will try."

"Lil' Adam, you and Lillie Mae get some clothes on, so you can help your Momma."

* * *

The doctor stopped Violet before going into the hospital room, "Mrs. Williams."

"Yes sir," she answered calmly.

"Your husband is heavily sedated. He was in a serious car accident, and in addition to that," he paused lightly touching her on the shoulder. "He has a gunshot wound to the head."

"Oh Lord," she gasped, Lil' Adam catching her from falling. "I must see him."

"Vee, are you sure," asked Ruby turning to the doctor. "She is pregnant, do you think she should?"

"Only for a few minutes," he answered turning towards Violet.

"I'll go in with her," said Grandma Mae arriving with Poppa John and Rose.

"Momma," cried Violet immediately hugging the three of them. "Something terrible happened to Adam. I don't understand, I don't know what happened, he was shot Poppa."

"It's all right baby," she said patting her softly on the back. "Don't worry about it now, we'll figure it out somehow."

"Come on, we'll be in the waiting room," said Ruby hugging Lil' Adam and Lillie Mae, as Rose followed behind them.

* * *

Tranquility filled the dimly lit room, interrupted only by the regular beep of the heart rate machine. Adam's body lay on the bed cold, stiff, distant. Liquid dripped from a plastic bottle into his once strong and muscular arms, now appearing weak and feeble. White bandages wrapped around his skull and under his chin, his handsome face no longer recognizable.

"There must be some mistake?" Her chest visibly lifted with every breath, searching for air. Weak, she reached for the bed frame, unable to stand. "Momma, I can't do this."

"Baby, sit here on the bed."

"Why would someone want to shoot him? Nothing makes sense. So many questions, how will I know?"

"No matter what happened, remember it is Adam, your husband you love," said Grandma Mae holding her strongly. "Talk to him."

"I don't know if I can…"

Finally, despite her hesitations, she slowly reached and gently took his hand, whispering, "Adam, I am here baby, it's me, Vee. Please, don't leave me. How would I go on without you? I can't. This pain is unbearable. The thought of losing you… Please stay with me."

His eyes moved but did not open. "Adam, I love you so much." She squeezed his hand softly as tears rolled down her cheeks. "I always have, and I always will love you. You are my life. You inspire me and protect me. Please don't let this be goodbye."

Gradually his eyes opened, trying to focus, he painfully turned his head towards her, their eyes met. "Vee," he tried to speak, his lips dry and cracked, quivering. His voice soft and sincere, "I'm sorry."

"Don't try to speak baby."

"Violet I love you," he whispered. A tear rolling down his cheek, "please forgive me."

"Baby, please, I forgive you, just don't leave me. Please stay."

"Kiss me."

She leaned over their lips touching, tenderly, romantically. Once again, two hearts beat in unison, together again. Looking in his eyes a flash of memories flooded her mind as they walked to school holding hands, laughing, hopelessly in love. Peace surrounded them, the room filled with tranquility…

His eyes slowly closed. His hand went limp beneath hers. An alarm sounded, continuous, nonstop. The nurse rushed into the room. "Mrs. Williams, we are going to have to ask you to step out."

"Momma," she sobbed heartbroken, laying her head on his chest. "I won't leave him."

"Baby we have too," she said rubbing her daughter's back.

The children rushed into the room, crying, heartbroken to see her in agony yet not ready to believe their father was no longer with them.

A nurse patted her gently on the shoulder. "Please step out Ma'am."

Lil' Adam stepped forward placing his arms around his mother's shoulder, and slowly began guiding her out the room. Glancing back he saw the doctor and nurses pounding frantically on his father's chest, the heart machine continued with one long piercing beep. "Come on Mom, I got you."

EPILOGUE

Sunlight crept into the room warming Violet's face. She smiled to herself thinking of a morning, not too long ago when a 'pesky fly' interrupted her sweet dreams. Touching the empty spot on the bed sadness gripped her heart. Tears flowed freely down her face as she remembered him, his smile, his laughter, constantly teasing her. She felt empty.

Tap, Tap, Tap – someone knocked on her bedroom door. She quickly tried to wipe away the tears, taking a deep breath, she called, "yes come in."

"Baby you awake?" Her mother entered with a plate of food in one hand and a glass of orange juice in the other.

"Momma, you didn't have too, I was fixing to get up and get dressed..."

"I know," she interrupted softly smiling. "I wanted you to eat something before we left. You'll need your strength today."

She sat on the side of the bed with her head in her hands. "I don't know if I can do this… I feel so alone."

Putting her arms around her, she kissed her on the cheek. "Baby you are not alone. God is always with you. Your Poppa, your babies, and me, are here." She rubbed her stomach only slightly protruding, "and this little one here needs you more than anyone."

"I am going to miss him Momma," she wept tears rolling down her cheeks. "When he died, something inside me died. I feel so empty."

"And I pray one day the good Lord will fill that empty spot, just keep your faith baby, God will work it out. Don't worry."

Violet turned to her mother with a small smile, "I used to say that to everybody, it almost sounds strange hearing my words spoken to me."

"The truth is good no matter who says it, in every life some rain will fall." Putting a spoonful of grits and eggs to her mouth, "here baby, eat this. When I was a chap and didn't understand something, my mother would always sing this song to me."

What a fellowship, what a joy divine,
Leaning on the everlasting arms;
What a blessedness, what a peace is mine,
Leaning on the everlasting arms.

Violet sat quietly eating while her mother continued singing:

Leaning, leaning,
Safe and secure from all alarms;
Leaning, leaning,
Leaning on the everlasting arms.

By this time, they both were beginning to feel better. Then Rose, Adam, and Lillie Mae came and sat on the bed next to them, followed by Poppa John. Soon everyone was singing the song with uplifted hearts. Before you knew it, they began patting their feet and clapping their hands, church was going on.

Oh, how sweet to walk in this pilgrim way,
Leaning on the everlasting arms;
Oh, how bright the path grows from day to day,
Leaning on the everlasting arms.

Violet stood to hug her father. He patted her on the back and whispered in her ear, "be strong baby, we're here with you."

Kissing him on the cheek, she replied through tears, "Thank you, Poppa."

Hugging the children altogether as they sang the chorus once again, she tried to speak through the tears. "I know we will miss your father. I wish things were different, but they not. I do know, and feel deep in my heart, that as long as we are together, we are going to make it through this."

"How Momma," asked Lillie Mae her eyes filled with tears.

"One day at a time, baby," she answered pulling her closer. "One day at a time."

ABOUT THE AUTHOR

Lori Elise is a Teacher, Writer, and Grandmother who wrote the Potato Patch to share a piece of history from a different perspective. She enjoys gardening, sitting on the beach, bike-riding, painting, cooking, and Bible study with friends and family.

ElonEnam.org
(God loves me, God gave it to me)

Share your memories of how your family dealt with difficult times because of your ethnicity at
ThePotatoPatch@roadrunner.com

UPCOMING BOOK

Torn Between

The saga continues as the Williams family journeys into the 60's, a turbulent time of change in America, where choices were made for prosperity, peace, love and war.

Please join our mailing list at
ThePotatoPatch@roadrunner.com

Made in the USA
Middletown, DE
23 September 2018